Praise for
the Black Cat Bookshop Mysteries

Words with Fiends

"Brandon again creates a lively whodunit . . . An endearing entry in a sturdy series, *Words with Fiends* should find many friends." —*Richmond Times-Dispatch*

"[A] finely tuned whodunit that quickly became a page-turner . . . nonstop action . . . great cast. This is one of the best books yet in this delightfully engaging series."

—*Dru's Books Musings*

"A really fun part of this book is that during Darla's spare time she plays the popular word game Words with Friends . . . The role that the online game plays in the mystery . . . is extremely clever . . . This is a sensational cozy mystery series that just gets better and better."

—*Melissa's Mochas, Mysteries, & Meows*

A Novel Way to Die

"Our favorite sleuthing cat is back . . . This series really does have it all: [a] bookstore, cats, likable, relatable characters, and a strong mystery." —*Cozy Mystery Book Reviews*

"The story line keeps you guessing and there's even some romance thrown into the mix. The words flow from page to page with ease and make for a delightful way to spend an afternoon. This book is fun, fun, fun! Ali Brandon is a great voice in the cozy mystery world!" —*Socrates' Book Reviews*

continued . . .

"Fun to read . . . The mystery was very good and the cat really added some interest to the story." —*Fresh Fiction*

"Cat fanciers will love the role Hamlet plays in the investigation and his strong personality; others will enjoy Darla's investigation as she learns more about her new environ."

—*The Mystery Reader*

Double Booked for Death

"A fun mystery that kept me guessing to the end!"

—Rebecca M. Hale, *New York Times* bestselling author of *How to Paint a Cat*

"Clever . . . Bibliophiles, ailurophiles, and mystery fans will enjoy *Double Booked for Death*."

—*Richmond Times-Dispatch*

"A charming, cozy read, especially if cats are your cup of tea. Make sure the new Black Cat Bookshop series is on your bookshelf."

—Elaine Viets, national bestselling author of *Catnapped!*

"Hamlet is a winner, and so is his owner. The literary references in this endearing debut will make readers smile, and the ensemble characters hold promise for fun titles to come."

—*Library Journal*

"An engaging new series . . . Definitely the start of something great."

—Sandra Balzo, award-winning author of the Main Street Mysteries

"[An] outstanding debut to a very promising new series . . . The characters are interesting and smart, the mystery is clever and provides clues the reader will notice but [doesn't] let the cat out of the bag prematurely . . . I had such fun reading about Darla and her cohorts, and found Hamlet's antics made me smile . . . If you enjoy a cozy mystery, a clever cat, a bookstore setting, and smart, realistic characters, you are sure to enjoy *Double Booked for Death*."

—MyShelf.com

"This first entry in the Black Cat Bookshop Mystery series is a harbinger of good books to follow . . . In case you are wondering, Hamlet fulfills his role as sleuth by knocking down books containing hints about the killer's identity. [Brandon] does a fine job with the plot and execution here—and even incorporates an element of romance as she introduces a potential love interest in the form of a hunky cop . . . who will undoubtedly be making an encore appearance in the next Black Cat Bookshop Mystery."

—*Mystery Scene*

"Those who like clever animals but draw the line at talking cats will feel right at home."

—*Publishers Weekly*

"The first Black Cat Bookshop Mystery is an entertaining whodunit starring a brilliant feline (who does not speak in human tongues), a beleaguered new store owner, and an ex-cop. The story line is fast-paced as Hamlet uncovers the clues that the two females working the case follow up on . . . Fans will enjoy."

—*The Mystery Gazette*

Berkley Prime Crime titles by Ali Brandon

DOUBLE BOOKED FOR DEATH
A NOVEL WAY TO DIE
WORDS WITH FIENDS
LITERALLY MURDER

LITERALLY MURDER

ALI BRANDON

BERKLEY PRIME CRIME, NEW YORK

THE BERKLEY PUBLISHING GROUP
Published by the Penguin Group
Penguin Group (USA) LLC
375 Hudson Street, New York, New York 10014

USA • Canada • UK • Ireland • Australia • New Zealand • India • South Africa • China

penguin.com

A Penguin Random House Company

LITERALLY MURDER

A Berkley Prime Crime Book / published by arrangement with Tekno Books

For information, address: The Berkley Publishing Group,
a division of Penguin Group (USA) LLC,
375 Hudson Street, New York, New York 10014.

ISBN: 978-0-425-26154-5

PUBLISHING HISTORY
Berkley Prime Crime mass-market edition / October 2014

PRINTED IN THE UNITED STATES OF AMERICA

10 9 8 7 6 5 4 3 2 1

Cover art by Ross Jones.
Interior text design by Kristin del Rosario.

This book is dedicated to the memory of my mother,
Helen Janet Ponewczynski Smart, one of the most
brilliant and talented women I have ever known.
I feel privileged every single day to be her daughter.
Love you and miss you, Mom.

ACKNOWLEDGMENTS

Special thanks to the dedicated folks of rescue, whose tireless and often unsung efforts change the lives of so many lost and discarded pets. And a big nod of appreciation to my friend Al Hallonquist, who graciously answers my random midnight emails about police procedure and is merely the suggestion for my character of the same name. Any law enforcement errors, omissions, or glaring bloopers are mine alone!

And paws up to the fine folks of Fort Lauderdale, whose city I have borrowed for this latest outing with Darla and Hamlet. The keen South Florida reader might notice that I've taken a few liberties with building names and locations. Be assured it is strictly for story purposes—you'll find everything in order again after you finish the book.

ONE

DARLA PETTISTONE FROWNED AS SHE PAGED THROUGH THE sheaf of blueprints spread atop the table in her bookstore's upper floor lounge. Seeing the shop's planned coffee bar neatly laid out on paper was one thing. Being confident that the design would translate into satisfactory reality was another.

"I'm still not sure, Cecil," she told the beefy construction superintendent seated across the table from her. "Maybe we should change the angle of the main seating area. Oh, and are you sure we should put the sinks right there?"

Cecil heaved a patient sigh redolent of the sausage breakfast sandwich he had been eating when he'd arrived thirty minutes earlier. His bald, black head gleamed with sweat despite the fact that it was late February in Brooklyn and the temperature outside was hovering in the teens. He swiped said shiny dome with a yellow bandana and then crossed bulky, sweatered arms over his ample gut.

"Here's the deal, Ms. Pettistone. You want to turn your

kitchenette into a nice little coffee bar for your store like you asked for, this is it," he said, and stabbed a stubby finger at the blueprints. "You want the Taj Mahal, I'll build that instead. But if you want us to get started this weekend, you gotta sign off on the design now. Otherwise, it might be another couple of months before Mr. Putin has a break in his schedule to fit your job in."

"But that's part of the problem," Darla explained with another worried look at the drawings. "I'm leaving tomorrow morning for Fort Lauderdale. I'm going to be in Florida for more than a week, so I won't be here to keep an eye on things."

"True," came a voice from behind her, "But remember, I will be."

The speaker was Darla's store manager, Professor James T. James. The unflappable retired university instructor had run Pettistone's Fine Books for more than a dozen years, well before Darla had inherited the business the previous spring from her late great-aunt, Dee Pettistone. In addition to his managerial duties, James was an expert on rare and collectible books, which in the past couple of years had become a major revenue source for Pettistone's. The new coffee bar that Darla was commissioning would, she hoped, be yet another cash stream. Given the current unsettled business climate facing independent bookstores, serving specialty brews would be another way to draw in customers—and, with luck, keep them in the store long enough to encourage a book purchase along with their lattes.

"The timing actually is rather fortunate, if you think about it," James went on in the same sonorous tones that, back in his teaching days, likely had held the attention of even the most lackluster student. "Not only did Mr. Putin assure us that will the job be finished in under two weeks—quite an amazing feat in itself—but the bulk of the construction will take place while Hamlet is safely with you at the cat show."

Darla shot a fond look at Hamlet, the bookstore's oversized feline mascot, who was snoozing on the arm of a nearby love seat like a small black panther lounging on a tree branch. She had inherited Hamlet along with the bookstore, and their initial relationship had been rocky, to say the least. Darla had never been much of a cat person, but then Hamlet wasn't the kind of bookstore feline that curled up in cute wicker baskets and purred nicely for customers.

Rather, he ran the place with an iron paw, stalking up and down the aisles like a furry potentate when he wasn't sprawled on a shelf somewhere. Darla's regular customers all knew their place in the Hamlet hierarchy and did not dare pet him or call "kitty, *kitty*" without his lordship's express permission. More than one innocent transgressor had found himself unceremoniously chased to the front door for violating those rules, to the point where Darla finally had posted a not-so-tongue-in-cheek sign reading, "Beware of Cat."

In fact, Darla often wondered just who was in charge at Pettistone's, her or Hamlet.

But in the year since Darla had owned the bookstore, the two of them had developed a bond. Not that she'd yet made Hamlet's BFF list, Darla told herself in amusement—James and her teenage goth salesclerk, Robert Gilmore, likely ranked above her—but she and Hamlet now coexisted in a mutually respectful manner that, given the fact Darla had never considered herself a "crazy cat lady," was good enough for her.

And James had a point about the advantages of her and Hamlet being gone during the construction, she realized. Hamlet was used to having free rein of the three-story brownstone that housed Pettistone's Fine Books in its first two floors and Darla's apartment on the third. (This didn't count the garden apartment below rented by Darla's best friend, Jacqueline "Jake" Martelli.) Hamlet was a moody enough feline on good days. Chances were that construction in the bookstore would send the finicky cat into a major snit that could last for weeks.

"You're right, James," Darla agreed with a determined toss of her red braid. Then she turned to the superintendent again. "It's settled. We might as well do this now, while Hamlet is busy being guest of honor down in Florida."

Cecil flashed crooked teeth in an approving smile as he plucked a pen from the pocket of his flannel shirt and handed it to her. "Good decision, Ms. Pettistone. We'll get the job knocked out in no time. You and your little kitty will come back to a fancy new store, and everyone will be happy."

At those last words, the "little kitty" in question slit open one emerald green eye and shot a baleful look in Cecil's direction. Darla paused in midsignature and gave Hamlet a warning look of her own. Cecil had not yet had the dubious pleasure of meeting the store mascot up close and personal. Last thing she needed was for Hamlet to take offense at the man's innocent words and give him feline what-for, putting the kibosh on the project before it even began!

Fortunately for the future coffee bar, the finicky cat had apparently decided to let the superintendent's lapse slide. After briefly flexing one oversized paw to display a formidable set of claws—just for effect—Hamlet shut his eye again and went back to his nap. Darla allowed herself a relieved smile at the reprieve. She finished signing the documents and wrote out the requisite deposit check to Putin Construction.

Darla had hesitated to use the company at first, given Alex Putin's reputation in the neighborhood as the "czar-father" of construction with rumored ties to the Russian mob. But her NYPD detective friend, Reese, had assured her that the man was a legitimate business owner with no criminal record beyond the usual parking violations. Jake also had given Putin the thumbs-up, as she'd done a little PI work for him (and gotten a bit too chummy with the man, in Darla's opinion). Since his online reviews for his construction work were uniformly positive, Darla had decided to give his company a shot.

As Darla and James escorted Cecil downstairs, Darla said, "You saw the alley and courtyard behind the building. If you can bring in all your materials that way, that would be great. But just in case you need to use the front door, too, we can move the bookshelves out of the way so you have a clear path either way to the stairs."

"That'll work fine, ma'am."

While Cecil pulled on a bright blue down coat big enough to fit her and James both, Darla pointed out the projected pathway. Once the maze of bookshelves filling the store was realigned (Great-Aunt Dee had cleverly had casters added to each shelf unit), it would be a straight shot from the front door, past the stairway to the room beyond, and then to the back door. In fact, the brownstone's layout reminded Darla of what back home in Texas they called a shotgun shack. Not that the elegant Federal-style building which housed the bookstore resembled anything shacklike.

The shop's main room—originally the brownstone's parlor—opened into what previously had been the dining room. Other than replacing the connecting doorways with open arches, Great-Aunt Dee had basically left the parlor intact, meaning that a majority of the original, ornately carved wooden built-ins remained. Now those built-ins served as additional bookshelves as well as display space for old crockery and bric-a-brac. The parlor had undergone a slightly greater revamping, with much of its original mahogany wainscoting repurposed to build a narrow, U-shaped counter near the store's front window, where the register was located. Overall, the bones of the old brownstone were clearly visible, unlike with other similar buildings that had been totally gutted and modernized.

"Don't worry, Ms. Pettistone," Cecil assured her again, tugging a crimson knit cap over his bald pate and sticking out a calloused hand to shake. "We'll get you taken care of just fine."

Refusing to hear anything ominous in that promise, Darla shook, smiled, and saw him out. She hurriedly shut the door after him, but not before an insidious blast of frigid air whipped its way in.

Florida can't come too soon, Darla thought with a shiver as she straightened the "Sale" sign that the wind gust had blown away from the nearby display of cookbooks. Given the fact that she'd lived in Dallas for most of her thirtysomething years, she was not yet acclimated to the frigid weather in New York.

Then she heaved a sigh. "Well, it's done. In another couple of weeks, Pettistone's will be entering a new era. Books con coffee . . . you know, like *café con leche*," she explained when James raised a gray brow. "I wonder what Great-Aunt Dee would have thought about this."

"Dee was quite the businesswoman, so I am sure she would have approved," the man assured her, adding, "And may I again thank you for not asking me to take on barista duties? Much as I enjoy a nice latte, I would not relish serving them all day . . . particularly if I would be expected to draw—ahem—cartoons in the foam."

"Don't worry, that's Robert's department," Darla told him with a smile. Then, spying her clerk unpacking a box a few shelves away, she called, "Robert, wasn't last night your final class in barista training?"

Robert poked his head around the shelf and grinned back, his dyed black hair flopping over one kohled eye. Darla bit her lip but didn't say anything about the black eyeliner. Since the youth had diligently followed her rule these past months about no visible piercings while on the clock, she had finally relented and allowed him a minimum of goth makeup at work.

As long as you don't scare the customers, had been her main stipulation.

"Yeah, last night was our final exam, and I, like, aced

it," he bragged. "They gave me a certificate and stuff. I even got first place in latte art because I drew a picture of Hamlet's face in the foam that everyone thought was sick."

Knowing that "sick" was a major compliment, Darla gave him an approving nod. "That's wonderful. Maybe that cat face can be the Pettistone's Coffee Bar trademark."

Robert's black-rimmed eyes widened. "Hey, great idea, Ms. P.!"

James gave a genteel snort as he headed toward the rear of the store. "Yes, a great idea. I suppose we will also be ordering coffee cups with Hamlet's image upon them."

Logo coffee cups?

Darla was about to echo the "great idea" sentiment in regard to James's cynical suggestion when Robert abruptly spoke up again. "Wait, I almost forgot. While you and Professor James were upstairs with Mr. Cecil, some guy brought a package. I left it on the counter. And it's not, you know, books or stuff."

Before Darla could inspect her package, however, the string of small bells hanging on the front door jingled. In hurried a small female figure wrapped in a full-length, balding mink coat and an incongruous pink-and-orange scarf that swaddled her from throat to eyes. Then, like a thrift-store houri, the woman raised a gloved hand and, clutching one fringed end of the scarf, gave it a swirl. The pashmina promptly spun away to reveal a familiar, wrinkled face.

"Mary Ann!" Darla exclaimed as she recognized her elderly neighbor. "You shouldn't be out in this weather."

The old woman gave a dismissive wave. "Really, Darla, I've lived in Brooklyn all of my life. I'm used to a little cold. Besides, young Robert does an excellent job of keeping our steps free of snow and ice."

She smiled in the youth's direction. Robert had finished unpacking his box and was headed to the back toward the recycling pile. Hearing his name, however, he paused and turned and gave the woman an enthusiastic wave.

"Hey, Ms. Plinski. Great coat."

Mary Ann tittered as she gave a little pirouette to better show off the garment.

"Of course, I would never purchase a new fur," she confided to Darla while Robert trotted off. "I found this one boxed up in our storeroom. Who knows how long it's been sitting there? Brother probably bought it in an auction years ago and forgot all about it."

Mary Ann and her older brother owned the brownstone next door to Darla. In addition to the apartment the two shared, their building also housed their antiques and collectibles shop, Bygone Days. Robert helped out the elderly pair on occasion with the heaving lifting. In return, Mary Ann had leased out her garden apartment to the youth at a substantially reduced rate. She had even waived her "no pets" rule on his behalf, allowing him to keep his tiny Italian greyhound, Roma, there with him.

"So what brings you here on a freezing cold day like this?" Darla asked her with a smile.

The old woman gave her a wide-eyed look. "Why, I wanted to know all about your upcoming trip to Florida. Robert said it had something to do with Hamlet, but for the life of me I couldn't guess what."

"I don't know why he made it sound so mysterious. Hamlet is going to be the guest of honor at this year's Feline Society of America National Championship show."

"How exciting! But however did you ever manage that?"

"Remember that video of Hamlet at the martial arts tournament that Robert and I competed in last year? You know, the one of Hamlet out on the mat mimicking me as I did my karate routine? Well, the video went viral. That means—"

"Really, Darla, I know what viral means," Mary Ann replied with a smile, cutting Darla off with another wave of her gloved hand. "I am quite Internet savvy, if I do say so, myself. Why, I even have three boards on Pinterest now."

Since Darla had no clue what Pinterest was, she conceded the win to the older woman.

"Sorry, Mary Ann. Anyhow, when you combine all the different videos of Hamlet's performance at the tournament that people uploaded, he had close to a million online hits, and that was back before Christmas. When Jake saw that, she called her mother in Fort Lauderdale. Apparently, Mrs. Martelli is good friends with the man who is president of the Feline Society of America, which is headquartered there. Jake suggested that her mom should tell the FSA folks to bring Hamlet down to Florida as their celebrity guest for this year's annual championship show."

Darla smiled. After all, who could resist a cat who mimicked his human with such sly accuracy? Even she laughed every time she saw the video, and she was the one who'd been unknowingly mocked. She'd even forgiven Hamlet for the fact that his performance at the tournament had caused her to be disqualified from her first and only karate competition.

Darla had scoffed when Jake first mentioned the cat-show idea, but her friend had been of the opinion that it never hurt to ask. *Hey, kid, they can only say no* had been her brash response. Still, the cop-turned-private-investigator had been as surprised as Darla when, a couple of weeks later, a registered letter arrived inviting one Hamlet the Cat to serve as the FSA guest of honor at the end of February.

"I still can't believe I'm going to leave all this snow behind and go to Florida," Darla went on. "They're paying all my expenses to bring Hamlet down, and they even arranged for a plus one, so Jake is coming with me, too. She's going to act as Hamlet's official bodyguard. The cat show is on Saturday and Sunday, and FSA will put us up in the conference hotel for three nights starting Friday, but Jake and I decided to stay the whole next week and make it a real vacation."

"What fun," Mary Ann agreed. "I've often wondered if Brother and I should sell our place and move to Florida with all the other old people, but I know he would never leave the shop. So you and Jake will just have to enjoy the sunshine for me."

"I'll bring you back a souvenir," Darla promised. Then, with a look around the empty bookstore—only two customers had stopped in since she'd unlocked the doors more than an hour ago—Darla added, "And maybe I should bring back some of that sunshine, too. Who wants to go out shopping in all this gloom? I swear, I don't know how Great-Aunt Dee kept the place going in the winter."

"Things will get better, my dear. We're just having an unusually unpleasant season this year, is all. And once your new coffee bar is built, I'm sure scads of people will stop in for a nice hot drink, if nothing else."

They spent a few more moments chatting about the remodeling job, and then Mary Ann pulled on her scarf again. "I'd better not leave Brother for too long. He might do something foolish, like try to shovel the walk outside the building."

After the woman had made her good-byes, Darla spent a few minutes helping a customer who had come in just as Mary Ann was leaving. Once she'd rung the gentleman up and sent him on his way, she excitedly reached for the box waiting for her on the counter. Given that she'd be officially representing Pettistone's Fine Books while at the Florida cat show, Darla had decided to do a little branding for the event, and when she had discovered a custom embroidery shop only a few blocks away, she had placed a rush order.

She opened the package and pulled out the topmost item—a polo shirt in an appropriately tropical pink—and gazed in appreciation at the logo: a black silhouette of a cat set against a blue book and encircled by the bookstore's name in gold thread. Neatly stitched right above where the breast pocket would be on a dress shirt, the design looked crisply professional . . . classy, as her good-old-boy father would have put it. Indeed, the polos had turned out even better than she'd expected, so much so that she wish she'd done this months ago.

"James! Robert! Come see our new corporate shirts," she called, eager for their approval, too. As the pair joined her at the register, she held up a lime green one and gushed, "Aren't they great?"

Obviously, the unspoken answer to that question was a resounding *no.* James and Robert exchanged twin looks of horror before turning back to Darla, eyes wide as they stared at the polo shirt. Disappointed by their obvious lack of enthusiasm, Darla shook her head.

"Look, y'all, I told you I was thinking about doing this. Right now, no one can tell us from the customers. This will give all of us a nice professional look, especially now, when we've got the coffee bar to bring in a whole new crop of customers.

"But—but they're girly pink," Robert squeaked, holding out crossed forefingers in the universal "back off, Evil" gesture.

James was more restrained if equally to the point. "While I understand your thought process, Darla, surely you do not wish me to appear as if I worked as a greeter at a discount retailer. Short sleeves are not, as they used to say, my thing."

"Aha! I knew you would say that."

With a chuckle, Darla set aside the pink shirt and reached into the box again, pulling out a flat, tissue-wrapped bundle and then handing it to James.

As if he were disarming a bomb, the ex-professor gingerly peeled off the wrapping. Within was a crisp, white long-sleeved dress shirt neatly folded to display a smaller version of the Pettistone's logo embroidered high upon the garment's left sleeve.

"See, you can even wear your sweater vests with this," Darla told him, referring to the man's personal uniform, one that he'd worn every day she'd known him.

James briefly held up the shirt to gauge its size, the snowy fabric a bright contrast to his mahogany features. Finally, the frown that creased his broad brow relaxed, and he allowed himself a slight smile. "Perhaps I would not be averse to wearing this particular style."

"Good, because there's also one in pale blue for you," Darla told him, knowing her manager favored that shade. Then she turned to Robert.

The youth had dispensed with the makeshift cross gesture but still wore an expression of dismay. "Uh, no offense, Ms. Pettistone, but I don't think I'd, you know, look good in one of those shirts with all those sleeves, either."

"That's what I figured," Darla told him with a smile. Feeling rather like a magician with a top hat filled with rabbits, she reached into the shipping box again and pulled out yet another shirt, which she tossed to Robert. "Maybe you'll like this one better."

"Sweet!"

Robert nodded in appreciation as he caught the black polo and held it up to admire. While he occasionally topped his work outfits with a bright-colored vest in good-natured imitation of James's personal style, the rest of Robert's wardrobe was strictly goth black, enlivened by the occasional gray. Knowing that, Darla had ordered him a couple of black shirts and reserved the bright colors for herself.

"I'm not going to be a real stickler about it," she told them, "but I'd appreciate it if you'd wear your new shirts to work at least a couple of times a week. Oh, and I bought a few extras in different sizes and colors. I figured once the coffee bar is up and running, we can display a couple and maybe sell them to our customers."

"I would agree there might be a market for such a thing," James observed, refolding his new shirt and wrapping it again in its paper. "For some reason, much of the shopping public seems to enjoy purchasing logoed items. Of course, there is no accounting for—"

"Me-ROOW!"

The unmistakable cry of a cat ignored for far too long interrupted James's platitudes. Hamlet had stalked down the stairs toward the register. He paused, and then, with a single graceful bound, lightly landed upon the countertop next to Darla's box of shirts.

"Hey, little goth bro!" Robert exclaimed. This was the usual greeting between him and Hamlet, and it normally was followed by a fist bump . . . or, on Hamlet's part, a paw bump. No matter how many times Darla had tried to get Hamlet to follow suit with her, however, the cat had stubbornly refused to play along.

For now, however, Hamlet didn't appear interested in hanging with his human "bro." Instead, his attention was fixed on the shipping box. He leaned closer for a sniff at the cardboard, only to rear back with a hiss almost as loud as a big rig releasing its air brakes.

"I do not think he approves of the shirts," James observed.

Robert shook his head. "No, he's mad because he knows there's not one in there for him. Right, Hamlet?"

Hamlet slanted the youth a cool green look that Darla translated to mean *Did you seriously just say that?* Then, to further illustrate his feelings on the matter, he swiped one back paw back and forth atop the counter, like he was burying something in his litter box. Finally, with a swish of his long tail that sent the topmost of the nearby stack of free newspapers flying, the cat leaped off the counter and strolled his way toward the games section.

"Do you think he figured out about the T-R-I-P?" Robert asked, carefully spelling out the last word.

Darla shrugged. "He saw me take my suitcase out of the closet last night, and I've got a couple of Florida guidebooks upstairs in my bedroom. Even worse, he caught me putting fresh towels in his cat carrier. A free vacation sounded like lots of fun when Jake and I first planned it, and it's good publicity for the store, but maybe Hamlet isn't up to traveling."

"He will be just fine," James assured her. "You have that calming spray from our friends at the rescue organization, and since he walks quite well on a leash, you will be able to exercise him outside when you get there. Besides, the construction noise and mess would likely be far more stressful on a cat than staying in a nice hotel."

"Yeah, and it's, you know, probably safer," Robert said. "Those guys on the crew, they do a great job, but they don't always pay attention to stuff. What if they were, like, bringing in tools from outside and left the door open for a minute? Hamlet could run outside and get lost and maybe freeze or something."

While Darla didn't doubt Hamlet would be able to make his way home should he escape the brownstone—to her past dismay, he'd done just that a time or two—she realized that James and Robert did have a point about the construction. The finicky feline would never put up with that sort of disruption to his personal stomping grounds. On the other hand, while Florida would be a strange new world for this Brooklyn-born cat, he'd be under her watchful eye twenty-four/seven the entire time, either on his leash or in his carrier. What kind of trouble could he get into that way?

Her earlier good spirits returning, Darla reached again for her bright pink polo.

"You're right," she told them as she refolded the garment and packed it away with the others. "It'll be a couple of days watching Hamlet play Mr. Celebrity at the cat show, and the rest of the time it's going to be nothing but sun and fun. I'll probably be so relaxed I won't even get around to sending out a bunch of postcards bragging about how warm it is in—"

Splat!

The unmistakable sound of a book hitting the wooden floor cut her short. Darla gave an exasperated sigh and turned in the direction where Hamlet had headed. The cagey cat had a habit of occasionally knocking books from their shelves. Of course, when she went to investigate, Hamlet invariably would be innocently sleeping far from the scene of the crime, or else would be nowhere to be found at all. In fact, she had yet to catch him in the act, but he remained her prime suspect in what she'd come to call "book snagging."

While it was an annoying bit of mischief on his part (and hard on the books, to boot), picking up after him wasn't the problem. Rather, it was the fact that, more often than not, the book titles that mysteriously ended up on the floor had something to do with whatever might be happening at the time. While everyone else attributed Hamlet's apparent insights to coincidence—at least publicly—Darla was convinced by now that the clever cat knew exactly what he was doing every time he sent a particular volume flying.

While Robert and James resumed their duties, Darla hurried over to where she guessed the most recent book had fallen. Sure enough, in front of the shelves that held the various trivia, puzzle, and other game-related books lay a single slim paperback. As for Hamlet, she spied him snoozing on one of the overstuffed reading chairs two aisles over.

Playing innocent or legitimately not guilty?

She picked up the wayward volume and glanced at it in surprise. What had she just been telling James and Robert about the upcoming Florida trip? Something about fun and relaxation? She shook her head. If the book she held was Hamlet's prediction of what was to come, then apparently she'd spoken too soon. For this instructional guide to playing poker was titled *Want to Bet?*

TWO

"THE SKIES HERE IN FORT LAUDERDALE ARE CLEAR, AND THE temperature is a balmy seventy degrees . . . sweater weather for us Floridians."

The news was met with a murmur of approval from the passengers as the plane taxied toward the gate. Darla had stuffed her coat into her checked luggage as soon as they'd reached the airport. She was set for the southern weather with white denim jeans, which she now cuffed to her knees, and a blue-and-white striped shirt she'd chosen for its distinct sailor vibe.

Darla had left the store that morning in James's capable hands, reminding herself that a) she was due a vacation, b) Hamlet would be happier far away from the construction, and c) she'd be crazy not to jump at a chance to get out of the frigid temperatures dogging New York. But she still had a few niggling doubts about her decision that hadn't been helped by the text from James that had come right before she had boarded the plane.

Construction crew is here. Union plumber is MIA.

Her message back had been a terse *Boarding now, will call for an update once in FL.* Not that there was anything out of the ordinary with a construction job starting off slowly; still, it put a damper on things to know her project wasn't starting off smoothly.

The engines shut down as the plane halted at its assigned gate, and even before the familiar *ding* sounded as the captain turned off the seatbelt light, passengers were already on their feet and scrambling to retrieve their baggage.

"*This* is why I hate to fly," Jake good-naturedly grumbled as she unfolded her six-foot frame from her aisle seat and began fishing in the overhead bin. "By the time I get all the kinks out, it'll be time to head back to Brooklyn again."

"Hey, you've got over a week to unkink," Darla reminded her friend with a sympathetic smile. "We're here until next Sunday. Besides, I read online that our hotel is right next door to a day spa, if you want to book a massage."

She refrained from mentioning that at least the older woman had had the space beneath the seat in front of her free throughout the trip. Not that Darla begrudged her friend the leg room, since the ex-cop-turned-PI's bum leg—courtesy of a shoot-out with a bank robbery suspect a few years earlier—had left her with a permanent limp and caused her early retirement from the NYPD. Still, Darla had spent the three-hour flight competing with a cat carrier for foot room. She would wager she had just as many kinks as Jake, despite being a good six inches shorter than her friend.

While Jake pulled down their carry-ons from the overhead, Darla slipped into the seat Jake had vacated. Flipping her auburn braid over her shoulder, she leaned down to pry the cat carrier in question from where it had been lodged since the beginning of the flight. Then, with an effort, she hoisted the soft-sided container up onto the center seat and anxiously peered through its mesh side to see how the official FSA Guest of Honor was faring.

"You okay in there, Hammy?"

A groggy but decidedly peeved growl was her reply.

"Uh-oh," Darla said to Jake, who was now busy with her cell phone. "I think the herbal calming spray is wearing off."

"Well, give him another spritz of it," Jake advised. "Who knows how long it'll take first class to clear out so all us little people back here in economy can get off. Besides, we still have to collect our checked luggage, and then we've got the drive to the hotel. Let's just hope Ma isn't late."

So saying, she put the phone to her ear and began talking. Darla overheard snippets—"No, Ma, I said outside baggage claim!"—but her attention was on the oversized feline, whose protests were becoming more and more vocal.

"Come on, Hamlet," she coaxed, giving the spray bottle a couple of quick pumps. A faint scent of brandy tinged with something herbal promptly perfumed the air around the carrier. "Hold on just a little longer, and then we'll be in a nice hotel room where you can stretch out."

Though she had to give the cat props in that he'd been more than cooperative to that point. Feeling somewhat foolish, she had explained to him the previous night that the carrier was not a harbinger of a visit to the vet's—a bad place, to his mind—but a means to take him off to meet his fans. Whether it was that explanation or the fact that she'd baited the carrier with shrimp snacks, Hamlet had surprised her by climbing in on his own this morning. And several good spritzes of calming spray had kept him sleepy and mellow . . . that was, until now.

"Mee-roooow!"

Despite the renewed application of the herbal spray, Hamlet was rapidly rousing out of the relaxed state he'd been in for the greater portion of the trip. Now his muzzy cries could be heard over the bustle of passengers around them, impatient to deplane. Apparently, the calming concoction had a half life, at least when it came to this particular cat. The sooner she got Hamlet off the aircraft and into the terminal, the better.

"Mee-roooooow."

Hamlet gave a low, threatening rumble, which, had Darla heard it while wandering a veldt instead of sitting trapped in a 747, would have spurred her to flee for her life. The sound seemed to trigger a similar primitive reaction in the nearby passengers, for a space miraculously opened in the aisle beside her seat as people scuttled back.

By now, Jake had ended her call. Before Darla had a chance to update her on the situation, however, her friend gave her a conspiratorial wink and then spoke up.

"Now, now, we don't want a kitty meltdown," she addressed their fellow passengers within earshot. "Maybe we can squeeze by everyone else and get the poor little fellow out of here right now, before things go really bad." Jake shoved the phone into her jacket pocket and started up the aisle, both of their carry-ons in tow.

"Gangway—ferocious cat coming," Jake called as she began plowing her way through the queue before her. "Outta the way, folks, if you value your flesh! Ferocious cat! Make room! Hide the children."

Choking back a surprised laugh at her friend's chutzpah, Darla grabbed Hamlet's carrier and, hoisting the case on one hip, promptly followed after her. Unlike Jake, however, she didn't need to assume a carnival barker's spiel to clear a path. Hamlet was doing all the talking for her.

"Me-ROOW! Hissssssssssssss!"

Those passengers who'd been stubbornly ignoring Jake and continuing to block the aisle were not so quick to disregard Hamlet's warning cries. Most beat a hasty retreat back into their seats. A few more hardy souls broke into a trot in the direction of first class and the plane's open door, Jake on their heels. Darla moved behind them as quickly as she could, given that she was hauling a struggling twenty-pound cat. It wasn't until she'd reached the front that she paused long enough to set the carrier down with its unwilling occupant and extend the telescoping handle.

Thank goodness for wheels, she thought with a sigh, glad that she'd spent the extra money for a rolling carrier. Waiting at the door and the jetway beyond were the usual contingent of flight attendants and gate personnel. Jake, with a regal nod, had already sailed past them.

"You and your kitty enjoy your vacation," the male flight attendant who'd made the earlier arrival announcement told her.

"Me-ROOOOW!" was Hamlet's reply, the outraged sound making all of them jump.

"Thanks. Sorry," Darla managed with a weak smile as, leaving behind the stunned airline employees, she hurried into the jetway.

She'd left Hamlet's harness buckled on him for the journey. Still, in the mood he was in, she didn't dare unzip the carrier enough to snap on his leash and let him trot alongside her. Knowing Hamlet, the minute her back was turned, the wily feline would probably slice the lead with a claw and make a break for freedom.

"Jake, wait up," Darla called as she hurried through the tunnel, the sound of the carrier's wheels rumbling loudly behind her. The air in the jetway was warm and humid, unlike the cool, uncirculated air of the plane. If this was a preview of weather to come, she'd done well to pack away her coat.

"I'm going to have to remember that ferocious-cat trick the next time I fly," Jake said with a grin in the direction of Hamlet's carrier as Darla caught up. "I don't think I've ever gotten off a plane that fast before."

"Yeah, it worked pretty well," Darla conceded with a smile of her own as they headed to the baggage claim area. "And Hamlet seems to know we're on terra firma. He's quieted down again."

"Well, let's not stress him any more than we have to,"

Jake said. "Why don't I wait for the luggage, and you can take Hamlet outside to the curb to look for Ma."

"But how will I know her? What does she look like?"

"Everyone in the family says she and I look alike, except I have more gray hair. She dyes hers," Jake said with a wink.

Darla chuckled. "Okay, that helps. What kind of car does she drive?"

"Last time it was a blue Mustang convertible. Before that it was a big yellow pickup. She swaps out her car every couple of years, though, so for all I know she's got a Jeep now," Jake said with an indulgent shake of her curly head, adding, "But don't worry, I described you to her, so she'll find you if I'm not there yet when she pulls up."

They parted ways at the baggage carousel, with Darla wheeling the cat carrier through the glass doors leading outside to the passenger pick-up area. As the doors closed behind her, she was enveloped by a warm breeze redolent with the scent of tropical blooms overlaid by diesel fumes.

"Welcome to South Florida," Darla told herself, wishing now she'd gone for shorts and a tank top. This might be sweater weather for Floridians, but she'd been up in New York long enough that her blood had thickened. To Hamlet, she added, "Hang in there, boy. I'll get you some water the minute we hit the hotel."

She walked a short distance to the passenger pick-up area, where a steady stream of cars was trolling slowly past, their drivers looking for arriving friends and relatives. No old women who looked like Jake, however. No doubt she was still circling around the airport, Darla decided.

Resigned to the wait, she sagged onto a bench and took a deep breath. Immediately, tension she didn't know she had been holding seemed to seep from her very pores, along with a fine coating of sweat that abruptly enveloped her. She unzipped a side pocket on the carrier and pulled out the in-flight catalogue she'd taken from the plane. She used it to fan a little air into the carrier, relieved to see that the feline showed no further signs of distress as yet. For herself, she dug into the pocket again for the small clutch purse she'd stashed there. She fumbled through it until she found a tissue, which she used to blot her damp forehead.

"Hey, *chica*, like they say, it's not the heat. It's the humidity."

Darla looked up to see a short, handsome young Hispanic man dressed in knee-length khaki cargo shorts and a Hawaiian-style shirt grinning down at her. His teeth were bright against his neatly cropped black beard, as precisely trimmed as his short black hair. She couldn't see his eyes behind the pair of designer sunglasses he wore, but he exuded an air of friendly good humor that reminded her of people she'd known back home in Texas.

"Need a cab?"

He gestured to the vehicle behind him with the usual oversized phone number in block numerals along its side and the requisite triangular sign on its roof advertising some expensive gentlemen's club.

Darla gave a cautious shake of her head in return—she had a rule about not letting herself be chatted up by strange men—and answered, "Thanks, but we've got someone picking us up."

"You sure? What, you got a little doggie in that bag? You don't want to wait around, let the doggie get too hot."

"Actually, he's a cat, and we're okay," Darla assured him, smiling as she decided he was likely harmless if persistent. "Our ride should be here any min—"

A sudden blare of horns and squeal of tires echoed in the tunnel-like passage, the sound cutting her words short. Fluent now in the art of being a defensive pedestrian—living in NYC did that to one—Darla reflexively leaped up, grabbed the carrier's handle, and ducked behind a column. But feeling morbidly compelled to meet possible death head-on anyhow, she ventured a peek around her concrete barricade. She was in time to see a sporty, dark green Mini Cooper convertible zip around the other passing vehicles and slide to a stop mere inches from the taxi's rear bumper.

The cabbie's genial grin vanished, and he spouted a litany of outraged Spanish in the driver's direction. The coupe's top was down, and for a stunned instant Darla thought the Mini Cooper was driverless. Then, as she eased her way back around the column for a better look, she glimpsed a shock of bright stop-sign-red hennaed hair barely visible over the top of the steering wheel.

"Keep yer pants on, kid," came an elderly woman's voice from the convertible's direction, the accent almost stereotypical "Joisey." "It's not like I hit ya."

The cabbie made a shooing gesture to the unseen driver. "Hey, lady, this is taxi parking only. Get outta here!"

"Shame on you, treating an old lady with such disrespect," replied the woman. "I'm picking up someone. I got as much right here as you."

Proving her point, she shut off her car's engine, as if prepared to wait.

The cabbie gave his head a disgusted shake.

"Snowbirds," he spat, referring to the hordes of (mostly elderly) people from Canada and the Northeast—most particularly, New York and New Jersey—who made annual pilgrimages to Florida for the winter months before returning home again in the spring. "They can't drive, and they sure don't tip." He turned back to Darla. "This is what you got to look forward to in sunny South Florida. And, word to the wise, *chica*: Don't go near a restaurant around four-thirty in the afternoon. Those crazy snowbirds, they'll stomp their walkers over their own grandkids to make the early bird dinner special."

With that parting advice, he hopped back into his cab and pulled off in a cloud of exhaust, leaving the unseen elderly driver waving bony arms to dispel the fumes while shouting a few pithy curse words after him.

Wincing, Darla looked around, praying that either Jake or her mother would show up before any further drama ensued. Said prayers were promptly answered, as the terminal's automatic glass doors slid open again, and she saw Jake stride out, followed by a skycap wheeling a cart with their bags.

"Hey, kid, why are you sitting there? How come you're not in the car?"

"What do you mean?" Darla replied. "I'm still waiting for your mother." She looked toward the loading area in confusion. Then, as realization dawned, she focused back on the green Mini Cooper.

The old woman driving it had popped up from the convertible's front seat like a prairie dog checking out the surrounding. She waved her arms again, and her spiky hennaed hair fluttered like a cockatoo's crest in the sudden draft of a passing limo. Bright red lips spread in a thin grin, she called, "Jacqueline, *bambolina mia*, come give your old mama a kiss!"

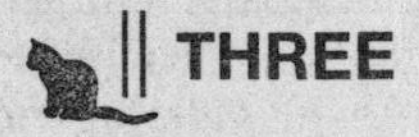

THREE

"YOU SAID SHE HAD RED HAIR," NATALIA MARTELLI SHRIEKED to her daughter over the sounds of interstate traffic. Glancing in the rearview mirror at Darla, she yanked a handful of her own cropped scarlet mane, and added, "That's not red hair. *This* is red hair."

"Both hands on the wheel, Ma!" Jake yelled back as the Mini Cooper swerved precariously close to the next lane, currently occupied by a semi. "You kill me in a car wreck, and I swear I'll come back to haunt you!"

"Eh, I'm a wonderful driver," the old woman protested, though to Darla's relief she returned her arthritic hands to the ten-and-two position on the wheel. "I'm the only one in the condo association who hasn't gotten a ticket yet this year."

"That's nothing to brag about, Ma. It's not even spring yet!"

While the two Martellis bickered, Darla shut her eyes and hugged the cat carrier on her knees more tightly. The one benefit of being crammed into the low backseat of the Mini between two oversized suitcases was the feeling of having additional protection in the event that the little convertible went flying off the highway. On the other hand, it was going to take Jake, her mother, and probably a crowbar to pry her out of the car again once they stopped . . . assuming they made their destination in one piece.

Hamlet gave a questioning meow, and Darla returned it with a reassuring little cluck. Lucky for him, the feline had no idea of the peril he was in. A whiff of his calming spray might have helped her endure the ride with similar aplomb. Too bad that she'd zipped the little spray bottle into her carry-on, now in the trunk behind her. Instead, she was going to have to go the Zen route and breathe deeply while conjuring peaceful images in her head.

Several verdant meadow visualizations and many deep breaths later, the vehicle began to slow. Darla cautiously opened her eyes again. She saw in relief that they were exiting the freeway, not that she was prepared to let her guard down yet. Didn't the old truism hold that most accidents happen ten miles from one's house—or, in Darla's case, hotel?

"You and Hamlet okay back there?" Mrs. Martelli called over her shoulder.

The old woman's initial introduction to the feline had taken place as they'd loaded the luggage into the Mini. Hamlet had managed not to hiss or growl, seemingly accepting Mrs. Martelli as extended family, being Jake's mother. In return, Mrs. Martelli had made the appropriate noises of approval while also confiding to Darla that she wasn't a cat person per se, but did the cat-show thing as a lark.

In the scheme of things, Darla deemed that encounter a great success.

Now she nodded. "Hamlet is snoozing, and my heartbeat's almost back to normal. No offense, Mrs. Martelli," she hurriedly added, catching the old woman's glance in the mirror.

The latter grinned again. This time, Darla saw the unmistakable resemblance between Jake and her mother despite their almost comical height difference. Both had the same strong features and heavy-lidded dark eyes, and both women had more than a hint of wickedness in their smiles.

"None taken, kid. And call me Nattie; everyone else does."

Nattie drove at a more sedate pace now that they were on the surface streets. Darla began to relax a bit, enjoying the warm breeze and sun on her face. "We're not in Brooklyn anymore, Hamlet," she murmured, gaping like the tourist she was.

And it *was* a whole new world, from both Texas and New York: art deco modern office towers and lofty condo buildings, tropical scents intermingling with auto exhaust. Of course, there were numerous fine examples from that same architectural period in New York City, Darla reminded herself, but here the buildings seemed so much more . . . well, deco. It had to be the use of color, she decided.

For, almost as if she had landed in Munchkinland, she was seeing colors she wasn't used to seeing—at least, not on homes. Stucco ruled this architectural world in lieu of brick or brownstone, in shades of pink and blue and green and yellow. In fact, so common were these sherbetlike colors that the occasional white structure stuck out like the proverbial opposable digit, as James would have termed it. Overall, the city appeared to be quite a splendid place to take a vacation.

A sense of excitement washed through her like an unexpected ocean wave. Nothing boring about this place. Heck, maybe she should open a second Pettistone's Fine Books location in South Florida, just to have an excuse to come back on a regular basis.

"Up ahead is the downtown business and historic district, where yer hotel and the convention center are at," Nattie announced as she slid through a yellow traffic light. "We're looking for Las Olas Boulevard. That's where the hotel is, and it's the street where all the tourists go. You got yer restaurants, yer bars, yer fancy-pantsy shops. Oh, yeah, and there's the Riverwalk, too."

"Riverwalk?" Darla echoed in surprise, recalling their hotel's name, the Waterview. "I thought we were going to be near the ocean."

"Sure, we keep driving, and we'll be at Port Everglades in a few minutes, if you want to hop a cruise ship. But this is Florida. You got yer water everywhere you look. The hotel's on the New River that comes out of the Everglades and dumps into the Atlantic not far from here."

Darla nodded, feeling a bit let down. With her hazy grasp of Fort Lauderdale geography, she'd assumed their accommodations would be overlooking the Atlantic, with plenty of sand and surf. Instead, it seemed the hotel had a view of some placid stream that meandered through the city.

"Don't worry, it's not yer run-of-the-mill river," Nattie assured her, seeming to sense her disappointment. "It runs fast, and there's all kinds of eddies and whirlpools in it. And they say that, back in the old days, the water was clear enough you could see sharks swimming up it."

"Sharks?" Jake interrupted. "Are you sure about that, Ma?"

"Would I lie to you?" Nattie gave her scarlet-crested head a vigorous shake, her expression offended. "Last year, I took a part-time job on one of them river taxis that rides up and down for the tourists. The boat people gave me a mike and this whole big spiel to memorize. I got to talk all about Fort Lauderdale history. Why the stories I learned—"

She broke off and swerved around an immense fallen palm frond that practically blocked the lane. The unexpected lane change drew a horn blast from the lumbering sedan behind them.

"Ah, keep yer pants on," Nattie muttered. To Darla and Jake, she added, "Them fronds, it's a full-time job keeping 'em picked up off the street. But it's the falling coconuts you really gotta watch out for. One hits you on the head, and it's lights out, permanent-like."

"Thanks for the warning, Ma," Jake said with an amused look back at Darla, who reflexively glanced skyward. Having lived in both Dallas and the New York City area, she thought she'd heard of every big-city hazard that could befall one, but killer coconuts wasn't one of them.

Nor were sharks in the water outside one's hotel window. And while the old woman hadn't mentioned anything about alligators, Darla was going to keep an eye peeled for those, too. From what the guidebooks said, you could assume you'd find one in any Florida body of water, no matter how small—and sometimes in people's swimming pools, too. No way was she going to let herself or Hamlet become gator bait!

When the little convertible halted at a red light, Darla checked out her surroundings while Jake and her mom chatted up front. The street had narrowed, and both car and pedestrian traffic had picked up. She spied, interspersed between the restaurants and bars, several of Nattie's so called "fancy-pantsy" shops, many with self-consciously clever names like Stuff (an antique store) and Your Tropical Bird (a women's chic apparel shop). Others were more to the point, like the enticing-looking Jennie's Bakery, which Darla vowed to check out during their stay.

"Here we are, the Waterview Hotel," Nattie said.

She pointed beyond the next traffic light toward a ten-story, art deco building that appeared to take up most of the block. While the hotel boasted a demure, sand-colored stone exterior, jaunty turquoise stripes raced skyward along its far corner, and bubble-gum pink awnings shaded its series of street-side entries. As they drew closer, Darla could pick out other typical art deco touches: the "eyebrows" over the windows, rounded corners instead of square, and the stepped upper stories that gave the place a vaguely pyramidal look. *This* was a hotel, she decided in satisfaction.

Nattie echoed Darla's thoughts. "Yer lucky they put you up here. I stayed here once, and it was great. Pool, sundeck, the whole smash. Good lookin' bellmen, too," she added with a wink for her daughter. "Oh, and the convention center where they're holding the cat show is the next block over. You can walk, no problem."

With those words, Nattie took the next corner and slid the Mini Cooper up a breezeway-covered drive that led to the hotel's main door. With the car stopped, the humidity that had been kept at bay by the moving air descended on Darla. Discreetly, she dabbed at the beads of sweat that formed again despite the shade. Not that she really was complaining. Warm and humid definitely trumped cold and snowy.

A balding, middle-aged bellman with a bright grin and dark tan made swift work of unloading their luggage onto a cart. When he went to take Hamlet's cat carrier, however, Darla smiled and shook her head.

"Sorry, live kitty inside. You'd better let me handle this one."

The grin remained in place. Apparently, he was used to such requests—at least, this week. "Yes, ma'am."

"Looks like we're not the only cat-show people booked at the hotel," Darla observed to Jake and Nattie.

The old woman nodded, flaming crest bobbing. "This show is a big deal. Lots of folks come from outta town. There'll be tons of cats staying here."

She turned to the bellman and handed him her keychain with a dangling zebra-striped stuffed heart the size of Hamlet's paw. "And don't let the valet run off with my car," she declared as she slung a red plaid canvas purse almost as big as she was over one skinny shoulder. "I'm just here dropping off the girls."

The three of them trooped through a pair of open frosted-glass doors, where Jake paused a moment to grimace at her reflection as she tried to smooth down the nimbus that her curly hair had become, courtesy of the convertible ride. Once inside the hotel lobby, they went in search of the front desk.

The wheels of Hamlet's carrier whirred loudly against the smooth, pale pink marble floors randomly inlaid with bits of mosaic: a seahorse here, a marlin there. Across the lobby, Darla could see that the doors leading out to the Las Olas Boulevard street front were propped open, as well. The long-ago architects obviously had designed the ground floor with the tropics in mind, for a mild but constant cross breeze kept the ambient temperature inside a good ten degrees cooler than outdoors.

The one thing that made her pause, however, was an odd, echoing buzz of sound that seemed to shimmer through the open floor plan. For a moment, it reminded her of the final minutes of a yoga class she'd once taken, when the class in unison had let loose with an unexpected series of guttural *oms*. The combination of voices had filled the room with a vibrating hum, much like what she was hearing now. And then, as she tuned into the lobby's acoustics a bit better, she realized what she was hearing.

Meow. Meow. Meow. Meow.

"Holy cats, talk about a lot of cats," Jake muttered as Darla zoomed in on the source of the mournful cries. Near the elevator, a luggage cart held four large animal carriers. An overly tanned middle-aged woman dressed in a sparkly T-shirt and too-short tennis skirt bent over them, seemingly trying to comfort the frightened felines. Darla wasn't sure how many cats actually were in the carrier, but she counted at least five paws waving pitifully from the carriers. To her relief, Hamlet gave but a single *meow-rumph* in return.

Obviously, he was going to be a real pro at this cat-show thing, she proudly thought.

By now, they'd reached the front desk, behind which stood a handsome, dark-skinned woman wearing a burgundy-colored skirted suit complete with a fancy gold "W" embroidered on the breast pocket of her jacket. Her black hair was slicked back into a smooth bun, which Darla eyed enviously. Darla's own auburn hair had immediately begun to frizz in the humidity, and she suspected that the minute she unbraided it, she'd be rocking Jake's same nimbus look. Which looked free-spirited on Jake, but a bit too Orphan Annie on Darla.

"Welcome to the Waterview Hotel," the desk clerk—Chantal, by her name badge—greeted them, her warm smile only slightly frazzled around the edges. Listening to a cat chorus who knew how many times over probably did that, Darla decided. Eyeing the carrier Darla was wheeling, the desk clerk added, "You must be one of our cat-show guests."

"Not just any guest," Nattie answered for her, drawing herself up with an important air. "This here is Hamlet the Karate Kitty. He's a real celebrity. He's on YouTube and everything!"

Chantal made the appropriate noises of interest as she input the pertinent information into her computer.

Seizing the opportunity, Darla reached into her bag and pulled out one of Hamlet's "paw"-tograph fliers—bookstore fliers featuring a photo of Hamlet and stamped with a cat paw print, which she'd made for their cat-show appearance. While obviously they weren't going to get a lot of walk-in customers that way—except for maybe a Brooklyn-based snowbird who happened to be at the show—she had added a coupon for free shipping. Besides which, she suspected that the children attending the show might enjoy something actually signed by the famous Karate Kitty.

"Courtesy of Hamlet," Darla said as she handed it over.

Chantal's smile broadened. "Thanks. And you tell Mr. Hamlet that if he needs anything special while he's here, just meow."

"As if she could hear him over the other cats," Jake muttered.

Chantal handed over two key cards and indicated the elevators. "You're on the sixth floor, overlooking the river. Enjoy your stay. We've told our staff not to disturb any of the cat-show rooms, so be sure you phone down here if you want your room cleaned or need extra towels or anything."

"What I need is a pit stop," Jake declared as the three women and feline headed to the elevator, whose ornate brass doors were scribed with scrolls and flowers, yet another example of the old building's art deco flair.

Hamlet meowed his agreement and Darla gave a sympathetic nod as the elevator door *ping*ed open. "Sounds like Hamlet does, too, after being stuck in the carrier half the day. I brought a bag of scoopable cat litter, so that should last us the week."

"Seriously? I was wondering why your suitcase was so much heavier than mine."

"You do know they sell cat litter in Florida, don't you?" Mattie added.

"I didn't want to take any chances that we wouldn't find a store near the hotel," Darla answered a bit defensively as they stepped inside the elevator, adding, "And on the bright side, at least we won't need to bring it back with us."

As the doors opened on the sixth floor a few moments later, they were greeted by a fainter version of the cat chorus from the lobby, now coming from multiple directions. Apparently, the hotel had booked all of the cat-show guests on the same level. *Not a bad idea*, Darla conceded as they made their way down the marble-tiled hall. It would be pretty hard for any of those guests to complain about the noise when they had cats of their own in their rooms. Hopefully, once everyone settled down, quiet would reign again.

The bellman had arrived ahead of them and had already begun unloading their luggage into what turned out to be a comfortable suite. Darla gave the place an appreciative once-over, deciding that being a feline guest-of-honor's lackey wasn't a half-bad gig. The main room held a love seat and two armchairs, along with a work desk and a table large enough to squeeze in four, plus a large flat-screen television mounted on one wall and a small fridge and coffee station. An adjoining alcove held two double beds and an armoire. The décor was what Darla pegged as "old-school Florida," with plenty of bamboo and pastels, framed travel posters from decades past, and even a potted palm tree situated near the sliding door that led to the balcony.

Before checking out that tempting view, however, Darla knew Hamlet had first priority. Once the bellman was out the door with a twenty-dollar tip—courtesy of Darla's kitty litter guilt—she concentrated on getting Hamlet comfortably set up in the oversized bathroom.

"Sorry, Hammy, but you'll need to stay in here at night and whenever we're not at the cat show," she told him once all his kitty gear had been situated. "It's too risky to leave you in the main room. I know no one is supposed to disturb the cat-show rooms without permission, but someone might open the door by mistake, and out you'd go to explore South Florida on your own. You know we can't have that."

Her cajoling tone had little effect on the cat. Perched upon the fluffy bath towel she had arranged atop the Jacuzzi tub's edge in imitation of his favorite sofa in her Brooklyn apartment, Hamlet shot Darla an emerald glare. He turned his back to her, crouching in an obvious display of feline pique, and looking obstinately in the direction of the sea foam–green tile wall.

So much for being a pro.

Darla sighed and tried again. "Hey, Hamlet, we're on vacation, so try to suck it up. Your food and water bowls are there under the sink, and your litter box is beside the people toilet. Oh, and your feather wand and catnip mouse are there on the towel shelf next to that big glass seashell. All the comforts of home, right?"

A knock sounded in reply. Jake opened the bathroom door a crack and peeked inside. "Is Hamlet settling in?"

"I'm afraid he's still pretty ticked off, though at least he's not making a lot of racket about it. Hopefully he'll get over it by morning."

"I'm sure he's just jet-lagged, kid. Let him nap and then take him for a nice walk when it cools down a bit. Speaking of which . . ."

Jake hesitated and gazed over her shoulder toward the hotel room before returning her attention to Darla.

"I hate to ask this, especially since we just checked in, but do you mind if I ditch you and Hamlet for a few hours? Ma's real anxious for a little one-on-one family time. She wants to show me her condo and introduce me to some of her friends. I figured we could do that, and then I can take her to the early bird special. She'll be in bed by eight, and I'll be back here in plenty of time to join you and Hamlet for a nightcap."

"Actually, I'd love to have a few hours to rest up from the flight and do a little Hamlet spoiling," Darla replied. "I thought I'd take a little nap of my own and then put him back in his harness and wander a bit."

"Perfect. Thanks for understanding."

Leaving Hamlet to indulge in his snit for a few minutes, Darla followed Jake back to the main sitting area, where Nattie was busy loading her purse with hotel stationery and pens from the desk. The hotel's complimentary magazine was already rolled up and tucked beneath her arm. At the sound of Jake loudly clearing her throat, her mother looked up with a guileless expression.

"Whaddaya looking at? They *expect* you to take this stuff."

"Sure they do, Ma," Jake agreed with a sigh. "Just don't start packing up the throw pillows, please."

"They are nice, ain't they?" Nattie said, wandering over to the sofa. She picked up one of the sherbet pink concoctions trimmed in little cranberry pom-poms and gave it a speculative look. As Jake began to sputter, Nattie shot her a grin. "Don't worry, I ain't gonna take it. Purse ain't big enough."

"And thank goodness for that. C'mon, Ma. Darla and Hamlet decided they'll hang out here while you give me the grand tour. I'll even take you to dinner."

"You mean it? Hey, I know the perfect spot. The restaurant across the street from my condo puts on a great buffet. The crab croquettes are to die for."

To Darla, Nattie added, "Thanks for indulging an old lady, Darla. I've missed my little girl since I've been down here. It'll be nice to catch up, just the two of us."

Darla smiled as she watched them leave the hotel room, Jake's arm around the old woman—though whether it was an affectionate gesture or simply a move to keep her from absconding with the official Waterview Hotel–branded coffee cups she was eyeing, Darla wasn't certain. In some respects, they made a comically mismatched pair, the Amazonian Jake and the pixielike Nattie. But in the short time that she'd known Nattie, Darla could see that Jake and her mother were more alike than either probably cared to admit. And she had no doubt that under their constant bickering was genuine love.

Suddenly feeling a bit homesick for her own family back in Texas, Darla distracted herself by wandering over to the sliding glass door, which led out to the balcony. With a quick look over her shoulder first, to be sure the bathroom door was still firmly shut, she unlatched the slider and stepped out into the Florida afternoon sun.

At six stories up, the view was at once exhilarating and relaxing. On the next block over to her left sat a squatter version of the hotel, which had to be the conference center that Nattie had mentioned. Beyond it, she could see office towers (mere spires, really, compared to the gargantuan edifices of New York City) along with the city's older buildings. Intertwined, they made a colorful architectural patchwork held together by the same palms and tropical flowering trees she'd spied on the drive in. In the distance, directly in front of her, she glimpsed what she realized were the white funnels and antennae of a docked cruise ship.

Below her snaked the river Nattie had told her about. It was no placid stream, but a broad and seemingly deep beast of a river that raced its way past her. The boaters appeared to be out in full force: small cruisers, fishing boats, even a modest yacht or three. A few kayakers braved the waters, as well, along with placarded tour boats and water taxis. As Darla watched, what she guessed was a chartered party boat slowly drifted past, tanned young women in microscopic bikinis and young men in baggy board shorts gripping beer bottles and hurricane glasses while the sound of steel drums blasted from what had to be a dozen speakers.

Spring break time, she thought in indulgence as she did an impromptu dance step in response to the calypso music. Leaving the sliders open, she went to unpack her own bags.

Remembering that she'd promised to check in with James once she was settled into the hotel, Darla stopped unpacking and reached for her cell phone. Despite her worry over what might be going on back at the store, however, she had to suppress a laugh as James's voice mail recording played.

Professor James T. James here. If you have reached this digital approximation of my voice, it is an indication that I am occupied with other duties. As I will not succumb to the prevailing societal rudeness that demands one answer a cellular phone to the detriment of more pressing obligations, you have no choice but to leave a message, which I will return at my convenience. Good day to you.

"Hey, James," Darla said after the beep, with only a hint of a snicker, "this is Darla. Hamlet and I made it to the Waterview Hotel just fine."

Before she could say any more, however, she heard the

sound of a call coming through and checked the caller ID. "James," she said, having hurriedly hung up on the original call, "did the plumber ever show? Are we still on schedule?"

"And hello to you, too, Darla," came his familiar mellow tones. "I trust your flight was without incident?"

"No problems. Florida is great. Now, what about the coffee bar? I'm still annoyed that Alex Putin never even stopped by in person to introduce himself before I signed the contract." Darla complained.

She stopped her diatribe when she heard a small sigh on the other end; then James replied, "As a matter of fact, Mr. Putin stopped by soon after I sent you the message this morning. He resolved the issue with the plumber, and all is back on track. Indeed, the basic bar is already roughed in."

"Really? That's fantastic!" Darla replied in relief. "Why don't you text me a picture? No, don't," she interrupted herself. "I'm supposed to be focused on the cat show. If you start sending me pictures, I'll just obsess over that. I'd rather wait and see the finished product when I get home again."

She went on to give James their room number. "I'll phone again tomorrow afternoon and let you know how Hamlet's debut went," she finished. "Call me on my cell if you or Robert need anything in the meantime."

With that duty out of the way, she resumed unpacking. By the time she'd hung her last pair of slacks in the closet, Darla found herself yawning. No doubt the long plane ride and the tropical breeze were to blame, she told herself.

Checking on Hamlet once more and finding him snoozing in the bottom of the Jacuzzi tub, she returned to the balcony. Compared to the room, the balcony was a bit spartan: a broad U of railings with just enough room for two lounge chairs and a round table between them. The balconies on either side were almost touching distance from hers, but fortunately none of the other rooms' occupants were taking advantage of the afternoon sun. Which meant that she could relax on one of the lounge chairs without worry of being disturbed. All she wanted to do was shut her eyes for a moment and listen to the breeze and the now-distant sound of calypso music.

Darla awoke with a start some time later to realize that the calypso music had long been silent, and the sun had fallen behind the taller buildings, leaving her balcony in shade. *So much for closing my eyes for a minute*, she thought in dismay. She must have slept for over an hour, she realized as she sat up and checked her watch. Yep, five o'clock. Time to check on Hamlet, and then—

She stifled a cry as she glimpsed something black out of the corner of her eye, like a small shadow . . . something that most definitely hadn't been with her when she'd first settled on the lounger. Carefully, she turned her head toward the balcony to her left, visions of building-scaling sharks and errant coconuts swooping through her sleep-fuzzy brain.

And then she froze.

For there on her balcony, perched six floors up on a railing no wider than her hand, sat Hamlet.

FOUR

"HAMLET," DARLA SOFTLY CAJOLED, BARELY DARING TO breathe. "Good boy, Hammy. Come down off that railing and sit with me, okay?"

From his narrow perch on the balcony rail six stories up, Hamlet blinked and stood. Then, while Darla watched in growing dread, he turned toward the river view and slid his front paws forward on the railing to stre-e-e-e-tch, tail and rump high in the air. Then he daintily began walking his makeshift balance beam, following along the short side. Not missing a step, he turned to march halfway down the railing in front of her, where he paused, silhouetted most artistically against the skyline and setting sun.

Darla winced as she took in this display, her heart beating wildly. How Hamlet had managed to get out of the closed bathroom, she could not guess. But she had no doubt that this show was being purposefully put on by the cagey feline, most likely in revenge for the plane ride and bathroom banishment. She should be furious with him, but terror was the only emotion she could summon at the moment. Even as athletic a cat as Hamlet could lose his balance. A six-story fall would likely mean his death.

Gulping back her fear, she softly called to him again. "Hamlet, come on back. You made your point, and you're scaring me. Let's go back inside, and then I'll take you out for a nice supper downstairs."

Hamlet stared back at her, green eyes wide, before glancing back at the river view behind him. As Darla watched in growing fear, he bunched himself up in preparation for a jump. Obviously, he had decided that freedom was worth the risk.

No, Hamlet, no! she silently screamed, fearing that if she lunged for him, he would tumble from the railing. As if in slow motion, Hamlet gathered himself for the leap . . . and then turned and lightly bounded onto her lounge chair before trotting back inside the hotel room.

"Hamlet, you little so-and-so!"

Darla did a little bounding of her own, leaping off the chair and rushing back inside after him. She stopped, however, to shove the slider door closed behind her, latching it and then dragging the desk chair up against it for good measure. No way was that balcony door getting opened again during their stay!

By the time she'd managed the door and turned back around, Hamlet was nowhere to be seen. Darla did a quick reconnoiter of the place and found him lying on her bed atop the decorative pillows that had earlier been arranged in a strategic pyramid of tropical hues. Now they'd been tumbled into an untidy heap upon which His Catship lounged, green eyes innocently wide and long black tail flicking ever so slightly.

"Hamlet, you gave me a freaking heart attack!" she scolded him, wagging a finger for emphasis. "Don't you ever pull another stunt like that again, hear me?"

Hamlet merely blinked as if to say, *Why so upset? This was all just an unfortunate misunderstanding.*

Darla wasn't buying what he was selling, however. Stomping from the room, she went over to examine the bathroom door, which stood ajar. She was certain she'd closed the door tightly when she'd left, but maybe the clever cat had figured out a way to open it.

Taking another look at the door, she noted that it opened with a lever-style handle. Stretched to his full length, Hamlet could likely just barely reach that handle, she judged. With a nice vertical leap, he'd easily be able to grab it between both front paws and, with his body weight hanging from it, click loose the catch. Since the bathroom door opened outward into the main room, the momentum of his moving body would be enough to swing the door wide open.

Given the way he'd commandeered her bed, it was obvious Hamlet had no intention of being banished to the bathroom again. Bowing to the inevitable, Darla left that door open so that he had access to his litter box and food. So long as the balcony door remained shut, and the "do not disturb" sign remained on the hallway door, she judged it would be safe enough to leave him free to roam the room while she was there.

"Fine, Hamlet. You win," Darla told him as she returned to the bedroom alcove. "I won't lock you in again, but you have to swear you won't try to run off, okay? Now, how about I change, and then we'll go downstairs. Maybe they have crab croquettes here, too."

A few minutes later, Darla had exchanged her jeans and top for a cute yellow-and-white striped sundress with a matching yellow sweater.

"All right, your turn," she informed the cat as she held up his harness and leash.

Despite his earlier bad behavior, Hamlet was surprisingly agreeable about being fastened into the black harness and matching lead. He'd learned to walk on a leash a few weeks earlier at the recommendation of a self-styled "feline behavioral empath" named Brody Raywinkle. Darla had consulted with the young man (whom she privately referred to as a "cat whisperer") to help rouse Hamlet from a dangerous funk he'd fallen into following a recent trauma. Whether or not Brody had actually been responsible for getting Hamlet back on track emotionally, she wasn't sure. But he'd definitely been the one who had schooled the feline in the fine art of the harness, and daily walks had become part of their routine ever since.

A few minutes later, Darla and Hamlet were striding across the pale pink marble of the lobby. A few people—mostly the attractive bellmen Nattie had mentioned, though also a few hotel guests—were scattered about the open hall. Darla was immediately aware of attention turning quite blatantly her way. She wasn't vain enough to think that she was the cause of the turning heads, appealing as the thought was. Obviously, it was the unexpected sight of what appeared to be a miniature panther walking on a leash that was drawing all the looks.

"Mama, Mama, look!" came the high-pitched cry from across the lobby. Darla glanced over to see a dark-haired boy, perhaps ten years old, pointing in her direction.

Darla gave the boy, who was wearing a green and orange Miami Dolphins T-shirt over red shorts, a friendly little wave in return. *Cat lovers—indoctrinate them while they're young*, she thought in amusement. His mother, however, appeared less thrilled than he. Dressed in a plus-sized version of her son's T-shirt, she continued dragging him in the direction of the elevators.

But the young man had other plans.

"Wait, it's the Karate Kitty, the one on the computer!" Darla heard the boy stubbornly insist. "I want to meet him."

He broke from his mother's grasp and started running in Darla's direction, his flip-flops slapping frantically upon the marble. "He really is the cat in the video, isn't he?" the boy excitedly demanded of Darla as he skidded to a stop before her. "The Karate Kitty?"

Darla smiled. "You're right; he really is. You're pretty smart to recognize him. Hamlet thought he could go undercover down here in Florida."

The boy, meanwhile, had dropped to his hands and knees before the feline. Hamlet sat back on his haunches and gave the child a cool green look in return. The boy widened his own eyes, but to Darla's relief kept a respectful distance, even though he was literally bouncing with excitement.

"Wow, this is better than meeting Mickey! Can he do karate now? Can he?"

"I'm afraid Hamlet doesn't do karate on demand. He's very stubborn that way. But don't worry, you can have his 'paw'-tograph." Darla pulled one of the fliers from her bag.

The boy stared in awe at the stamped paw print and then leaped up.

"Wow! Thanks!" he yelled, and then ran to meet his mother, who was still trudging toward them. The woman gave Darla a sour look as she grabbed her child's hand and swung back around toward the elevators once more. The boy seemed not to notice his mother's pique, however, for he was busy explaining to her how he'd just met the famous Karate Kitty.

"Sorry, Hamlet. I guess not everyone is a fan," Darla told the feline. "Come on, let's get a little exercise while it's still light, and then we'll grab some supper."

Their first stop was the hotel gift shop, which offered, in addition to the usual snacks and emergency pharmaceuticals, an upscale collection of coastal-themed souvenirs. Several were items that Darla had seen in her own room: the embroidered guest robe, the tropical prints, the glass seashell sculpture, and even one of those pastel throw pillows Nattie had admired. Darla bought a handful of postcards to mail to friends and family. She also purchased a guest robe each for Robert and James, which she scheduled to be delivered up to her later that evening once she returned to the room. Then she and Hamlet—who had indicated his boredom with shopping by plopping down in the middle of the store and flinging one leg over his shoulder while he licked the base of his tail—headed for the great outdoors.

Leaving the hotel lobby, the pair headed down the sidewalk, making their way along picturesque Las Olas Boulevard. A mild breeze along with a setting sun made Darla glad she'd grabbed her sweater. The boulevard was stop-and-go with shoppers headed home and hungry diners headed in; still, the street traffic was far less frenetic than she was used to back in Brooklyn.

The pedestrian traffic, however, was a different story.

Feeling a bit smug now that she'd lived a year in a city where walking was the norm, Darla could immediately spy those tourists who rarely left the confines of their cars. These were the people who stopped smack in the middle of the sidewalk to discuss dining options, or who walked three and four abreast, so that anyone coming from the opposite direction had to step off the curb to let them pass. Not to mention the ones walking with travel brochures clutched in their hands, their heads bent back to ogle their surroundings.

"Hey, *chica*!"

The vaguely familiar-sounding salutation came from the street behind her. Darla tore her attention from a store window to see if she were the *chica* being hailed. Sure enough, she saw behind her a taxi whose bearded young driver was leaning toward the open passenger window, one tanned, tattooed arm waving in her direction.

"Looks like you found your ride," the cabbie from the airport called with a grin. "And that must be *el gato*—the cat—you had in your bag. So, you and your *gato* need a cab now?"

"No, we're just out enjoying a little walk," Darla replied with a smile. "And I hate to tell you, but that snowbird lady who almost rear-ended you at the airport turned out to be my ride."

"Seriously?"

The look of dismay he gave her made Darla laugh outright, her amusement earning her a slanted look from Hamlet. "Yeah, I know, but we made it here in one piece, so all's well."

"Well, be careful. You read the paper, and the police, they're always pulling those old people's cars out of canals and crashed buildings," he warned. Pointing at the phone number on the cab door, he added, "Next time you need a ride, call and ask for Tino T. I'll get you where you want to go. No crashes, I promise."

"I'll keep that in mind," Darla told him, not sure whether he was kidding about the canals and buildings. But having recently experienced the road with Nattie at the wheel, she was inclined to believe him.

He nodded. "Oh, if you and your *gato* get hungry later, that's my sister's place," he added, indicating a shop a few doors down. The sign said "Jennie's Bakery," the same place Darla had noticed on the drive to the hotel. "She makes the best Cuban pastries in town. Tell her I sent you and she'll give you a sample."

"I'll do that," Darla assured him.

Tino nodded and waved again before blending back into traffic. Still smiling, Darla turned her attention back to Hamlet. "Okay, that talk about pastries was the last straw. How about we call it quits on the walk and grab a bite at the hotel?"

Fifteen or so bistro tables on the sidewalk along the hotel comprised the outdoor dining at the Waterview's restaurant, fenced in by waist-high wrought iron and leaving the rest of the walkway clear for pedestrian traffic. Each table was appointed with crisp white napkins folded into crowns and green glass chargers that matched the empty imported water bottles serving as vases for single red hibiscus blooms. Seats were already filling up despite the early hour, so Darla felt fortunate to score a table with a clear view of the street and activity across the way.

At the end of the row of tables, a column supported the permanent overhang sheltering the sidewalk dining area. Behind that column, a saxophonist was playing something light and breezy that made Darla think of piña coladas and ocean surf. Inspired, she waved down her server, a petite girl dressed in black slacks and a gold Waterview blouse topped by a long black apron, and ordered one—a drink, not an ocean.

"And water for my cat, please," she added to the departing girl as she looped Hamlet's lead around the leg of her chair. Unimpressed by the ambiance that so pleased Darla, the feline responded by leaping up onto the seat next to her and plopping into an inky heap.

"No sulking," she told him. "I'll buy you a nice shrimp cocktail to make up for the flight."

A few minutes later, the frosty rum, coconut, and pineapple concoction in her hand and Hamlet's bowl of water safely under the seat, Darla ordered their suppers and settled in for a bit of people watching. There was plenty to see from her vantage point. Most of the passersby were dressed in either tourist regalia: logo T-shirts (variations on the Mouse predominating) and shorts or jeans for both male and female; or what she'd dubbed "South Florida casual": flirty sundresses like hers for the ladies, and Hawaiian shirts over cargo pants or chinos for the men.

Her favorite wardrobe category, however, belonged to the twentysomething girls parading up and down the sidewalk and slyly glancing about to see if they were being noticed. The uniform consisted of short shorts, a dressy blouse falling off at the shoulder, and fuzzy boots better suited to northern climes than the temperate weather in Fort Lauderdale.

Now this is Reese's kind of Fort Lauderdale, she thought with a smile.

Reese was NYPD Detective Fiorello Reese, with whom Jake had once worked. Darla had met him when Jake had brought him in to help work off-duty security at an event at the bookstore. He and Darla had clashed initially, mostly because he thought books were only good for propping broken furniture, and she thought he didn't give enough credit to her and Hamlet for helping the police solve more than one unsavory crime in their neighborhood.

It didn't help that Darla had never been into blond, blue-eyed guys built like a young Ah-nold, while Reese—a stereotypical Italian guy despite his corn-fed, Midwestern looks—had a decidedly retro attitude toward women. But over time, and with Jake's admitted encouragement, their relationship had morphed into a friendship that, once or twice, they'd tried to take to the next level. The result, however, had been vaguely uncomfortable, to the point they had mutually decided that perhaps they did better simply as friends.

Still, a bit of a spark remained between them, making Reese the closest thing to a "boyfriend" that Darla currently had.

Making a mental note to pick up a tacky souvenir T-shirt for him, Darla turned to casually scan her fellow diners, wondering if any were cat-show attendees. No one seemed to fit the mold, however, she decided in disappointment. No cat jewelry, no stray fur on fabric. And Hamlet appeared to be the only cat enjoying al fresco dining. No doubt the other owners weren't going to risk bringing their show cats out in public. But surely that didn't mean they were all holed up in their hotel rooms with their furry charges.

Abruptly, she recalled that the cat-show itinerary she had been provided had said something about a welcome cocktail party on Friday night. Doubtless that was where the action was tonight.

She momentarily considered having her food packed to go, leaving Hamlet in the hotel room, and heading to the social instead. But after Hamlet's high-wire act earlier, she figured it was better to keep him close. No way would she ever forgive herself if something happened to the curmudgeonly kitty.

The server interrupted her musings. "Tilapia for you, ma'am, and a shrimp cocktail for the, uh, gentleman. Can I bring you another drink?"

"One's plenty. We have an early morning tomorrow," she told the young woman, appreciatively eyeing the arrangement of delicate fish and colorful sauce on the plate before her.

Tempting as it was to dig right in, however, Hamlet came first. The scent of fish had quickly reached his sensitive nostrils, and he was sitting up in his chair, whiskers quivering. Darla plucked the half-dozen cocktail shrimp from their ice bed and lopped off their tails; then, feeling artistic, she arranged them in a neat pinwheel on a plate, which she set on the ground beneath his chair.

"Here you go, Hammy. Bon appétit."

The feline needed no further prompting and leaped down and dug right in, making little *nom-nom* noises of appreciation as he chomped away. Darla did the same, minus the sound effects. And in short order, both she and Hamlet had cleaned their respective plates.

"That was wonderful," Darla said with a sigh, pushing her plate away.

Hamlet apparently agreed with the assessment. Leaving his empty plate on the ground, he lightly leapt back up into his chair and began cleaning his whiskers with an oversized paw. Darla reached for the remains of her piña colada and took another sip before glancing at her watch. It was only six-thirty . . . a good hour and a half before Jake had expected to return. No way could she nurse the final two inches of her drink that long, and she didn't really feel like wandering back up to the room yet. And with the cocktail party already nixed . . .

Feeling only a bit guilty, she sucked down the rest of her

piña colada and flagged down her server for a second one after all. Hamlet voiced no opinion of her overindulgence, busy as he still was with his après-dinner bath. Once the drink arrived, Darla settled back into her chair and lazily sipped.

"*This* is what we'll do when we retire, Hammy," she told the cat, listening in appreciation as the saxophonist switched gears to a more bluesy set. And then Darla noticed the sole occupant at a nearby table.

She sat perhaps a dozen feet from Darla, at the opposite end from where the sax player lurked. Her table was half-hidden by one of the columns but partially illuminated by a nearby street lamp. Now that the diners at both tables between them abruptly stood and began heading out, Darla had a relatively unimpeded view of the woman seated there.

She appeared to be about a good decade or more older than Darla, maybe in her late forties, her dark, bobbed hair liberally frosted and blown out to jaw-length perfection. She was dressed a few steps up from Darla's South Florida casual, her beige linen shirtdress belted with a heavy gold chain that matched both the bangles on her arms and her gold strappy sandals. She clutched a martini glass in one hand while two other empty ones sat abandoned on the table in front of her.

Drinking alone.

The judgy thought flashed through Darla's mind, though she promptly felt a bit hypocritical—after all, she was alone herself, and on her second drink. But the way the woman was protectively hunched over her martini seemed to indicate serious imbibing going on.

Not my business, Darla scolded herself.

Even so, morbid curiosity kept her sneaking glances that way. By now, the server had brought the woman drink number four and collected the evidence of the other three. Hopefully, the Martini Lady, as Darla dubbed her, was a hotel patron who wouldn't be hopping into an automobile anytime soon.

Darla was contemplating walking over to offer a friendly word when she saw a girl in a ragged version of the twentysomething wardrobe wander over to the woman's table.

The newcomer planted herself there and stood with hand out. Her back was to Darla, but from the aggressive stance and outstretched palm, Darla pegged the girl as a panhandler. No doubt she had seen the older woman sitting alone as an easy mark, likely because the latter had been drinking. Between the sax player and traffic noises, Darla couldn't make out what was being said between the two women, but it was obvious the two were arguing.

The situation abruptly set off Darla's hinky meter. Hamlet's finely tuned feline radar must have sensed that something was off as well, for he paused in midlick and swiveled his furry black head in the direction of the woman's table. Concerned now, Darla looked about for the server so she could point out the situation. Hopefully, the waitress could contact someone in hotel security to be on the alert in case things escalated.

As things abruptly did.

While Darla watched in shock, the girl snatched up the water bottle vase from the table, the water and hibiscus blossom tumbling out. Gripping its narrow end, she raised it in an intimidating manner.

Darla's eyed widened. This was like a bar brawl in a bad movie!

To the older woman's credit, however, she did not appear frightened by the threat. Instead, sloshing down another gulp of her martini, she pushed back from the table and rose, an admonishing finger pointed at the girl. But although the contentious pair were the same height, the girl still had the advantage of her makeshift weapon, while the older woman was backed against the hotel wall.

Darla glanced frantically around again. None of the other diners seemed to notice what was going on, and the waitress had apparently disappeared for parts unknown. If anyone was going to intervene to halt the fight before it happened, it would have to be Darla.

Hamlet, meanwhile, had abandoned his bath and raised up on his haunches so that his front paws leaned against the table as he kept his emerald gaze fixed on the pair. Darla hesitated, then determinedly slid her own seat backward. While she had some rudimentary martial arts training, she wasn't equipped to go up against someone with a weapon. And, tempting as it might be to let Hamlet take the lead in this—she'd already seen the feisty feline in action once before—she couldn't put him in harm's way. But she did have one weapon of her own that she knew the panhandler couldn't defend against.

FIVE

"IT MUST HAVE BEEN THAT SECOND PIÑA COLADA," A chagrinned Darla explained to Jake a couple of hours later. "I know I should have waited on hotel security to handle the situation, but there wasn't time. So I did the only thing I could think of to scare her away."

Jake looked up from stocking the mini fridge with leftovers courtesy of Nattie, and grinned.

"Hey, you get points for originality, if nothing else. And I have to say, I would have given up my whole plate of crab croquettes—which were lovely, thank you very much—to see you jump up on that chair and yell at her to cease and desist."

"Well, it worked. The panhandler didn't even look my way. She just dropped the bottle and tore off down the street," Darla answered in satisfaction. "And don't worry, Hamlet had my back."

From his spot atop the sofa back, Hamlet gave a small *meow-rumph.*

"Not that I got any thanks for making a fool of myself," Darla continued. "Here I saved the woman from being beaned with a Perrier bottle by some crazy street person, and she acted like *I* was the insane one. You should have seen the nasty look she gave me before she ran into the hotel. And the other diners weren't much better."

Jake shut the refrigerator door and rose, nodding in commiseration.

"Like they say, *no good deed*, et cetera," she agreed, popping a bite-sized piece of chocolate cheesecake into her mouth and offering one to Darla. "But don't worry, you handled things the best way you could have under the circumstances."

"Try telling that to the Martini Lady."

Sighing, Darla accepted the cheesecake consolation prize, and added, "Poor Hamlet. I almost gave him a heart attack, shouting like that. I hope he forgives me."

"Frankly, it sounds a little tit for tat," Jake observed, slanting a disapproving look at the feline in question, who merely gave an innocent blink in return. "What you said he did to you on the balcony was pretty darned bad."

"Well, Hamlet will be with us pretty much all the time, so hopefully there won't be an opportunity for him to try his high-wire act again," Darla said, mentally crossing her fingers that she was right. "And if I'm really lucky, I won't bump into the Martini Lady again."

"That's the spirit. And even if you do run across her, once she's sober, she'll probably thank you for getting involved . . . assuming she remembers what happened."

Darla gave a rueful nod. "So, stick a fork in this one, right? Now, your turn. How did things go with you and your mom?"

Jake snorted. "As usual, Ma has a hidden agenda to everything. The dinner part of it was fine, but turns out we finished up at the buffet just in time for her monthly condominium association meeting. There are some rumblings that someone on the board of the directors is skimming money from the association, taking kickbacks from the subcontractors, stealing pennies out of the poor box. You get the idea. The association is down a good fifty thousand dollars that they know of, maybe more. Ma wanted me to sit in on the meeting with her and see if I could ID the culprit."

"Wow, fifty thousand dollars? That's a lot of money! So, did you figure it out?" Darla asked, truly curious.

Jake shook her head.

"I'm a PI, not a psychic. Unless someone breaks down and confesses, these things can take a couple of years to sort out. You've got to go through the paper trail and see what's there—and what's not there—and then you can start building a case," she explained. "I told Ma she needs to check the association bylaws to see what her rights are, then she can request records from the board and get a CPA to review them. But here's the kicker."

Jake paused to grab the sherbet-colored throw pillows from the sofa and, one by one, Frisbeed them into the corner before flopping onto the now bare couch.

"It turns out Ma is the lone voice questioning the identity of the guilty party. All the other condo owners think it's the condo association president, this guy named Billy Pope, who's doing the embezzling. Ma claims that Billy's being falsely accused."

"Ouch. Not good."

"Oh, it gets better," Jake added with a grim smile as she arranged her long legs over the sofa arm. "Not only is this guy Ma's good friend, he's also the head judge for the Feline Society of America and the one who's pretty much running the National Championship."

"Double ouch," Darla replied, wincing. "Plenty of room for all kinds of fraud and underhanded stuff there. So, did you meet him? What was your impression—crook or not crook?"

"Hard to tell. He seemed like a nice enough old guy—your basic white-haired, twinkly-eyed grandpa type. And he didn't get all twitchy when she told him I used to be a cop. But on the other hand, that Madoff guy fooled a lot of people for a lot of years. And some of those other board members sure were giving him the stink eye all night."

"So your mom wants you to spend your vacation doing a little PI work?"

Jake shrugged. "I reminded her that I'm here to keep an eye on Hamlet, at least until the cat show is over. Not to mention I'm not licensed to do a darn thing in the state of Florida. But Ma swears that Billy's being set up, so I told her I'd keep an eye peeled this week and see if I spot anything funny going on."

Darla gave her friend a considering look. "You know, the cat-show folks are only footing the bill through Sunday night. If you want, we can cancel the reservations I had here for the rest of the week and camp out at your mom's place until we leave. You know, so we can be in the thick of all the condo action."

"Darla Pettistone, you're the bravest woman I know," Jake said with a chuckle. "I'd never volunteer to do that, and she's my mother." Then, sobering, she added, "But tell you what, let's see how things shake out after the show. If I think we've got a shot at uncovering any dirty dealings, we might do just that. Plus it will save us a buck or two."

"Me-ooow" was Hamlet's contribution from the discarded pile of sofa pillows that he'd made his own.

Darla shot Jake an amused glance. "Think someone has a theory about Nattie's embezzler?"

"That, or he's saying he'd rather stay at the hotel," Jake replied.

MEOW. MEOW. MEOW. MEOW.

"It's like the hotel lobby all over again, multiplied a hundred times," Darla exclaimed the next morning over the noise reverberating through the convention center floor.

Jake winced in sympathy. "I don't suppose you packed any earplugs, did you?"

"Eh, you get used to it," Nattie assured them from behind the check-in table. Her scarlet hair neatly subdued today into a slicked-back bob, she looked professional in her official purple FSA polo shirt, adorned with a giant beribboned button that proclaimed "Volunteer." "It bothered me a little the first time, but this is the third show I've worked now. Once the cats are all settled in their cages and covered up, things will quiet down."

"They don't sound very happy to be here," Darla observed.

Nor did Hamlet, she realized as she looked down at the feline. While he'd been cooperative on the walk over, seemingly enjoying the temperate early morning breeze, he was now hunkered down on the floor between Darla and Jake, twitching his tail and softly grumbling. As an only cat, he wasn't used to sharing his space with other felines . . . certainly not a couple of hundred of them. No doubt he would have appreciated the earplugs Jake had mentioned, Darla thought in sympathy.

Nattie shrugged. "That's how cats are. It's mainly the first-timers making the most noise. Take a look around, though, and you'll see which ones are the veterans. They just curl up and go to sleep until it's their turn in the ring."

"Well, let's hope the sandman flits through here pretty darned quick," Jake declared, a finger in one ear to muffle the sound.

Nattie grinned. "An hour or two, max, and it'll settle down." Then, with a huff, she added, "Say, did you get a load of the kids picketing outside the front door? We didn't have time for that sort of nonsense in my day," she declared, which Darla thought unlikely considering that the protest-filled 1960s were likely Nattie's "day."

"Well, you know, Ma . . . free speech, and all that."

"Free speech, my patootie! If they really cared about the

animals, they'd be scooping poop in a shelter somewhere," Nattie complained in return.

On this point, Darla was inclined to agree with the older woman's assessment. Thankfully, their encounter with said picketers had been brief. Jake had declared that her bum leg was recovered enough from the previous day's airline torture to handle the short walk to the Waterview's convention facilities, so she, Darla, and Hamlet had hoofed it . . . drawing, of course, the expected attention. Early morning joggers and office workers walking their way to their jobs paused to smile and stare at Hamlet, who was in his official harness and looking very much the feline YouTube sensation.

Strategically placed signs along the convention center building had directed them to the exhibition hall where the cat show was taking place. Unfortunately, to reach the main entrance at the top of a broad series of steps, they'd been forced to walk past three college-aged girls flaunting protest signs—and quite a bit more.

"Show flesh, not fur!"

The trio of chanting young women were all dressed in thong bathing suits despite the cool morning temperature. The "Flesh" slogan was repeated on one young woman's placard, along with the more basic "Cats Don't Belong in Cages," brandished by another girl. Yet another sign read, a bit more crudely, "If You Want to Breed, Ask for My Number." Obviously, the girls were members of some animal rights group, but what their beef with the cat-show circuit was, Darla wasn't certain.

"You with the red hair—unchain your cat and set him free!" one of the girls had shrieked at Darla as she, Jake, and Hamlet strode past. The shrieker had been a bleached blonde—a good two inches of black roots were showing—wearing a pink-sequined thong bikini, a bleeding heart literally tattooed over one breast.

"Don't engage the crazy," Jake had muttered. "You start

a conversation with one of these types, and you about have to chew off an arm to get free."

Darla nodded in agreement, though her primary thought at the moment was to wonder just how uncomfortable a sequined thong must be. But while she and Jake studiously ignored the group, Hamlet had other ideas. Once they'd reached the top step leading in, the feline had abruptly flopped down and flung one leg over his shoulder before giving his hindquarters a lick. The gesture was what Darla always considered the feline equivalent of a middle-finger salute.

"Guess Hamlet doesn't want to be liberated," Darla had observed with a chuckle, drawing a matching grin from Jake. By that point, the protesters had found other show attendees to heckle, so the trio made it inside without further incident.

Now, Darla told Nattie, "They were being pretty obnoxious about the whole thing. Do you have any idea why they're picking on the cat show?"

"Eh, they say that breeding purebred animals means shelter cats can't get adopted, which is a crock of poop. You seen the price tags on some of these cats here? I want a cat, I can get one at the shelter when they adopt 'em out half-off to seniors. Besides, we even have a rescue group with cats for adoption here at the show. I hope those girls don't scare off the public."

"Think of it as free publicity," Jake said with a shrug. "As soon as the news outlets start posting videos, you'll get a crowd. But I hope your volunteers are keeping an eye out. I've heard these crackpots deliberately let animals out of their cages just to cause trouble."

"Oh, I'll keep an eye out, all right," Nattie promised, slapping the rolled up judging schedule she held against her palm. "But forget about them. We got a special place set up for Hamlet."

She used her schedule to point past the sea of caged felines that took up the center of the hall. "You head all the way to the back, behind all the exhibitors. There's a stage there, and in front of it is Hamlet's official VIP area, where people can come by and see him. Look for my friend Mildred—she's dressed like me—and she'll take care of you. Say, did I tell you that Mildred was an alternate for the 1960 US women's gymnastics team? It was the summer games, and—"

"Ma, why don't you tell us about that tonight? We've got to get Hamlet settled. See you later."

A grumpy Hamlet in tow, Darla and Jake began making their way through the rapidly filling exhibition hall. Darla wore her official Pettistone's shirt and beige slacks in anticipation of a sea of cat hair. Jake was in full bodyguard mode, hair slicked back in a bun and wearing her black pantsuit and mirrored sunglasses. All the woman needed was an earpiece, Darla thought in amusement, and she could pass as a Secret Service agent.

The check-in and information tables where Nattie had given them their VIP lanyards sat to the left of the entryway. Behind those tables stretched a double row of vendor booths taking up perhaps a quarter of the floor space. From what she could see of the merchandise on display, one could pretty much find all things cat there.

"Check those out," Darla told Jake, nudging her and pointing to a series of cat-shaped pillows in plaid fabrics. "Wouldn't they look great in the bookstore?"

"Sure, but remember I'm here as Hamlet's bodyguard, not as your personal Sherpa. You buy it, you lug it."

Promising herself a closer look at all the feline paraphernalia later, Darla turned her attention to the opposite side of the hall.

Here were the "rings": six judging areas arranged one after another down the wall and separated from each other by side curtains. In each ring space, twenty or so chairs for spectators were arranged in rows in front of the judging table, a waist-high platform the size of a desk, topped with a smooth white surface and a lighted wooden canopy—Darla later read that the bulbs were required to be full-spectrum to properly show off the cats—with one leg wrapped with sisal to make a scratching post. Behind each of those tables was a U-shaped arrangement of broad benches lined by a series of wire cages. No doubt this was where the cats being judged awaited their turns. Right now, however, all the cages were empty, for the first classes had yet to be called.

But the greatest portion of the show hall was taken up by the cats themselves. Darla made a quick mental estimate, guessing there were close to three hundred meowing, purring, hissing felines gathered there. The competitors spanned all breeds, from hairless Sphynx kittens that could pass as little extraterrestrials to fluffy Maine Coons the size of bear cubs. Rows of tables had been set up down the center of the floor, each topped with wire cages similar to what Darla had seen in the judging rings. Here was where the competing cats would stay during show hours when they weren't in the ring.

"And I thought people who spend a fortune on their dogs are crazy," Jake said. "Look what they've done to those cages! The place looks like a toy shop filled with doll houses."

Each small kennel was covered on the top and three sides. A few exhibitors made do with towels, but most of the cages sported custom covers that reflected the owners' tastes. Some were covered in big cat prints in homage to the felines' larger cousins; others were more girly, with down-home ruffled gingham or upscale lace-trimmed satin; still others simply had the owner's cattery name embroidered on canvas. But Darla's favorite was an elaborate concoction that resembled Sleeping Beauty's castle, except in sparkly purple.

"I think they're cute," Darla countered as they continued up and down the aisles, nodding to the exhibitors as they passed and accepting compliments on Hamlet's good manners. "And, look, some of the cats even have little kitty vanities set up beside their cages!"

The vanities in question actually were either small folding tables set at right angles to the cages, or else full tabletops that the exhibitors had reserved next to their respective wire kennels. The temporary grooming areas were basic towel-covered spaces with an array of combs, brushes, and other trappings that far surpassed what personal grooming tools Darla herself owned. Some of the exhibitors had their gear stored in hanging travel toiletries bags, while others had cosmetic cases brimming over with tools and products, enough to outfit a dozen human salons.

Many of the tabletops featured short wooden or cardboard screens positioned to form a rear wall and give the tables a stage-like appearance. Adding to the ambiance, those screens were adorned with past show ribbons or championship photos of the competing felines. Some even included "kittens for sale" notices with pictures of roly-poly future champions posed on lush lawns or in beribboned baskets. Despite what Nattie had indicated, Darla was still shocked at the asking prices.

Maybe in addition to coffee, she should start selling registered kittens at the bookstore, Darla told herself.

As they walked the floor, they saw the feline beauty show contestants undergoing a final, pre-judging grooming session—fur brushed against the grain until it fluffed to gleaming perfection, claws trimmed, and faces and hindquarters mopped with damp clothes.

Darla watched with interest as one owner brushed out her female Himalayan from merely fluffy into a silvery white, seal-pointed feline powder puff. A nearby Russian Blue was submitting less docilely to his regimen and grumbling in response to every move his owner made.

Major spritzing of fur went on, as well—"conditioning

spray" Darla overheard the product being called. And she puzzled over why a few tables even held boxes of dryer sheets, until she saw one exhibitor make a couple of quick passes with a sheet over her Persian's coat, doubtless to keep the static down.

"Talk about a lot of work," Jake observed as they watched one cat owner with a pair of cuticle scissors painstakingly clip a few stray hairs from between her Abyssinian's front toes. "These people must really want to win."

"Oh, yes," a voice spoke up behind them. "They most certainly do. Shows are a serious business."

The speaker was a helmet-haired woman with tiny, steel-rimmed glasses. Since she was about the same size and age as Nattie and also wore a purple shirt and a big "Volunteer" button, Darla guessed this must be—

"Mildred? Hi, I'm Darla Pettistone." With a gesture at Jake, she added, "And this is Nattie's daughter, Jake Martelli. And of course, this is Hamlet," she finished, proudly indicating Pettistone's Fine Books' official mascot.

Mildred gave them all a wide smile, revealing a smear of pink lipstick on slightly bucked front teeth. "Nice to meet you ladies. And we know all about Hamlet." She leaned over and gave him a quick visual once-over. "He's a beautiful boy. Such a glossy black coat. Are you going to show him in HHP?"

"HHP?" Darla echoed, giving her a confused look.

"The Household Pet category," the old woman clarified. "Our shows aren't just for registered cats. A fine specimen of your basic domestic shorthair, like Hamlet, would fit right in there. As long as he's neutered and hasn't been declawed, he can compete with other everyday cats and even win ribbons."

"That sounds like fun," Darla agreed, intrigued, "but we'd better let Hamlet concentrate on his guest-of-honor duties this time around. Nattie said you had a special area set up for him?"

"Oh, we do. It's right in front of the stage."

Mildred led them past the final row of exhibitors to an open area. In the corner behind the vendor booths, Darla saw a small concession stand serving coffee and breakfast sandwiches. The whiteboard menu also promised hot dogs and nachos for lunch.

In the opposite corner, a portable stage had been set up, complete with a large wooden podium and an oversized, flat-screen television mounted on a stand. The back third or so of the stage was curtained off, the heavy blue drapery forming a colorful backdrop. The stage rose waist high from floor level and was angled so that anyone who climbed up there would have a view of the entire hall. For the moment, however, the only person in the figurative spotlight was a chunky bald man in a maintenance worker's uniform fumbling with a series of cables behind the podium. A teeth-gritting squawk of feedback momentarily drowned out the meow chorus, which, Darla noticed, had grown far quieter.

Or maybe, like Nattie had said, Darla had just gotten used to it.

A vaguely pie-shaped section of floor space that could accommodate perhaps a hundred standing spectators lay between the stage front and the exhibitor area. Since the hall was still filling up and no activity was happening to draw attention, only a few people milled around, examining a large structure made of wire and wood situated just in front of the stage.

Easels on either side featured bunting-draped white posters that proclaimed in red and gold letters: *The Feline Society of America National Championship Welcomes Its Guest of Honor, Hamlet the YouTube Karate Kitty!* A glossy black-and-white photo of Hamlet was affixed to each placard, reminding Darla of the "coming attractions" posters in movie theater lobbies.

It wasn't until they were standing right beside the temporary digs, however, that Darla realized what else the show folks had done with Hamlet's quarters.

"I can't believe it! Look, it's a little bookstore," she pointed out to Jake and Mildred, bending to examine the pen more closely.

The cage was a good ten feet long and half again as wide, and tall enough that Darla could easily kneel inside it. Short wooden bookshelves filled with actual hard covers were arranged along the back of the pen to form a wall of books, while a couple more bookshelves had been set at right angles to divide the pen into three sections. A tufted gold footstool and a couple of pillows suspiciously similar to the sherbet ones in their hotel room were neatly scattered on the blue linoleum floor that had been cut specifically to size.

"His potty is back there"—Mildred pointed to a litter box discretely hidden by one of the divider shelves—"and his food and water are over there. The shelves are short enough that he can walk along top of them without bumping into the top of the cage. We even left spaces between the books if he wants to sleep on the shelves instead of one of the cushions."

"Mildred, this is marvelous," Darla exclaimed while Jake whipped out her cell phone and snapped a couple of shots. "I wouldn't mind hanging out here all day myself. I'm sure Hamlet will love it. Right, Hammy?"

The cat deigned to give her a small mew that could have been interpreted a couple of different ways. Darla chose to believe it was a definite "you bet!"

"Now, we figured Hamlet would stay here most of the time while the show is going on," the old woman went on, "but maybe every couple of hours you can take him out on his lead and walk him through the hall. Oh, and I almost forgot," she went on. "This morning is all the preliminaries, but after lunch we're going to have a little ceremony up here on the stage to formally introduce Hamlet and play his video. I think someone from the newspaper might even show up. So I need to be sure that Hamlet and his entourage"—she giggled at that last word—"are back here a little before two p.m."

"Loose cat!"

The cry came from the exhibitors' area. Reflexively, Darla glanced down to make sure she still had Hamlet's lead firmly in her grasp. She did, which meant that some other wily feline apparently had escaped its owner.

"Don't be alarmed, this happens at least once each show," Mildred explained, all business now. "If you'll excuse me, I'll be back in a few minutes. I need to join the search team."

"We'll be glad to help look, too," Jake offered, while Darla nodded her own willingness to jump in.

Mildred shook her head. "No, dear. Please stay right here. We ask that only the designated search team and the owner look for the cat. Too many people running around will frighten the poor thing more than it already is. I'm sure you understand."

"Of course," Darla replied, "but isn't that the cat right there?"

She pointed to a tiny tortoiseshell kitten crouched beneath one of the grooming tables in the last row of the exhibitor area.

Mildred glanced from the cat back to Darla and smiled. "Why, it certainly must be. My, you have sharp eyes. I'd better signal the team."

While Darla and Jake watched, the old woman moved casually toward the table. A few more volunteers wearing the official polo and oversized lapel button were nearby, and Mildred waved an arm to gain their attention before pointing toward the bench. With military precision, the team moved in and surrounded the wayward tortie. Then, in a quick move, Mildred swooped down and scooped up the kitten before it realized what was happening.

A smattering of applause from the nearby spectators greeted Mildred's capture of the kitten. The cat's owner, meanwhile, rushed to join them. A sixtyish man with a tie-dyed T-shirt and blue bandana over lank gray curls smiled as he took his cat from Mildred. Snuggling the orange-and-black kitten tightly to his chest, he hurried back to his spot among the exhibitors.

"I guess she's done that a time or two," Jake said in approval as Mildred, dusting her hand together in a "that's finished" gesture, headed back to where they waited.

"Well, that was a little excitement," Mildred said a bit breathlessly as she rejoined them. "Now, where was I?"

"Two p.m. for the video. We'll be ready," Darla promised, hoping that if the press did show up, she could get a few minutes' interview time to publicize her store. Then, with a look down at Hamlet, she said, "So, Hammy, you want to try out your new place?"

Setting him inside the pen and unsnapping his lead, Darla let him loose and fastened the door behind him again. Jake, meanwhile, was taking her bodyguarding duties seriously, making a careful round of the pen to check for any cat security breaches.

"Hamlet's an escape artist," the PI warned Mildred, "so either Darla or I will be here with him at all times." Pointing to a second opening at the other end of the cage that Darla hadn't noticed, Jake added, "And we need to make sure every door on this cage is double-fastened."

"Don't worry," a woman's cool voice abruptly spoke up behind them. "Our local FSA organization has been handling cats for years. You'll find this pen as secure as Fort Knox. The earlier escape was strictly the owner's fault."

Darla had been kneeling beside the kennel, watching Hamlet tentatively sniff at the books. Reflexively, she glanced up and rose to greet the speaker. As she took a second look, however, she realized that she'd met the woman before . . . at least, in a manner of speaking.

Catching Jake's gaze, Darla took advantage of Mildred's nervous laugh and her burbling, "Oh, you startled me, Mrs. Timpson," which momentarily distracted the newcomer. She mouthed three swift, panicked words in Jake's direction.

The Martini Lady!

SIX

"OH, DARLA," MILDRED EXCLAIMED, CLUTCHING DARLA'S arm, "I was hoping I'd be able to introduce you. This is our show committee chairwoman, Mrs. Alicia Timpson. She's the one who arranged for your Hamlet to be our special guest. She even oversaw the design of his pen. Mrs. Timpson, this is Darla Pettistone."

Darla met the woman's cool amber gaze and noted her jaw-length frosted hair and pale blue linen skirted suit, which had yet to wrinkle despite the humidity. Definitely the Martini Lady from the previous night. Now, however, she appeared stone-cold sober—and, unless she was one heck of a poker player, she appeared not to recognize Darla. *Thank goodness!*

"Ah, yes, the bookstore owner," Alicia replied with only the faintest of patronizing airs. "All of us on the local FSA board are thrilled that you and Hamlet were able to accept the invitation to our little event."

She put out impeccably polished but surprisingly beefy fingers for a languid handshake.

"Thank you for providing such lovely accommodations. The hotel is first-rate," Darla managed as she accepted the proffered hand, only to release it as swiftly as she politely could.

"We may not be New York City," the woman conceded in a tone that indicated she was quite glad of it, "but we do have our certain small charms here in South Florida." Turning to Jake, she added, "And who is your, ah, friend?"

"Jake Martelli, Martelli Investigations," Jake said and handed over a business card. "I'm handling personal security for Ms. Pettistone and Hamlet."

"I see," the chairwoman replied, tucking Jake's card into her leather clutch without bothering to look at it. "Of course, the Waterview provides for security both here and at the hotel. But extra protection for our special guests can't hurt."

The niceties out of the way, Alicia gave a regal nod. "It was lovely meeting all of you. If you need anything at all, don't hesitate to ask Mildred or another of the volunteers for help."

With that, she turned on her spiked heel and started back toward the exhibitor area.

"Wasn't that lovely?" Mildred said, rushing to fill the sudden gap in the conversation. "Mrs. Timpson has chaired this show for the past four years, and she's also in charge of our annual benefit that we put on in the fall. Because of her, we've doubled the amount of money we can distribute to various pet rescue organizations."

"Impressive," Jake agreed while Darla simply nodded, still processing the unexpected encounter with the Martini Lady. It seemed like that whole event on the patio was a "no harm, no foul" situation. Even so, instinct told her to watch her back around the woman.

"Of course, it helps that Billy Pope is a multimillionaire," Mildred went on in a confidential tone.

At Darla's confused look, she clarified. "Mrs. Timpson's father. He made a fortune in real estate before the bubble burst and everyone lost their shirts. He used to show cats himself as a hobby, but he retired back in the nineties, and now he judges. He has tons of rich friends who wouldn't dream of saying no to his daughter when she asks them to give to the cause."

Another screech of feedback drew their attention to the stage again.

Darla jumped. Hamlet, who had gone from checking out the books to lazily batting the tassels on the tufted footstool, shot an annoyed look behind him before returning his attention to tassel batting.

"Oh, look, it's time to begin," Mildred declared with a glance at her watch. "Let's move closer so we have a better view." Pointing to a zaftig middle-aged blonde in a tight pink skirt suit who had climbed onstage and was now wielding the mike, Mildred went on, "That's Shelley Jacobson, our announcer and events coordinator working with Mrs. Timpson. She'll be introducing all the judges and pointing out the rings. If you have any questions, she can help you out, too."

Darla nodded in recognition at the name. Shelley Jacobson had been the one who'd sent the official letter of invitation to Hamlet, and she'd been helpful over the phone in coordinating arrangements. Together, Darla and Shelley had agreed that the odds of a meteor striking the cat show were better than trusting Hamlet to recreate his famous kitty karate kata. Instead, Shelley assured Darla that they had a version of the viral video that had been specially enhanced for the event. What that entailed, Darla couldn't guess, but she was taking it on faith that the cat-show crowd would find it entertaining.

Shelley, meanwhile, now flapped open a sheet of paper and bellowed into the microphone, "Test one, two. Test one, two. May I have your attention?"

The woman paused while the crowd began drifting in her direction. In another minute or so, sixty or seventy spectators started to fill the area in front of the stage. From babes in arms to elderly folks steering walkers, all ages and both genders were well represented.

As the crowd settled in, Shelley called, in slightly less deafening tones, "Welcome, everyone, to the Forty-third Annual Feline Society of America National Championship, being held for the ninth year in a row here in beautiful downtown Fort Lauderdale, Florida!"

Spectators and exhibitors alike clapped enthusiastically. Smiling, Shelley went on, "For all you first-time show attendees, we have a nice brochure at our front table that explains all about our cats and the judging process. And remember that the show lasts the whole weekend. If you have fun today, be sure you come back tomorrow to see even more wonderful cats."

She paused to gesture a group of six men and women up onto the stage, and then went on, "Now, before our first events start, let me introduce our show judges."

More applause followed as she read the names from her list. "Ms. Jane Trent, Mr. Robert Pyle, Ms. Cecilia Levin, Ms. Ida Greene, Mr. Mitchell Paul," she called, with each respective judge nodding and waving to the crowd. "And, of course, we can't forget our head judge, who has been part of this organization since its founding. Everyone knows Mr. Billy Pope."

The applause increased as a white-haired man who looked to be in his seventies stepped forward, smiled, and waved. He was dressed in a tan, European-cut suit worn over a surprisingly whimsical orange-and-yellow shirt that Darla figured probably cost more than her whole outfit. Even better, Darla spied a pair of white wingtips peeping from beneath his trousers cuffs. Though she vaguely recalled an old sartorial rule about no white shoes before Memorial Day, she had to give the old man props for not dressing like a stuffy real estate baron.

"Love those shoes," she muttered to Mildred with a smile.

"They're Mr. Pope's trademark look," she whispered back. "You know, like Tom Wolfe and his white suits."

With that bit of trivia, Mildred gave her a friendly nod and vanished back into the crowd. Jake, on her other side, gave Darla a nudge.

"That's him, Ma's friend," she said. "Now, you tell me if he looks like an embezzler."

"You're right. He's the kindly old guy who fixes your kids' bikes and has the best candy on Halloween," Darla agreed with a smile. "Though, actually, that makes me doubly suspicious of him."

But, she wondered, why would Mr. Pope steal condo association money? It didn't make sense. Hadn't Mildred said earlier that the man was a multimillionaire? For him, a cool fifty thou would be chump change, hardly worth risking freedom or reputation over.

"Snap decision," Jake replied with a matching grin. "The correct answer is: *I'm withholding judgment until I have more information.*"

"Fine. I'm withholding judgment until I have more information," Darla obediently parroted, adding, "but in the meantime I'm going to keep an eye on him."

"That shouldn't be hard. I'm sure Ma will make a point of introducing you to him later today."

Shelley continued, "And most of you know already that we have a very special treat this year. Hamlet the Karate Kitty of YouTube fame is here with us"—she gestured to the pen where said feline was lounging atop the footstool, looking more like a couch potato than a martial arts star—"and he'll be walking the aisles meeting his fans throughout the day. And at two p.m. we'll have a special playing of his video, so be sure to stop back here after lunch. Now, enjoy the show!"

While a good portion of the crowd filtered back toward the rings in anticipation of the judging, a small flock of children migrated to see Hamlet the Karate Kitty in person. To Darla's surprised relief, rather than playing reclusive celebrity, Hamlet seemed to be relishing his fifteen minutes of fame. He rose from his perch and, leaping atop one of the bookshelves, posed politely for photos.

"I can't believe how well Hamlet is taking to all this attention," Darla told Jake in amazement. "If this was happening back at the store, there would be all sorts of hissing and pouncing. Maybe I should look behind the litter box for a pod."

"Yeah, he's certainly on his best behavior," Jake agreed, sharing a smile at Darla's old sci-fi movie reference. "Either he's still zoned out from that spray of yours, or he's decided it's more fun playing to his fans. Let's just hope it lasts."

"Speaking of lasting, I'm already almost out of 'paw'-tograph fliers." Darla waved the stack of folded brochures, the thickness of which had diminished appreciably over the past few minutes. "I've got the file on a flash drive. Maybe there's a copy shop somewhere on the block where I can print up some more before this afternoon."

"Check in with Ma. She'll probably know."

As Darla nodded, more feedback sounded from the PA system, as the various ring clerks summoned cats to their respective stations.

"Long-haired kittens to Ring One. Entrants number one through sixteen. Household Pets to Ring Two. Entrants number three through eighteen," came the announcements, one after another. While the remaining ring assignments were called, Darla turned to Jake and stared at her with puppy dog eyes, hands lifted high on her chest to imitate begging.

"Can I please, please, please go see the kitties while you watch Hamlet?" she wheedled in the same tone she'd heard her nieces use.

Jake laughed outright. "Go ahead, kid. I've got things handled here. Just don't get carried away and decide to buy a show cat."

"Oh, no danger of that. Hamlet is about all the cat I can handle."

Leaving the fliers with Jake and giving Hamlet a final wave, Darla grabbed up her tote bag and followed the stream of spectators toward the judging rings. The ring clerks were repeating ring assignments, and Darla watched as a few tardy exhibitors gave their cats final quick brush swipes before trotting them over to the judging area.

Unable to resist, Darla made her first stop the long-haired kitten ring. The judging cages each held a single fluffy kitten—mostly Persians and Himalayans—the majority of whom seemed less than thrilled to be there. Tiny fuzzy paws reached through the cage wire and waved wildly, while the meow chorus moved up a register to a refrain of squeaky mews.

"So cute," sighed a glasses-wearing brunette teen to her pimpled boyfriend, who seemed impervious to the sight.

Atop each cage now was a numbered card, alternating blue and pink around the ring. *Boy, girl, boy, girl,* Darla realized after a moment. While it might not matter much with kittens, no doubt such spacing was necessary for unneutered male cats.

Darla recognized the ring judge from the earlier introduction as Ms. Ida Greene. *Poor kittens,* she thought as the woman, who looked like every child's scariest grade-school teacher, stalked over to the first cage and opened it. Darla hoped the little felines wouldn't be traumatized by the woman's brusque manner and sour expression. Feeling a bit indignant now, she wondered why someone would choose to judge cats—particularly kittens!—if she didn't actually enjoy the job.

While the gray-haired, African American ring clerk busied herself with paperwork beside the judging table, Ms.

Greene removed a smoky gray Persian kitten from his cage and carried him over to that platform. There, she plopped the little fellow into place, lightly hefting him a time or two as she ran her hands along his body. Her touch was efficient yet surprisingly gentle, and Darla wondered if perhaps she'd misjudged the woman.

"This one has sound coat color," Ms. Greene murmured to the spectators, and then pulled back all the fur from around the kitten's little face to better examine its eyes. Nodding in approval, she added, "Very nice head style."

With efficient moves, she gave each tiny paw a little squeeze to reveal the required claws and checked under his tail for the requisite boy parts. Then, setting him down once more, she again felt along the length of him, brushing his fur backward to look more closely at his undercoat. Finally, the judge picked up a feathered wand similar to the one Darla had for Hamlet and began teasing the little Persian with it. The kitten promptly snared the feathers between two fluffy paws and wrestled with it for a moment before letting it go and flying halfway up the scratching post.

At the sight, Ms. Greene cracked what Darla was stunned to realize was a smile as she gently disengaged the kitten from the post. Then, to Darla's even greater delight, the stern judge gave the kitten a little kiss atop his fuzzy head before returning him to his cage.

Darla had noticed a stack of paper towels piled on one corner of the judging table. Now, Ms. Greene spritzed down the white laminate surface with a spray bottle of disinfectant, wiped it clean with a couple of paper towels, and then did the same with her hands.

The judge spent a few moments afterward making notes in a three-ring binder; then she repeated the process with the next kitten. Throughout the handling of each small cat, she took time to share with the spectators her murmured thoughts on each entrant. While none of the other kittens in the ring scaled the scratching post like the first feisty boy had done, most of them played with the proffered feathered wand or dangling mouse on a string. Only one shy cream-colored female turned up her flat nose at all the toys. Ms. Greene waited until she'd put the little girl back in her cage to try the feathers again. This time, the kitten responded with a polite bat of one paw through the bars, drawing a genuine smile from the woman.

When the final kitten had been judged, the judge made one last walk past the cages, using her feathered wand to play with each as she walked past. Then, after making final notes in her book and filling out a three-part form, she swiftly hung a series of colored ribbons—blue for first, red for second, and yellow for third—on various cages. In addition were two more ribbons: Best of Color and Second Best of Color. Since the kittens were divided by color as well as gender, that meant that by the time the judge finished, a regatta's worth of ribbons flew in the judging area. Darla was glad to see that both Feisty Boy and Shy Girl, as she'd mentally dubbed them, had taken first place in their respective color classes.

The exhibitors removed their kittens from the judging cages, which were then spritzed and dried by a small crew of teenaged volunteers. Darla moved on to another ring, where the judge was evaluating the Household Pets. Since this was the category Mildred had mentioned Hamlet could qualify for, Darla eagerly grabbed an open seat in front of the judging table.

The first thing she noted was that all colors and breeds were represented in a single judging category, from orange tabbies to white longhairs to calicos—even two sleek black cats that resembled miniature versions of Hamlet. The male judge had a flamboyant if genial air about him. Tall and almost painfully thin, with hair that had been bleached to an unnaturally pale yellow, he was dressed in a smart, powder blue suit. Paul something . . . or maybe he was something Paul, Darla thought, flipping through the handout she'd picked up at the door. She found his name finally: Mitchell Paul.

While Mr. Paul's judging procedure was almost identical to Ms. Greene's, he kept up a running spiel with the spectators that was worthy of a seminar presenter as he efficiently made the rounds of the pets.

He addressed the spectators as he picked up the first entrant, a male tuxedo cat. "Now, I always like to know if it's their first time." Then, with a mock look of shock at a few answering snickers, he stuck one hand on his hip and clarified. "No, not that, you naughty people. I mean, is this our young fellow's first cat show? Who's his mom or dad?"

A black-haired young man, whose bulk spilled over onto the folding chair beside him, raised a tentative hand. Paul smiled. "Now, tell me his name and his story."

The banter went on in a similar vein with all the owners, most of whom were new to the show ring. His comments were kind as well as constructive, Darla decided, pleased to see that Mr. Paul found at least one positive characteristic for each cat that he claimed set it above the others. Only when he reached the tiny calico girl, who was hunched up in the back of her cage, did the patter change. He paused, frowned, and said, "Now, I see a little crazy in those eyes. Owner, come take this cat out for me, just in case."

An old woman who looked remarkably like Nattie—except twice her size—hobbled her way to the cage. The cat cooperated, and the woman carried her to the judging table, where she—cat, not old woman—behaved quite nicely. Praising both cat and owner, Mr. Paul let the old woman return the calico to her spot; then, after a quick cleanup of hands and platform, he opened the final judging cage.

"Oh my. My, my, my," he mused in obvious interest as he carried the cat over to the table.

Oh my, was right. Darla studied the unusual feline with its batlike ears and fawn-colored fur that seemed almost painted on. And where was its tail? This was no basic domestic shorthair, à la Hamlet.

"Owner, tell me about this unusual little fellow," the judge went on. He indicated the tailless hind quarters, which were raised a bit higher than the front legs, giving the cat a rabbitty look. "He appears to have a bit of Manx in him. Was he a stray? Do you know anything about his parentage?"

"Actually, I bred him myself," the owner spoke up, standing.

While most of the spectators and exhibitors wore T-shirts or polos over jeans or shorts, this man looked like he'd come from an executive meeting: beige dress slacks, long-sleeved pale yellow shirt, and a striped tie that picked up both colors. In his late fifties, he had the tanned, self-assured look of a man who spent as much time cutting deals on the golf course as he did in the boardroom.

"He's a cross between a Manx and a Sphynx," the owner went on. "I call him a Minx."

Better than calling him a Spanx, Darla thought with a smile.

"I've been perfecting the breed for more than five years now," the man went on in a self-important tone. "You can see that the fur is like velvet, and far shorter than the usual feline coat. People who might have been turned off by the Sphynx's hairlessness but can't keep a regular cat because of allergy issues do quite well with these fellows. And with the Manx hindquarters, they tend to want to leap rather than run, so they're easier to keep in an apartment or condo. I'm going to present the Minx for inclusion in the FSA later this year."

"Really," the judge replied, his tone approving as he ran his hands over the odd cat. "I must say, it's a fetching little thing. And you're right—the coat feels just like velvet."

He flicked the feathered wand in front of the Minx,

smiling as the cat gave the toy a swipe. Then he returned the Minx to his cage and spritzed the platform and his hands before making his final notations in his book. Handing the clerk his filled-out form, Mr. Paul reached for a handful of ribbons, saying, "All of you should be proud. You groom and put these guys together as well as any pro. Every one of these cats deserves a merit ribbon."

Swiftly, he hung a bicolored ribbon on each cage and then returned to the judging table. "Now comes the hard part. I must choose Best through Fifth Best."

Starting with Fifth Best, the judge began hanging colored ribbons on the cages. First went to a white longhair belonging to a freckled, twentysomething girl who had brushed her pet into snowy perfection. The tuxedo, the calico, and a Siamese that Darla had admired also placed. The Minx came in third . . . much to the apparent displeasure of its owner. When the call came to remove the cats from the judging cages, he stalked over and, tucking the cat beneath his arm, strode off without another word.

"There's always one," Mr. Paul observed with a disapproving moue as Darla went up to thank him for sharing his thoughts with the spectators. "There's more to a win than just coming up with a clever mix of breeds."

She gave a commiserating nod. "Well, I thought you made the right choice. That white longhair was beautiful."

"To be truthful, underneath all that fur it had stubby legs and a head too big for its body," Mr. Paul said with a shrug, "but the owner obviously takes excellent care of it. Seven years old, and not a spot of tartar on those teeth. And, of course, she had him brushed to perfection. It had to have taken her hours. I prefer to recognize the true pets, and the true amateurs."

Darla thanked him again; then, glancing at her watch, she headed to check in with Nattie about the copy shop.

A few minutes later, Darla informed Jake, "Your mom said there's a copy place a couple of doors from the bakery I told you about. If you think you can hold out a bit longer without me, I'll pick up some pastries to tide us over until lunch."

"We're good here," Jake assured her. "The first wave of excited kiddies has passed, thank goodness. And Hamlet is on his second nap," she added, indicating the sleeping cat, who'd stretched out between stacks of books on one of the back shelves.

Darla nodded. "Well, if he wakes up by the time I'm back, we'll make another round of the exhibition hall. Don't want him getting fat from lack of exercise."

Leaving Jake and Hamlet to their own devices, Darla went out the main door. She'd forgotten about the animal rights protesters lurking on the broad concrete stairs, however, until she was accosted a second time.

The pink-sequined girl was apparently on break, for Darla didn't see her; however, her sisters-in-thong were there to fill the gap. A chunky brunette with an unfortunate farmer's tan and a tiny African American girl with an armful of colorful bangles rushed up as Darla made her way down the steps.

"Cat shows are cruel!" the latter cried, waving her sign in Darla's direction.

Don't engage the crazy, Darla reminded herself. Still, she couldn't help asking, "Uh, why are they cruel?"

"Because they put them in cages," the Farmer Tan Girl declared.

The bangle girl vigorously nodded. "And it's not right to put the cats on stage to, you know, perform."

She suspected the girls were confusing the show exhibitors with backyard breeders, but as far as she had seen, the greatest number of the exhibitors didn't fall into that category. And since Hamlet had done the whole performing thing on his own—hence, his YouTube appearance—Darla wasn't buying that one. That, or she was guilty of cat cruelty. But she politely replied, "Oh, then I agree with all that. Now, can you tell me where the copy shop on Las Olas is?"

"Oh, sure," the brunette agreed. She trotted back down the steps and, tucking her sign under her arm, pointed down the street. "It's over there by Jennie's Bakery. She has the best Cuban pastries."

"So I've heard. Good luck with the demonstration."

Leaving the bathing-suited girls to their protest, Darla made her way to the copy store and paid for another hundred fliers. While they were being printed, she slipped into the bakery. A young Hispanic woman about Darla's age was at the far end of the counter arranging pink coconut cupcakes on a tiered glass plate. Her black hair was pulled back in twin ponytails and covered by a striped green bandana that matched her striped apron.

"Hi, are you Jennie?" Darla asked. "Your brother, Tino, said I should stop by."

"He did, did he?"

The woman gave a tiny smile, tweaking the final cupcake and then sliding shut the glass case door. Leaning with folded arms atop the case, she said in lightly accented tones, "My brother, he's my best advertising. The only problem is that he comes by and eats as much inventory as he helps sell. Don't tell me you were brave enough to ride with him!"

Darla smiled with her. "Actually, we met at the airport when my ride almost rear-ended his cab. And then I saw him last night while I was taking a walk. I hear you have great Cuban pastries."

"The best in town! Tino's not the only one who thinks so, either."

Jennie pointed to a large framed photograph prominently displayed on the far wall. It was taken on what appeared to be a reality television stage set, and it showed Jennie exchanging hugs with a celebrity chef whom Darla recognized from one of the cable food channels.

"I was a finalist last year on *Pastry Battle*," Jennie explained, the smile proud now. "I would have won, but the cupcake girl sabotaged my oven, and my temperature was off."

"*Pastry Battle*!" Darla echoed in appreciation. "I've watched that show. You must be great just to get on at all. So what are Cuban pastries? I've never tried them before."

"Here." Jennie moved to the center of the case Darla was standing before and pointed to what looked like fluffy turnovers. "I make a few different flavors. There's cheese, kind of like a cheese Danish. And if you want more of a meal, there's spicy meat. But my favorites are the guava"—she pronounced it *wah-vah*—"and a special strawberry jam pastry for the kids. Here, I have some samples."

She pulled out a plate that held turnovers sliced into bite-sized pieces. Darla took a sample of each, proclaiming all of them tasty. "It's hard to decide," she said, wiping crumbs from her lips, "so let's go with a meat, a cheese, a jam, and a guava . . . not all for me, of course. I'm bringing back some for my friends."

"Sure, no problem." Jennie pulled out silver tongs and quickly bagged them up; then, with another smile, she added a fat macadamia nut cookie to the bag, and said, "A little something extra on the house, since Tino recommended you."

Darla pulled out her wallet to pay; then, glancing down the pastry case again, she impulsively said, "How about a dozen of those fancy donut holes in a separate bag, too?"

She paid Jennie and, promising to return the next day, picked up her fliers at the printers and then headed back to the exhibition hall. As Darla started up the steps, she was once again accosted by Farmer Tan Girl and her buddy, Bangles. Before the pair could begin their spiel, however, Darla smiled and held out the bag of donut holes.

"You've already indoctrinated me, remember? Now, how about a little something from Jennie's? You know, to help keep your strength up."

And to keep you off my back the rest of the show, she silently added.

Farmer Tan Girl gave her a suspicious look as she gingerly accepted the white bakery sack. As she peered inside, however, suspicion morphed into delight. "Look, Talina, donut holes . . . the fancy kind," she breathed in awe. To Darla, she added, "Wow, like, thanks!"

"Bon appétit," Darla replied, and trotted up the steps.

Once inside, she stopped at the check-in desk, where Nattie was presiding. The woman was on the opposite end and busy speaking with a man Darla belatedly recognized as the Minx breeder. Their tones were low, and it was difficult to hear them over the cat chorus and the occasional PA announcement, but something in their huddled stance made her think the conversation was not a friendly one. She didn't have long to wonder over it, however, for the man abruptly straightened and stalked off toward the exhibitor area. Nattie muttered something after him, her accompanying hand gesture one Darla recognized from some of the rougher Brooklyn neighborhoods.

Curious, Darla wondered what the two could have been discussing to lead to Nattie's extreme reaction. While she was sure the old woman could hold her own against the breeder, she thought maybe she should find out what had gone down in case Nattie took it a step farther and went completely "old neighborhood" on the man.

"Pastry?" she asked in a bland tone, sidling up to where Nattie stood and waving the remaining bakery bag in the old woman's direction.

Nattie gave her a genial smile. "Well, maybe one," she replied, reaching in and pulling out a guava pastry, "but that's it. I already ate four donuts out of the box Mildred brought. Gotta save some room for lunch. Besides, I don't digest too good when I'm riled up."

"Oh, that," was Darla's noncommittal response. With a swift look around to make sure they weren't being overhead, she casually went on, "I saw you having words with one of the exhibitors. Who is he? Is anything wrong?"

"That was Mr. Fancy Pants Ted Stein." Nattie's tone made it clear she didn't approve of fancy pantsers, be they people or shops. "He thinks he got robbed in the HHP category and wants to file a complaint against the judge."

"I saw that category being judged, and I think Mr. Paul did a fine job. The cat that won was lovely."

"Yeah, well, Mr. Stein thinks *he* shoulda won. I told him if he has a complaint, he needs to take it to Billy."

"You mean the head judge, Mr. Pope?" At Nattie's nod, Darla asked, "Well, did he go complain, then?"

Nattie lifted her penciled-in brows. "No way is he gonna complain to Billy. Once they were friends, but now there's bad blood between them two. That Stein fellow, he's on the condo board where I live. He's the one accusing Billy of stealing the missing condo association money."

Before Darla could question her further, Nattie went on in a stout tone, "Billy's innocent, of course. He never touched a cent of our association money that he wasn't supposed to. But that Stein character, he's a whole other bucket of goldfish."

"I did get the impression that Mr. Stein was kind of a jerk," Darla agreed, failing to understand the woman's muddled metaphor but pretty sure she knew where Nattie was trying to go with it. "Do you think he's trying to frame Mr. Pope on purpose?"

The old woman nodded.

"Bingo. I think he's trying to make Billy look bad because Billy wouldn't invest in Stein's Minx scheme. Billy says Stein's a charlatan out to make some fast money, and that new cat breed ain't for real. It got pretty nasty at the board meeting last night. They about got into a fight in the parking lot. Me and Jacqueline, we had to break it up."

Now it was Darla's turn to lift her brows. Jake hadn't mentioned that part of the evening's excitement to her. "I can see where you don't want to be in the middle on this one. Should I mention this little run-in with Mr. Stein to Jake?"

"Nah, don't worry her. I can take care of myself." Grinning, Nattie flexed a scrawny bicep before glancing past Darla, and adding, "Oops, gotta go. Some people need tickets here."

Leaving Nattie to help the young family that had stepped up to the table, Darla left with her pastries and started through the exhibition hall toward the back. She was just congratulating herself on her restraint in walking through the vendor area (simply eyeing a cat tote bag surely didn't count) when a scream of pure terror made her almost drop her pastry bag.

Darla and everyone else within earshot—which pretty much was the entire exhibition hall!—whipped around, frantically looking for the source of that chilling cry. Darla spied her almost immediately: the freckled girl whose cat had won first place in Household Pets. The young woman stood out from the rest of the crowd, mostly because she was spinning about like a cat chasing its tail in the aisle where Darla stood. Her hands, however, were the most noticeable thing about her, coated as they were with something wet and red.

And then the girl stopped spinning long enough to shriek, "Someone's murdered my Cozy Kitty!"

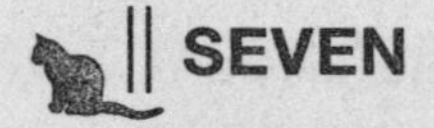

SEVEN

MURDERED HER CAT?

Instinctively, Darla rushed forward to where the girl stood sobbing uncontrollably. Already, four other nearby exhibitors converged on the girl and were huddled protectively about her.

"No, stay back," one of those women called in a shaky voice, raising a hand, palm-out, in a "stop" gesture. "It's—it's too awful."

At the woman's words, one young family made a swift retreat in the opposite direction, parental hands shielding toddler eyes. A few other spectators had already hurried to the scene with Darla to see if they could help. They all prudently halted a good ten feet back from the carnage, maintaining a respectful silence while the cat owner sobbed.

"I was only gone for a few minutes," the girl wailed softly to the women comforting her. "She was just fine then, but when I came back she was like, like . . . that."

The girl dissolved into fresh tears, and Darla felt her own

heart sink in sympathy. More than once had she feared the worst for Hamlet, and each time the thought had sent a burning little dagger of disbelief ripping through her very core. At least the girl was among people who understood that a pet was far more than just an animal.

"Coming through, coming through," Darla heard a man's voice abruptly call behind her, and she reflexively moved aside.

The speaker was a young Hispanic man with slicked-back black hair wearing a blue lab coat and carrying a medical bag. He must be the show's official veterinarian, Darla realized. Behind him, she spotted Billy Pope trotting along as fast as he could go, followed by his daughter, Alicia Timpson, aka the Martini Lady.

Darla held her breath as the vet reached inside the wire enclosure. His body blocked her view of the cat, for which she was grateful. Then he abruptly straightened and turned to Billy for a few quick words. Billy took a step back, his expression one of outrage as the vet lifted a red-streaked palm. A collective gasp rose from the spectators alongside Darla. Before she could wonder what in the heck was going on now, the vet leaned into the cage again.

He dragged out the limp white cat, covered in red . . . and thrust the feline into her owner's arms! Darla watched in horror and then sagged in relief as the cat squirmed in her owner's grip. Her meows weren't yowls of pain, but merely indicated irritation at being unceremoniously dragged from her cage.

Darla turned to the stocky middle-aged woman wearing a "Cats Rule, Dogs Drool" T-shirt standing next to her.

"Look, she's alive!" Darla exclaimed, instinctively grabbing the woman's hands as the two of them did an impromptu happy dance there in the aisle.

"False alarm," Billy Pope called in a reedy voice. Waving his hands in a dismissive gesture at the surrounding crowd, he clarified. "You can go back to what you were doing. Dr. Navidad assures me that the cat's fine . . . just a little messy."

And, indeed, Cozy appeared quite hale. Her dance over—and feeling slightly embarrassed at her impulsive show of emotion with a stranger—Darla saw Alicia Timpson grab a towel from one of the grooming tables, wrap it around girl and cat, and begin escorting them away from the onlookers.

"But what about all the blood?" demanded Darla's temporary dance partner. The cartoon feline on her T-shirt ballooned alarmingly as the woman heaved an indignant breath and pointed. "It's like the Saint Valentine's Day Massacre in that cage."

"Ketchup," Dr. Navidad answered as he headed back in the direction from which he'd come, wiping his hands on another towel and shaking his head in disgust. "Watered down so it looked more like blood. Just a prank, but pretty darned cruel."

"Attention, everyone," Shelley's voice boomed across the hall. "We had a minor situation, but everything is just fine now. Let's finish up the next rings before we break for lunch. And remember, at two p.m. we'll have a special appearance by our guest of honor."

Hamlet!

Making a quick good-bye to her new friend, Darla hurried in the direction of the stage, grateful that Jake had been with Hamlet while all this had gone down. The so-called prank hadn't been funny at all. And what if this joker planned further disruptions? Another cat—maybe even Hamlet—could be the target of something far worse.

Jake was stationed at the side of Hamlet's pen, arms crossed and looking even more badass than usual, given the frown plastered beneath her mirrored sunglasses. Obviously, she'd been keeping tabs on the disturbance. At Darla's approached, she whipped off the shades.

"What the heck's going on?" she demanded. "I heard all the screaming, and then the rumor flew around that a couple of cats had been butchered and hung from one of the judging rings. And then Shelley hops up on the stage to spout a bunch of sunshine and unicorns, without a word about what went down."

"It was just a really rotten prank," Darla assured her, pausing to take a look in Hamlet's cage. To her relief, the feline was snoozing peacefully on his back atop the footstool, paws curled to his fuzzy chest. Apparently, neither screams nor PA announcements could pierce his Zenlike nap mode.

"Someone poured watered-down ketchup on the cat that won the household pet category," she went on, plopping into one of the folding chairs. "Her owner saw her lying in her cage all covered in what looked like blood, and she went into hysterics. The show's vet, Dr. Navidad, checked the cat out, and said nothing's wrong with her, except she needs a good bath. The Martini Lady is on the job, getting it handled."

"That's a relief. So, what do you think? The second-place owner taking a little revenge on the winner?"

Recalling how Stein had argued with Nattie over his Minx's showing, Darla shrugged. "Maybe more like the third-place owner. He definitely wasn't happy. Oh, and also he happens to be someone Nattie says you met last night: Ted Stein. You kind of forgot to mention breaking up the fight."

"Eh, it was just a little argument," Jake replied with a wave of her hand, sounding like her mother. "But what happened with the judging?"

When Darla had finished describing what had gone on, the PI said, "Yeah, Stein is a loose cannon. But from a logical point of view, it would have made more sense to dump ketchup on the cat before the judging, not after. I'm more inclined to think it might have been one of the animal rights protesters. From what I hear, that's the kind of mischief they go in for."

Darla nodded. "That's a possibility. When I left the building to get the printing done, I noticed that the girl in the pink thong wasn't protesting with her friends anymore. And she was still MIA when I got back. Maybe she threw on some clothes and sneaked into the exhibition hall for a little guerilla activism."

"And here I thought bodyguarding Hamlet at a cat show was going to be a quiet gig," Jake said with an ironic smile. "Don't worry, no one's going to pull that sort of stunt on Hamlet while I'm on the job. Speaking of which"—she paused and glanced at her watch—"my contract says I get a break right about now."

"Go ahead, I'll keep an eye on things here. Oh, and I brought you back some pastries, as promised. The owner wrapped them in foil, so they're still warm."

While Jake headed out to the floor, pastry in hand, Darla pulled out her fliers and busied herself stamping Hamlet's "paw"-tograph on each before stacking the folded sheets neatly atop Hamlet's pen. He'd finally awakened from his nap and was pacing about, much to the delight of the three grade-school-aged girls who were kneeling in front of the cage.

Darla spent the next half hour chatting with folks and munching on the cheese pastry while Hamlet did his Hollywood routine and posed for photos. By the time Jake returned, Darla had all but forgotten the unfortunate ketchup incident. But the sheepish expression on her friend's face made Darla sit up and give the woman a wary "What?"

"Oh, nothing."

Jake gave an airy wave, which only intensified Darla's suspicions. Obviously, something was up. Then she spied a series of silvery hairs glinting against the black lapel of Jake's jacket, and she opened her eyes wide. "Wait! Don't tell me. You bought a cat!"

"What makes you say that?"

Jake glanced down, noticed the hairs on her jacket, and then gave a rueful smile. "I didn't buy, but I admit it, I was looking. Not at the show cats," she hurriedly clarified before Darla could say anything. "There's a rescue group that has a few of what they called 'un-adoptables.' You know, cats with problems . . . too old, too ugly, health issues. There's a Siamese kitten named Trixie who's missing a back leg, but she's a feisty little thing. I'm thinking about bringing her home with me."

A three-legged cat named Trixie.

"Hey, that's great," Darla replied, her sentiment sincere. Then, switching to a deliberately innocent tone, she mischievously added, "You think your landlady will mind you bringing a pet home with you?"

"Oh, jeez, I didn't even think of that. Uh, Darla, any chance I can keep a cat in my apartment? Please?" the PI asked, turning the same puppy dog look on Darla that Darla had earlier used on her.

Darla laughed. "Of course you can."

"Don't worry, it's not a done deal, yet," Jake assured her. "Most you can do here at the show is call dibs on the cat you want and fill out the paperwork so they can do a background check on you. They won't let you take home the cats during the show since they don't want impulse buys, which makes sense. I'll check again tomorrow, and if Trixie's still there, I'll fill out the papers and let the rescue people do their background check. And I'll still have until the end of the week to be really sure I want to do this."

"That's a good idea, thinking it over for a few days. Believe me, being a cat owner is tougher than it looks. Right, Hamlet?"

The feline paused in his pacing to shoot her a cool green look that seemed to say, *Ha! Being the cat is tougher.*

Darla exchanged looks with her friend. "See what I

mean? Hammy," she addressed the cat again, "how about we make another round of the hall before it's time to show your video? Maybe we can even meet Trixie."

Snapping the lead on Hamlet again, Darla left Jake to finish off the remaining pastry while she and Hamlet once more went out to greet his public. As before, the sleek black feline was met with praise and laughter, the latter coming from those who'd already seen the YouTube video. Darla had to disappoint more than one person who asked if she and Hamlet would be recreating their tournament performance during the cat show by explaining that Hamlet performed only when and if it suited him. She assured them, however, that they *would* be seeing Hamlet in action that afternoon, via the video presentation.

Darla found the rescue exhibit Jake had mentioned tucked alongside the vendor tables. Tropical Adoptables, it was called, with a cute cartoon logo featuring a big-eyed tabby peeking out from behind one side of a palm tree, and a goofy beagle peeking out from the other.

Trixie was easy to pick out from the cluster of ten or so kittens playing together in an open pen, since she was the sole Siamese of the bunch. A petite little girl with classic seal point markings and the biggest blue eyes Darla had ever seen on a cat, Trixie seemed unfazed by the lack of one rear limb. When Darla paused near the pen for a closer look, Trixie and Hamlet exchanged polite sniffs through the mesh. A good sign, Darla thought to herself.

Leaving Trixie to her kitten game, Darla and Hamlet continued to make the rounds, finally stopping at the judging area and the ring where Billy Pope was presiding over a group of Russian Blues. To her mind, they were striking cats: a solid blue coat—which was actually gray—the tips of which hairs were a shimmering silver. And their eyes were deep bottle green, far darker than Hamlet's emerald orbs.

Darla took a seat in the back row so as not to disturb the cats with Hamlet's presence and watched with curiosity. Hamlet eyed the proceedings with seeming disapproval, whiskers and tail flicking every so often, but sat quietly in the chair beside her.

She was a bit surprised at Billy Pope's judging technique, which was nothing like the other two judges she'd witnessed. Despite his grandfatherly image, the man was all business when it came to sizing up each feline. It didn't help that all of the Russian Blues seemed exceedingly ticked off about being in the show, displaying their displeasure with much pawing and meowing as they were taken out to be evaluated.

"These Blues sure are pistols," the middle-aged gentleman with a cane sitting on the other side of her softly observed with a small chuckle.

When Darla nodded her interest, he went on in a stage whisper, "They're one of the smartest breeds out there. If they don't want to be shown, they figure out real quick that if they act up with the judge, they get put back in their cages faster. There's a saying with Russian Blue breeders that they breed for dumb. The smart ones, they're too hard to show."

Sounds a lot like Hamlet, Darla thought with no little amusement as she thanked him for the insight. And the Russian Blue 101 lesson likely explained why there were no head kisses or silly asides with this breed.

Still, she wished Billy could be more like the other judges in that they'd explained their reasoning with the spectators. Billy Pope judged in silence, his poker-face expression giving away none of his thoughts as he poked and prodded each cat before making copious notes in his binder. When the last entrant had been judged, he grabbed up a handful of colored ribbons and quickly hung them on the cages, leaving it to the ring clerk to dismiss the group.

"Well, Billy got it right again," Darla's neighbor conceded above the applause that greeted the winner. Leaning heavily on his cane, he lurched to his feet, and added, "You get a win from that man, you deserve it."

Darla considered those words as she and Hamlet made their way back to the stage. Surely a man so scrupulous about judging a cat show would be equally on the up-and-up in his other doings, she decided. Still, it would be nice to have a consensus from a group other than the condo owners. Once the Russian Blue category had been judged, Shelley had fired up the PA system and called the lunch break. That meant an hour before it was time for Hamlet's video airing. She could grab a couple of hot dogs from the concession for her and Jake and maybe casually ask around for opinions on Mr. Billy Pope.

When Darla said as much to Jake after unleashing Hamlet and closing the cage door behind him, the other woman shrugged.

"Go ahead, kid, if you think you can keep your motives for asking on the down-low. People like to gossip, so you never know what they might spill. Heck, you might even mention Stein's name and see what pops up."

"Uh-huh," Darla replied, momentarily distracted by the sight of a slim, oversized volume lying faceup in Hamlet's pen beside one of the shelves.

She could see the familiar illustration on the orange-and-white front cover, so she didn't even need to read the title to know it was a copy of the Dr. Seuss classic *How the Grinch Stole Christmas*. A gap in the row above it seemed to indicate it had come from that collection. She gave Jake a questioning look.

"Was that book on the floor a minute ago?"

Jake shook her head. "Didn't notice it. Hamlet must have accidentally knocked it down when you took him out to go touring."

Accidentally? When it came to books, Hamlet never did anything by accident. Darla slipped her hand through the wires of the pen and, with a bit of careful maneuvering, retrieved the book. Was the cagey feline trying to tell her something? Or had this been a simple slip of the paw?

Probably the latter, she decided.

"You're right. He probably just knocked into it while he was sniffing around," Darla agreed. "Now, what do you want on your hot dog?"

THE LINE AT THE CONCESSION WAS LONG, GIVING DARLA PLENTY OF opportunity to casually chat with people about the head judge and innocently wonder about the Minx cat and its breeder. The few people who personally knew either all shared basically the same opinion as Darla: Billy Pope was tough but fair, and an all-around nice guy; Ted Stein was a blowhard jerk. Of course, Darla had to give the latter a bit of credit for his concern over the condo association's lost funds, even if—according to Nattie—he was barking up the wrong tree as far as the culprit. Iffy as his motives might be, presumably Ted was trying to do the right thing.

When Darla finally headed back toward the stage, food and soft drinks balanced in one of those flimsy cardboard trays, she was halted by the sight of Billy Pope near one of the vendor booths talking to a young woman. Her back was to Darla, but something about her was very familiar—the short shorts, the blouse falling off at the shoulder, the fuzzy boots. Then the girl stuck out a hand, and the pose jogged Darla's memory.

It was the same panhandler who had threatened Alicia Timpson last night! And now she was threatening the woman's father!

Darla eased her way toward the pair, taking care to screen herself behind a hanging display of cat tote bags. Surely the girl wouldn't try something in the midst of this crowd, she told herself. But if something did happen, at least Darla would be a witness to it.

"C'mon, I know you have the money." The girl's wheedling voice also seemed familiar, though Darla didn't recall having heard the panhandler speak last night. "I wouldn't ask if I didn't really, really need it."

Darla tightened her grip on the cardboard tray. She could see Billy's expression of furtive resignation wash over him as he reached a gnarled hand into his jacket. *Why is he doing this?* she wondered in frustration. *What hold can this girl have over him?*

But Darla was not the only one watching the pair. As Billy pulled an oversized wallet from his coat, Alicia Timpson swooped down upon them.

"What are you doing in here?" she demanded, grabbing the girl's arm and giving her a shake. Then Alicia pointed at her father. "Don't you dare give her any money, Dad. You know what she's going to do with it."

"Yes, but—"

She cut the old man short. "No buts. We agreed we're not going to enable her anymore."

"But I can't just abandon her," he protested, sounding like a sad old man instead of a retired real estate tycoon who'd spent years eating other businessmen for lunch. "Cindy's my only granddaughter."

Granddaughter?

Darla almost dropped the tray. The panhandler who'd threatened Alicia Timpson was Billy Pope's granddaughter? Did that also mean that Cindy was Alicia's daughter? Darla wasn't sure if Billy Pope had any other children besides Alicia, but she didn't have time to mull over the implications, for the argument was continuing.

"All the more reason not to indulge her," Alicia snapped. "Give it to her now, and she'll be back for more tomorrow, and the day after. She's my daughter; I should know."

She whipped back around to the girl and went on, "And as for you, don't think I don't know what you did. Now leave, before I call security on you. I'll be informing everyone at the door that you're banned from the exhibit hall."

Cindy spouted off a few colorful epithets in Alicia's direction, ending with a hand gesture cruder than Nattie's before spinning about and stalking away right toward Darla, giving her a good look at the girl as she hurried past.

She was young, pretty, petulant . . . and when her oversized top slid lower, it revealed a familiar bleeding-heart tattoo peeking out of a skimpy sequined bikini top. Not only was Cindy the panhandler from the night before, she was also the pink-thonged animal rights protester who'd accosted Darla and Jake that morning!

Which also meant she was the person likely responsible for pouring ketchup on Cozy Kitty, the HHP winner.

Feeling suddenly foolish that she hadn't recognized the girl earlier—though, in fairness, she hadn't seen the panhandler's face the previous night, having only glimpsed her from behind—Darla assumed as nonchalant an air as she could. Pretending to give a cat toile tote bag a final look, she casually turned and continued on toward the stage area.

She'd have to let Jake know what she'd learned, Darla told herself. She suspected that sparks might continue to fly if Cindy managed to sneak back in again. With Hamlet being the guest of honor, he'd be an obvious target for some sort of dramatic animal protest statement.

She didn't have a chance to enlighten Jake about the dysfunctional Pope-Timpson family, however. As soon as she reached the stage area, Jake snatched her drink and hot dog from the tray and took a big bite of the latter.

"Sorry," she mumbled, pausing to wash down the cheese and chili with a big gulp of diet soda. "I gotta eat and run. It's almost time for the video."

Jake indicated Mildred, who was standing beside Hamlet's cage talking into her walkie-talkie.

"Mildred and I hammered out a plan. As soon as you finish eating, you get Hamlet all leashed up. I'll take him behind that curtain"—Jake used her hot dog to point to the split swag of fabric that divided the final quarter of the stage area from the rest of the space—"and we'll wait there. You stand out front with the rest of the adoring public until Shelley introduces you and brings you up on stage to say a few words."

"That's right," Mildred interjected with an eager nod, hanging the walkie-talkie back on her belt. "Shelley said that you and she discussed this on the phone. All we need is a minute or two to hear a little about your store, and then you can talk about how Hamlet learned karate."

"When you're finished talking," Jake went on as Darla continued working on her hot dog, "they'll play his video. Apparently, this is a special music-video version the show commissioned, so it will run two or three minutes."

"Right, Shelley mentioned that," Darla confirmed, shooting a look at Hamlet lounging in his makeshift bookstore. *What's next, Hamlet on MTV?*

"Once the video is over," Jake continued, "I'll bring Hamlet out to prance around the stage for photos and take his bows. Who knows? Maybe we'll get lucky and he'll do a few karate punches. Then it'll be back to cat judging."

She paused and looked at her watch, and then reached for her drink. "Chugalug. We've only got a few minutes before we have to take our places."

They made quick work of their remaining lunch, Darla pretending not to notice the growing crowd of show attendees gathering near the stage. Mildred, however, wasn't shy about keeping count.

"Oh, look—there's at least a hundred people already, Darla," she said in satisfaction. Leaning in with a confidential air, she added, "Now, remember, if you get nervous when it's your turn to talk, just picture everyone out there naked. They say that's a perfect cure for stage fright."

"I'll keep it in mind," was Darla's wry response. The bikini protesters had already filled her quota of naked—or, at least, mostly naked—people so far that day. A whole exhibition hall of them, even imaginary, might permanently scar her eyeballs.

She headed to Hamlet's pen, scanning first for any wayward books the wily feline might have tossed about. To her relief, all the volumes were neatly in place, so she snapped on his lead and handed it over to Jake. "Remember, keep the loop over your wrist all the time."

"Hey, kid, I'm a pro. I've got it."

"Now, Darla, go ahead and stand over there by Shelley," Mildred said, making little shooing gestures toward the crowd. "Jake, you and Hamlet come with me. There's a door right here that leads to a little hallway behind the back wall. I'll show you a ramp you can walk up that will take you right to the stage behind the curtain. We want Hamlet to make a dramatic entrance, don't we?"

Darla watched as the two women and Hamlet slipped out the side door. Then, checking the lock on the pen a final time, she went over to Shelley.

"Nervous?" the woman asked her with a smile. "No need to be, but if you get a little stage fright, just picture everyone out there naked. It works for me every time."

"Great idea," Darla agreed, suppressing a smile.

Giving Darla a reassuring pat on the arm, Shelley bounded up the short staircase at the side of the stage and whipped out the mike again. "Attention, everybody. We're about to start."

When the crowd had settled down so that only a soft undercurrent of meowing could be heard, she began. "First, I hope that everyone is having a wonderful time so far!"

When the obligatory applause died down, Shelley continued. "As you know, every year we have a guest of honor join us at the show. This year, we have a very special treat for you. Unless you've been living under a rock the past couple of months, you must have seen him. He's an Internet sensation . . . Hamlet the Karate Kitty!"

This time, the applause was punctuated by laughter and whistling, and Darla found herself grinning. Hamlet really had made a name for himself. Depending on how things went at the cat show, she might have to start a fan club for him, or at least set up his very own Facebook page.

Shelley was gesturing for quiet. "Now, if you haven't met Hamlet here at the show yet, we'll be showing his famous video and bringing him out on stage in just a couple of minutes. But first, let's hear from Hamlet's owner. She's the proprietor of Pettistone's Fine Books in Brooklyn, New York. Please welcome Ms. Darla Pettistone."

Naked people, Darla reminded herself as she climbed the steps onto the stage and took the mike from Shelley. The crowd had grown to close to two hundred people . . . not a mob, but quite large enough for her usual stage fright to kick in. It didn't help that she could see Billy Pope and Alicia Timpson standing to the front of the spectators. While apparently they had put aside their earlier argument—at least, for the sake of appearances—their presence reminded her of the recent unpleasantness marring what should have been a carefree couple of days playing celebrity.

Then she caught sight of Nattie standing to one side. The old woman gave her a big grin and a thumbs-up, and that bit of support was enough to allow her to say, "Hi, I'm Darla Pettistone. Hamlet and I are thrilled to be here in Ft. Lauderdale with you for this fabulous show. Now, let me tell you a little about Hamlet before he became—what did Shelley call him?—an Internet sensation."

Swiftly, she related the story of Hamlet as James had first told it to her: how, as a tiny black kitten he'd shown up on the doorstep outside the bookstore and had made himself right at home when Great-Aunt Dee let him inside. And how, after he'd had a makeshift meal of milk and a bit of Dee's tuna sandwich, he'd wandered over to the bookshelves and curled up on a fallen copy of one of Shakespeare's tragedies, earning the name Hamlet. The story earned a few indulgent *ahh*s from the audience, so Darla mentioned some of his more memorable store antics—chasing customers, claiming the best reading chairs, even once stopping a shoplifter.

"Thank you, Darla," Shelley said as the applause for her short speech died down. "Now, let's take a look at the video that brought Hamlet to everyone's attention."

She escorted Darla to one side of the stage as the lights dimmed and then proceeded to press a few buttons on a video player Darla now noticed was hooked to the large screen television. A blast of music sounded, and Darla grinned. She recognized the opening notes to the 1980s hit song "Eye of the Tiger." It was definitely appropriate.

The video that followed was slicker and far more produced than anything she'd yet seen online. Someone skilled at videography had taken the original upload of Darla doing karate katas at a tournament with Hamlet imitating her in the background and turned it into a comical music video. Hamlet's image had been pulled to the forefront, with Darla now but a background character as the cat leaped and feinted to the music.

While the music blared, quick cuts of the "fighting" feline were interspersed with slo-mo, with Hamlet seemingly performing the more elaborate stunts common to martial arts movies. One moment, he was sparring with Darla, who'd been shrunk down to his size; the next, he was fighting a small army of Hamlets rushing him from every direction. He even did the invisible wire-flight routine, seeming to walk across towering treetops. Each new stunt brought more laughter from the spectators, who by the end of the video were all but screaming in hysteria.

Darla was also impressed, and through her tears of laughter she spied Billy Pope in the front row wiping his own eyes with his handkerchief. Even the Martini Lady had cracked a grin, making her appear quite human for a change. When the video finally ended, the ovation lasted a good minute, with a smiling Darla vowing to get her hands on a copy.

She shouted as much to Shelley over the sound of the applause.

"Great, wasn't it?" Shelley shouted back. "Alicia will get you a copy later."

Taking up the mike again, Shelley quieted the crowd. "That was fabulous, wasn't it?" she asked, drawing another cheer. "Now that we've seen him on the silver screen, let's meet him in person. Ladies and gentlemen, Hamlet the Karate Kitty!"

Beaming, she swept an arm toward the curtains behind her, where Jake and Hamlet were to enter center stage. When they didn't, Shelley raised the mike again, and said, "I guess Hamlet is a little shy about meeting his public. Hamlet, come on out!"

The spectators had begun to murmur among themselves, while Darla watched the wall of curtains in some concern. If Hamlet had gotten stubborn about making an appearance, surely Jake would have popped out to let her know.

Then the heavy blue drapes moved, and Darla smiled in relief. *Showtime!* Her smile promptly faded, however, when Jake staggered out onto the stage alone. As for the official karate cat, he was nowhere to be seen.

"Jake," Darla cried, rushing to her friend and grabbing her arm to support her. "What happened? Are you hurt? Where's Hamlet?"

"I'm fine," Jake mumbled, clutching her head. "Don't worry about me. Hamlet's the one in trouble!"

"What do you mean?" she demanded, reaching past her friend to flick aside the curtain to check on Hamlet. A glance was all she needed. Save for a couple of folding chairs, the space was empty.

Voice trembling now, she went on, "What happened? Did he get loose?"

Jake shook her head, wincing at the motion. "No, it's worse than that. We were sitting back there waiting for the video to end, when someone hit me on the head from behind.

I don't think I was out for more than a couple of seconds, but when my head cleared, Hamlet was gone, leash and all."

"Gone! You mean—"

Jake nodded, wincing again. "Yeah. I think he's been kidnapped."

EIGHT

"KIDNAPPED?" DARLA ECHOED IN DISBELIEF.

Somehow, she couldn't picture a cat of Hamlet's size and disposition simply being snatched, not without leaving behind a trail of blood and fur. But she hadn't heard any caterwauling over the blare of the video, and nothing behind the main stage area had appeared unusual . . . other than the fact that there had been no sign of the feline. Obviously, Jake wouldn't make up a wild tale about being attacked just for the fun of it.

Then, realizing she was about to lose her grip on Jake, Darla snapped, "Quick, Shelley, have someone grab a chair and bring it up here. We need some medical help right now!"

Shelley, however, had already gauged the situation and was on her walkie-talkie. "Yes, the police and an ambulance," she clarified to the person on the other end. "It wasn't a fall. She says she was attacked."

Flipping off the walkie, she pointed at two burly young

men near the stage, and said, "You, sir, and you—bring a chair up here right now."

By now, the crowd realized that what was happening on stage had nothing to do with the video and had begun to mill uncertainly about. Shelley grabbed the mike again.

"Everyone, please remain calm. Everything is under control. Don't worry—we'll reschedule our official appearance by Hamlet for later. But if there's a doctor here at the show, we need you at the stage at the rear of the exhibition hall. Everyone else, please stay clear of the area. And while we're waiting for the judging to resume, why don't you visit our vendor booths for all your cat needs."

While Shelley made her announcements, the two men she'd recruited had found a folding chair at the concession area and lifted it onto the stage. Darla gave them a grateful nod as she guided her friend over to it.

"Quick, Jake, sit down. You look like you're about to pass out."

"I'm fine," Jake mumbled, even as she sagged heavily into the chair. "It's Hamlet I'm worried about. We need to lock the place down and find whoever took him."

"We're doing that right now," Billy Pope declared in his reedy voice. He'd made his way up the stage steps, accompanied by his daughter. "Alicia has already notified all the volunteers at the front doors that no one is to leave without all bags and boxes and carriers being searched."

"What about the back way?" Darla demanded, trying to keep her voice from shaking. *Better to stay mad than dissolve into a weeping mess*, she told herself. *Crying about it isn't going to help find Hamlet.* Taking a steadying breath, she went on, "Mildred said there were a couple of doors leading out to the hall behind the stage. That's how the kidnapper must have gotten back there."

"Perhaps, but there's no place for them to go other than back out into the hall again," Alicia said, her tone cool, though her expression betrayed her concern.

Concern for the show's reputation, not for Hamlet. Darla had seen a fleeting look of dismay on Alicia's face when Shelley had mentioned that the police were on the way. All Darla wanted to do was rush backstage and try to track the kidnapper herself, but she didn't dare leave Jake. And yet, for every minute she couldn't search, Hamlet could be farther from the exhibit hall.

Alicia went on, "I'm quite familiar with this building. The only exterior doors that are unlocked besides the front entry are the emergency exits. An alarm would have gone off if someone tried to flee through any of them. So it only follows that whoever has Hamlet must still be here inside the hall."

"Jacqueline, *bambolina mia*!"

Nattie, carrying a chili cheese dog and an oversized soft drink cup, came rushing onto the stage. "I sneak off to get something to eat, just a little nourishment for an old woman, and I come back to find this?!"

Shoving the drink and hot dog into a bemused Alicia's hands, Nattie dropped to her knees beside her daughter. "Oh, I'll never forgive myself bringing you here to die like this!" she wailed, reaching up to examine Jake's skull.

Jake gently batted away the old woman's hands. "Ma, I'm fine. It's just a little bump. See, not even any blood," she said, displaying an un-bloodied palm for Nattie's scrutiny.

Meanwhile, the show veterinarian who'd earlier attended Cozy Kitty had rushed up on stage, medical bag in hand. Nattie straightened and gave him an outraged look. "What, an animal doctor is going to take care of my baby?"

"I'm just here as a Good Samaritan," the vet assured the old woman as he reached into his pocket for a penlight. "The EMTs will arrive in a minute."

Sidestepping Nattie, he shined a light into one of Jake's eyes, and then the other, while remarking to no one in particular, "Actually, the first two years of veterinary training are virtually identical to what you get in med school." Then, addressing Jake, he asked, "How are you feeling, ma'am?"

"Like someone smacked me in the head."

The vet's lips twitched, though whether in amusement or impatience, Darla couldn't tell. "Yeah, I kind of figured that. The headache's a given. I meant, any nausea . . . double vision . . . flashing sparks when you look around you?"

"Maybe a little at first," she admitted, "but it's pretty much just a rotten headache now."

Her voice was stronger now, sounding like her old self, Darla thought in relief. Maybe it really wasn't anything worse than a bump.

"Oh dear, this is terrible!"

The wavering voice came from Mildred, who had joined the growing crowd on the stage. Rushing over to Jake, she cried, "My dear girl, I never would have left you and Hamlet alone backstage if I'd had any inkling something might go wrong." Her eyes watery behind her steel-rimmed glasses, Mildred turned to Nattie. "I am so sorry. Please forgive me."

"Eh, it's not yer fault, Millie," the other woman said a bit brusquely, though she gave Mildred a reassuring pat on the arm. "We Martellis all have hard heads."

"Shelley, do you copy?" a tinny male voice abruptly squawked from Shelley's walkie-talkie. "The cops and paramedics are here. I'm bringing them back to you now."

"Ten-four," was Shelley's reply. With an apologetic glance at Jake and Darla, she asked Alicia, "Not to be insensitive here, but if we delay much longer, the show will be running behind. Should I go ahead and have the ring clerks announce the next categories?"

"Yes, let's stay on schedule," Alicia said. "If nothing else, it will keep the spectators and exhibitors occupied while we deal with the police. We don't want to spoil everyone's good time with . . . unpleasantness."

Darla shot Shelley, Alicia, and Billy an outraged look as the trio huddled in a hurried CYA session. She couldn't help but wonder if Cindy had had a hand in this attack.

Darla glanced toward the front of the hall. From her

vantage point, she could see two police officers in short-sleeved, navy blue uniforms making their way toward the stage, a trio of EMTs with a gurney following after them. Swiftly, she leaned toward Jake.

"If you think you'll be all right with your mom, I'm going to take Mildred and have her show me that back hall," she said in a low tone. "Maybe Hamlet's still back there. I can't see him letting someone carry him off that easily, so maybe he got away and is hiding."

"You're right. Go look for him," Jake urged. "We should have already been doing that. I hate to say this, but when it comes down to it, the cops will treat Hamlet's disappearance as a property theft."

"Property theft!" Darla glared at the approaching officers, unable to believe Hamlet's catnapping was on par with a stolen bicycle.

"Sorry, kid. That's the law. And it's not like they have the authority to search the crowd. They're lucky that Alicia's volunteers are doing the dirty work for them. If someone stuffed him in a cat carrier and tries to haul him out of here, the polo shirt squad will stop them."

"But what about you? You were attacked. Won't they investigate that?"

"Yeah, that'll be aggravated battery. Throw Hamlet into the mix, and if you've got some real gung-ho cops, they might stretch it as far as armed robbery. But unless a witness to the whole thing comes forward, or someone in the crowd caught something on video, it's going to be on us to find Hamlet."

"Then I'd better get moving."

Darla turned to leave, only to have Jake grab her arm. "Before you run off, I have to tell you how sorry I am about this. I—I let you and Hamlet down."

"You didn't let us down. It's no one's fault, except the jerk who hurt you and took Hamlet."

Jake released her arm, though Darla could see she looked

unconvinced. Not that Darla blamed her. In Jake's place, she would have felt the same way. Turning to Mildred, Darla said, "Quick, I need you to show me the back hallway and all the exits."

The older woman's gaze hardened behind her glasses, and she nodded. "Come with me."

The hallway held no surprises. Strictly utilitarian, the passage ran the length of the rear of the convention center, allowing facilities and set-up personnel access without their having to wander the main exhibition area. Darla could see at a glance that Hamlet wasn't lurking anywhere along its length.

"This is the way Jake and Hamlet got backstage," Mildred explained, and pointed to a black-curtained entry at the top of an open ramp that ran parallel to the backstage wall.

The actual door, Darla saw, opened inward to the hall and had been propped in place, with the ramp and curtain obviously temporary add-ons. For now, the door served as a handy backstage access. When the ramp and curtain were removed, however, and the stage taken down, the entry would simply be a tall doorway between hallway and exhibition area.

Darla bent down to look beneath the ramp, using her cell phone as a makeshift flashlight.

"Hamlet, are you under there?" she called, praying she'd see a glint of eyes to indicate he was crouched in the shadows there. Unfortunately, all she spied were a couple of discarded bottles and what appeared to be candy bar wrappers.

"Nothing," she told Mildred, trying to keep the disappointment from her voice. It would have been too much to expect that it would that easy to find the missing cat. Still . . .

Straightening, she gave the corridor a closer look. Halfway down was a roll-up door that Darla assumed led to a loading dock. Hurrying to examine it, she saw that both it and the main door beside it were padlocked shut. Even if someone had had the keys to open them, no way could they have relocked them.

That left the emergency exit doors, one at either end of the hall. Both displayed the required signage overhead, and both opened with red crash bars that had alarm warnings stenciled on them. Alicia was right, Darla reluctantly conceded. Had the catnapper actually left the building by way of the back hall, a siren would have blared in warning.

"I don't suppose there's much else to check out back here," she told Mildred. "We might as well go back out onto the floor and start looking. Let's go that way"—she pointed to the ramp—"just in case there's anything backstage that might be a clue."

She hurried up the ramp, Mildred trudging behind, and slipped behind the black curtain onto the platform. The backstage area was nothing more than perhaps a quarter of the full stage separated by the wall of blue drapes that served as backdrop for the main stage area. The background sounds of the cat show were once more loud and clear, though Darla could also hear conversation coming from beyond the blue curtain, probably the police and EMTs still dealing with Jake and the others.

A quick look showed that the backstage area was bare save for a couple of folding chairs. Both were situated side by side right in front of her, facing forward. One of the pair, however, had been knocked askew. That must have been where Jake had been sitting when she was hit from behind, Darla reasoned. And, given that Jake had been sitting down when she'd been attacked from behind, that left the police with a large pool of potential assailant-slash-catnappers. Had Jake been standing, it would have narrowed the field considerably. They'd need to look for someone tall enough to have dealt a significant blow to a six-foot-tall victim. Instead, practically anyone at the show was a potential suspect.

"Oh, look," Mildred exclaimed, bending near the blue curtains and reaching for something. "Do you suppose this is the weapon the catnapper used on poor Jake?"

"Mildred, don't touch anything!"

Darla's cry was a heartbeat too late, however, for the old woman had already picked up a glass bottle half-hidden by the curtain folds and was examining it.

"Quick, put it back down," she urged. "If that bottle is the weapon, then you've just tampered with evidence."

"Oh dear!"

The woman hurriedly set down the bottle again and took a step back, hands over her heart as she stared in sudden misery at the glass container. "I wasn't thinking. Oh dear, I am so sorry."

"You didn't do it on purpose," Darla assured her, tamping down her impatience with the woman that, she knew, mostly stemmed from her fear for Hamlet's well-being.

Then Darla frowned. If she wasn't mistaken, the empty bottle that Mildred had found was the same brand of bottled water as the makeshift vase that Cindy had wielded at her mother the night before. Coincidence? Or was this a weapon of choice for the girl, which then pointed to Cindy as the most viable suspect?

"Come on, let's go back out there and tell the police what we found."

They made their entrance on stage to find Jake doing her best to convince the paramedics she was fine, while the two burly cops—one female and Hispanic, the other male and African American—were talking with Alicia and Billy. Shelley had apparently gone back out onto the floor. As a group, they looked up at Darla's approach.

"Any luck finding Hamlet?" Jake asked hopefully, holding an ice bag to the back of her head.

Now that she knew Jake was relatively unharmed, Darla's concern for Hamlet rose to the forefront. Striving for an even tone, she replied, "No. Alicia was right. There's no way out except the emergency exits, and nothing to show he was ever back there. But Mildred might have found the weapon that was used on you. It was an empty glass bottle."

Darla deliberately focused on Alicia as she said this last, waiting to see if the woman would have some reaction. But Alicia's poker-faced mask was once again firmly in place.

"Ma'am," the female officer spoke up, turning to Darla, "why don't you show me this bottle."

"Sure, it's right behind the curtain, but Mildred accidentally picked it up before she realized it could be evidence."

The two uniforms exchanged glances, and Darla could practically hear the unspoken epithet passing between them: "civilians." Still, the cop—Garcia, according to the silver name badge pinned over her shirt pocket—retained her professionally noncommittal air as she said, "We'll collect it anyhow and send it to the lab."

Darla left the officers to poke around a few minutes longer while she returned to where Jake sat. To the obvious displeasure of the paramedics, the PI was handing back the ice pack while reaching for a clipboard one of the EMTs held.

"You're not going to let them take you to the hospital." It was a statement, not a question, since Darla already knew the answer.

Jake finished signing the release form they'd given her with a flourish. "I'm fine—just need to take it easy for a couple of days. Right, boys?"

The "boys" muttered under their breaths but gave her a copy of the paper; then, tossing bags and boxes onto their gurney, they began rolling toward the exit. As for the cops, they had returned with the bottle safely bagged for evidence. After getting Darla and Mildred's version of what they knew regarding the assault and catnapping, the male cop—"Officer Cory Johnston," Darla read off the business card he had handed her—flipped his notebook closed.

"Well, folks, you can see we don't have much to go on

here. Ms. Martelli didn't see who hit her, and no one saw anyone walking off with the cat. And you've got a few hundred people here, and almost that many cats to sort through. The best we can do at this point is hope a witness comes forward, or that someone managed to get something on video," he finished, practically repeating Jake's earlier estimation of the situation word for word.

"What about the protesters outside? They seem to have a grudge against the show. And then there was that incident earlier, when someone poured ketchup on a cat and made it look like they'd butchered it. Oh, and someone's cat escaped, too. Luckily Mildred caught it, but what if it had been let out on purpose?"

"Really, Ms. Pettistone," Alicia coolly interjected while the two officers again exchanged looks. "I know you're upset about your cat—we all are worried about Hamlet, of course—but I think you're blowing these other incidents out of proportion. We often have protesters at our shows, and it's not uncommon for cats to escape from inexperienced handlers. As for that ketchup incident—it was unpleasant, but no animal was actually harmed."

The female officer penned a few final words and then looked up at Darla.

"Ms. Pettistone, we saw those college kids with the signs when we came in. Don't worry, we'll talk to them on the way out . . . throw a little scare into them, see if they'll admit to anything. But, I'd be really surprised if one of those kids was the person who assaulted Ms. Martelli. That's just not their usual modus operandi."

Then the female cop gave Darla an encouraging smile. "Try not to worry about your cat, Ms. Pettistone. We have your cat's description. We'll notify Animal Control to keep an eye out in case he's loose somewhere on the street. And if those protesters turn out to be the ones who took him, I can almost guarantee they'll leave him somewhere for you to find before the end of the show today. Most of those kids who do the animal rights thing, their hearts are in the right place."

Before Darla could mutter her first reflexive response, which was what she'd do with certain thong-wearing protesters' hearts if she found out they were the culprits, the male cop jumped back in.

"Oh, and I'm sure the show people will want to offer a reward for the cat's safe return, as well as for information regarding Ms. Martelli's assault," he said with a glance at Billy and Alicia. "Money—that's what usually does the trick in situations like this."

"Of course," Billy hurriedly agreed. "We all want Hamlet back as quickly as possible. Alicia, why don't you have Shelley come see me, and I'll arrange that right now."

The officers took their leave, followed by Alicia, presumably in search of her announcer. Billy, meanwhile, turned his attention to Darla and Jake.

"Ladies, I can assure you that nothing like this has ever happened at one of our shows before. Believe me, we'll do everything we can to make it right. Ms. Martelli, why don't I have the hotel send one of their golf carts over here to carry you and your mother back to the Waterview so you can relax for a while?"

"That's a great idea, Billy," Nattie spoke up even as Jake opened her mouth to protest. "She needs a bit of rest right now."

"Ma, I'm fine. Darla needs me here."

"No, Jake, your mother's right," Darla replied. "It's bad enough I have to worry about Hamlet. It'll be worse if I have to worry about you, too. I'm going to search this place top to bottom for him, and then I'll meet you back at the hotel after the show is over."

Jake threw up one hand in surrender. "Fine, I'll go," she muttered, earning an approving pat on the arm from Nattie.

Billy headed off to procure the promised golf cart, and

soon thereafter Jake and Nattie clambered on board. Billy waved the women off, then turned to Darla.

"We've established a one-thousand-dollar reward both for Hamlet's safe return and information about the assault, no questions asked," he told her. "Shelley has already made the announcement on our various social media sites. And, of course, our volunteers will be continuing to check bags and boxes as people leave the show, just in case."

"I appreciate that, Mr. Pope. But what about your granddaughter, Cindy?" was Darla's blunt reply.

At her question, Billy's expression of genial concern hardened.

"I can assure you, Ms. Pettistone, that my granddaughter has nothing to do with this unfortunate incident. Now, if you'll excuse me, I need to get back to the judging. My people will keep you informed if we learn anything."

He turned and headed back toward the judging ring, while Darla silently fumed. Maybe Nattie's loyalty to the man was misplaced. The fact that Billy had an obvious blind spot when it came to his granddaughter likely meant he was weak in other areas, as well. Maybe he'd channeled the missing condo association money to Cindy.

"Well, that's the rich for you."

The surprisingly bitter sentiment came from Mildred, who was standing beside Darla. "They think because they have money, the rules don't apply. And they don't have much sympathy for all us 'don't haves,'" she said in a quavering voice.

Then, apparently realizing she'd spoken out of turn, Mildred waved a dismissive hand.

"Oh, don't mind me, I'm just letting off a little steam," she said, managing a smile. "Mr. Pope and Mrs. Timpson have been very generous patrons of the FSA. I don't know what the organization would do without them."

"Well, you'd think they'd be trying a bit harder to find Hamlet," Darla countered, not quite as willing as Mildred to give the pair a pass. "Why haven't they had Shelley make an announcement over the PA that Hamlet's been taken?"

"Oh, my dear, you wouldn't want to do that," the old woman replied, her expression faintly horrified.

Gesturing to the crowd, she went on, "If Shelley started telling people that Hamlet was catnapped, the place would be in an uproar. The exhibitors would all be worried something could happen to their cats, too. And then you'd have all these Helpful Hannahs thinking every black cat at the show was Hamlet. No, believe me, dear, it's much better for everyone—Hamlet included—if we're a bit subtle about this."

Subtle, my butt, was Darla's reaction, though she grudgingly admitted that Mildred had a point. She could just imagine people rushing up to her with sundry black cats, all hoping to get the reward money.

"All right, Mildred," she conceded. "We'll keep it low-key. But before I do anything else, I'm going outside to talk to those protesters. The catnapper might have made it out the door before Alicia had time to put her volunteers on pat-down mode. Those kids might have seen something important."

"Weren't the police already going to question them?"

"Yeah, but did the cops bribe them this morning with donut holes? Maybe they'll be more forthcoming with me."

Darla's timing proved fortunate, for the protest seemed to have broken up. Bangles and Farmer Tan Girl were off to one side of the walkway, fully dressed now and stuffing their signs into garbage bags. There was no sign of Cindy, but it was probably for the best. Maybe separated from her, the other girls would be willing to divulge what, if anything, they knew about Hamlet's disappearance.

"Hey, girls, wait a minute," Darla called, waving the pair down as the students shuffled off in the direction of the main sidewalk. "I really need to talk to you."

Bangles looked back, and then poked her friend, drawing

her attention to Darla. To her relief, the girls waited while she caught up to them.

"Hi," Darla breathlessly greeted the pair as she caught up to them. "Remember me? I brought you the donut holes this morning."

"Yeah, they were, like, awesomely good," Farmer Tan Girl said with a smile. Pointing to her friend, she added, "Talina ate three of them."

"Did not," Talina muttered, though her grin gave away the lie.

Darla smiled back. "Believe me, I'd have eaten three myself if I hadn't had breakfast already." Then, sobering, she went on, "Girls, I'm in real trouble and need your help. Did the police ask you about the cat that's been kidnapped?"

NINE

AT DARLA'S QUESTION, BOTH PROTESTERS IMMEDIATELY dropped their friendly air.

"We didn't have nothing to do with that, right, Lilly?" Talina declared, her expression threatening.

Lilly gave Darla an equally thunderous glare. "Yeah, like we told the po-po, we don't know nothing about it."

The pair swung about and continued down the steps. Determined not to lose this opportunity, Darla trotted after them. "Look, girls, this is really important. I know you didn't take the cat, but maybe you saw something . . . maybe even the person who did it. The cat that's missing is mine, and I really want him back."

She couldn't help the slight catch in her voice as she said that last. The girls must have heard the quiver of emotion as well, for they paused and looked at each other. Darla persisted. "Maybe you've heard of him before. His name is Hamlet. He's the Karate Kitty on YouTube."

"OMG! Karate Kitty is *your* cat?" Lilly gave a little jump

of excitement. "I've seen that video, like, a hundred times. The *Star Wars* version is my favorite."

"No way, girl. The one with the Jay-Z song is the best," Talina countered, giving the other girl a friendly little push. Then, turning to Darla, she said, "Say, you do kinda look like the lady in the video. So, he really is your cat?"

"He's mine. He's the official mascot of my bookstore. See?"

She reached into her tote bag and pulled out the "paw"-tograph fliers, handing one to each of them. "Look, I know the police already asked this, but did you maybe notice anyone leaving the building about"—she paused and consulted her watch—"say, about an hour ago, carrying a big black cat? He might've been in a carrier, or maybe in a backpack or gym bag. You might not have even seen him, but he'd probably have been meowing. And he weighs a ton, so he's not that easy to handle, even when he's in a good mood."

The two girls stared at the fliers and then each other before reluctantly shaking their heads. "No, I didn't see him. Sorry," Talina said, her expression now one of dismay.

Lilly added, "No, it was pretty slow an hour ago, so anyone who walked out, we would've seen. Sorry."

Darla gave a disappointed sigh. It had been too much to hope that the catnapper had been spotted leaving the scene of the crime. On the bright side, however, that might mean he was still somewhere in the hall. She'd team up with Mildred again and check out every row of the exhibitor area in case Hamlet was locked in somewhere.

Making her farewells to the girls, who promised to call the cell phone number Darla scribbled on the fliers if they heard anything of interest on the protester grapevine, Darla headed back inside the hall. Mildred was waiting for her at the information table.

"I already checked all the restrooms and the storage area

near the concessions, but no sign of Hamlet," the old woman told her. "Were those young people outside any help at all?"

Darla shook her head. "They said they didn't notice anyone, and I'm pretty sure it would be obvious if anyone was carting out a cat his size. I guess the next thing to do is search the exhibitor area."

"Good idea, dear. How about you start here, and I start in the back, and we meet in the middle? That way, we can cover more area in a short period of time."

"That would be perfect. Thanks so much for helping me out like this. Without Jake and Nattie, I'm kind of on my own here."

Darla hastily blinked back the tears of frustrated worry she had been trying hard to suppress ever since she'd learned Hamlet was missing. She was already late checking in with James and Robert at the bookstore. If they didn't find Hamlet by the time the show ended for the day, she'd have to let her manager know that their mascot was officially a crime victim.

Mildred, meanwhile, gave Darla a reassuring pat on the shoulder. "Buck up, dear. I know we'll find him. Be sure to look underneath the tables as well as in the cages."

They spent the next little while separately scouring the exhibition area. Some of the exhibitors recognized Darla and already had heard the rumors about Hamlet. They offered advice and condolences, and all vowed to keep an eye out for the missing cat.

As she continued the search, it occurred to Darla that maybe they'd been looking for motives in all the wrong places. Maybe the person who'd taken Hamlet had no agenda other than wanting to own a famous cat. The feline's appearance at the cat show had been well advertised; heck, she had even helped spread the word all over social media that Hamlet was going on tour. It would have been easy enough for the catnapper to buy a ticket to the show and simply wait around for an opportunity; then Hamlet's video had proved the distraction needed.

By the time Darla and Mildred finally met again in the predetermined center point, both of them empty-handed, Darla was feeling discouraged and more than a little fearful that she might never see Hamlet again.

"I'm sorry, my dear," Mildred told her. "Hamlet wasn't hidden away in any of the cages, and none of the exhibitors has seen tail or whisker of him."

"I didn't have any luck either. Maybe I should try outside, in case he did get away and is waiting for me to find him."

"That's a good idea, dear. I'd join you, but I really have to get back to work," Mildred explained, looking faintly guilty at the admission.

Darla nodded. "I understand, and I'm grateful for all the help you've given me."

"You can thank me when we've found your kitty. Now, you know the Riverwalk, which runs right behind the convention center? I suggest you go down to the corner and turn right"—the old woman pantomimed the route Darla would take—"and you'll run right into the walkway. The city has done a lovely job of landscaping there, and you'll find all sorts of bushes and groundcover for Hamlet to hide in, if he's out there."

Leaving Mildred to her volunteer duties, Darla exited the exhibition hall and started in the direction the woman had indicated. She wondered if she should try to recruit someone else from the show to help her, but then she decided against it. Hamlet was touchy enough when things were going well. If he had escaped his presumed abductors and was outside the hall, he'd probably be wary of any stranger attempting to catch him. She'd likely have more success alone.

She came across the Riverwalk almost immediately, a broad concrete path that ran parallel to the water. Rather that the bird's-eye view she'd had the previous afternoon, this look at the New River was up close and personal. Darla could hear the rapidly flowing water lapping against the banks, and actually saw a fish or two flash by in the clear water. The river smelled of rain, overlaid with faint notes of mud and fish and the ocean. Many of the bushes lining the walk were in bloom, and their perfume, carried on a cool breeze coming off the water, bathed her in a bit of calming aromatherapy.

On the opposite side of the river, Darla could see homes—some charming, others elegant, almost all with their own private boat docks. As with the other structures she'd passed the day before, the homes spread along the riverbank were painted in tasty sherbet hues that contrasted with the pewter-colored waters. On her side of the river were commercial buildings interspersed with the occasional vintage home. Most of the latter were fenced off and appeared to have been converted to businesses and—in at least one case—a museum. Maybe later in the week, if things got back to normal, she'd take a closer look.

The walkway was busy with clutches of wandering tourists. Normally, Darla would've summoned a smile and a nod as she passed each group, but for the moment her attention was focused at a lower level. Not caring how it looked, she crouched here and there to peer beneath a clump of greenery and call Hamlet's name.

More than once, she was startled when a green or brown lizard popped out. Most of those reptiles were cute enough, reminding her of the so-called chameleons that many of her classmates had kept when she was in grade school. A few, however, were decidedly less cute—fat and the size of small rats, with long tails that curled over their backs as they scampered past. It took all her effort not to let out a girlie shriek every time one of those creatures skittered across her path.

Darla spent a good hour pacing up and down the Riverwalk, growing more discouraged with each passing minute. Surely if Hamlet had escaped to the great outdoors, she would have spotted him by now; that, or he would have heard her calling and ventured out. Whoever had taken him must still be holding him captive, she told herself stoutly, forbidding herself to speculate on any other potential fates.

The sun had dropped behind the taller downtown buildings, leaving her in partial shadow, and the temperature had dropped as well. Darla wished she had a sweater to toss over her polo shirt. She glanced at her watch and saw that it was already five o'clock. The cat show would be over for the day, with all the exhibitors gathering their cats for the trip back to their respective homes or hotels. Even though she and Mildred had already combed through every owner's spot searching for Hamlet, Darla wanted to take one more look about the place before they locked the doors for the night.

Darla bent to check behind a final green-and-yellow-foliaged bush before she headed back, when she heard an unexpected *beep beep* behind her, and Jake zipped up beside her in a golf cart. Darla stared at her friend in surprise. Her first thought was to hope Hamlet had been found; her second, that Jake had no business tooling around in any sort of vehicle after that blow to her head.

"Mildred told me you were out here on the Riverwalk searching for Hamlet. I guess you haven't seen any sign of him?"

"No. Any news from anyone at the cat show?"

"None." Jake shook her head, her expression grim. "They're closing the hall down for the night, so I figured we'd take another look around the place. Come on, hop in."

Darla did as she was told, and Jake wheeled the cart around, retracing the route to the convention center. Darla clung to the pole supporting the overhead canopy as Jake negotiated the curves at a swift clip.

"So, what are you doing driving around? I thought you had a concussion," she demanded, trying to use righteous indignation to distract herself temporarily from thoughts of Hamlet. "Does Nattie know you're out here?"

"First, getting hit on the head does not equal concussion," Jake countered. "I was just a little woozy for a couple of minutes. And, second, what Ma doesn't know won't hurt her. I left her napping in the room with her beloved throw pillows."

Before Darla could come up with a retort to that, Jake drove up the handicapped ramp to the exhibition hall entrance. She halted the cart there, since a steady stream of cat owners was moving out of the building now and pretty well blocking any incoming traffic. Some of the participants were wheeling their cats in carriers similar to the one Darla had used on the plane, while others had several cages stacked on luggage carts. The scene had a *Grapes of Wrath* vibe to it . . . at least in that hunger definitely drove these travelers, Darla thought with a fleeting smile, hearing the meow chorus of kitties ready for their suppers.

Shelley Jacobson and two male volunteers stood in the doorway supervising the exodus. The former looked up at Darla and Jake's approach.

"No luck, ladies?" she asked in sympathy. When Darla shook her head, Shelley added, "If you want to give the exhibition hall another look, we'll have the doors open for another fifteen minutes or so."

While Shelley played traffic cop, Jake fired up the golf cart again. She dropped Darla off at the stage. "I'll check out the judging area. You take another look back here, and at concessions. Who knows? If Hamlet really is on the loose, maybe he found some leftover hot dogs to chow down on and has been napping all afternoon." The women exchanged wan smiles and went their separate ways.

They were still searching a quarter of an hour later when the overhead lights began shutting down. Darla scrambled out from beneath one of the vendor tables, and Jake zipped over to pick her up again.

"Don't worry," Jake said as they headed back to the main doors. "That Hamlet is a smart, resourceful cat. He can take care of himself, even in a strange town."

Darla nodded, doing her best not to give in to defeat. "When we get back to the hotel, I want to talk to Chantal at the front desk and let her know what's going on in case the catnapper leaves a message for us."

"Good idea."

Making their good-byes to Shelley, Darla and Jake rode off in silence toward the hotel. The shadows were gathering in earnest now, with the setting sun throwing a final blanket of pink light across the surrounding buildings. The stress of the afternoon weighed on Darla, and once again she found herself blinking back tears. After all that she and Hamlet had been through together the past year, how could he suddenly be gone from her life?

"Jake, what are we going to do?" she softly wailed as they approached the hotel. "We don't even have the beginnings of a clue as to who took him. And you know the police won't do anything to find him, not without some sort of solid lead to follow."

"Hang in there," Jake reassured her. "Remember, I was a cop for almost twenty years. I've solved cases starting out with less than we have now. When we get back to the hotel, I'm going to see if I can't call in a few favors. There's got to be someone down here who can—"

She broke off and hit the brakes on the cart, so that Darla had to grab the canopy pole with both hands to keep from sliding out. "What's wrong? Why are we stopping?"

Jake held up a cautioning hand. "Shh, listen. I swear I heard . . . maybe it's just because I've been listening to cats crying half the day . . . but it sounds like—"

Me-ooooow!

"Hamlet!" Darla exclaimed and pointed up to the sixth floor. "There, on the balcony! No, not our room, the one at the corner. Look on the railing."

Despite the gathering dusk, there was still sufficient light for Darla to make out a dark shape crouched upon the balcony, the silhouette familiar.

"Hang on," Jake said and stomped on the accelerator.

The golf cart rocketed toward the valet stand at the corner of the breezeway. The same balding bellman who'd carried their luggage the day before was chatting with a young Hispanic valet. Both men looked up in alarm as Jake stopped the cart inches from where they stood.

"Hey, Jake, they teach you to drive like that in Jersey?" the bellman demanded with a grin, fluttering his hand over his heart in mock palpitations. "Last time I let you—"

Jake interrupted his banter as she scrambled from the cart, Darla on her heels. "Clyde, quick, we've got to get into a room on the sixth floor! You know the stolen cat I told you about earlier? I'm pretty sure he's on the balcony up there!"

Joking forgotten, Clyde followed them out from under the breezeway to the curb beyond so that he could look up and see for himself. Another meow—this one more demanding—drifted down to them.

Definitely Hamlet, Darla thought in fearful relief, clasping her suddenly sweaty hands together as she saw the cat take a few impatient steps along the railing. How in the heck he'd gotten up there, she couldn't guess. All that mattered for the moment was getting him down again.

"That's room 624," Clyde confirmed after doing a quick count of rooms and floors. "C'mon, I'll get one of the housekeepers to let us in there."

Leaving the valet to deal with the golf cart, the trio hurried inside the lobby, where Clyde grabbed up a staff phone behind the bellman's desk and quickly dialed.

"Rita, it's Clyde. I need you to meet me at room 624 right now with your master keycard. No, I don't care if you're in the middle of eating supper. It's an emergency. Thanks."

He slammed down the phone and gestured them toward the elevator. "She'll meet us up there. Let's go."

Earlier, Darla had found the art deco–style elevator's leisurely pace quaintly amusing, but this time the ride seemed excruciatingly slow. She was almost screaming with impatience when they finally reached the sixth floor.

"This way. Room 624 is one of our luxury suites. I think one of the cat judges is staying there," Clyde said as they exited the elevator.

He motioned Darla and Jake down a corridor in the direction opposite their room. For the moment, the hall appeared empty, no doubt because it was the supper hour. Chances were the cat-show folks were all gathered in a bar or restaurant somewhere. Even the earlier feline chorus was subdued, with only a single mew coming from behind one of the closed doors. But as they rushed past the bend in the hallway, they spied someone fumbling with a door at the corridor's end . . . leaving or entering, Darla wasn't certain.

"Is that the room we're looking for, where that woman is standing?" Jake demanded as they headed down the hall at a brisk pace.

Clyde nodded. "Yeah, corner room."

Darla broke into a run. Hamlet's perch on the railing was precarious enough. All they needed now was for the woman to barrel unexpectedly into the room. Her sudden appearance might startle the cat enough to send him tumbling off the balcony.

"Wait!" she called, waving her arms to get the woman's attention. "Don't open the door, not yet!"

The woman jumped and spun about. Only then did Darla get a clear look at her face. *The Martini Lady . . . aka Alicia Timpson!*

Darla stared at her in surprise. This was Alicia's room? Still, it made sense that, as the chair of the show committee, Alicia might want to stay onsite for the duration of the event.

"I beg your pardon," said Alicia as Darla halted in front of her, panting a little from her sprint. "Is there something I can do for you, Ms. Pettistone? If it's about your cat, I can assure you that we are continuing the search for him."

"Sorry, I didn't mean to yell," Darla breathlessly explained.

"But we found Hamlet. He's out on the balcony of your hotel room. I didn't want you to frighten him when you walked in."

Alicia gave her a look of cool astonishment. The look went on to take in Jake and Clyde, who had now joined Darla there at the door.

"You say your cat is on my balcony? But I'm staying on the fifth floor. This room is my father's."

"Okay, then Hamlet is on your father's balcony," Darla said with an impatient shake of her head. One would think that the show's chairwoman would be relieved to know that Hamlet was alive and presumably well, if only to preserve the organization's reputation. It couldn't be good publicity for the FSA for an invited feline guest of honor to go missing under their watch. But the woman seemed almost reluctant to resolve the matter.

"I don't understand. What would he be doing in there? Are you suggesting that my father is responsible for Hamlet's disappearance?"

Darla hesitated. She wasn't suggesting that, was she? She reminded herself that she'd seen both Billy and Alicia at the front of the crowd the entire time that Hamlet's "Eye of the Tiger" video was playing. Therefore father and daughter could surely be eliminated from her suspect list.

"Of course not," she assured Alicia. "I'm certain Hamlet ended up there by accident. But could you please ask your father to let me inside so I can collect my cat?"

Alicia shrugged. "I don't think he's in there. I already knocked and he didn't answer, so I presume he's at supper. But I can hardly let you waltz in without his permission simply because you claim your cat is inside."

Darla exchanged a swift look with Jake, who, from her irate expression, appeared ready to go all bodyguard on Alicia. But for the moment, they needed diplomacy, not brawn. Even on short acquaintance, Darla knew that Alicia wasn't the type to be intimidated into cooperation, even by an ex-cop. She'd frostily dig in her heels and deny them access to the room, just because she could. But Darla suspected that the woman thrived on feeling herself to be magnanimous. All Darla had to do was exploit that weakness.

"Maybe you can call Mr. Pope and get his okay," she suggested.

Alicia shook her head again.

"I already tried calling him, and he didn't answer, so either he's busy or else he left his phone here in the room." Then, with a thoughtful moue, she added, "But if the cat's inside, I suppose I can bring him out to you."

Darla swiftly assumed a conciliatory air. "I don't claim to be as experienced as you are at handling cats, Mrs. Timpson, but I understand Hamlet. For all his tough attitude, he's really rather skittish. I know you understand how delicate the situation is. The fastest way to resolve this is simply to let me and Jake go in to retrieve him by ourselves. Don't you agree?"

Alicia's response wasn't quite as gracious as Darla might have hoped, but it would have to do.

"Fine," Alicia huffed, sounding not fine at all as she slapped the keycard into Darla's hand. Then, with a genteel snort, she settled onto one of the pair of sleek padded benches at the hall's end. "Good luck getting the key to work. It doesn't seem to want to open the door for me."

"Let me try, ma'am," Clyde smoothly suggested, holding out a hand to Darla and then adding to Alicia, "You know, sometimes people put the keycard in their wallets, and that can demagnetize them. So I'm certain it's nothing you're doing wrong at all."

He tried the card a couple of times himself, but the tiny red light on the automatic door lock remained unchanged. In the interim, however, Darla heard the elevator doors down the hall ding as someone else arrived on the floor. A moment later, a very large Hispanic woman wearing an abundance of red lipstick came jogging toward them, waving a keycard. *Rita*, Darla decided, her guess confirmed when the woman drew closer and Darla saw her name embroidered on her uniform.

When Clyde tried the door again with the key Rita provided, the light turned green. Before he could open it more than a couple of inches, however, Darla stuck out an arm to block him.

"Just me and Jake," she reminded him. "Once we have Hamlet safely bundled up, we'll let you know."

Clyde hesitated. "You know, technically, I shouldn't be doing this," he said with a look around at everyone. "I mean, this is Mr. Pope's room."

Rita clamped plump hands over her ears. "La-la-la-la, I hear nothing, I see nothing. Me, I'm going back to my supper. Bring me back my keycard when you're done," she proclaimed, and promptly trotted back toward the elevator.

Alicia, meanwhile, gave a disgusted *tsk*. "You can blame me. Let's just get this over with."

Clyde nodded and gestured for Darla and Jake to go on inside the dimly lit suite, which proved a larger and more luxurious version of Darla and Jake's own. Darla set her tote bag down on the pale green carpet and gave the place a quick once-over. The main area was arranged into three areas: a work station with an oversized desk, a dining nook with a small bar, and an entertainment area with an immense flat screen television twice the size of the one in her room and a pair of cushy black leather love seats set into an L and flanked by glass-topped end tables. The former was piled with so many of the familiar pastel throw pillows that most of them had cascaded off into a heap on the floor.

Jake nodded in the direction of the overstuffed couch. Behind it, the sliding door to the balcony was wide open. It was too dark by now to make out anything on the balcony, but the open door let in the faint echo of traffic and a cool evening breeze lightly perfumed with night blossoms and the scent of the river.

"Hamlet," Darla softly called in the direction of the

balcony, praying he was still out there. "It's me. Come on inside where it's safe, and then we'll go back to our room and order up shrimp cocktails."

To her relief, Darla heard a soft but insistent *meow* in reply. She waited breathlessly, and then heard a faint thud and metallic scrape from the balcony, the sound of a large cat landing upon a metal table. Another meow drifted to them, followed this time by a familiar furry black face peering past the open balcony doorway.

"Hamlet," Darla sighed in relief. "It's really you!"

Displaying more confidence than she actually felt—what if Hamlet decided he liked it on the balcony?—Darla casually walked toward the open slider. She kept her gaze fixed on the cat as she circled around the couch and its accompanying glass table to softly talk to the skittish feline.

"Hey, Hammy. Everyone at the show loved your video. They thought you were brilliant. And I've given out tons of your 'paw'-tographs already today. If you're up to it, we'll go back to the show tomorrow and you can meet some more of your fans. Oh, and we can visit Jake's new friend, Trixie, again. What do you say?"

By that point, she'd reached the table where Hamlet perched, his black form barely visible in the artificial light coming from the suite. He still had on his black harness, though the leash was missing. Someone had to have removed it, she realized—most likely whoever had spirited him away from the stage. As clever as Hamlet was, no way could he have unhooked it by himself. Luckily, she'd thought to put a spare lead in with his kitty gear.

She put out a cautious hand and gave him a little scratch on the head. When he didn't protest, she turned the little scritches into actual petting, letting her hand drift down to the harness. Weaving her fingers around one nylon strap, she moved in on him and gently hefted the cat into her arms.

To her immense relief, Hamlet didn't protest. Gripping

him more firmly, she finally let loose the afternoon's tension in a whoosh of breath.

"Got him," she said in triumph, turning back around. "Jake, get ready to open the door as soon as I—*eeeek!*"

Darla's reflexive shriek made Hamlet squirm in her arms. Still, she managed to maintain her grip on the cat even as she almost stumbled into the glass table in the process. Jake abruptly released the door handle and gave her a questioning look.

"What? Did Hamlet scratch you or something?"

"It—it's not Hamlet," she choked out, sidestepping away from the couch. "Jake, you know how Alicia said she thought her father had gone out for supper? Well, I don't think he ever left the room."

Pointing, she indicated the space between the couch and the sliding glass doors. Darla had been so focused on Hamlet when she'd entered the room, she hadn't ever looked down. And so it wasn't until she turned around that she had noticed a pair of legs wearing tan trousers and white wingtips sticking out from the spill of throw pillows at the other end of the couch. And she was pretty certain the man those legs belonged to wasn't napping.

In fact, unless he had spilled most of a bottle of red wine onto the pale green carpet beneath him, Billy Pope was almost certainly dead.

TEN

"OKAY, DON'T TOUCH ANYTHING," JAKE WARNED HER—NOT that Darla had any intention of doing any such thing. "Move back and let me take a look."

Still clutching Hamlet, who had settled quite comfortably in her arms again, Darla promptly scooted toward the door. She waited while Jake bent and assessed the situation.

"Is he, uh, you know?" she finally choked out, not quite able to manage the actual words.

Jake straightened and nodded, and then winced a little at the gesture, absently putting a hand to the back of her head.

"I didn't want to disturb anything, but I felt his leg and checked his skin reaction. If I had to guess, I'd say he's been dead for an hour or so. Given all the blood and where he's lying, it's possible he hit his head on that glass table. Maybe tripped, maybe a heart attack. You can lose a lot of blood with an injury like that, and if he never regained consciousness . . ."

Jake trailed off with a meaningful shrug, and Darla swallowed hard. From her short acquaintance with Billy Pope, he'd seemed a decent enough man, and Nattie had true affection for him, which surely meant something. And while he appeared to have an occasionally contentious relationship with both his daughter and his granddaughter, Darla suspected that breaking this bad news to them would not be easy.

"All right, let's get out of here," Jake told her. "I'll call 9-1-1 from the hallway."

Barely had she said the words, however, when the hotel room door clicked open, and Clyde thrust his bald head inside.

"Hey, Jake, can you hurry? Mrs. Timpson is getting real impatient out here, and your mother just came down the hall to see what all the commotion was. Oh, hey," he added with a glance and smile at Darla, "looks like you got your kitty—"

"Clyde." Jake cut him short. "I need you to stop right there and go back out into the hall now. We've got a situation going on here."

"Situation?"

The frosty word came from Alicia, who had shoved past the bellman and strode into the room in time to catch Jake's comment.

She halted near the sofa, addressing Darla now as she continued. "I am quite relieved to see that Hamlet is safe and sound. I hope that means we can put all this unpleasantness behind us and continue on with his appearance at the show tomorrow."

She paused and glanced at Jake. "And do not worry, Ms. Martelli. I promise we will continue to cooperate with the police while they investigate who attacked you."

"Yer darn tootin' you will." Nattie rushed in on Alicia's heels, her expression mutinous until she spied Hamlet safe in Darla's arms. "You found him! Oh, that's just grand. How did he get in here?"

"We don't know, Ma. But right now, it's important that we head back to the hall."

"Yes, please, everyone exit the room now," Alicia ordered.

"You, too, Mrs. Timpson," said Jake.

"Ms. Martelli, what right do you have to tell me to leave my father's room?" Alicia demanded, looking around and wrinkling her nose. "I don't know what that smell is"—she paused and shot Hamlet a suspicious look—"but I really must air the place out. So if you don't mind," she finished, gesturing them toward the front door while she started for the balcony.

"No!" Darla and Jake shouted in unison, both moving to block the woman's path.

Alicia shot her an indignant look, while even Nattie raised her penciled-on eyebrows in surprise. Hamlet chimed in with a warning growl from Darla's arms. Jake, meanwhile, caught the woman by her arm.

"Look, Mrs. Timpson, like I said, we've got a situation here," Jake clipped out. Then, turning to Clyde, she added, "Help me get her out of here so I can take care of that 9-1-1 call. We really need to wait out in the hall until the police arrive."

"Police?" Alicia echoed in seeming confusion.

Then, seeing Darla's reflexive glance toward the sofa, the woman's perfectly made-up eyes widened while the beginning of realization dawned. "Wait—does this have to do with my father? I—I assumed he was out at supper. Did something happen to him?"

Not waiting for a reply, Alicia elbowed her way past Jake for a look behind the couch. She gave an ear-piercing shriek, which sent Nattie rushing over, too. Catching sight of Billy's prone form behind the couch, Nattie gave an echoing scream and promptly slid down in a faint. For her part, Alicia had managed to stay upright, but she was hyperventilating to the point that Darla expected her to come crashing down at any moment as well.

Jake shot Darla an authoritative look. "Take Hamlet back to our room," she said, "then get back here quick as you can."

Darla didn't wait for further instruction. Gripping Hamlet tightly, she snatched up her tote bag and rushed out the door. Two rooms down, a portly Asian man stuck his head out his own door and stared at her in concern.

"I thought I heard a scream. Is everything all right?"

"Just a cat emergency," she lied, hurrying past him. The burden of a twenty-pound cat in her arms made her sprint down the hallway more a labored race, however, so that she was panting by the time she reached her room. Juggling cat, tote bag, and keycard, she managed to get the door open.

"Here you go, Hammy," she exclaimed and set him down on the sofa to unbuckle him from his harness. Giving him a swift hug, which he promptly wiggled free of, she went on, "I hate to leave you like this after we just got you back from wherever you were, but Jake really needs my help. We'll be back as soon as we can get this situation sorted out, and then we'll figure out what actually happened to you."

Hamlet shot her a slanted green look that said, *Don't worry, I'll make you feel guilty about it later*, and then sauntered off to the bathroom. A moment later, Darla heard the sound of loud kibble crunching as he made up for his missed supper.

At least he didn't seem overly traumatized by what had happened, Darla thought in relief. She double-checked that the balcony door was securely locked with the desk chair still in front of it. Then, grabbing up her tote once more, she rushed back to Billy's suite.

By the time she got there, Nattie and Alicia were both huddling on the benches in the hallway outside the hotel room. The former sat with her head between her scrawny knees and her red crest bobbing like a drunken rooster, while Alicia sat stonelike, staring at the art deco wallpaper opposite her. Jake and a pale Clyde flanked the suite door.

Darla sank onto the cushion beside Nattie, who raised

her face and sighed. “I can’t believe this is happening. It’s too much for an old woman to take.”

“I know,” Darla replied, putting a supporting arm around her shoulders, “but try to hang in there. The police will be here soon, and they’ll figure out for sure what happened to Mr. Pope.”

As if on cue, the elevator down the hall dinged, that bell followed by the sound of purposeful footsteps headed in their direction. A big, middle-aged man wearing a burgundy sports coat with the hotel’s requisite fancy gold “W” embroidered on the breast pocket rounded the corner and marched toward them. *Hotel security*, Darla decided. He was followed by a pair of officers whom she promptly recognized as the same two, Garcia and Johnston, who had responded to Jake’s attack and Hamlet’s kidnapping.

“Here come the uniforms,” Jake said unnecessarily while Clyde hurried to join the newcomers. Stepping from her post at the door, she leaned toward her mother. “Ma, you holding up okay?”

“I’m fine, Jacqueline . . . fine as I can be after losing a friend,” she said with another sigh, making a swift sign of the cross.

While Jake and Nattie were speaking, the police had exchanged a few words with Clyde and the hotel security man. Now they headed toward where Darla and the others were waiting.

“Looks like the cat show is getting a bit exciting this year,” Officer Johnston observed as he halted before them; then, glancing Jake’s way, he went on, “Ms. Martelli, you want to show us to the scene? The rest of you please wait right out here.”

Taking the keycard from Clyde, Jake ignored the annoyed look the head of security shot her and did the honors on the door, holding it open and explaining to the officers where they would find the body. The pair went inside, then quickly came back out into the hall. Garcia moved to one side and muttered a few quick words into her shoulder microphone, a couple of which Darla caught: "homicide" and "coroner."

Hearing those words didn't rattle her; she knew that the police considered any death that occurred outside a doctor's care suspicious until proven otherwise. Even so, it likely meant they were going to be stuck in the hallway awhile.

Johnston, meanwhile, had flipped open his notebook again.

"All right, can anyone tell me the identity of the gentleman inside?"

"He's my father, Billy Pope—prominent Fort Lauderdale real estate mogul and head judge for the Feline Society of America," Alicia mechanically spoke up from her seat on the bench. "You interviewed him at the cat show this afternoon after Ms. Martelli was attacked, and the cat was stolen."

The officer gave a meaningful nod. "Of course. I remember speaking to him earlier. My condolences, ma'am."

Alicia accepted the sentiment with a stony nod and lapsed back into silence. Looking uncomfortable, Johnston glanced at the rest of them and went on, "So, who actually found Mr. Pope's body?"

"That would be me and Ms. Pettistone," Jake replied.

Garcia took Jake aside, while Johnston motioned Darla to join him a bit farther down the hall. "All right, Ms. Pettistone," he began, flipping open his notebook, "can you tell me how you came to find the deceased?"

Darla gave the cop a quick rundown of the situation, from when she and Jake had spied Hamlet out on the balcony to the cat's recovery and the subsequent discovery of the body. Just as she finished her account and rejoined the others, Darla heard the elevator arrive on the floor again.

A tall, dark-haired woman who Darla judged to be in her late forties, wearing a black pantsuit and with a gold shield glinting at her waist, was striding toward them. She was trailed by two men in plain clothes wearing police windbreakers and carrying equipment cases. *The homicide detective and crime scene investigators*, Darla thought, a bit dismayed that she was familiar enough with the process to know this and hoping that they'd be able to quickly determine it had all been just a tragic accident after all.

As the female detective drew closer, Darla noticed that she looked vaguely familiar—then, with a glance over at Jake, she realized why. Both women were close to six feet tall with similar strong features made more prominent by the way they wore their curly black hair pulled back into tight buns. And, apparently, they'd both found the identical black pantsuit at their respective outlets of the Intimidating Tall Gal's Shop. The only difference in wardrobe was their footwear. Jake wore her standard high-laced Doc Martens, while the newcomer strutted in a pair of impractical high-heeled black pumps.

Darla wondered if the woman carried a pair of sensible running shoes in the black leather tote she had slung over her shoulder, just in case a foot chase ever ensued.

The detective halted with her crew and gave a crisp nod to Darla and the others before focusing her attention on the two uniformed officers.

"The body in there?" she asked, jerking a thumb toward the suite.

Johnston nodded. "Good to see you again, too, Detective Martinez," was his bland reply. Indicating Alicia, he went on, "The deceased gentleman inside the room is Ms. Timpson's father."

Martinez flicked a gaze in Alicia's direction.

"Sorry for your loss, ma'am," she said, sounding not a bit sorry at all, in Darla's estimation.

More like annoyed that her evening was disturbed.

Turning to the CSI guys with her, the detective went on, "Let's do a quick walk-through, and then I'll let you boys get down to work while I talk to our witnesses. Officer Johnston, you and Officer Garcia keep these people entertained."

Entertained? Darla silently fumed. She was already picking up bad vibes from the detective. Surely the fact that a person lay newly dead just a few feet away from them should rate a bit more respect.

With Clyde obliging again with the keycard—this time, he flipped the security latch to keep the door from automatically locking again as it closed—the newly arrived trio went into the hotel room. Garcia and Johnston, who had exchanged silent if telling looks while the detective gave out commands, remained in the hall with the rest of them.

Jake moved over to the bench where Nattie was sitting and leaned against the wall. Nattie looked up and then patted the spot beside her. "Here, *bambolina mia*, come sit by your mother."

"I'm fine," Jake protested, though she accepted the seat anyhow.

Immediately feeling guilty, Darla softly exclaimed, "Why didn't you say something? I forgot you were supposed to be taking it easy after what happened this afternoon."

Clyde, meanwhile, sidled over. Sotto voce, he asked Jake, "So, why didn't you tell me you had a twin sister?"

Despite the somber circumstances, Darla had to suppress a snicker. She'd been debating whether to make a similar quip herself and had finally erred on the side of prudence. Which was probably what Clyde should have done, she told herself as Jake shot the bellman a look that would have quelled a lesser man.

Clyde apparently had developed a thick hide from his time spent dealing with the public, for he grinned. Still, he held up both hands in a gesture of surrender as he added, "Just kidding."

"Uh, folks," Garcia spoke up, "no kibitzing, if you don't mind. You're all considered witnesses until Detective Martinez says differently."

That comment from the officer abruptly quashed any amusement Darla was feeling. Her trepidation grew when

Detective Martinez pulled open the hotel room door again and strode a few feet out into the hall.

"All right, ladies and gentlemen. I need to know what everyone knows about this situation. Who are our witnesses here? Anyone?"

"Those two ladies are the ones who found him," Garcia spoke up, indicating Darla and Jake.

The detective turned her laser gaze on them and whipped out her business cards. "Detective Sam Martinez, Fort Lauderdale Police," she said, officially introducing herself and handing a card to Jake. "And you are . . . ?"

"Jake Martelli, Martelli Investigations, Inc.," Jake said, rising to hand over her own card. "NYPD, retired. Licensed by the state of New York as a PI."

"Not licensed in the state of Florida, I see," Martinez observed as she squinted at the credentials printed on Jake's card.

Jake shook her head. "I'm not on the clock. I'm here on vacation and doing a little unofficial personal security for Ms. Pettistone and her pet, since they are guests of honor at the cat show next door."

"And you would be Ms. Pettistone?" Martinez asked, turning to Darla.

Darla nodded. "Darla Pettistone, owner of Pettistone's Fine Books in Brooklyn, New York," she said, handing over both a business card and one of Hamlet's "paw"-tograph fliers. "My cat, Hamlet, is why we're here."

There was a fractional defrosting of the detective's attitude as the woman glanced at the flier and appeared to bite back a reflexive smile. "Yeah, I heard something about a little dustup there." Martinez squinted more closely at the flier Darla had handed her. "So this is the cat someone stole from the exhibit hall. That happen on your watch, Ms. Martelli?"

"What, you're sayin' my daughter's no good at her job?"

Nattie broke in, popping up from the bench before Jake could respond.

Martinez raised a brow. "And, ma'am, you are . . . ?"

"Uh, that's Ms. Martelli's mother," Johnston spoke up, flipping back through his notes. "Ms. Natalia Martelli."

"It wasn't her fault," Nattie went on. "Some lousy, rotten catnapper snuck up behind her and hit her on the head and stole Hamlet!"

"Ma, I got this." Jake put out a warning hand to Nattie, who muttered under her breath but grudgingly returned to her seat beside Darla.

"Yes, we had an incident at the show," Jake continued. "Someone assaulted me backstage and took off with the cat. These officers"—she indicated Garcia and Johnston—"responded, so they should be able to give you all the details, but the cat has since been recovered. Darla and I spotted him on this room's balcony about an hour ago. Since we were told the gentleman wasn't in the room, the bellman let us inside. That's when we retrieved the cat and discovered Mr. Pope's body. Unfortunately, Mrs. Timpson and my mother came into the room before we could secure it, and they saw the deceased, as well. We immediately vacated the premises and called the authorities."

Martinez scowled, and Darla wondered which she was more concerned with: the body, or the fact they'd tromped all over her crime scene. What she asked, however, was: "Why would anyone steal a cat? Is it valuable?"

"*He* isn't valuable, per se, except to me," Darla spoke up. "But he's something of an Internet celebrity these days. I suppose someone could've wanted him for that reason. Or maybe they'd planned to hold him for ransom."

"Did you actually get a ransom note? A call asking for money?"

"No," Darla admitted, trying not to sound resentful at the detective's apparent dismissal of her theory. After all, it was a viable possibility. Maybe she and Jake had found Hamlet before the kidnapper had a chance to dictate terms.

"So you think this Pope guy is the one who stole the cat, then?" Martinez said as she scribbled in her notebook.

"I *beg* your pardon?"

The clipped words came from Alicia, who rose with icy majesty from her spot on the bench. Out-frosting Martinez's chilly manner, she went on, "My father was a prominent man in this city. Not only was he a successful real estate magnate, he served as head judge for the Feline Society of America. He would never stoop to such an action; besides which, he was standing beside me when the kidnapping incident occurred, with at least two hundred other witnesses there who can attest to that fact. Now, can you tell me why we are speaking about this instead of trying to find out who killed my father?"

"Killed?"

If Martinez had been a cat, her ears would have flicked forward at the word. As it was, the detective raised a dark eyebrow and flipped her notebook closed again.

"Mrs. Timpson, is it?" she went on, earning a nod from Alicia. "All indications so far are that we're dealing with an accidental death. Why would you think your father was murdered?"

Alicia gave an audible gulp, her carefully made-up features turning ashy. "I—I don't know. I saw the blood. I—I just assumed . . ."

The glacier promptly melted into a puddle of uncertainty as Alicia dropped back onto the bench and clamped her lips shut. Darla exchanged swift glances with Jake. Her friend gave her a fleeting nod, which Darla took to mean, *Hang on. We'll talk when we're back in the room.*

But Darla wasn't going to wait to come up with theories of her own. Why had Alicia immediately jumped to the conclusion that her father had been murdered? Was it because Jake had been attacked earlier that day? Or maybe it was because her daughter had threatened both Alicia and Billy, and Alicia feared that Cindy was somehow involved? Or maybe Alicia hadn't been trying to enter the room when she and Jake had first spied the woman fumbling with the door. Maybe she'd been leaving the room, instead.

The detective, meanwhile, let her cold, dark gaze sweep over them all before focusing on Jake. "Anyone touch anything on or around the body that you know of?"

Jake shook her head. "I only touched his exposed calf to confirm whether or not he was dead. Beyond that, except for closing the balcony door and taking Hamlet with us, we left everything as we found it."

"So how were you able to ID the body?"

"Well, it *is* his hotel room," Darla began. "Besides, we saw his wingtips."

"His shoes?" Martinez asked.

Darla nodded, "Apparently, Mr. Pope is known for wearing white wingtips all year round . . . you know, like a trademark."

"Yes," Alicia confirmed in a small voice. "He started wearing them when I was a child. Except when he's on one of his boats, I don't think there's ever been a public occasion where he hasn't worn a pair. They're his signature look."

"All right, but we'll still need a formal ID." The detective held up her smart phone. "The CSI team is still at work, so I can't let anyone in the room, but I took a photo of the gentleman that shows his face very clearly. Mrs. Timpson, are you up to looking at the photo and confirming that it is your father in there?"

"I—I think so."

Alicia rose on unsteady feet and took a few steps forward toward Martinez. The rest of them stood, too, and formed a semicircle behind her—whether in support or curiosity, Darla couldn't be sure. She uncharitably suspected Nattie of simple nosiness, despite her grief.

Martinez held the phone out to Alicia. For the first time

since her arrival on the scene, the detective's words held a note of kindness as she said, "It's all right, ma'am. I cropped the picture so it's his face only. He looks like he's asleep."

Alicia nodded and took a deep breath.

"I can do it," she said, sounding more like her usual imperious self. She straightened her shoulders and took the phone, but before she even looked at the small screen, she abruptly screamed.

Darla gave a little shriek of her own at the unexpected sound, while Officers Garcia and Johnston jerked to attention as well. Both Jake and Martinez appeared equally startled, with the latter clipping out, "What the—"

"Here, gimme that," Nattie said, snatching the phone from Alicia. "If yer not gonna look, I will."

Alicia made no protest at the old woman's action. Instead, she clamped her hands over her mouth and was staring in seeming horror down the hallway toward the elevator. *As if she'd seen a ghost*, was Darla's reflexive thought.

And then a man's reedy voice demanded, "What in the hell are all you people doing standing in front of my hotel room?"

"Billy!" Nattie shrieked, grinning as she shoved past Alicia to rush over to the man. "We thought you was dead, but you're alive! Unless you're a ghost," she added with a suspicious look at him while she gripped his arm to apparently satisfy herself he was indeed corporeal.

"Well, I almost did starve to death, wondering why my daughter didn't meet me for supper downstairs," Billy Pope replied as he disengaged from Nattie's grasp. "I finally figured out I left my phone upstairs, so I came back to the room to get it, only to find this."

"Hold on," Martinez interjected while Alicia went over to give her father a stiff hug before returning to her spot on the bench again. Plucking her gold shield from her waistband, Martinez flashed it at him and went on, "Detective Martinez, Fort Lauderdale PD. Are you telling me you're Mr. Billy Pope and this is your room?"

"Yes, and yes. Now, would someone mind explaining why the police have taken it over?"

While Martinez gave him the CliffsNotes version, Darla reflexively glanced down at the man's feet. *White wingtips, just like he always wears.* She shot a look at Jake, wondering if the PI had noticed this, too. The wingtips were the reason they'd assumed the dead man in Billy Pope's room was Pope himself. Not only had someone other than the judge been wearing that unique style of footwear, but that person had somehow managed to die in Billy's hotel room.

"We were just about to have your daughter make a positive ID from a photo," Martinez was continuing, "when you showed up, alive and well."

"So who's in there, then?" the old man demanded, his thin voice barely audible now.

Jake gestured her mother over. "Ma, give the phone back to Detective Martinez so she can pull up the picture again. We need to figure out who the dead guy is."

The detective punched in her passcode and handed the phone to Nattie, who squinted at the screen before handing it back, shaking her head. "I don't have my reading glasses with me. He just looks like a blurry blob."

"Ma'am," Martinez replied, "why don't you give the phone to Mr. Pope? It's his room after all."

The old woman handed off the phone to Billy, who stared at it for a long moment.

"C'mon, Billy," Nattie urged. "Who is it? Do you know him?"

Billy briefly shut his eyes. Then, looking like he'd been punched in the gut, he nodded and held out the phone.

Darla stood to the other side of him, so she took the cell and cautiously looked at the photo herself. If the dead man had any connection to Hamlet's kidnapping, she wanted to put a face to the criminal.

Her first thought on seeing the image was that Detective Martinez was right—the middle-aged man in the photo did look like he was just sleeping. Her second, and far more surprising realization, was that she actually *did* know the man . . . by sight, if not by actual acquaintance.

Darla promptly handed the phone back to the detective, but it was Billy Pope she addressed when she said, "I recognize him, too. I saw him at the show today. He's the guy who raises the Minx cats. What was his name again?"

There was a pause before Alicia spoke up.

"Stein," she said in a soft voice. "His name is Ted Stein."

ELEVEN

AFTER DARLA GAVE HER WITNESS STATEMENT, SHE HEADED back to the suite to wait while Jake and Nattie took turns being questioned by Detective Sam Martinez. Nattie returned last from the grilling, around eight o'clock, and dramatically declared her intention to stay the night in the suite with Darla and Jake rather than go home alone to her place.

"After all this shock, I wouldn't sleep a wink tonight back at the condo!" the old woman exclaimed with a shudder as she plopped onto the sofa with a proprietary air. "What if I saw Ted's ghost floating around there? Me, I'm an old woman. I see something like that, and I get the angina and drop dead myself."

Jake raised a brow. "Ma, I hate to play Captain Obvious, but aren't you forgetting that Ted died right down the hall from us? You see any ghosts tonight, chances are they'll be right here at the hotel."

"Yeah, but here I'll have my Jacqueline to protect me," Nattie countered with a determined air.

Jake exchanged glances with Darla, who nodded her agreement. In Nattie's place, she probably wouldn't want to go home alone, either.

"Fine, Ma. If you'll feel better sleeping here tonight, we understand. You can get up early and run back home to change before the show starts tomorrow."

"I knew I could count on you, *bambolina mia*," Nattie said in satisfaction. Then she frowned. "Wait—I don't have a nightie or a toothbrush."

"Don't worry, there's a toothbrush in the bathroom along with all the complimentary toiletries. And you can wear one of my T-shirts for a nightgown," Jake told her.

"Then it's settled. I sure hope you girls can stay up all night with me. It'll be fun, like one of them slumber parties you had when you were a little girl."

But despite Nattie's assertion that she'd be up all night, by nine she was passed out in the bedroom alcove.

"I'll take the couch," Jake volunteered, ruefully adding, "Sam Martinez asked me to meet her in the bar downstairs around nine to kick around a few ideas, off the record. You know, shop talk. I didn't realize that we'd be babysitting Ma. . . . Not that I mind, of course."

"You go," Darla insisted. "I'll stay here with your mother. Besides, after all that happened today, I really don't want to leave Hamlet again."

"You sure?"

"Go!" Darla told her. "But remember, tomorrow is a school day."

"I'll keep that in mind," was Jake's reply as she pocketed her keycard from off the coffee table again and headed for the door.

To the accompaniment of Nattie's rhythmic snoring, Darla spent the next thirty minutes lounging on the floor playing with Hamlet and his feathered kitty wand. Despite her earlier concern, the cat seemed none the worse for his abduction, kicking and gnawing at the bright plumes with feline glee.

Then, hearing new commotion outside in the hallway, Darla scrambled to her feet. How many people were needed to take pictures of a bloodstain on the carpet? And, more to the point, how many more cops and various law enforcement people could Detective Martinez crowd into that small corridor?

"Hammy, let's give those poor feathers a rest for a minute. I want to check this out."

Leaving the cat sprawling beside his toy, she hurried to the door and squinted through the peephole, just in time to see a gurney bearing Ted Stein's covered body wheeled past.

Darla shivered. The stark memory of seeing the man lying dead behind Billy Pope's sofa had been bad enough. The sight of his shrouded form oddly distorted by the peephole's wide viewing angle was enough to give her the heebie-jeebies.

Darn Nattie and her ghosts. The next thing she knew, she'd be imagining seeing phantom figures and get the angina herself!

"Come on, Hammy," Darla said, swiftly turning from the door and back to him. "While we're waiting for Jake to come back, let's order up a good old pay-per-view comedy, and—"

She broke off. The feathered wand was still lying where she'd left it, but Hamlet was gone.

Tamping down sudden fear, she shot a quick look at the balcony door. It was still tightly shut and barricaded, just as she'd left it earlier. Then she glanced at the bedroom alcove. Enough light from the suite's main room shone into that alcove for Darla to spy the feline curled upon the foot of her bed, apparently asleep. As she moved closer to check on him, she saw that he was using Nattie's copy of the hotel magazine as his personal mattress topper.

"Here, Hammy. That can't be comfortable," she whispered to the feline, and tried to slip the open periodical out from beneath him.

Hamlet slit open one green eye and put out a swift paw, his razor-sharp claws slicing away a couple of crisp, four-color pages before Darla got the magazine away from him.

"Hammy," she softly scolded, but he made no other protest. Instead, the emerald eye shut again, and he gave an audible snore.

Shaking her head, Darla left him with Nattie and picked up the torn paper from where it had drifted to the rug. She carried both pages and magazine back into the other room to toss them into the trash, when an inch-high headline on one torn page caught her eye.

Deconstructing Condo Association Theft.

The article unfolded like a soap opera. It named no names or associations but was heavy on scares. The offenses varied from condo board members absconding with association funds—much as Ted had accused Billy of doing—to predatory condo associations slapping liens on owners who'd fallen behind on their dues. All in all, it sounded like certain boards ran their associations like private fiefdoms, with the lowly owners at their mercy, sometimes to the point of losing their homes over a few hundred dollars in unpaid dues.

"Wow," she softly exclaimed when she'd finished reading. She stuck the article into her tote bag. Given the uproar about Billy Pope and the missing condo money, she'd have to tell Jake about this.

A knock sounded from the hallway, making her jump. No doubt it was Jake—maybe her keycard didn't work, either. But when she peered through the peephole in the door just to be sure, she was surprised to find instead a pale-faced woman staring back.

"Alicia?" Darla exclaimed as she unlatched the door. "What's wrong? Are you all right?"

Two stupid questions, given the circumstances.

But Alicia merely asked, "May I come in?"

"Of course," Darla told her, opening the door wider, and adding, "But we need to be quiet. Nattie is sleeping in the other room."

A sudden, loud snore from that vicinity underscored her words.

Alicia nodded. "This will only take a minute," the woman assured her as she stepped into the suite's foyer area. "I simply wanted to urge you all to stay for the second day of our little show."

"Stay? But—"

"I realize that having Hamlet go missing, if only for a few hours, was a traumatic experience," Alicia rushed on before Darla could finish asking why she thought they were packing up. "And certainly what happened in my father's room tonight was upsetting, to say the least. But let me reassure you that we are redoubling our security efforts for tomorrow. You, Hamlet, and Ms. Martelli will be perfectly safe with us."

Alicia paused expectantly, and Darla nodded. *Might as well play along.* "I appreciate your saying that, Alicia. All right. We'll all be there tomorrow."

"Thank you. Now, I'd better go help my father. The police are allowing him back into his room long enough to retrieve his things." Alicia gave her a cool nod and turned to go.

Impulsively, Darla put out a hand. "Wait," she said. "I didn't get to say it before, but I'm sorry for your loss. It's always hard losing a friend."

"Oh." Alicia paused, her expression even blanker than before. "That's very kind of you, Darla, but Ted was my father's friend . . . at least, he was once. I have to say, I didn't really know the man, at all."

"ARE YOU SURE YOU'RE OKAY? YOU LOOK WORSE THAN WHEN WE LEFT the room. How's your head?" Darla asked the next morning with a concerned look at Jake, who sat in the folding chair beside her.

The PI winced a little and put a hand to the back of her skull. "I really shouldn't've had those beers with Sam Martinez last night. And all this meowing isn't helping any, either."

"Yeah, well, you're not supposed to drink with a head injury. That one's on you, so you're not getting any sympathy out of me."

"Ma? Ma, is that you?" Jake asked with a snort, pretending to look around the exhibition hall for her mother, who once again was manning the information table.

Darla grinned. They were back at the cat show, and the place was already humming with the sounds of exhibitors and spectators rushing about, along with the now-familiar chorus from a few hundred cats randomly mewing.

Hamlet, of course, was above it all . . . both figuratively and literally. Ignoring the hubbub, he once again was lounging in his guest-of-honor quarters, atop one of the bookshelves. To Darla's relief, he seemed none the worse for wear after his abduction.

That was, assuming he'd actually been catnapped.

Darla's smile faded. It was possible that he'd somehow simply escaped from Jake . . . and, in fact, she suspected this was the police's theory. But no way would her friend have lied about that, or about being hit over the head. And there was no mistaking the fact that, when they'd found Hamlet again, he'd been minus the leash that had been attached to his harness right before his disappearance. A human had definitely been somehow involved.

"Burmese numbers fifteen through twenty-eight to Ring Three," came the announcement over the PA, bringing her back to the moment. *"Tonkinese numbers one through sixteen to Ring One."*

"I'm glad for all the exhibitors' sakes that things are

going on as planned," Darla observed in a low voice while turning a friendly smile on two preteen boys who'd stopped to meet Hamlet. "I was hoping we could go under the radar today, but I've already had a couple of the show people ask me about Ted Stein. I guess it's hard to keep something like this under wraps."

By way of illustration, the stocky woman Darla had commiserated with over the supposed murder of Cozy Kitty the day before came trotting over. Today, her ample bosom sported the words "Really Crazy Cat Lady" on a tentlike pullover.

"Oh, honey," she gushed, plump hand over heart, "I heard all about that breeder . . . what was his name, Stern?"

"Stein," Darla corrected, bracing for the barrage of questions sure to come. To her relief, however, the woman didn't sink to the expected level of nosiness, saying only, "Such a terrible thing. But don't worry. I'm sure this had nothing to do with Hamlet or our nice little show."

"Maine Coon numbers three through eighteen to Ring Six," came another announcement over the loudspeaker, drawing the woman's swift attention.

"That's me. Gotta go," she proclaimed. "Wish me and my big boy good luck!"

Darla waited until Ms. Really Crazy had rushed off again and then sighed. "I hope everyone else is too busy worrying about their cats to connect Ted's accident with the show."

"Accident?"

Jake's tone indicated that an accident it was not. Darla shot her friend a surprised look. "Wait. I thought yesterday you said he probably tripped and hit his head on the coffee table, then bled to death."

"Sure, but that's when we thought the dead guy was Billy Pope. Since it's Ted Stein, that puts a whole other spin on things. Let's just say I don't think there's anything accidental about how he was killed."

"What did Martinez tell you last night?"

Jake hesitated long enough that Darla figured she was going to invoke some kind of cop confidentiality, but then she said, "I heard the media already know this, so I guess it won't hurt to tell you, too. You know that big glass seashell sculpture on the shelf in our bathroom?"

Darla nodded. "You mean the one the size of a salad plate and looks like it could be from that Botticelli painting of Venus? It's kind of cute. They sell them in the hotel gift shop if you want one to take home with you."

"They'll be selling like hotcakes once word gets out that a guest at the Waterview was murdered with one of them."

As Darla stared at her wide-eyed, Jake said, "According to Sam, they found one of those shells with significant blood spatter on it under the pillows on the floor next to Stein's body. With luck, they'll pull some prints off it, too. Chances are pretty darned good the ME is going to find that to be the cause of death."

Darla winced a little as she pictured the whimsical glass souvenir being used in so brutal a fashion. Then she suppressed a shiver. If Ted's death had indeed been murder rather than a simple accident, did that mean he'd been deliberately targeted? Or had Billy been the intended victim?

But when she asked Jake as much, the PI shrugged.

"Out of my jurisdiction, kid. And now that Hamlet's back safe and sound, it's not our problem. Sam and her people have everything under control. Our only job here is to get through the rest of the cat show and then squeeze in a little beach time before we have to head home again."

Darla was about to press her for more, when she abruptly recalled the magazine article. Digging into her tote bag, Darla pulled out the torn pages from last night.

"Hold that last thought, and check this out first," Darla told her friend as she handed over the article. "Last night while you were gone, Hamlet decided to do a little light reading. He ripped this out of the hotel magazine."

Jake pulled her reading glasses from her jacket pocket and scanned the pages.

"What do you think? Could this put our friend Billy Pope on the suspect list in Ted Stein's murder?" Darla asked when her friend finally looked up from the tattered article.

The PI promptly shook her head.

"For my sake, I hope he's not. If Sam so much as Mirandizes the man, Ma won't let me hear the end of it unless I try to prove him innocent."

Which Darla knew that Jake couldn't technically do without being a licensed PI in Florida. She considered this a moment, and then replied, "You know what you said a minute ago about none of this being our concern? Well, I think you're right. Let's get through today in one piece and then do some sightseeing. We're supposed to be on vacation. If Detective Martinez needs anything more from us, she knows where to find us."

"Sounds good to me, kid."

"Good." Setting down her empty *grande*-sized paper cup, Darla stood. "You know, we did promise the show folks that we'd take Hamlet through the hall a few times each day so everyone can see him. Why don't we take him on a quick stroll past the vendor tables before it gets too crowded? Besides," she wheedled, "we need to visit with Trixie again so you can make up your mind whether or not you want to adopt her."

The mention of the three-legged recue cat was apparently sufficient for Jake. The trio made their way through the slowly growing crowd, dodging the exhibitors who were rushing their furry charges from cage to ring and back again. Darla noticed as they passed him that Billy Pope was back in his usual judging spot in Ring One, looking dapper. He glanced up as they strolled past, giving no indication his room had been the site of a grisly murder scene the evening before, with the victim a known colleague of his. But either he didn't see them—though a redhead and a six-foot-tall brunette walking a cat were hard to miss—or else he thought it best not to engage, for his gaze swept quickly past them with no sign of recognition.

Aloud, Darla wondered, "Shouldn't he be lying low for a few days? I mean, if whoever killed Ted Stein meant to kill him instead, do you think it's safe for him to be out in public?"

"Since whoever it was got up close and personal with Ted, I'd lay odds the killer knew who he was whacking over the head. Right now, my big question is: What was Stein doing in Pope's hotel room?"

"Maybe he saw Hamlet on the balcony before we did and let himself into the room to rescue him?"

"Maybe," Jake replied, "though from what I saw, Ted wasn't really the rescuing type." She gave a quick look around, just in case they could be heard over the bustle of the cat-show crowd, and then went on, "Unless he's as good at climbing railings as Hamlet, someone had to have let Ted inside the room. And those wingtips he was wearing? They were Billy's. I've seen a lot of strange things in my day, but that one is at the top of the list for weirdness."

"It's not at the top; it's on a whole different crazy chart," Darla replied. Pausing to look at an orange tabby Cornish Rex, she added, "I wonder if the police returned them to Billy. Though all I can say is that if those were *my* wingtips, they'd be in a trash bin somewhere right now. You think Ted had some kind of shoe fetish?"

"Beats me. I can't come up with any good reason for a grown man to be wearing another man's shoes like that."

Darla thought a moment, and then snapped her fingers.

"Wait—I've got it. I know how this whole thing went down. Ted snuck into Billy's room because he wanted those wingtips. Billy caught him wearing his precious shoes, freaked out, and killed him, then went down to the restaurant to create an alibi. He planned to go back up to the room and 'find' Ted dead, not expecting us to have found him first. Billy is the killer. Slam-dunk case."

"Interesting motive," Jake replied with a grin, "but slow down, Nancy Drew. Taking the wingtips out of the mix, if Pope *had* killed Stein and was trying to create an alibi for himself, he sure blew it, coming back up to the room alone like that. He had no way of knowing that Stein's body had already been found, and half the Fort Lauderdale PD was already there to witness him walking up after the fact. If he was the killer, he would have made sure that Alicia or someone from the show was with him when he came back to the room. That way, he'd have an eyewitness who could testify to his shock at discovering the body."

"Oh, right."

Feeling deflated that Jake had so readily punched holes in her theory, Darla decided to give crime fighting a rest for a minute. Instead, she encouraged a toddler who'd given a happy little shriek at the sight of Hamlet to come closer. After the boy's parents had snapped the obligatory camera photo of the little boy flashing a gummy grin at the oversized feline, Darla tried again.

"So does Detective Martinez have any idea of a motive, or a suspect?"

"If she does, she's not sharing. Though, from what everyone says, Stein was a class-A jack wagon who ticked people off right and left, so any number of folks might have wanted him dead. I know *I* wanted to strangle him while I was sitting in at that board meeting the other night at Ma's condo."

"But that still leaves Hamlet's kidnapping. The fact that Hamlet was in Billy Pope's room has to mean something." Darla halted long enough to scoop up Hamlet and snuggle him protectively in her arms . . . only to set him right back down again when he gave a little rumble that definitely was not a purr.

"Maybe, maybe not," Jake replied. "Hamlet could have escaped from whoever took him and just happened to be on

Billy's balcony when we found him. Those balconies are close enough that you could hold hands with the person on the one next to you. He could have hopscotched around out there for a while until we noticed him."

Darla considered that a moment. "That could explain why I never got a ransom note or call. The person who took Hamlet didn't have him as a hostage long enough to do anything."

"Maybe. But now that Hamlet is safe and sound with us, all that is Sam's problem."

By unspoken agreement, they dropped the subject of Ted Stein's death as they browsed the vendor tables, the occasional ring announcement the only interruption to the murmur of voices—human and feline—that was the soundtrack of the show. Darla finally broke down and bought the cat-shaped pillows she'd been lusting after. And then it was off to pay another visit to the Tropical Adoptables rescue booth.

Trixie was still there, the little Siamese bounding about the pen on her three legs with her fellow kittens. Darla noticed that all ten of the tiny cats now wore bright paper collars, eight of them blue, and Trixie's and a little black female's both yellow.

"The ones in blue are spoken for," the middle-aged blond rescue woman, who had introduced herself as Marie, explained. "Their prospective new owners have filled out their paperwork and put down a deposit, and once we do the background checks, they can pick up their new kitties from our shelter and take them to their forever homes. The other two are still waiting for someone to adopt them."

"I can't believe no one wants that little black one," Darla exclaimed. "Look how sweet she is. She looks like a miniature Hamlet."

The rescue woman shook her head. "Special needs cats like Trixie, and black cats like Nera, are our hardest placements. Most people don't want to take a chance on a cat that has issues, even if that cat can live a perfectly long and healthy life. And in the case of Nera, you won't believe how many folks still think black cats are unlucky and refuse to own one."

"Ridiculous," Darla muttered. It was hard to fathom that some people still clung to such medieval beliefs, though she'd seen for herself the occasional bookstore customer steering clear of Hamlet simply because of his fur color. Although to be fair, in Hamlet's case, there might have been a number of other possible reasons to stay out of the feline's way.

Jake, meanwhile, pulled a pen out of her jacket. "Hand over the clipboard, Marie," she addressed the rescue worker. "I'm going to adopt Trixie."

"Fantastic! You won't regret it, believe me."

Digging out a clipboard with a long form attached, a smiling Marie gave Jake the paperwork. Then, while the PI began filling in the blanks, the woman shot Darla a hopeful look. "That just leaves Nera. You sure that handsome fellow of yours doesn't need a little sister? I've got another clipboard."

By way of answer, Hamlet leaned closer to the cage and hissed at the would-be sibling. Darla winced and pulled him back from the pen.

"Sorry, I think that's a no. Hamlet is pretty much an only cat. But if you give me your contact information, I'd be happy to post something on my website for any of our mail-order customers in this area."

By the time Jake finished her paperwork, Darla and Marie had exchanged cards and were swapping cat stories like old friends. Jake set the clipboard down and leaned into the pen, scooping the tiny Siamese into her arms.

"How's tricks, Trix?" she asked in a high-pitched voice that an amused Darla had never before heard out of her friend. "Does hers want to come home with me?"

Trixie seemed on board with that suggestion, for she promptly snuggled against Jake's shoulder, leaving a new sprinkling of silver cat hair on the black fabric.

Darla smiled. "You don't have to worry about contacting

Jake's landlady," she told Marie. "That's me, and I officially give her permission to keep a cat in her apartment."

She signed the approval block on the form that Marie indicated and then turned her attention to Hamlet. "Looks like you're getting a new neighbor," she informed the cat. "I hope you like her better than Nera."

Hamlet flicked a whisker but made no comment, which Darla took as a good sign. "All right, boy. If Jake can say good-bye to her little friend, we've got to head back to your pen to greet more of your fans."

With seeming reluctance, Jake returned the kitten to Marie, who had pulled out a blue paper collar. Bending down to tear the kitten's yellow collar off, she then fastened the blue one around Trixie's neck.

"Another happy ending," she exclaimed, looking close to tears as she handed Jake a sheet of paper. "Here are the directions to the shelter. Assuming everything goes well with your background check, you should be able to pick her up anytime after Thursday."

"Our flight leaves Sunday morning, so how about Saturday a.m.? Darla and I plan to do some sightseeing for the rest of the week, and it wouldn't be fair to Trixie to bring her to my mother's condo just to leave her there alone."

"Perfect. We'll see you Saturday morning. Enjoy the rest of the show and your stay here in Florida."

Leaving the kittens to pounce upon each other like tiny tigers, the two women plus Hamlet headed back in the direction of the stage. Darla glanced at her friend and saw Jake grinning like a kid who'd won a prize at the state fair.

"Looking forward to litter boxes and shedding cat hair, are you?" Darla asked with a matching smile.

Jake nodded. "Yeah, it's gonna be fun. Would you believe Trixie will be my first pet ever?"

"Seriously?"

"Ma didn't want to take care of a bunch of animals when we were growing up, and once I was accepted into the academy, I knew I wouldn't have time to take proper care of a cat or dog. But now that I'm my own boss, I'll be able to work my schedule however I want to. And since Robert is right next door with Roma, I'm sure I can persuade him to swap pet-sitting duties with me and Trixie."

"Sounds like a plan," Darla agreed. "And I'll be your backup."

They returned to Hamlet's pen, where a small group of kids and their parents were waiting for the famous feline. Darla set him back inside the cage and unhooked the leash from his harness. Freed of his tether, Hamlet hopped onto the nearest bookshelf. Then, to the delight of the children, he leaped from that shelf to the next one, and all the way to the end, and then jumped his way back again, just like a circus cat.

Jake snorted. "If there was ever any question why that cat was named Hamlet, this explains it . . . at least, the 'ham' portion of it."

"He's definitely enjoying his fifteen minutes of fame," Darla agreed. "I don't know what we're going to do with him when we get back to Brooklyn."

Then she glanced down at the floor of his bookstore cage. "Wait, where did that book come from?"

"I don't know. It probably fell down while he was doing his Cirque du Soleil routine."

"Watch the cage door for me while I grab it, will you?"

Not waiting for Jake's reply, Darla opened the cage and, to the further amusement of the children, quickly crawled inside. Apparently not on board with sharing his spotlight, Hamlet shot her a disapproving look but made no other protest. While Jake held the door firmly closed behind her, Darla scooted her way around one shelf and grabbed the fallen volume before scooting backward in the direction from which she'd come.

"That lady thinks she's a cat, too," one of the grade-schoolers piped up, prompting giggles from the rest of the kids.

Darla crawled out and rose, tucking the book under her arm and giving the children a fair imitation of Hamlet's meow. She waited until the group had their fill of posing with him and moved on before she took a look at the book she had retrieved.

"*The Shoes of the Fisherman*," she read aloud. A heraldic crest was the sole illustration on the cover, which gave her no clue as to its content. She looked at Jake. "I vaguely recognize the title, but I don't know what it's about. Wasn't a movie made of it?"

"Yeah. Ma loved that film, so I had to watch it about a hundred times when I was growing up. It's all about electing a pope."

Not noticing that Darla was staring at her in alarm, Jake continued, "The whole title is symbolic. St. Peter was the first pope, and he was a fisherman, so all the popes that followed were said to be stepping into his shoes. And it was kind of eerie, because the book was written in the sixties, but it almost predicted Benedict . . . you know, the pope who resigned a while back. And then—"

She finally broke off when Darla waved at her to stop.

"What? Oh, sorry. It's just that when you grow up in a Catholic household, you kind of absorb all this stuff."

"It's not that," Darla exclaimed, and held up the book so Jake could see the cover. "We're talking shoes, and according to you, we're also talking about popes. Maybe Hamlet is trying to tell us something—as in, Billy Pope and the infamous wingtips!"

Before Jake could reply, however, they both heard a familiar voice rise over the sounds of cats and humans. "No, you're wrong. I know you are!"

"Ma?" Jake gave a quick look across the exhibition hall and then shot Darla a look of concern. "I can't tell what's going on, but that sounds serious. Quick, get Hamlet's leash on him, and let's go check this out."

"I'm way ahead of you," Darla replied. At the sound of

Nattie's voice, she'd set the book on top of Hamlet's pen and grabbed the lead. Already tiring of his audience, the feline had settled down for a nap on one of the bookshelves, so it was an easy matter for her to snap on the leash. It took a bit more to coax him out again, during which time Jake was shifting from one foot to the other, obviously wanting to come to her mother's aid, but equally unwilling to shirk her duty to Darla and Hamlet.

Darla waved her away. "Go. I'll be right behind you as soon as I get Mr. Lazy Boots moving."

Jake gave a reluctant nod and rushed off in the direction from which Nattie's strident voice had come.

"Come on, Hammy," Darla urged him. "Jake's mother needs our help."

The feline gave an irritated hiss but rose and followed Darla at a swift trot to Ring One, where Billy Pope had been presiding. But the judging there apparently had ceased. Instead, the spectators and exhibitors there had all bunched to one side where Officers Garcia and Johnston were forming a human blockade. Detective Martinez was talking with Billy, though her voice was too low for Darla to make out any of the discussion. Jake, meanwhile, was physically holding back her mother, who was no longer shouting but was wearing a mutinous expression. Alicia Timpson was there, too, though appearing far more restrained than Nattie in her reaction.

Abruptly, Martinez gestured Johnston over. As Darla watched in dismay, the cop whipped out his handcuffs and fastened them around Billy Pope's wrists, though Martinez did allow him to keep his hands in front, rather than being cuffed from behind. Martinez was speaking again, and this time Darla caught a few words: "silent" . . . "court of law" . . . "attorney."

She glanced down at Hamlet, who sat nonchalantly beside her. He looked up and blinked at her before raising a paw to lick. He seemed completely unfazed by the arrest.

But then, he'd probably known who the killer was all along, Darla told herself—the wily feline may have even been in the room when Ted Stein was murdered. But what had Martinez learned since last night that had led her to arrest Billy Pope for the crime?

"Freedom!" shrieked a woman's voice from the front of the exhibition hall.

The unexpected cry made Darla jump. Catching her breath, she exchanged swift glances with Jake. Was someone about to stage a revolution of sorts and wrest Billy from the arresting officers? Martinez must have been wondering the same thing, Darla realized, for she saw the detective gesture to Garcia and Johnston, who quickly moved in front of the man.

"Freedom!" echoed a second, nearer voice, this cry even more strident.

"Freedom!" a third voice called, though this time the challenge was followed by a series of high-pitched squeals and screams. And then, over the PA system came the announcement that Darla had come to dread—*"Loose cat! Loose cat!"*—followed by an even more chilling cry from the exhibitors' rows.

"Eek! Mouse!"

TWELVE

"ON THE BRIGHT SIDE, CHASING DOWN ALL THOSE LAB MICE and loose cats let Billy Pope do the perp walk out of the exhibition hall with hardly anyone noticing what was going on," Jake observed the next morning as she and Darla were packing up to leave the hotel.

Darla looked up from folding her Pettistone's polo shirts. "Speaking of perps, I'm glad the show committee pressed criminal mischief charges against those girls . . . Cindy included. They're lucky none of the cats—or none of the people, for that matter—got hurt. That's the closest I've ever come to being in a riot."

Though the term "riot" was a bit of an exaggeration, she admitted to herself. Before the situation could devolve into more than a small disaster, Alicia Timpson had swiftly rallied. Despite seeing her father being arrested right in front of her, she'd grabbed one of the microphones and launched a full-scale counterassault to the mouse attack.

Assisted by the remaining judges—and with Nattie's,

Shelley's, and Mildred's help—they had corralled the five or six loose kitties within a few minutes, much to their respective owners' relief. The counterassault team also managed within another quarter of an hour to scoop up eleven of the admitted twenty lab mice that the protesters had let loose in the exhibit hall. Three were discovered too late, having already being chowed down upon by certain of the AWOL cats.

Six mice remained at large in the exhibit hall but, given their laboratory origins, were deemed not a hazard to the attendees. In addition to the rodent casualties, three "I ♥ Cats" mugs and two ceramic cat sculptures in the vendor booths were broken in the confusion; hence the criminal mischief charge.

"Well, at least the show managed to go on," Jake said. "That was pretty smart of Mildred to suggest they play Hamlet's video while everyone got situated again." She paused and grinned. "I think almost everyone, down to the judges, forgot what had just gone down by the time they finished laughing at you and the Karate Kitty."

"If I can help bring world peace by looking like a total idiot, then that's the price I'll pay," Darla replied with an answering glance at the cat in question. While she and Jake were doing the heavy lifting getting all the packing done, Hamlet was lounging, paws up, on the sofa, surrounded by the sherbet-colored pillows. And, as far as Darla could tell, he did not appear at all dismayed to be judged as a feline slacker.

Then she sobered. "I have to say, I really have a hard time believing Billy Pope killed Ted Stein. I wonder what evidence Martinez found that made her confident enough to arrest him."

"I don't know, but she's a smart cookie. It's got to be something pretty damning."

Darla considered this as she continued packing. Since the rest of their time in Fort Lauderdale was officially vacation, she'd again donned the cuffed white denim jeans, though she'd exchanged the striped top for a silk Hawaiian shirt in shades of blue, green, and yellow. Jake was equally casual—for her—in a pair of black cropped pants and a red-and-white polka-dotted top, her usual Doc Martens swapped for black boat shoes.

The PI had already packed her clothes and was collecting her toiletries from the bath. She came out with an armful of combs and shampoos and various sprays . . . along with the glass seashell sculpture, a twin of which had sent Ted Stein to that great cat show in the sky.

Darla tried to ignore a squeamish feeling when Jake, after first dumping the toiletries onto her bed, began examining the scalloped-shaped sculpture from all angles. It was the general size and shape of a small salad plate, and broad enough at its base that it could stand upright. Made of Murano-style glass with swirls of blues and greens accenting its ridges, the piece was just elegant enough not to be dismissed as a simple tourist's souvenir.

She couldn't help wincing when Jake experimented a bit further, hefting the shell with one hand—it had to weigh a pound and a half, maybe two, from Darla's best estimate—and simulating smacking someone over the head with it. Then the PI raised it with both hands and repeated the exercise before setting it down on the bedside table.

"So how's Nattie taking things?" Darla asked to distract herself from the uncomfortable images that Jake's pantomime had set loose in her imagination.

"So far, so good," Jake said with a shrug. "She's with Alicia now trying to get Billy bailed out."

"No offense, Jake," Darla said, "but I've been wondering this whole time what a multimillionaire like Billy is doing hanging out with your mother in the first place. I mean, I think she's great, but she doesn't seem to be the type to be rubbing elbows with real estate magnates."

"Kid, you'd be surprised whose elbows Ma has rubbed,"

Jake replied with a wry smile. "I learned a long time ago not to ask questions about her friends. But I know they met on the condo board, even though he doesn't actually live there, he just owns a couple of units that he bought as investments before the big real estate bust."

"Wait—if his condos are investments, where does Billy actually live?"

Jake gave a deprecating snort. "Word is he's got some sort of mansion on the Intracoastal Waterway, some place where he doesn't have to mingle with the hoi polloi. Oh, except when he's dictating condo policy."

"Gotcha. Though I have to say Billy is a pretty decent sort compared to some of the rich people I've run across. I mean, assuming he didn't actually embezzle the condo funds and kill Ted Stein," she hastened to add when Jake shook her head and rolled her eyes.

Darla zipped up her suitcase. All that was left for her to do was to pack up Hamlet's gear, and she'd be ready to head out. Then another thought occurred to her.

"Jake, any idea what happened to Ted's cat . . . you know, the Minx? Surely the poor little thing didn't get left behind at the show!"

"Don't worry," Jake replied, fastening her own bag. "Ma said that Alicia or someone would keep the cat until Ted's sister can come pick him up."

Deciding that was enough talk about Ted Stein and Billy Pope, Darla switched the conversation to where they'd have breakfast the next few days, since the official hotel breakfast buffet and Jennie's Bakery would no longer be in walking distance. They also discussed the state of Jake's headache—pretty much gone—and whether they should buy Nattie one of the throw pillows she'd so admired as a hostess gift.

The pillow got a yes vote, with Jake volunteering to pick it up from the gift store on their way out of the hotel. Darla, meanwhile, finished collecting Hamlet's things and then managed to coax the feline into the carrier for the ride to Nattie's condo.

"Sorry, fellow," she apologized to the cat as she dialed the cab company, "but it's safer for you to be in there while we're driving. Besides, Tino probably won't want cat hair in his taxi."

While Jake waited in the room for Clyde to bring up a baggage cart, Darla wheeled the sulking Hamlet down to the lobby to check out. Meows echoed through the lobby again, with other cat-show attendees also on their way home. She got in line behind the owner of a male Maine Coon who had been judged Best in Show at the end of the previous day's event.

"Congratulations," she told the elderly man. "Seaside Sunset Sailor is a beautiful cat and definitely deserved the win."

"You can call him Sunny, my dear," the man replied with a smile and a fond look down at the cat in the carrier he was wheeling. "And yes, we are very proud. It was a wonderful show."

Then his smile faltered a little as he apparently realized what he'd just said.

"Except, of course, for all that unpleasantness," he hurried to clarify. "I didn't know Mr. Stein, but we consider our fellow exhibitors family. And I have to say, I've known Billy Pope for years. He's one of the best judges on the circuit. I certainly hope he had nothing to do with it."

"Me, too," Darla murmured as the man nodded his goodbyes and took his turn at the front desk.

When it was finally Darla's turn, she and the clerk—this one young, male, and with hair as red as hers—exchanged bland pleasantries regarding her stay. By unspoken agreement, they made no reference to the past days' occurrences despite the stack, there on the desk, of free daily newspapers, whose headline blared: *Real Estate Mogul Arrested for*

Murder. It was accompanied by an unflattering picture of Billy Pope caught climbing from the backseat of a squad car. A second, smaller headline noted that the dearly departed was being buried that afternoon with a public memorial to follow the next day.

Darla signed off on her incidental charges, then folded one of those newspapers and slipped it under her arm. She'd add it to her copy of yesterday's edition, with the headline *Local Businessman Murdered in Downtown Hotel.* James and Robert would definitely be interested in reading those issues firsthand, she was certain.

Jake was already waiting by the main lobby door with Clyde and their luggage and holding a hotel gift shop bag as Darla and Hamlet approached. Beyond the glass doors, Darla could see a familiar cab pulling up beneath the breezeway. Clyde opened the door and gestured them out, towing the luggage cart behind him.

"Hey, *chica*!"

Popping open his trunk, a grinning Tino hopped from the driver's seat and started around front to the passenger side. He was wearing his same uniform of baggy cargo shorts and a florid Hawaiian shirt. Arms crossed to better show off his tats, he lounged against that door while Clyde loaded the trunk. "You got your *gato* with you?"

"Yes, Hamlet's here," Darla replied with an answering smile, indicating the wheeled carrier beside her.

Tino lowered his sunglasses to give her a look of mock disappointment. "I thought he could ride shotgun in the front seat with me. Oh well, maybe next time."

"Probably not," was Darla's reply. "We had a little scare with him getting loose while we were at the cat show."

"Yeah, that was you? I heard someone tried to steal a *gato* from the show. Ana told me about that."

"Ana?"

"Yeah, *mi prima*—my cousin—Ana Garcia. She's a cop."

Doubtless the same Officer Garcia who, along with Officer Johnston, had been dispatched every time something went wrong in Darla's vicinity. While she digested this bit of information, Clyde put the last bag in the trunk and shut it.

Jake moved closer to the bellman and slipped him a few bills. "Thanks for all your help these past couple of days, Clyde. And sorry about the ding I put in your golf cart."

"No problem." Then, ducking his head a little, he added, "So, uh, if you need a guide around town, I've lived here all my life. And, uh, I'm off on Wednesday."

Jake smiled and slipped on her mirrored shades. "I appreciate the offer, but I really need to spend the time with my mother. You understand."

"Oh, sure, sure. It's been a pleasure meeting you, Jake. Oh, and you, too, Darla," he added with a nod in Darla's direction as he grabbed the cart and pushed it back toward the lobby.

"Your tall friend there, she's a real heartbreaker," Tino observed to Darla as the lobby doors opened and then closed behind the bellman. To Jake, he added in a cheeky tone, "Hey, *chica*, why'd you shoot the poor guy down? You shoulda given him a chance."

Jake turned the mirrored shades his way, her expression unsmiling. Even without her usual stacked-heel boots, she still towered over the cabbie. In precise tones that would have done Professor James proud, she said, "If you wish to earn your tip, you will address me as ma'am. Understand?"

"Yes, *ma'am*," Tino obediently echoed, snapping to attention and opening the passenger door for her. To Darla, he said in a low tone, "Ex-military?"

"Ex-cop," Darla cheerfully replied as she loaded Hamlet, inside his carrier, after Jake. Preparing to slide in beside the cat, she added, "Like your *prima*, Ana."

"Uh-oh. I know what that means."

Closing the door after her, Tino trotted back around to

the driver's side, jumped in, and then swung about to face them. "And where can I take you lovely ladies? I mean, you fine women—er, you two ma'ams?"

Still wearing her shades and still channeling James, Jake gave the cabbie Nattie's address. Tino turned back around again and snapped on his seat belt before resetting the meter. As he pulled out from under the breezeway and onto the street, Darla exchanged quick glances with her friend. She saw the faintest quiver of a smile on Jake's lips before the PI resumed her stern visage. Obviously, she was enjoying yanking the young cabbie's chain.

"So, should we go the shortcut or the scenic route?" he called back to them.

"Shortcut," Jake declared.

"Scenic route," Darla countered.

Tino gave an exaggerated sigh and glanced at them via the rearview mirror. "Okay, which one of you ma'ams is paying the fare?"

"I am," Darla told him with a smile, "so scenic route it is. But just hit the highlights. Hamlet will start getting restless if we drag it out too long."

"Scenic but short. Gotcha. Say, how about I show you the mansion of that old guy that killed that other old guy at your hotel?"

"You know where Billy Pope lives?" This from Jake, whose casual tone, Darla knew, belied her actual interest.

Tino nodded. "I know where all the rich people live. We'll swing by when I show you one of the water-taxi launches."

The cabbie proceeded to take them on an eclectic tour that rivaled their recent drive with Nattie. Hamlet, safely in his carrier, gave a couple of questioning meows the first few blocks but apparently decided that if he'd survived a ride with Jake's mother, he'd survive Tino, too.

Zipping through the crowded streets with the flair of a man who did it for a living, Tino pointed out some of the obvious tourist sights: the art museum, the nearest college, even a supposedly haunted pioneer home. He also rolled past a few more offbeat places: a gloriously campy art deco movie theater (where, Darla presumed, they showed fancy-pantsy art films); the International Swimming Hall of Fame, and a dive bar and a restaurant where, according to Tino, was served the world's best rum runner and the best Cuban sandwich, respectively.

They passed the promised water-taxi launch—"Not as good as riding with me," Tino told them, "but it's pretty fun, and you can carry your own booze on"—and Darla recalled Nattie saying that working on one of those Intracoastal tourist boats had been a previous part-time job of hers. Then Tino took a little jog off the main boulevard, sliding down a twisting narrow side street that ran parallel with the water not far from one of the marinas.

Riding down this particular road felt almost like driving through a tunnel. Along one side of them, newly greening deciduous trees, combined with various palm species, canopied a portion of the lane. On the opposite side, concrete walls six feet tall and a scant couple of yards from the curb stretched down the road, serving as a barrier between passing traffic and the million-dollar-plus residences that faced out onto the Intracoastal.

Despite the seeming out-of-the-way location, it was a busy little thoroughfare, full of vehicles ranging from beat-up box trucks to luxury sedans. At intervals, other smaller lanes lined with still more homes pointed like narrow fingers directly toward the water. Most of those streets were marked "Dead End" and required crossing over small bridges.

"Sorry," Tino spoke up. "You can't really see the homes from here. You gotta ride the water taxi for that. But we're lucky to get this close. Parts of this road are gated off, and you can't get through unless security lets you pass."

Still, at each property's driveway, the gates—a few wooden, most others wrought iron—allowed tantalizing glimpses of what lay beyond. This close to the water, there was little room for a yard, so most homes were built right up against the road. Darla's favorite, she decided as Tino slowed for another speed bump, was a salmon-colored, Mediterranean-style beauty with a red-tiled roof and numerous covered porches and balconies.

A moment later, the cabbie pulled off onto the narrow shoulder in front of a painted wooden gate that was almost a parody of the traditional white picket fence.

"That's Mr. Pope's place," he said, pointing to the two-and-a-half-story pale yellow stucco home visible between the gate's broad pickets.

For a mansion, it looked refreshingly humble, Darla thought. True, it featured a matching detached garage, a mother-in-law quarters, and what appeared to be a pool house; still, the various structures' lines were clean and simple, just fancied up a bit with white trim and white-tile details. Still, no one was getting in who didn't belong; the gate was mounted with one of those metal boxes with an intercom and a keycard slot, like at a hotel.

"He's got a really nice garden, and there's a dock out back where he has a boat," Tino told them. "And there's at least three cars in that garage. One of them's a Bentley, but I think it's leased."

"You sure know an awful lot about the man," Jake observed.

Tino shrugged. "Hey, we cabbies, we get around. No one pays us much attention, or questions us when we're stopped like this."

As if in illustration, a Jaguar slid up behind them. The driver beeped, reminding them that most of the taxi still hung out into the street, halfway blocking the lane. Tino stuck out a tattooed arm and waved the driver on.

"See," he said as the Jag beeped again and, once the opposite lane traffic cleared, zipped around them, "for all he knows, we're just waiting on the hired help to open the gate for you ma'ams."

Before Darla could reply, a sudden and very irritated meow issued from the cat carrier.

"Oops. Hamlet says it's time to get a move on," Darla told the cabbie. "Let's cut the tour short here and head to the condo."

"You got it."

He pulled back onto the road and took the next left since, as predicted, a large security gate now spanned the road, making the section beyond private. And with that turn, they were now driving through what appeared at first glance to be a decidedly lower-middle-class neighborhood. But Darla spied a construction crew removing what remained of one demolished house, and she realized that the value of these homes was in the lot and location and not the structures themselves. One of those tear-downs likely ran into the mid-six figures just as it stood.

They reached Nattie's condo just a few minutes later. And while the complex wasn't an elegant manor like Pope's place, it still had a certain upscale style of its own.

The stone sign plunked between two bushy palms at the edge of the semicircular drive read "Lauderdale Tropics." In smaller words below that name was carved "A Fifty-Five-and-Better Community." A little reverse ageism, Darla thought in amusement. The complex seemed less like an apartment building and more like an office tower, five stories tall with plenty of glass and balconies. With a little squinting, she told herself, someone looking out the fifth-floor window could probably just make out a glimpse of the Intracoastal Waterway.

A three-tiered fountain big enough to swim in squatted halfway up the drive, right in front of the portico where Tino was pulling up. The driveway itself was stone rather than concrete, while the oversized glass doors leading into the building were etched with an elaborate tropical jungle scene. For all of Nattie's disdain of things fancy-pantsy, the old woman appeared to be living in quite the nice situation, Darla thought.

"Here you go, ma'ams," Tino said, throwing the cab into park and popping the trunk.

He hopped out and pulled open both passenger doors. While they climbed out and Darla wrestled Hamlet's carrier onto the drive, the young man started unloading their bags onto the walkway in front of the lobby.

"Can you manage all this luggage on your own?" he wanted to know.

Darla nodded. "We got it on and off the plane, so we should be fine. Now, what do we owe you?"

He quoted her a price, and she paid him and added a generous tip, earning a grin in return. "Forget about Clyde at the hotel," he told her. "You two need a tour guide, you call me again."

"I'll keep that in mind."

With a snappy little salute, he jumped back into the cab and headed out, narrowly missing an elderly woman and her equally aged white standard poodle who'd chosen that moment to cross the driveway without first looking both ways. Jake shook her head as she watched him go.

"Kids these days," she lamented, sounding an awful lot like Nattie, Darla thought in amusement as she slung her tote bag across her chest.

Dragging Hamlet's carrier behind her in one hand and her suitcase in the other, Darla followed Jake as the PI unlocked the foyer entry with Nattie's spare key. The inside was equally fancy-pantsy, with lots of cool white tile and a calming palette of sand and sea green for the walls and ceiling.

Rather like a hotel lobby, the foyer was empty save for a large round table in tile and brass that held a frighteningly spiky dried flower arrangement. Two small conversation groupings—each with a pastel floral love seat, matching chair, and tile-and-brass coffee table—took up the wall to Darla's left. Ahead she saw three frosted-glass doors: the right one marked "Laundry," the left one "Health Club," and the center one "Pool." To her left were two elevators as well as an alcove, which she saw served as the combination mailroom and business center.

"Nice place," Darla said in approval. By her guess, the condos this close to the water had to cost in the mid–six figures; she'd always had the idea that Jake came from a working-class background, but maybe there were some rich relatives in the Martelli family tree that no one had mentioned.

"Yeah, it's pretty nice," Jake agreed as she pressed the elevator button. Then, answering Darla's unspoken question, she added, "Ma has a decent pension on top of what she got of Dad's. And she got really, really lucky one night at the casinos."

They took the elevator up to the second floor, accompanied by what sounded like the Mantovani cascading strings version of Jimmy Buffett. Darla tried not to laugh as Jake rolled her eyes, and muttered, "Would it kill them to pipe in a little heavy metal?"

Darla promptly sobered, however, as she caught sight of a notice posted on the elevator announcing a memorial service being held for Ted Stein that evening out by the pool. Apparently the condo association used the elevator as the community bulletin board, no doubt going on the assumption that all residents would eventually have to go up or down in it.

She had no time to discuss the planned gathering with Jake, however, since the condo elevator was significantly swifter than the one at the hotel. When the elevator door dinged open, Jake barreled out to flee the sentimental music. In the process, the PI all but stumbled over a familiar-looking old woman who stood right outside the door.

"Mildred, good to see you again," Darla said with a pleased smile while Jake and Mildred did an impromptu if necessary dance around each other. Darla dragged Hamlet and her suitcase out of the way. "I forgot Nattie said you lived here at the condo, too."

"Oh, yes. I was one of the first to buy. My place is down the hall from your mother," Mildred said a bit breathlessly as she straightened her ruffled blouse. Properly rearranged, she smiled, revealing the usual spot of pink lipstick on her one bucktooth. "It's nice to see you girls again. Will you be staying for a while?"

"We're here through Sunday morning," Jake told her. "Our plan is to get in a little sightseeing, maybe hang out at the beach."

"How nice. If you girls need a guide, I've lived here for years. Why, I even worked on the water taxi with Nattie. I'll be happy to show you around."

Darla suppressed a smile. It seemed that the entire city of Fort Lauderdale was volunteering to play tour guide for them!

"Thanks, Mildred," Jake told the old woman, "but I think Ma has the guide duties covered."

"Oh, I understand." Then, bending toward the cat carrier, she added, "And how is Hamlet today? Hopefully all recovered from his ordeal?"

"He's great," Darla told her, only to hear a distinctly not-so-great growl come from the carrier's occupant. Darla hurried to reassure her. "It's not you. Hamlet's probably just grumpy after that taxi ride."

"Not to worry, I've been growled at before," was her placid response. She stepped into the elevator, adding as the doors closed on her, "I'll see you girls later. Maybe at the memorial service tonight."

"Memorial service?" Jake echoed as she and Darla started down the hall, the rumble of their luggage wheels muffled by the faux Oriental carpet runner.

Darla nodded. "There was a sign in the elevator. Apparently the condo residents are having a little get-together around the pool tonight at seven to honor Ted Stein's memory. He might have been a jerk at the cat show, but I guess he had some friends here if they elected him to their board. Should we go?"

"Let's see what Ma wants to do. I'd rather try that bar that Tino was raving about, but since we found the body, I sort of feel obliged to do the memorial thing. Besides, it might be interesting to see who shows up."

Not that you intend to investigate the man's death or anything, Darla silently added.

They halted at the third unit on the left, and Jake pulled out the keys again. She opened the condo door, and Darla walked into what at first glance appeared to be a Florida souvenir shop, circa 1950.

A dozen kitschy Florida tea towels featuring variations on oranges, orchids, and palm trees had been framed and hung as art upon the pale green living room wall. Rattan furniture was upholstered in an oversized tropical floral pattern, heavy on pinks, which hues made more vibrant the faint rosy tinge to the broad beige tiles covering the floors. A matching rattan-and-glass bookshelf held Florida-themed souvenirs: snow globes, salt and pepper shakers, spoons, and decorative plates. A grouping of net-wrapped glass fishing floats were lit from within and hung from the ceiling near the sofa. Those makeshift lights competed with an arrangement of rattan hanging lamps over by the television set.

But Darla's favorite touch was right next to the front door. There, a bamboo-framed rectangle of weathered wood proclaimed the words "Tiki Bar" in fluorescent hues, accented by a wooden tiki mask nailed to one corner of it.

"Wow," was Darla's assessment of the décor. "I don't know that I could live with all this, but it sure is fun to visit it."

"Yeah, Ma got a little carried away with the vintage Florida theme. I think she watched too many beach movies back in the sixties."

Since, despite her love of heavy metal, Jake had a thing for vintage décor as well—her garden apartment was a veritable homage to the fifties and sixties—Darla refrained from comment. Instead, she looked toward the hallway. "Where do you want me and Hamlet?"

"You two take the guest room. Make a right at the hall door and you'll see it. The bathroom is yours, too . . . there's a connecting door to your room as well as to the hall, so you can set up Hamlet's things in there."

"What about you and Nattie?"

"There's a second bathroom in the master suite, so we're covered. I'll bunk with Ma, or else I'll take the couch if she gets too restless. Oh, and the balcony should be Hamlet-proof," Jake added, pointing to the sliding glass door. "Ma's got windscreens installed in all the openings. If they can hold up to a hurricane, they can probably withstand one cat."

Darla rolled Hamlet back to the carpeted guest room and let him out to zip around a bit to get the kinks out. While he did his crazy kitty thing, she took quick stock of the room that was hers for the duration.

The only true Florida kitsch in here was the white vintage chenille bedspread embroidered with bushel baskets of green-leaved oranges and topped with a giant accent pillow in the shape of a pineapple. The rest of the décor was tropical neutral: sand-colored carpet, pale blue walls with white trim, white rattan dresser and bedside table, and a watercolor of a fighting marlin "walking" the waves hung on one wall. While nominally a guest room, it also appeared to serve typical double duty as storage. The open shelving on either side of a quaint window seat held numerous lidded cardboard boxes neatly labeled with their contents. The double-door closet held more boxes along with a few winter coats and sweaters stored in plastic.

Leaving her suitcase at the foot of the bed to unpack later, Darla pulled out Hamlet's gear and set him up in the bathroom. When she was sure he understood where to find his food, water, and litter box, she gingerly opened the door to the hall again and let him out to explore the rest of the apartment.

As she suspected, he made a beeline for the balcony sliders.

"Jake, we're going onto the balcony," she called to her friend, who was busy unpacking in Nattie's room. "You hear any screams, it's me trying to drag Hamlet back from the brink when he proves he's tougher than a hurricane."

But to her relief, the balcony did seem impervious to felines. The moment she slid open the door, Hamlet scampered out onto its concrete surface and then bounded onto a garish orange wicker lounge chair. After an exploratory sniff in all directions, he leaped from the chair onto the balcony's broad rail and peered through the screen. He gave the material a tentative tap with one oversized paw, looking a bit surprised when the material bounced back at him. Finally deciding that it wasn't worth fighting the system, he lowered his paw and settled down onto his stomach. Paws tucked against his chest now, he shut his green eyes and began to purr.

"Score one for our team," Darla murmured as, careful not to disturb him, she moved toward the railing to check out her surroundings.

Nattie's condo lay at the rear of the building. Thus, rather than a view of the driveway and fountain in front, Darla was treated to the sight of a respectably large rectangular swimming pool almost directly below the balcony. Taking advantage of the water was one very old (and very large) man in a very blue (and very tiny) Speedo, who was swimming excruciatingly slow but perfectly executed laps. Despite an open tiki hut complete with bar and stools situated at the pool's shallow end, Darla suspected that Nattie didn't have to worry too much about the noise from pool parties in the wee hours of the night.

A nice bit of landscaped lawn lay outside the fenced and gated pool area. Darla spied what appeared to be the obligatory shuffleboard court, as well as a croquet lawn. At the moment, the only one outside besides the swimming gentleman were a couple of obvious retirees puttering around a small flower garden behind the pool. From what she'd heard Jake mention before, however, she knew there were ninety units in the building, which implied at least that many occupants.

Minus one now, of course.

With a final cautious look at the sleeping Hamlet, Darla walked back inside, where Jake was in the kitchenette, digging into the refrigerator. She pulled out two bottles of sparkling water and a lime, which she rinsed and then quartered with a knife that had a plastic lemon slice as its handle. Squeezing a lime wedge into each bottle, she strode out and handed one to Darla, and then raised hers in toastlike fashion.

"To not doing a thing except sightseeing for the rest of our vacation," Jake declared.

"To sightseeing," Darla agreed and clinked her bottle to Jake's. "How about as soon as Nattie gets back, we drag her out to that restaurant Tino told us about that makes the amazing Cuban sandwiches? And then maybe we can catch a water taxi and take a ride up and down the river."

"Sounds like just my speed. I tell you what, I am so looking forward to—"

"Jacqueline!"

The front door of the condo flew open, making them both jump. Nattie burst into the living room, her red cockatoo's crest fairly bristling in agitation. "Jacqueline, where are you? We have to talk about Billy! He's in real trouble!"

THIRTEEN

"MA, I'M STANDING RIGHT HERE IN FRONT OF YOU," JAKE replied, waving her water bottle like a signal flag. "Take a deep breath and tell me what's going on."

Darla, meanwhile, had recovered from her momentary surprise and rushed to close the door after the old woman. She'd have to tell Nattie about Hamlet's propensity for slipping out open doors and wandering where he didn't belong. Although he was still peacefully sleeping on the balcony, at any moment the wily feline might decide it was time to get up and get close and personal with life in South Florida.

Nattie stood wringing her veined hands. Apparently, something had not gone well with the bailing-out process. Though how much more trouble someone could be in after a murder arrest, Darla wasn't certain. Jake pulled another bottle of water from the fridge and, giving it the lime treatment, handed it off to her mother. "C'mon, let's sit down and talk."

Nattie let herself be led to the rattan couch, sitting beside

Jake and clutching the bottled water, from which she took a shaky sip. Darla, meanwhile, settled into the matching chair.

"So tell me what happened, Ma," Jake prompted her. "Did Billy's lawyer get him bailed out okay?"

"Oh, that was the easy part, though when Alicia and I went to pick him up from the jail, we waited around almost an hour for him to get out. You shoulda seen the kind of people coming and going there. Ugly, no teeth, tattoos . . . and that was just the women." Nattie sighed and took another sip of water. "And then Alicia's phone rings, and it's Billy. His lawyer had already taken him home."

"So he's bailed out, and he's got an attorney. Sounds like everything is on schedule. So what's the worry?"

"What's the worry?" Nattie gave her daughter an indignant look. "He's being charged with second-degree murder. But he's innocent! You gotta help him."

Jake sighed. "Ma, I explained this to you before. I'm not licensed as a PI in this state, so there's not a darned thing I can do for him. Besides, with all his money, your friend Billy can afford to hire himself a whole contingent of lawyers and private investigators."

"Yeah, but none of them are as good as my Jacqueline."

Jake smiled a little and gave her mother's hand an encouraging pat. "Ma, I'm sure everything is going to work out. Unless there's some really damning evidence against Billy, there's a good chance this won't make it to the grand jury, let alone to trial."

"Yeah, but get this: Billy told Alicia that rotten police detective—what was her name, Martinez?—figured out why Ted was wearing his shoes. And that's why she arrested him."

Darla and Jake exchanged glances. The whole odd footwear appropriation was what had stumped Darla from the first, and she had yet to figure out a logical explanation for it. She assumed Jake hadn't, either.

"Come on, Ma, spill. What did the shoes have to do with it?"

"They found a picture on Ted's cell phone of Hamlet sitting next to someone's legs, and those legs were wearing Billy's shoes!"

"Ma, that's not a motive for murder. Is he sure there's really a picture, or could Detective Martinez have been bluffing?"

Nattie gave a vigorous nod. "There's a picture, all right. Billy checked his phone and said that no-good Ted Stein emailed it to him, too."

Jake furrowed her brow, took a sip of water, and then leaned back against the new throw pillow she'd bought for Nattie.

"All right, since we don't have any better theories at the moment, let's assume that Ted was responsible for the Hamlet-napping. Here's how I see it went down."

She began ticking points off on her fingers. "Ted smacks me over the head, steals Hamlet, and manages to sneak him out of the exhibition hall before they lock the place down. He hides Hamlet in an unknown location for a few hours, then waits until after the show to somehow get into Billy's hotel room while no one's there. He digs a spare pair of wingtips out of the closet, snaps a selfie with Hamlet, and then sends the picture to Pope right before someone walks in on him. This person—or persons—unknown then proceeds to cosh him with the glass seashell. Does that about cover it?"

"So far, so good," Darla agreed.

Jake sighed. "Okay, here's where it goes from complicated to downright convoluted, and why I'm glad this case belongs to Sam Martinez and not me. We've got a handful of different offenses here, and various possible motives behind them. There's assault on me, theft of property—sorry, Hamlet—breaking and entering, and murder. And maybe blackmail, if that's the purpose of the picture Ted sent Billy. And that doesn't take into consideration the possible embezzlement going on here with Ma's condo association."

"Don't forget the whole cat-show brouhaha," Darla spoke up. "Ted was hoping to cash in on his Minx, and he wasn't pleased not to win his division. And, Nattie, remember how you said Billy called Ted a charlatan for trying to push that new breed?"

"Yeah, and that Ted wasn't taking it lying down," Nattie declared. "Only last week, Billy told me that's why he thought Ted was accusing him of stealing the condo-association funds. You know, revenge for Billy not helping him get the Minx cats recognized."

Jake gave an approving nod. "That wasn't on my radar, but it could be important. So to figure out who the killer is—and, Ma, sorry, I'm not prepared to take Mr. Pope off the list—we need to determine if all these various crimes and misdemeanors are all tied together, or if they all just happened to occur around the same time."

"Wait, wait. One more suspect to add to the list," Darla broke in, reflexively waving her hand as if waiting to be called on in class. "What about Alicia's daughter, Cindy? She's some sort of addict, from what I overheard Alicia say. Plus, remember that I saw her threaten Alicia with a bottle that first night at the hotel. And don't forget that she got arrested with the other girls for disrupting the cat show. Maybe she had a beef with Ted that no one knows about. Or maybe she was the one to find him in Billy's room, and things got out of hand."

"Wow, Darla's good at this," Nattie said with an admiring look at her. "Jacqueline, you should hire this girl as yer assistant."

"I think Darla has enough to do running her bookstore" was Jake's response. "But Cindy definitely has suspect potential. You did tell Sam about that incident with Cindy, didn't you?"

Darla nodded.

"Good. So we'll leave it to Sam to figure out. Now, I don't know about the rest of you, but I'm going to go ride the water taxi."

So saying, Jake rose and headed to the kitchen to dispose of her empty bottle. Nattie stared after her, her expression petulant. "So you're going to throw Billy to the dogs. I never thought I'd see the day when my own flesh and blood would do such a thing to a friend."

"Ma, if he truly didn't do it, I'm sure Sam will find the guilty party, and then he's off the hook permanently. Now, how about that water-taxi ride?"

When the old woman remained stubbornly silent, Jake added in a cajoling tone, "C'mon, it will be fun. You can even tell us all the stuff the water-taxi tour guide gets wrong."

"Oh, believe me, they'll get a lot wrong," Nattie proclaimed, looking a bit more chipper as she hopped up.

Then, to Darla, she added, "Say, where's that cat of yers?"

"He's out lounging on your balcony," Darla told her. "When we go out, I'll put him in the guest room and leave the bathroom door open so he can go in and out. I don't think he can open these doors by himself."

She briefly told Nattie about Hamlet's misadventures the first night on the hotel balcony and how he'd managed to hang from the lever-style handles to open the doors.

"Now that's one smart cat," the old woman said, her tone admiring.

While Jake and Nattie prepared to leave, Darla bit the bullet and rousted Hamlet from his balcony perch.

"Sorry, fellow. I can't take the chance that you'll figure out a way to undo the screens," she told him as she carried him into the bedroom. "But after we get back, I'll take you for a nice walk around the pool."

With a grumpy Hamlet settled in the guest bedroom—Darla crossed her fingers that he wouldn't use her luggage as a litter box to show his displeasure—the three women headed out. Nattie drove, the Mini Cooper again barreling down the road like a carnival ride. Darla clutched her seat-belt to her, wishing she had a medal of St. Christopher, the patron saint of travelers, to wear for the duration of this visit.

They parked near one of the launch stops and bought tickets for the water taxi. It was rather like riding a subway, Nattie informed them, each bright yellow boat with its scalloped Bimini top making stops along the Intracoastal Waterway and the New River.

"Just don't get in no hurry," she warned them as they boarded. "They're slow as Christmas, and if you get off, you can wait an hour for another one to come by. I think that's why they fired me. I tried to make them kids that crew the boats toe the line."

They spent the next hour bobbing gently down the Intracoastal and up the New River. They got a look at Port Everglades and the Fifteenth Street Fisheries and passed the Swimming Hall of Fame from its opposite side this time before hopping off at the Riverfront to find a place to eat an early lunch. Then it was back on the water taxi again for another hour's ride to gawk at mansions along what was called Millionaire's Row.

According to the pert young woman in gray shorts and a vaguely maritime-looking short-sleeved white shirt holding the microphone, "millionaire" was something of a misnomer. "Billionaire" was more accurate. Meaning, Darla presumed, that they wouldn't be cruising past Billy's place.

The accompanying commentary as they floated by the multimillion-dollar homes was cheesy but rather eye-opening. While Darla had expected a "tour of the stars' homes (nautical version)," she learned that most of the celebrities had places further south, in Miami.

Here the homes belonged to corporate bigwigs, attorneys, doctors—capitalism at work, though a couple of requisite movie directors did also own places along the waterfront. They floated past the marina where Spielberg and others docked their yachts for a thousand dollars per day—in contrast to the mooring buoys farther down, where humble fishing boats could tie up for a mere thirty-five dollars a night, making them quite the cheapest place to stay in the city, according to their guide.

They eventually disembarked again where they'd first climbed aboard. Somewhat windburned by the Intracoastal breeze, the three agreed to spend the rest of their afternoon on dry land.

"You'da thought she coulda pointed out Cher's old place," Nattie grumbled about the tour guide as they headed back to the car. "And you'd of missed that little red, white, and blue guest house if I hadn't of mentioned it. Oh, and she forgot to tell you about why the House of Butterflies is called that, because it's shaped like a butterfly. Though you can't really tell except from the air."

"Ma, everything was fine," Jake assured her. "We had fun, right, Darla?"

"It was great," Darla agreed, adding with a groan, "though I kind of wish I hadn't eaten that whole slice of cheesecake at lunch."

"Eh, don't worry," Nattie said. "We've got plenty of time to rest up before the memorial service tonight."

Jake gave her a considering look. "You really want to go to that?"

Nattie unlocked the Mini and nodded. "Of course," she said, hopping behind the wheel and putting down the top. "In all those mystery novels, the killer always comes to the memorial service to gloat. I want to go and see who's gloating so I can figure out who really killed Ted Stein. You girls can come along or not."

"I guess I'd better go and make sure you stay out of trouble," Jake said as she folded herself into the Mini Cooper's front seat. Glancing back at Darla, who was busy contorting herself into the back, she asked, "What about you, kid?

"Sure, why not? I've got some postcards to write, but I

can do them tonight. All I ask is that I get my Cuban sandwich, okay?"

Once back at the condo, Darla hurriedly reminded Nattie as they rode up in the elevator, "Take a peek first, when you open the door, and make sure Hamlet didn't get out of the guest room."

"All clear," Nattie proclaimed a few moments later after sticking her head past the front door. "Come on in girls, we'll—"

"Loose cat!" yelled Jake as a black flash whipped out the door and into the hallway.

"Hamlet!" Darla shrieked, making a dive for the cat and missing, instead landing in an ungainly heap upon the faux Oriental rug. Hamlet didn't give her another chance at capture but made a beeline down the hall toward the elevator's closing doors.

To her relief, the elevator door slid shut a heartbeat before the fleeing feline reached them. He stopped on a dime and stared a few moments at the metal door, as if willing it to open again. Then, when the elevator proved immune to cat telepathy, Hamlet gave a flip of his long black tail and turned. Looking quite pleased with his feline self, he trotted back to where Darla still lay sprawled on the floor. Ignoring her plight, he slipped past the condo door and went inside again.

"Are you okay?" Jake asked in concern, helping her to her feet.

Darla nodded. "I'll live." Limping a little, she hurried into the apartment to find Hamlet patiently waiting next to the locked sliders.

"You little so-and-so," she grumbled as she opened the glass door. "Fine, go out."

With another tail flick, Hamlet strolled out onto the balcony and made a graceful leap up onto the railing. There, he settled with paws tucked to his chest and turned wide emerald eyes on Darla. *Me, I'm a good kitty*, that innocent expression seemed to be saying.

Darla snorted. "Yeah, right," she said and turned to head toward the guest room. "Now let's see how in the heck you got out."

Nattie, however, had already solved the mystery.

"Gee, sorry, Darla. I forgot all about that linen cupboard," she said from the hallway, pointing to the open cabinet door on the wall near Darla's room. "You can get to it from inside the bathroom, too."

Darla went into the guest bath to find a similar cabinet door also standing wide open. Peering straight ahead past the towels, she could see the wall that separated the bathroom from Nattie's master suite. But, glancing to her left, she saw the second opening and the hall beyond, where Nattie stood looking back at her. Obviously, Hamlet had discovered this clever little architectural feature and played it to his advantage.

"Don't worry, dear," the old woman told her with a grin at the cat's cleverness. "Hamlet seems well behaved enough that I'm sure it's fine to let him wander the condo all he wants."

"Well behaved, my . . . posterior region," Darla muttered, editing herself at the last minute and channeling James. "But on the bright side, he'll be with us the rest of tonight, so I'll be able to keep an eye on him."

Darla shut the linen cabinet and marched into the guest room to make sure Mr. Claims-to-Be-a-Good-Kitty had not wreaked—or was it wrought?—any degree of havoc in her absence. To her relief, her luggage appeared intact, the pillows and comforter on the bed undisturbed, and the closet door closed.

Maybe he's a good kitty after all, she thought with an indulgent smile. And then she walked around the bed and saw the box of scattered paperwork.

What appeared to be paid bills, bank statements, and various legal documents blanketed the sand-colored carpet back there. With a groan, Darla dropped to her knees and started gathering the pages. How she would ever get them rearranged, she had no idea. The best she could do was scoop them up and then confess Hamlet's transgression to Nattie. She was straightening the first stack of paperwork when the old woman chose to check up on her.

"Darla, do you think it's okay if I take Hamlet—"

She broke off and stared at Darla, offended. "Hey, whaddaya doing with my papers? They're private, you know."

"Oh, Nattie, I'm so sorry," Darla replied. "Hamlet got into some trouble after all. He pulled down this whole box of paperwork. I was trying to clean it up for you."

"Eh, that's okay then," the old woman said, her expression relaxing as, with much cracking and creaking of joints, she knelt beside Darla. "Here, just toss it all back in the box, and I'll reorganize it another time."

They made short work of the cleanup and then regrouped in the living room, where Jake sprawled on the rattan couch. "It's four o'clock now," Jake said with a look at her watch. "Why don't we kick back awhile before we go out to dinner?"

"That will give me a chance to check in with James and catch up on email," Darla agreed.

Nattie nodded as well. "I wouldn't mind resting my eyes for a few minutes."

Since Hamlet made no objection, either, Jake flipped on a movie while Darla and Nattie each retired to their respective rooms. Darla finished unpacking and then set up her laptop on the dresser, dragging over the small cushioned Windsor chair in the corner to sit on.

James already had taken care of most of the store emails. And his message to her regarding the state of the Project, as she had begun thinking of the coffee-bar remodel, was briefer than usual . . . meaning only a single page on the screen.

> You will be interested to know that Mr. Putin himself came in again to supervise the progress today. Even though everything is now plumbed in, he had a few ideas for improving the design. I discussed that with him at length. I did not necessarily agree with all his suggestions; however, he does have the construction expertise, and so I granted him permission to make the below substitutions.

James went on to list the various construction options he'd approved, among them a beveled edge rather than a bullnose for the countertop; bronze trim rather than copper; a U-shaped counter rather than an L-shaped one. He ended with a postscript.

> I made an executive decision and ordered a gross of logo coffee cups, which should arrive sometime next week. While I, myself, would prefer fine china, these utilitarian mugs will be easier to clean and less prone to breakage. Besides which, I find myself agreeing with you regarding the marketing angle. JTJ

Smiling at that last, Darla went back and reread the message. She was tempted to ask him to send her pictures of the job after all, but she resisted the temptation. In matters of taste, she trusted James implicitly; besides which, it was going to be more fun to see the finished project for the first time in person. And so her reply to his message was simply, *Works for me*, followed by three smiley faces.

The second email from James, however, rated frown faces. It was in response to her message the previous night letting him know that Hamlet's debut hadn't gone quite as expected. She'd considered keeping him in the dark about that, at least until their return from Florida, but in the end had decided honesty—or, at least, an approximation of same—was her best bet. With her luck, he would have read something about it online and never forgiven her for saying nothing. And so she'd given him a sanitized version of events, earning the following reply:

> Both Robert and I continue to be concerned about Hamlet's well-being. I trust he is exhibiting no ill effects from his traumatic ordeal. Have the police determined a motive for his kidnapping? Oh, and we hope that Jake is well, too. James.
>
> Postscript: I suspect from the restrained tone of your missive that you have not given me all the details, but you can be assured I will expect a full accounting upon your return. JTJ

She was about to reply to that one, when a third email from her store manager abruptly popped up on her screen. The subject line, in all caps to indicate shouting, read: *WHY DIDN'T YOU MENTION THE MURDER?*

Since the precisely spoken Professor James only lapsed into shouting and the use of contractions when under extreme duress, Darla knew he was pretty ticked off about being kept out of this loop. Wincing, she opened the email to find a series of links to articles in Fort Lauderdale's major daily newspaper, the *Sun Sentinel.* She didn't need to click on them to guess to what news story they led. James's only other comment in the body of the email was: *It is amazing what one can find on the Internet these days by simply Googling an event.*

Darla debated whether she should call him to explain and beg forgiveness, or take the wimp's way out and email her apology. Rationalizing that he was probably busy with customers, she typed out said apology along with an account of what had gone on over the past couple of days.

Conscience temporarily appeased, she finished her other emails and dashed off postcards to her parents and sister in Texas, and to her other sister in Washington State. By the time she was done, it was time to choose something to wear to supper on the patio at the Cuban diner that was also suitable for a poolside memorial service. Luckily, one of the outfits she'd brought was a pair of lightweight black linen pants with a matching black linen top stenciled with turquoise and white fish silhouettes . . . beachy-looking, yet in requisite black.

"Hey, Darla. The bus is leaving," she heard Nattie call from the living room.

Grabbing up her purse and Hamlet's lead, Darla went out to the balcony to get the ornery feline. Apparently, his nap had agreed with him, for Hamlet seemed in an almost playful mood as she snapped on the leash and walked him inside. The short ride to the diner was equally uneventful—at Darla's request, they rode with the top up so as not to frighten Hamlet—and the diner's staff seemed quite pleased to have the feline join the trio at their outdoor table.

They went with the daily special, which was a Cuban sandwich with black beans and rice on the side. The Cuban proved as tasty as Tino had promised. Made with ham, pork, Swiss cheese, pickles, and mustard on Cuban bread, and then flattened and grilled, the traditional sandwich reminded Darla of a panini. Even Hamlet approved, nibbling bits of pork that Darla cut onto a saucer for him. And the mango ice cream they had for dessert made Darla glad her linen pants had an elastic waistband.

By unspoken agreement, they kept the dinner conversation light and away from such topics as murders and arrests. Once back at the condo, Darla set up Hamlet with a buffet of snacks, courtesy of the "kitty bag" that their admiring waiter had pressed on Darla as he presented the check. Leaving him happily gnawing on yet another bit of pork, she went to throw away the takeout container when an argument in the living room between Nattie and Jake stopped her short.

"Seriously, Ma, it's like wearing a long white dress to a wedding. You'll draw attention away from the dearly departed. No way can you wear that to the service."

"That" was a vintage-style picture hat in black straw, trimmed with black veiling, black satin roses, and black velvet ribbons that perched on Nattie's head. It looked like something that Mary Ann might sell in her antique shop, Darla thought in amused admiration, wondering where the old woman had found such a creation. Had Jake worn it, the six-foot-tall PI probably could have pulled off such dramatic headwear with aplomb; but on Nattie, it made her resemble nothing so much as an evil, pixielike mushroom.

"We're in Florida. When else am I gonna wear a hat like this, except a funeral?" Nattie stubbornly demanded. "Besides, look at Darla. She's wearing black."

"Right, but she doesn't look like Morticia Addams heading to the Kentucky Derby," Jake countered. "Darla, you tell her."

"Don't ask me to take sides," Darla said with a smile, raising her hands in a "not touching this" gesture. Then, promptly contracting herself, she added, "But if Nattie thinks she won't be properly dressed for the ceremony without it, then I say she should wear the hat."

"Fine," Jake said, rolling her eyes. "You stand next to her. I'll be in the next county over."

"Thanks, Darla. You know how to treat an old woman with respect," Nattie replied, smiling at Darla and then sticking her tongue out at her daughter. "Are we ready? I want to get a good spot so I can keep an eye on all the potential suspects."

"Give me two minutes to re-pin my hair," Darla told them, "and I'm set."

She went into the guest bath and did a quick restyling before going back into the bedroom for a final check on Hamlet. While she could have taken him down to the pool with her, she suspected it might appear less than respectful should she show up to a memorial service with a cat in tow. Not to mention that she still wasn't sure whether Ted had been Hamlet's catnapper. And in any case, Hamlet could always watch from the balcony if he was truly interested.

He was lounging on the giant pineapple pillow when she walked in, looking more than satisfied after a meal of sliced ham and pork. "This is vacation food only," she warned him. "When we get home, it's back to your usual kibble."

Darla turned to leave, when she noticed something white sticking out from beneath the bed. Apparently, they'd missed one of the far-flung documents that Hamlet had decided to decorate the guest room with.

She bent and picked it up, meaning to put it in the box with the other paperwork she'd packed, only to notice that the letterhead was that of the Lauderdale Tropics Condominium Board Association. She didn't mean to read any farther, except that several phrases were in bold, with a few pertinent words in red. Suddenly feeling uneasy, she read the letter from start to finish.

By the time she reached the final paragraph, her heart was beating faster. And when she read the letter's signature, she felt the Cuban sandwich do a little flip in her stomach. She folded the letter along its original creases, but instead of putting it back into the box, she tucked it into the pocket of her empty suitcase, which was sitting alongside the dresser.

Then she glanced up again to see Hamlet's unblinking green gaze fixed upon her. Could his spilling of the box have been deliberate? He blinked at her, and she heaved deep breath.

"Oh, Hamlet," she softly said. "I think may I know why someone killed Ted Stein."

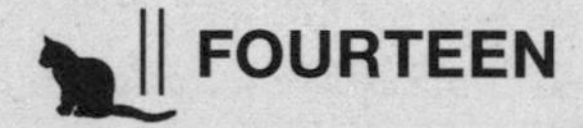

FOURTEEN

HAVING SEEN TED STEIN IN ACTION, DARLA HAD BEEN PREpared for one of those embarrassing memorial services, the kind where the few people who show up are relatives or coworkers who do so simply out of obligation. And maybe to do a little impromptu twerking on his figurative grave. So Darla was surprised to find what appeared to be close to the entire condo population gathered poolside to honor the late Ted Stein.

"Wow," Jake murmured as the three of them walked down a candlelit path to join the somber crowd. "I hope this many people show up for me."

"Yeah, me, too," Darla whispered back. "You think maybe they're serving drinks and appetizers afterward, and that's what everyone is here for?"

Jake glanced at the little poolside tiki hut, devoid of any extraneous items save a lit candle arrangement, and shook her head.

"Cupboard looks bare," she replied in the same low tones. "I guess they're here because they actually liked the guy."

"Eh, they didn't know him like I did," Nattie said, not bothering to lower her voice. Then, when a few others nearby shot her questioning looks, she pulled out a handkerchief and made a show of dabbing at her eyes.

"They didn't know him," she repeated with a dramatic sigh, "and now it's too late. Such a tragedy. I can't believe he's really gone."

"There, there," a man's quavering voice of approval spoke up from behind them. "Don't worry, Nattie. We all feel the same way."

The speaker was the same large old man Darla had seen swimming that morning in the pool. To Darla's great relief, he was now wearing more than just the Speedo. In true snowbird fashion, he had on baggy navy blue shorts and a tight white polo shirt stretched so taut over his stomach she could make out his belly button. Standing beside him in a matching outfit was an old woman of similar girth, though half his height. Her helmet of hair was hennaed the same bright shade as Nattie's.

"Georgie and I, we was just saying how awful it all is," the woman proclaimed in a nasal accent that immediately pegged her as being yet another "New Yawk" transplant. "You're not safe anywhere these days. Me, I carry the pepper spray everywhere I go."

"That's a smart move, Mae. I used to, until one day I didn't have my glasses on and thought it was hairspray." Nattie gave a little cackle; then, obviously recalling where she was, she sobered and went on, "You didn't meet my daughter yet, and her friend."

Nattie handled the quick introductions between them, adding, "That cat of Darla's, he's smart as a whip, and he can even walk on a leash. We'll bring him down to visit you later."

"Attention! Attention, everyone. We're about to begin the service."

The call came from the other side of the tiki bar, where someone had laid a spray of yellow carnations mixed with red snapdragons next to a propped-up poster board. Pinned to it were what looked like a series of Facebook pictures all featuring Ted—red drink cup or beer bottle in hand—hanging with people she assumed were various owners here at the Lauderdale Tropics. A few, she saw, were also of Ted and his Minx cats. Cute as the kittens looked, however, Darla got the vibe that the felines had been strictly business propositions for Ted.

The person who had called everyone to order was a middle-aged woman whose graying hair hung in two long braids. She wore khaki safari shorts topped by a matching short-sleeved jacket. Adding a punch of color to the drab outfit was a large, carved wooden necklace painted in primary colors that glowed in the artificial light.

"Rosalind Marcus," Nattie whispered to her and Jake. "She's on all the committees here. She likes to think she runs things, but she's not even on the board."

Rosalind, meanwhile, raised a hand for silence. Once the crowd settled down so that the only sounds were the rumble of nearby traffic and a chorus of peeping frogs, she began to speak.

"Thank you everyone for coming. We are here this evening to pay tribute to our dear friend, Ted Stein, who was heinously cut down in the prime of life."

She paused dramatically, not needing to speak Billy Pope's name aloud; plenty of the crowd murmured his name for her. Then, lifting a hand again, she continued, "But our purpose tonight is not to cast aspersions on . . . anyone. Instead, we pay homage to a man who worked tirelessly on behalf of his neighbors, looking out for their best interests, often to the detriment of himself."

Rosalind went on in that vein for a couple more minutes,

virtually asking for an "amen" every time she listed another of the man's supposed virtues. All they needed was a documented miracle or two, Darla wryly thought, and Ted could be put up for sainthood, or the rabbinic equivalent thereof.

She glanced over at Jake, whose expression was carefully neutral. Still, it was obvious to Darla that, despite the PI's claim of noninvolvement, she was discreetly gauging the reactions of the various condo owners. Nattie made no such similar pretense of casualness. Instead, her giant hat dipped this way and that as the old woman peered at friends and neighbors.

After finally hitting the five-minute mark—Darla had glanced at her watch when the woman started—Rosalind made a little bow and conceded the floor. "Please, if you have a memory of Ted you'd like to share, speak up."

There was the usual awkward few seconds where everyone waited for someone else to go first. Then an older gentleman in a golf cap and plaid Bermudas raised a hand.

"I'd like to say a few words about old Ted. Sure, he had his way about him, but he was the only board member who stood up for the rest of us. He's the only one who tried to find out what happened to the money that someone took out of our association account."

A general murmur of assent followed that pronouncement. Another old man stepped forward and talked about a weekly golf foursome with Ted. Still another mentioned the monthly cookouts sponsored by the association, which had been instigated by Stein when he joined the board. Then a spindly old woman in a shockingly short pink tennis skirt waved veined fingers.

"Ted took care of my Maltese, Mitzi, when I had to visit my sister in the hospital for a week. And once, when I was late on my monthly association dues, he paid them for me so I wouldn't get fined."

At that last, Darla opened her eyes wide in surprise. Why would Ted Stein have paid this woman's dues? For it had been his signature as board member on the letter Hamlet had snagged that she'd read—a letter threatening to place liens on all condominiums whose owners were in arrears when it came to monthly association fees.

"Oh, yeah?" another voice piped up, this one male. "Well, that son of a gun slapped a lien on my place because I missed *my* dues payment one month while I was on a cruise. He threatened to sell my condo right out from under me! I had to get a lawyer to stop it."

"He brought me cookies when I broke my hip!"

"He said someone else's dog poop was my dog's and made me pick it up!"

"He bought everyone a round of drinks one night at the Divers' Hut!"

"He made me repaint my door; said red wasn't on the approved-color list!"

With that, the somber service promptly devolved into a Team Ted versus Team Not-Ted bit of verbal flurry. Darla prudently retreated behind the tiki bar, hoping the bamboo barrier would keep her out of the way of retirees gone wild. Jake had the same idea, for she grabbed Nattie by the sleeve and pulled her out of harm's reach behind the bar as well.

"People, people!" Rosalind cried over the growing hubbub. "This is a hallowed occasion! Please stop fighting. You know that Ted wouldn't want us to—*STOP!*"

That final shriek was in response to a scrawny, six-foot-tall geezer with a tonsure haircut who had snatched the Ted poster board off the bar top and ripped it into quarters. Then, with a manic grin, the man flung the pieces skyward. As the poster board fluttered into the pool, he stomped off to a chorus of mingled hisses and cheers.

That act of petty vandalism was enough to send half a dozen retirees diving for the flower spray. The winner proved to be a little white-haired woman wearing a daisy print muumuu and compression socks. Before she could carry the flowers off, however, Mitzi the Maltese's pink-skirted owner rushed over. A struggle ensued between the pair until the arrangement they were fighting over erupted in a cascade of blooms that were promptly trampled beneath their sneakered feet.

And then a shrill whistle rent the air, the sound so piercing that Darla slapped her palms over her ears.

She looked around to see Nattie with two fingers in her mouth emitting the kind of whistle made to summon a cab from two blocks away. The high-pitched noise stopped the bickering condo owners in their respective tracks.

"You oughta be ashamed of yerselves," the old woman shouted. "Here, Rosalind tried to do something nice, and yer acting like schoolkids. Now go back to yer condos, all of you."

To Darla's surprise, the scolding worked. Attitudes deflated, and the crowd began to disperse shamefacedly. A few of the more responsible ones stopped first to blow out the candles and toss bits of crushed flowers into the poolside trash bin.

Mae patted Nattie's arm in approval as she walked by. "Good job. Someone needed to give them all a kick in the tush."

"We can always count on you for that," Georgie agreed with nod as he filed past.

Rosalind, still looking a bit shaken and carrying a few carnations that had survived the stampede, stopped long enough to say much the same thing.

"I know you and Ted didn't care much for each other," she added, "but it was good of you to break up that scene. You've got to wonder about people sometimes."

"Yer right, Roz. Me, I just try to do the right thing" was Nattie's pious reply. "Say, looks like we got a vacancy on the board now. Are you thinking about running?"

Linking arms with the woman, Nattie led Rosalind off toward the building, leaving only Darla and Jake remaining behind at the pool.

"And *that* is how you hold a memorial service," Jake said with an appreciative grin. "If mine goes that good, I'll be thrilled. I'll bet our buddy Ted is feeling pretty proud right now."

"Probably," Darla absently agreed, watching the man's floating images being chased about the water by the automatic pool sweeper. "You know, Jake, it seems like he sure stirs up a lot of strong feelings in people. Do you know if Detective Martinez is checking out any of the condo people as possible suspects?"

"I'm sure she's got all the bases covered." Jake gave her a keen look. "Why, did you notice something?"

"Not specifically, but Hamlet turned up something I think points at someone who lives here."

Ignoring Jake's smothered smile—the PI fluctuated between believing in Hamlet's seemingly psychic-kitty skills and dismissing them as coincidence—Darla settled on the pool's top step and pulled off her sandals so she could dangle her bare feet in the water. Jake joined her, casually kicking off her boat shoes to soak her feet in the cool water as well.

While the pool filters gently hummed, Darla explained how Hamlet had knocked down a box of Nattie's papers, revealing the letter written by Ted Stein. On the surface, the missive had seemed merely an impersonal notification of association policy. But reading between the lines, Darla sensed more than a little spiteful bullying at work.

"Something in the way it was worded. It was like he couldn't wait for someone to get in arrears with their payments," she explained with a moue of distaste. "And his signature was this big flourish, like he was almost giddy with excitement at being the one to set the policy. That's what some of the people here tonight were complaining about. He actually threatened to put liens on people's condos if they got behind on their association dues."

Jake raised a dark brow. "So you're saying Ted was the designated hitter, so to speak, for the board?"

"Right. Remember the article about corruption on condominium boards? I wonder if Ted Stein actually got his hands on any units and resold them for a tidy profit. Maybe one of those foreclosed-on condo owners was still holding a grudge."

Jake thought a moment, then grimaced. "Not a bad theory, but how would any of the condo people get into Billy's hotel room to kill Ted? It's not like the good old days when you could swipe a hotel room key off the pegboard." She leaned back on the pebbled concrete. "Those keycards have to be programmed at the front desk, and half the time they get demagnetized when people put them too close to their cell phones and so forth."

"What about Billy's granddaughter, Cindy?" Darla asked. "I saw for myself that she has a thing for threatening people with glass objects. And maybe she didn't like the way Ted tried to blackmail her grandfather. Billy could have given Cindy a key to his room."

Jake shrugged. "Could be, but from what you've told me about her, it seems more likely she'd try to get in on the blackmail action, not put a stop to it."

"How about Alicia?" Darla gave the surface of the pool an idle kick that sent a nearby floating stalk of red snapdragon bobbing. "Remember how she was standing right outside the hotel room when we went to rescue Hamlet? Just because she claimed to be going in doesn't mean we didn't actually catch her leaving after she'd done in Ted." Then, as another thought occurred to her, Darla added, "Oh, and she used to be a 'Pope' before she got married, so that still works for the *Shoes of the Fisherman* book clue."

"Good point."

Jake gave Darla an approving nod as she fished out part of the poster board that had drifted to the shallow end.

"Alicia would be high on the radar for me if this were my case. But sometimes the simplest explanation is the right one. And that pretty well narrows it down to Billy, despite what Ma thinks." Then the PI shook her head. "But we're still missing some of the basic puzzle pieces. We don't know for sure that Ted was the one who attacked me and took Hamlet, and we don't know how he got into Billy's room either."

"So all we really have is a whole bunch of 'don't knows'."

"Exactly.

Darla sighed. "We might as well settle on 'Mrs. Peacock in the library with the candlestick' and be done with it. Tell me again why we're doing this on our vacation?"

"Because you and Ma decided you wanted to play private eye." Groaning, Jake dragged herself upright again and picked up her shoes. "Let's leave the detecting to Sam, okay? We can go back upstairs and stream a Gidget movie or two to get us in the mood for the beach tomorrow."

"Works for me," Darla agreed with a final splash as she also stood and gathered her footwear. Glancing up at the screened balcony, she added, "And I owe Hamlet a walk, too. Let me see how restless he is when we get back upstairs."

They found Hamlet still peacefully snoozing, so Jake did as promised and downloaded the movie via Nattie's surprisingly sophisticated entertainment center. Nattie was already camped out on the sofa. The three of them settled in to watch a lighthearted little beach film, which Darla had never seen before. They'd just reached the part where Gidget hired one of the surf bums as her date to a luau to make Moondoggie jealous, when Hamlet decided he needed an evening walk after all.

"Me-oooow!" he called from where he had planted himself at the front door and was scratching at the panel with his front claws.

"Count on you to wait until I'm all comfortable," Darla grumbled, shooting the cat an aggravated look as he continued to meow and scratch. Finally, she rose from where she'd been curled up in the rattan chair. "Fine, we'll go for a walk, but it's going to be a short one."

"We can pause the movie if you like," Jake volunteered from her own cozy spot on the sofa next to Nattie, raising the remote control in preparation.

Darla shook her head. "That's okay. We won't be gone long."

Hamlet, satisfied that he'd gotten his way, deigned to sit quietly while Darla found his harness and leash, and then fastened them on him. The look he turned on her was angelic as, with a final pat on the door and a little *meow-rumph*, he waited for her to open it. Tapping into her inner Sandra Dee, Darla gave Jake and Nattie the "hang loose" pinkie and thumb wave—made famous by Hawaiians, surfers, and one president—then followed Hamlet out into the hall.

A brief elevator ride later, they were in the lobby. "Pool or driveway?" she asked the cat.

He didn't ponder the question but made an immediate turn toward the front doors. Hoping that Mitzi the Maltese or the old white poodle hadn't chosen this same time to take a potty break, Darla trotted after him and opened the doors.

The fountain splashed before them, its cascading water glowing blue from the underwater lights in each tier. She caught a faint whiff of chlorine, overlaid by the inviting scent of night-blooming jasmine that wafted from somewhere nearby. After the hoopla of the memorial service, it was nice to simply enjoy the South Florida night.

Hamlet seemed pleased with their little jaunt as well, trotting down the lighted drive with his black tail streaming behind him like a banner. Occasionally he stopped to sniff the night air, perhaps catching the scent of a Florida mouse on a night mission. It was cooler out now, but Darla didn't mind the faint chill. Apparently, she'd been in New York long enough that temperatures in the fifties constituted shorts weather, she thought in amusement.

Hamlet trotted over to the nearest patch of lawn,

springing back with cat surprise when an equally startled toad hopped away from the spot he'd been sniffing. He would have pursued it, but Darla gave a firm tug on the leash.

"No toads, Hammy. I overheard some of the people at the cat show talking about a nasty little toad species here in Florida that's deadly poisonous to animals who lick them."

Hamlet shot her a disappointed look but seemed to understand that amphibians were verboten. Still in search of adventure, however, he made a detour up a secondary drive. This one led from the showy circular driveway to the rear of the property, dead-ending at the condo building's single-level covered parking structure. The drive ran parallel, first to the building and then to the waist-high stone planter spilling over with broad-leaved tropical plants that separated condo traffic from the rear landscaping. The wrought-iron fence a few yards on the other side of the planter wall was the same fence that enclosed the pool where the ill-fated memorial had been held. Even at a distance, Darla could see in the blue-lit water the remains of the poster and a couple of blooms that still swirled there like garnish in an oversized cocktail glass.

For safety's sake, Darla coaxed Hamlet from the driveway onto the grass, though the uneven ground along the fence was not quite as conducive to walking.

Could use a few lights out here, Darla groused to herself as the toe of her sneaker caught on a protruding stone, almost tripping her. Hamlet, with his feline night vision, had no such difficulty and kept a steady pace going. Once or twice, he glanced back her way as if to say, *Pitiful human, can't you keep up?*

They had not gone far, however, when a movement from the corner of her eye drew Darla's attention. She glanced toward the pool again to see that someone—a woman—was walking around out there, carrying what appeared to be a cardboard box the size of an old-style computer monitor.

The newcomer looked up just then, light glinting off a pair of steel-rimmed glasses. It was Nattie's friend, Mildred.

Pleased, Darla gave her a little wave. She started to call out to the woman when Hamlet abruptly leaped in front of Darla as if pouncing on another toad.

Momentarily distracted, she checked to see that the feline hadn't caught some critter he shouldn't have. When she looked up again, Mildred had left the gated pool area and was moving toward the drive.

At first, Darla was certain the woman must have seen her and Hamlet standing there in the shadows. Then she realized the old woman's attention was focused on the parking garage. And something almost furtive in her body language made Darla hesitate to hail her now.

Scooping up Hamlet, Darla shrank back farther into the shadows. She watched as Mildred, still cradling her box, made her way through a gap in the wall and walked into the parking garage.

Hamlet began to struggle in her grasp, a sure sign he wanted down. Darla complied, reminding herself it was none of her business what Mildred was doing. Chances were the building's trash container was located nearby, and the woman was simply throwing something away. Still, given the strange events of the past few days, Darla knew she wouldn't be able to sleep that night if she didn't satisfy her curiosity.

Hamlet was already ahead of her on this plan. Crouching like a panther on the prowl, he moved forward toward the parking garage, putting one soft paw in front of the other without rustling a single blade of grass. Holding on to his leash, Darla trailed after him. She could see Mildred simply standing there, box still in her arms as she surveyed the half-empty structure.

Probably just throwing out some trash, she inwardly repeated. Though, if that were the case, why was she lingering there in an empty parking spot? And then a set of headlights a few rows from her blinked twice.

FIFTEEN

A SIGNAL?

Sure enough, Mildred started toward the car that had flashed its lights. Darla took a deep breath and then looked down at Hamlet. "Come on," she whispered. "Let's see what old Mildred is up to."

Hamlet gave a soft *meow-rumph* and led the way. Keeping to the shadows, Darla reached the parking structure as Mildred paused beside a rusty blue Volkswagen Beetle that had duct tape patching its torn cloth top. The driver had left the vehicle running, and even Darla's nonexpert ears could tell the Bug needed a tune-up. Not the sort of car the condo folks regularly drove, she noted, spying several dozen high-end automobiles parked in owners' slots.

Darla crouched lower and moved still closer. She was relieved that Mildred and the VW had chosen to meet in an illuminated spot; standing as she was in shadow, Darla knew she would be less visible to them. Hamlet, small in profile and already camouflaged in black fur, had no such worries.

Darla was a row away when the driver abruptly shut off the engine and opened the door, while Mildred handed over the box. Then Mildred turned and scampered back toward the pool area again before Darla ever got a glimpse of the driver.

Drat!

Darla hesitated, then slid a couple of more cars down the row until she was directly opposite the VW. Staring through the windows of a lower-end Lexus, Darla had a clear view of her target. Unfortunately, the driver was bent over the passenger seat so Darla still couldn't see the person's face.

Then two things happened almost simultaneously. The driver straightened, revealing herself to be a young woman with bleached-blond hair—Alicia's daughter, Cindy. At the same time, Darla heard a tiny but distinct *meow* emanate from the battered Beetle, the sound causing Hamlet's ears to flick curiously. The girl fired up her car and backed out of the parking spot. As she maneuvered around, Darla made a crouched sprint to the end of her row, arriving just in time to see the VW pass by.

"Darn it, Cindy's gone," she whispered to Hamlet, who appeared tired now of playing spy and was sniffing an interesting twig. The odd cat exchange she'd witnessed had to mean something . . . but what, she had no idea. Her best bet would be to brainstorm the situation with Jake later that night, after Nattie was asleep.

But when Darla opened the door to the condo, she saw that the conversation was going to have to be put off for quite a different reason: Mildred herself was sitting on the rattan sofa, looking comfortable and prepared to stay awhile. And there was no sign of Jake or Nattie.

"Hello, dear," the woman said with a friendly wave and a smile revealing the ever-present spot of pink lipstick. "I just popped in to ask Nattie about the memorial service. I see you and Hamlet have been out and about?"

Darla managed a smile and a wave back before leaning down to unbuckle Hamlet. The cat leaped onto the rattan chair and gave the old woman a baleful look, not even bothering to pretend disinterest. Darla could only hope that Mildred didn't question this obvious feline snub too closely.

"Oh, we just made a quick run outside so Hamlet could stretch his legs. Out front, to the fountain," she added, to make sure Mildred would have no reason to wonder if they'd been prowling around near the pool. "Where are Jake and Nattie?"

"Jake ran off to the powder room, and Nattie wants to show me some kind of trick, though I must confess I'm not certain this is a good idea."

"Eh, don't be a stick-in-the-mud, Millie," Nattie said as she came from the hallway dragging a large ironing board with a pink-flowered cover.

She propped it against the archway between dining and living room areas. As Darla watched in growing confusion, the old woman pulled one of the straight-backed dining chairs into the middle of the living room. Then she reached for the ironing board and laid it across the chair seat. A third of the ironing board overhung front and back, like a floral teeter-totter.

"Gidget did this on her bed," Nattie explained to Mildred as she gripped the seatback and hiked one foot up onto the makeshift surfboard, "but I think this will work better on a chair. It'll be more like real surfing, don't ya think?"

"Ma, get down and put the ironing board away before you hurt yourself!"

This from Jake, who stood at the hall doorway staring in horror at her mother. Nattie left her foot where it was and shot her daughter a peeved look. "You won't let me take a surfing lesson, so this is the closest I'll ever get to trying it," she said, and hopped up onto the center of the ironing board.

"See? I'm surfing," Nattie said, gaining her balance and striking a pose with arms flung wide. But her triumph lasted only a moment, as the ironing board began to wobble precariously.

Darla gasped and started toward her, and even Mildred sprang up from her seat. Jake, however, was faster than both of them. She grabbed Nattie just in time to prevent the old woman from taking a nasty tumble.

"Down," Jake demanded once Nattie regained her balancc. Shc continucd to hold on to hcr mother's arm until Nattie reluctantly clambered off her ersatz surfboard.

"Eh, I almost had it," the old woman said with very un-Gidgetlike snort. "I just need a little more practice."

"Practice, my rear end. You try that stunt again and break a hip, and I swear I'll put you in a nursing home."

"Why don't you ever want me to have any fun? I might be old, but that don't mean I'm dead," Nattie declared. "And Mildred was a gymnast. I bet she can do it."

"Oh, I'm sure I can," the other woman said with a smile and duck of her head, so that the overhead light flickered off her glasses. "But I always work with a spotter. And I'm sorry, Jake, but I really didn't think she'd try it."

"Not your fault, Mildred," Jake answered, giving her mother a stern look. "Now, why don't we all sit down and watch the rest of the movie like grownups."

"Oh, I can't stay," Mildred replied with a flutter of her hands. "As I told Darla, I just wanted to ask Nattie how the memorial gathering went."

"Hoo-boy, it was a doozy! And I even got some of it on video," Nattie declared with a grin, pulling her phone from her pants pocket and waving it in delight. "How about we get together in the morning and I tell you all about it?"

Mildred brightened. "Actually, the formal memorial for Ted is tomorrow morning at a synagogue in West Palm Beach. Do you want to come with me and tell me about it on the way?"

"Sure, that would be great fun. I haven't been to a good memorial in at least a month." Then, when Darla and Jake both stared at her in dismay, she added, "What? You get to my age and you'll like going to these things, too. It's like a game, seeing how many people you outlive."

Unsure whether to laugh or be horrified, Darla merely shook her head. As for Jake, she gave a longsuffering sigh.

"Ma, I thought you were going shell hunting on the beach early in the morning with me and Darla."

"Eh, I've got seashells out the patoot. You girls go, and when Millie and I get back, we'll drive around town and see the sights."

"I'll come over at nine o'clock and get you so we can be there early for good seats," Mildred agreed.

Nattie walked her to the door, the "surfing lesson" forgotten in her glee over Ted Stein's upcoming memorial. Jake shook her head and put the ironing board back herself, while Darla returned the chair to the table. Hamlet kept a cool green gaze fixed on everyone until Mildred was gone; then he jumped down from the chair again and slipped like a black shadow back into the guest room.

By the time the final credits rolled on the big-screen television, Darla had come up with a subterfuge to get Jake alone. . . . She'd say she lost a tag off Hamlet's harness during their walk and needed Jake's help outside to find it.

Fortunately, Nattie saved her the trouble, declaring, "I need to get my beauty sleep if I'm going to make that memorial in the morning. How about you girls lock up for me?"

"Will do, Ma. Sleep tight."

Jake waited until Nattie had disappeared down the hall, and the faint sound of running water came from the master suite, before she turned to Darla.

"All right, kid. You've been twitching like Hamlet's tail ever since you got back from that walk. What's going on?"

Darla gave a sheepish smile. "Sorry, I thought I was being pretty subtle. I hope your mother didn't notice anything."

"She only notices things when it suits her. Now go ahead—spill."

Darla needed no further encouragement to relate what she'd seen with Mildred, Cindy, and the mysterious box. Jake asked no questions, though her expression went from concerned to perplexed as Darla described the final, incriminating meow she had heard.

"I don't get it," the PI said when Darla finished. "Maybe some sort of clandestine rescue thing going on? Could it have been Ted's Minx cat?"

"I guess that's a possibility," Darla agreed. "But I think Ted's sister was going to take his cat. And Mildred was so . . . so sneaky about it. Maybe they're dealing in stolen champion cats?"

Jake gave her a slanted look. "What, you think Cindy is selling blue-ribbon kitties in some back alley to support her drug habit? And Mildred gets a cut of the action, too?"

"Well; when you put it like that . . ."

Darla trailed off with a reluctant smile and shook her head. "Okay, I agree. I probably overreacted. Chances are whatever happened between Cindy and Mildred was perfectly innocent."

"Don't worry, kid. Enough hinky stuff has been going on these past few days that I don't blame you for thinking the worst."

"Thanks. But speaking of hinky stuff, do you think Detective Martinez is any closer to figuring out who killed Ted Stein . . . and who hit you and stole Hamlet?"

Jake shrugged. "It's not like back home, where I'm still part of the good old blue rumor mill. But I'll put in a call to Sam in the morning, see if she's made any progress on the case. Besides," she added as she reached into her pocket and pulled out her own phone, "Ma's not the only one who did a little clandestine filming during the memorial service. I figure after we do our shell hunting in the morning that we meet up with Sam and show this to her."

"SERIOUSLY, DARLA, ARE YOU PLANNING ON CARRYING THAT WHOLE BAG of seashells back to Brooklyn?" Jake asked the next morning as they packed up their towels and other gear after a couple of hours on the beach.

Nattie had been the first to head out from the condo—wearing her funeral chapeau, as Jake had dubbed the flamboyant black hat—and had departed with Mildred for Ted Stein's official memorial. Once she'd left, Darla and Jake had thrown on their swimsuits and borrowed some of Nattie's beach gear before absconding in her Mini Cooper in search of sun and surf. Darla had left Hamlet behind at the condo contentedly lounging on the balcony and catching some rays.

Now, Darla looked down at the bulging plastic grocery bag she'd been diligently filling all morning. Her best find had been what another shell hunter had told her was a Scotch bonnet. Slightly larger than Hamlet's paw but cream colored and accented with rows of tan, rectangular splotches, it was a petite, sleek little cousin to those giant conchs whose pink-mouthed selves gaped from the shelves of every local gift shop.

"You're right. Once I got them home, they'd probably just sit in a box somewhere, anyhow," Darla said, pulling the Scotch bonnet out as a keeper. She handed the rest of her morning's collection off to a couple of nearby grade-schoolers who were delighted to add her shells to their collection.

She tucked the empty bag into her tote to properly dispose of later—a lifeguard had warned her that turtles frequently mistook floating grocery bags for their favorite food, the moon jellyfish, and swallowed them with often fatal results. Then she reached for the sleeveless, green batik tank dress that she was using as a cover-up and pulled it on over her pale green two-piece. Given that she had a redhead's typical fair complexion, which freckled and burned rather than tanned, Darla had slathered on plenty of sunscreen even though the sun hadn't reached its peak.

Jake, with her olive skin, had no such similar worry, not even bothering with a ball cap like Darla wore to keep the sun off her face. The older woman had gone for a classic black maillot, halter-strapped and ruched. On anyone else the suit might have looked frumpy, but Jake gave it a distinct bad-girl vibe, probably because the high-cut legs showed off the unmistakable scar that ran like a thin purple lightning bolt from hip to halfway down her thigh.

This was the first time that Darla had ever seen evidence of the woman's career-ending injury, though she'd watched Jake set off the metal detector at the airport security checkpoint because of the various pins in her leg. Jake caught her glancing at it and shrugged.

"Guess it kind of ruins my chances of a career in nude modeling," she said with a smile, "but compared to some of those nasty chest scars I've seen on the cops who've had open-heart surgery, this is nothing. But I've been thinking about maybe getting it tattooed . . . you know, turn the scar into a snake or a flower vine or something."

"Sure, why not? That could be interesting," Darla agreed. She wasn't keen on tattoos for herself, but she could appreciate the artistry in some of the more elaborate examples of body art.

"Maybe when we get back home."

"Well, whatever you do, don't get a tattoo while you're down here. You'll only encourage your mother to want a battleship inked on her chest," Darla said with a chuckle. "Speaking of Nattie, I've been meaning to ask—she seems like a typical Italian mom, right? So why in the heck did she name you Jacqueline, and not something like Isabella or Giovanna? I mean, Jacqueline is a lovely name, but it's not Italian. It's French."

"So was my grandmother," Jake explained with a smile.

"Ma named me after her mother, Jacqueline Prevot. That was my cross to bear in the old neighborhood, being a quarter French. On the bright side, though, I got a double dose of the foodie gene."

"Right. So how come I'm the one who always has to count calories?" Darla good-naturedly complained.

Jake laughed as she stuck her magazine into her woven red beach bag and then pulled out a matching red sarong. She wrapped and tied the textured cloth around her into a respectable-looking sundress. "All right, let's go. Sam's meeting us over at the restaurant in about ten minutes."

They set off the few yards up the beach to the wooden steps that would take them back up to the parking lot. Darla noticed that, without the benefit of her customary boots, Jake was limping more than usual through the uneven sand. That, in turn, reminded her of Trixie the three-legged rescue cat. They'd need a plan to pick Trixie up on Saturday.

Tossing their gear into the back of the Mini, they made the five-minute trip to the Porto del Sol diner. A ramshackle, tin-roofed wood structure about a block from the water, the restaurant was perched on short stilts. It featured a mural of boats docked beneath a blazing sun that illustrated the diner's name, though in Darla's opinion, the artist had had more enthusiasm than talent.

Jake agreed, it seemed.

"Either that's a brilliantly ironic example of South Florida primitivism," she said, "or else the owner saved himself some cash by having his kids paint the place for him."

"I'm betting on the kids, but I kind of like it," Darla said with a smile. "Maybe I should do something similar at the bookstore."

Leaving the mural behind, they walked around back and spied Detective Martinez at one of the painted white picnic tables on the deck. Once again, the detective was wearing a sober black pantsuit. This time, however, it was enlivened by a yellow blouse the same sunny hue as the tiny coffee cup on the table before her. Since it was almost noon, the remaining tables on the deck were all occupied, but only Martinez sat with her back to the distant view of the water, sunglasses pushed up on her head while she rapidly typed on her cell phone. She looked up as they approached, however, and gestured them to join her.

"So what's this about a brawl at Stein's memorial service?" she asked without preamble.

"It was more of a spirited discussion," Jake replied as she and Darla took the seats at her table, facing the water.

She pulled out her own phone from the red beach bag. "I only caught a couple of minutes of the action, but it gives you the gist of what was going on."

Jake pressed play and handed the phone to Martinez. The volume was turned up, so that Darla could hear a murmur of recorded conversation that she guessed was Rosalind. Next followed the sound of tiny shouted voices, as the pro-Ted and anti-Ted factions began to rally. She saw Martinez raise a brow, probably when the one old man had ripped apart the poster and flung it into the pool. The video lasted only a few moments longer after that and then cut off.

Martinez nodded and handed the phone back to Jake. "Mind emailing this to me? We're looking in another direction on this case, and your video might be useful."

While Jake typed out the email, Darla asked in surprise, "Another direction? Does that mean Billy Pope isn't under arrest anymore?"

Before the detective could answer, an excessively tanned waitress in cutoff blue jeans and a denim halter top that barely contained her assets sidled up with menus. Her entire right arm had been tattooed with all manner of flowers and skulls—a sleeve, as Darla had heard it described—and her black hair had a wide streak of turquoise in it.

Darla initially guessed the woman to be in her midforties despite her rebellious appearance . . . and then downgraded it by a decade when she spotted the year emblazoned on her class ring. Obviously, there was at least one major disadvantage to living in a semitropical climate. Still, the waitress's smile was warm as she asked, "You ladies need a little Cuban coffee to get started with?"

Darla and Jake exchanged glances before Darla nodded. "Since I've got that coffee bar going in at the bookstore, I might as well work on expanding my own coffee horizons."

"Two cups, coming right up," the woman replied, leaving behind the menus and sauntering back inside.

Jake, meanwhile, picked up where Darla had left off. "So, what's the word, Sam? Is Pope really off the hook for Stein's murder?"

The detective reached for her tiny yellow cup and slanted them both a cool look from over her coffee. "That decision hasn't been made yet."

"I've got to think the motive is pretty thin. You're not convinced Pope did it, are you?"

Martinez took a sip of her coffee. "I didn't say that."

"You didn't have to. There's someone else you're looking at, right?"

"Maybe."

The detective finished her coffee but played with the tiny cup a moment, rolling it between her palms as she seemed to consider her next words. Before she could speak again, however, the waitress once again interrupted them as she returned to the table bearing two more demitasse-sized cups.

"Two Cuban coffees," she cheerfully announced. She set a white cup with green and orange stripes on it before Darla, and a navy blue cup with what looked like a melted red heart on it in front of Jake.

The few ounces of coffee the cup held were dark like espresso with a hint of foaminess. Jake slugged hers down in a couple of gulps. Darla, however, decided that her cup deserved the wine-tasting approach. She took an experimental sniff and caught a whiff of what smelled like burnt socks.

Maybe Cuban coffee wasn't all she'd heard it to be. Steeling herself, she took a cautious sip, and then promptly changed her mind. The steaming coffee was strong and incredibly sweet, with just enough complexity of flavor that she had no choice but to take another taste.

Seeing her reaction, the waitress smiled.

"First time, huh? The stuff's addicting, and it'll get you through the day better than those little bottles of energy drink you buy at the convenience store. Now, can I get you ladies lunch?"

At Martinez's suggestion, Jake went for the blackened dolphin tacos—which, the waitress clarified, meant dolphin fish a.k.a. mahi mahi, and not Flipper or one of his porpoise friends. Relieved to have that misunderstanding cleared up, Darla decided to order the same thing. Once the waitress was out of earshot again, Jake returned the conversation to the subject at hand.

"Not to go off on a tangent," she said, "but Darla witnessed something else last night that might have some connection to all this."

When Jake nodded at her to take it from there, Darla gave the detective a brief explanation of the exchange she'd seen between Mildred and Cindy in the parking garage.

At Jake's first words, Martinez had pulled out a small notepad. Now, she jotted down a few lines as she listened to Darla's account.

"Interesting," she agreed when Darla finished, "but for the moment I'm not sure how it ties into Stein, if at all."

Jake shrugged. "All right, Sam, it's pretty obvious that something's up. Why don't you use us as a sounding board? We've kind of got a vested interest in figuring this thing out, too," she added, putting a fleeting hand to the back of her head.

Nice touch, Darla thought in approval. Martinez seemed to register the gesture, though she furrowed her brow a little as she glanced Darla's way. Noticing her unconvinced look, Jake hurried to reassure the detective.

"Don't worry about Darla. She's had more experience with this sort of thing than the average civilian."

Expression still skeptical, Martinez nodded. "Fine, I'll take a shot. What do you two know about the Minx Connection?"

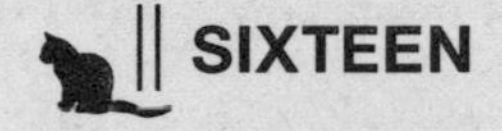

SIXTEEN

"THE MINX CONNECTION?"

Darla took another sip of coffee as she attempted to keep a straight face. *That's* what Stein called his cat breeding business? A little too precious for her tastes.

"It's what you get when you cross a Sphynx cat with a Manx," Darla offered, trying not to sound smug. "They're tailless and have fuzz instead of fur. Ted Stein was trying to promote the Minx as a new breed. And he was pretty ticked off when his cat didn't win its division at the cat show."

Jake seemed to be biting back a smile, too. "Yeah, Ma said that Billy Pope claimed it was just some sort of get-rich-quick scheme that Stein came up with, multilevel marketing with pets. But the cats were real enough."

Martinez shook her head and gave an inelegant snort.

"Good try, ladies, but no cigar. The late Mr. Stein had a scheme going, all right, but it wasn't only cats."

When Darla and Jake gave her a puzzled look, Martinez cleared her throat. "He was recruiting, ah, talent over at the local college and then advertising their 'services'"—she gave that last word air quotes—"online. He provided the empty condo and basically paid them by the hour. We had a warrant to search his place, and we turned up a nice paperwork trail. Could be he was using this cat-breeding business as a cover story in case the IRS or the bank questioned him."

"Wait," Darla interrupted. She'd obviously missed something here. "Exactly what kind of business was it you say Ted Stein was running?"

"Prostitution," Jake explained, her tone now one of disgust. "Ted Stein was nothing more than a pimp in cat breeder's clothing. Right, Sam?"

"You're kidding!" Darla choked out as the detective nodded. "Sure, I thought the guy was kind of skeevy, but to be involved in something like that . . ."

"Oh, that's only the tip of the iceberg," Martinez coolly assured them. "We're still putting the pieces together, but it's starting to look like some of that prostitution money was being laundered through your mother's condo association. And there's a good chance some of that missing money you told me about was being skimmed from the account at the same time. By the end of the day we should be bringing in the person who we suspect was Stein's silent partner."

"Sounds like Stein was an ambitious little perv," Jake observed. Then she asked the question Darla had been waiting for. "So who's the silent partner?"

The detective shook her head. "Sorry, I can't tell you. But let's just say that, at this point, Billy Pope is probably the least likely person at the Lauderdale Tropics condo association who might have wanted to see Ted Stein dead."

Before Darla could pounce on that one, the waitress showed up with their fish tacos, along with a greasy white paper bag that she set before Martinez. "Got your usual in there, Sam."

"Thanks, Farrah," the detective said, rising from the picnic table and reaching for the sack. "Tell my brother I said hi."

"Will do. Come over and see the baby sometime, okay?"

"If I can ever manage a day off, I will."

As Farrah sauntered off, Martinez slid her sunglasses back down onto her nose and gave Darla and Jake a final look. "Sorry, ladies. Gotta run," she said, indicating the bag. "If you hear any more interesting rumblings down at the condo complex, you know how to get hold of me."

Jake raised her cell phone and nodded. "We've got you covered."

Darla waited until the detective had disappeared around the corner of the restaurant before saying, "I wonder why she wanted to see your video. She said they were working on an arrest warrant, so it's not like she was still trying to find a suspect."

Jake shrugged and reached for a fish taco. "Maybe their case isn't as airtight as she'd like it to be. Maybe she thought something might show up in the video that could help. Or maybe she just wanted to know what we knew, and this was a good excuse to rope us back in."

Darla would have replied, except that she'd already taken a large bite from one of her own tacos. Rather than the lettuce, tomato, and cheese that topped a regular Tex-Mex beef taco, these flour tortillas filled with chunks of blackened mahi were stuffed with avocado, mango, and coleslaw. With a side of black beans and rice, Darla was in culinary heaven.

"So who do you think this new suspect is?" she finally asked once she could speak again. "I mean, after seeing how everyone reacted at the memorial service last night, I'd say there's probably a long list just of condo owners."

Jake reached for taco number two and shrugged.

"Not our problem, remember?" she said around a mouthful of blackened dolphin. "But what went down at the cat show is. So after I finish eating, I'm going to put in a call to Johnston and see if they've made any progress on the assault and catnapping. It would be nice to know that someone has been arrested for putting a kink in our vacation."

"Kink" seemed a mild way to describe the murder and mayhem that had punctuated their stay in Fort Lauderdale, Darla told herself as she picked up her second taco. Still, Detective Martinez seemed every bit as capable as Jake, while the other two officers had been professional and thorough in their investigations. If any of the week's crimes could be solved, surely that trio would do it.

They made short work of the remaining food. A few minutes later, Jake pushed away her plate with a satisfied groan and pulled out her phone, along with a business card with the local PD's logo on it.

"Fingers crossed," she said as she punched in the numbers.

The call went to voice mail, so Jake left a message asking about any progress on her assault case and the cat theft, rattling off the case number. "Would you call me when you can with an update?" She gave her cell number and then hung up.

Darla, meanwhile, signaled for the check and realized guiltily that she hadn't saved any of her fish tacos to take back for Hamlet. Though the feline had started out eating only kibble under her care, at some point bringing Hamlet a "kitty bag" had become a ritual for Darla whenever dining out. No doubt there'd be some cat sulking for a while when they returned.

Which meant they'd simply have to come back another time, Darla decided in satisfaction, already eager for a second round. She'd check on the way out to learn if pets were allowed on the deck.

When they returned to the condo, however, Darla found Hamlet crouched on the living room floor happily gnawing on what appeared to be a slice of pepperoni, as Nattie looked on indulgently from the rattan sofa. She was dressed in a black-and-white summer pantsuit, her gaudy black hat safely perched atop the dining table. And on the coffee table before her was the source of Hamlet's current bounty: a small paper plate heaped with cold cuts and cheese and topped with three pink-iced petit fours.

"Jeez, Ma, did you really raid the buffet table at a memorial service?"

Nattie gave an innocent blink that reminded Darla of Hamlet's "good kitty" expression. "They had tons of food. It woulda gone to waste if I left it there. Even Mildred agreed. Besides, that rabbi guy took a bigger plate than mine."

"Ma, if the man was officiating, I'm sure the family asked him to take a nice big plate home as a courtesy. That didn't mean everyone else was supposed to load up like that."

Despite her dismayed tone, however, Jake reached for one of the petit fours. When she caught Darla smiling, the PI shrugged.

"Hey, now that the deed is done, no point in letting good food go to waste," she replied before taking an appreciative bite of the confection.

"Good point," Darla replied and took one of the petit fours herself. After a taste, she added, "Heck, Nattie, you should have loaded up on more dessert instead of all the healthy stuff. These little cakes are heavenly."

"Eh, gotta watch my weight," Nattie answered and patted her small belly bulge. "So how was the beach, girls?"

"Nice, Ma. Lots of sand. How was the memorial service?"

"Nice." Then, when Jake gave her a sharp look, Nattie added, "Lots of people."

Darla gave her a considering look. In the short time she'd known the old woman, Darla had discovered that Nattie never passed up the chance for a gossip. And what better place to dig up a little dirt than when people had gathered to eulogize one of their own? She would have bet Hamlet's stash of catnip that Nattie was keeping quiet about something.

Jake was obviously thinking along the same lines, but

she took a different tack. Reaching for a couple of cubes of cheddar—*How in the heck does Jake not gain weight with all her snacking?* Darla wondered yet again—Jake assumed a "good kitty" expression of her own.

"Guess what, Ma? We ran into Detective Martinez over at the Porto del Sol diner. Keep this under your hat, but she's having second thoughts about Billy Pope's involvement with Ted Stein's murder."

Nattie snorted. "Well, it's about time. I coulda told her from the start that Billy had nothing to do with it. I *did* tell her."

"Well, looks like you were right. But Sam mentioned something else . . . something called the Minx Connection. Ever hear of it?"

"I think that's what Ted called his so-called cattery where he bred those poor Minx kittens. What, is the Humane Society after him now, too?"

"I don't know. It was just something she mentioned," Jake lied, flashing Darla a look that she interpreted to mean, *Fishing expedition, kid . . . Don't say anything.*

Darla gave her a swift nod of understanding, pretty certain the old woman knew nothing about Ted Stein's alleged prostitution ring. There was no way Nattie would have kept quiet about something like that if she'd suspected it. And since she was already dismayed over her friend's situation, no reason to upset her with more unpleasantness.

But that still didn't explain why Nattie was being evasive about the memorial service.

"Say, girls, are we still going shopping this afternoon?" the old woman mumbled around the petit four she'd popped into her mouth. Standing, she tossed Hamlet a final piece of pepperoni and picked up the plate. "I wanna rest up after that long trip up and back from West Palm—but I'll be raring to go in an hour or so."

"Sure, Ma," Jake answered with a sharp look after the old woman, who'd trotted off to the kitchen with her spoils.

"I'm going to take a shower and wash the salt off. I'm sure Darla will want to do the same. So just kick back for a while, why don't you?"

To Darla, she quietly added, "Do me a favor, kid, and chat her up about the memorial service while I'm in the shower. Something's going on in that beady little brain of hers, and we probably need to know what it is."

Darla nodded. Nattie had returned from the kitchen munching on a cube of Swiss this time. Darla sat on the rattan chair and picked up Hamlet's kitty wand, which he'd apparently dragged out in their absence. Flicking it back and forth for him, she brightly told Nattie, "The Porto del Sol was wonderful. I'm now a convert to fish tacos. How about you?"

"I'm not much for that fancy-pantsy food. Give me a nice lasagna, though, and now yer talking."

"Well, it looks like the food at the memorial service was pretty darned good. I wonder who catered?"

"Eh, who cares?"

Nattie paused and glanced toward the hallway. The sound of the running shower from the master bath was faintly audible.

"I didn't want to say anything in front of Jacqueline," she went on in a lower tone, "but that memorial service, it was a bust. The only good thing about it was the food."

"You mean no one flung flowers around?" Darla asked with a smile.

Nattie grinned back. "Hey, it woulda put some life into the service. I about fell asleep listening to all these people talking about what a good guy Ted Stein was. Oh, and get this—Alicia Timpson was there, snuffling into her hankie like he was her late husband or something. You'da thought she'd be more worried about her own father."

Alicia Timpson, mourning Ted? Yet hadn't she claimed that she barely knew the man?

While Darla was pondering that, Nattie went on, "I tell

you, that Ted, he was a Class-A jerk. It's all true about him putting liens on people's condos. Why, he even tried to foreclose on Millie when her pension check got stolen outta her mailbox one month and she was late paying her association fee. Me, I got mine set up so it comes outta the bank automatic, but I caught them one time charging me twice. It took me complaining to Billy to get it fixed."

"Well, maybe with him gone, that will put an end to the problems," Darla absently commiserated, even as she continued to muse over the Alicia-Ted connection. "Maybe once everything is settled about his murder, the condo association members can have the books audited once and for all."

Though if someone else—perhaps the Martini Lady herself!—had been a partner in Ted Stein's crimes, as Martinez had suggested, then stuff was about to hit the fan.

They chatted a bit about the proposed shopping expedition until Jake returned, dressed now in red capris and a nubby white cotton sweater that came down to her hips. She was blotting her curly hair with a fluffy pink towel.

"Plenty of hot water left," she said to Darla. "Ma and I will chat while you get your shower, and then we can figure out where we want to go."

Once in the shower, Darla washed a salt shaker's worth of salt from her hair and as much sand from various crevices and crannies. Fifteen minutes later she was clean, dressed in blue denim crop pants and a Hawaiian top with a towel wrapped around her head, realizing that she hadn't put on as much sunscreen as she'd thought.

"Ugh, sunburn," she declared as she gingerly made her way back into the living room, where the other two women waited. "I didn't realize I got that much sun until the shower got hot."

"Keep in mind yer in the tropics," Nattie told her. "That sun can be a real killer, even in winter. I'll get ya some aloe gel from my bathroom."

She hopped up without waiting for Darla's response and

headed toward her bedroom. Jake waited until she'd disappeared down the hall to softly ask, "You get anything out of her about the memorial service?"

Darla shrugged. "Maybe. Food was good, but all anyone did was talk nicely about Ted. The only really interesting thing was that Alicia Timpson was apparently mourner-in-chief."

"Great, put her back to the top of the suspect list," Jake muttered, but by then Nattie had returned carrying a clear plastic jug filled with bright green gel and topped with a plunger.

"Here ya go, Darla. It's the economy size. I bought it at one of those membership clubs."

With the sunburn starting to sting in earnest, Darla gratefully pumped a handful of gel and began slathering it on all exposed skin. Hamlet, who had been lounging beneath the coffee table washing up after his second slice of pepperoni, gave her a curious look through the glass. Then, with a blink of his green eyes that seemed to say, *Humans—can't even bathe correctly*, he returned to his ablutions.

Jake, meanwhile, had pulled out her phone and was paging through a few screens. "This app shows the supposedly best shopping in the downtown Fort Lauderdale area. But our big question is, are we going to be looky-loos, or do we intend to buy?"

"Both," Darla and Nattie chorused, and then smiled at each other.

"Works for me," Jake agreed. "I'm going to check off a few stores here, plus if Ma has any she wants to add to the list, we can—"

"Beautiful dreamer, wake unto me," a man's saccharine voice trilled from the vicinity of the kitchen, cutting Jake short.

Startled by the unexpected music, Darla looked around for the radio, until she realized she was hearing a ring tone. "Starlight and dewdrops are waiting for thee." Apparently, both generations of Martellis had a penchant for downloading corny songs to their respective phones. And if she wasn't mistaken, the singer on this one was none other than Roy Orbison.

Nattie, meanwhile, leaped from her chair.

"Oops, that's mine," she said and trotted to the kitchen, where her cell phone lay plugged in on the countertop.

Darla heard her answer with a "Hello?" promptly followed by a merry-sounding "Oh, hello."

"Sounds like Gidget has a boyfriend," Jake murmured. "Too bad there's not an extension where we could listen in."

Darla snickered, but her amusement swiftly faded as she heard the old woman say, "No," in a sharp voice that lacked any hint of flirtation. Jake must have caught it, too, for she looked up from her phone and stared toward the kitchen.

"No. Yes. Yes. No. All right," they heard Nattie say in curt succession.

Darla glanced at Jake and stage-whispered back, "That sounds like in the movies, when someone on the other end is asking if you're alone, is so-and-so with you, and giving instructions on where to drop the ransom money."

Jake shook her head and raised a hand for silence, frowning as she listened.

"Yes, I understand," Nattie clipped out. "Good-bye."

A few moments of silence hung over all of them before Nattie finally returned.

"Ma, is everything all right?"

Nattie waited until she'd settled on the sofa again to answer. "Oh, sure, sure, everything's fine. That was just one of the girls from the Bunco group. She had a death in the family, so we won't see her this week. She asked me to watch her Maltese while she's gone."

Maybe it had been Mitzi the Maltese's human mom on the phone? Still, Nattie seemed more upset than the phone call warranted. Looking over at Jake, Darla wasn't sure that her friend was buying it, either.

Nattie apparently realized she was being scrutinized, for

she grinned and gave a wave as if dismissing the momentary gloom.

"Girls, yer taking things too seriously. We're supposed to be having fun. Besides, Doris's aunt had to be ninety if she was a day."

"If you're certain everything is all right . . . ," Jake replied, her expression still concerned.

"Seriously, Jacqueline, it's fine."

Then she snapped her fingers, as if recalling something. "Maybe you girls wouldn't mind going down to my mailbox. I always get lots of coupons from the local shops. They might be having some specials, so that could help decide where to go."

Darla shrugged. "Actually, I wanted to take Hamlet out to stretch his legs again for a few minutes anyhow, since he didn't get to go outside this morning. Jake, do you want to go with me?"

"Sure," Jake agreed—a little too swiftly, in Darla's view. She suspected the PI wanted to discuss the Alicia situation without Nattie knowing.

While Nattie went to find her mailbox key, Darla retrieved Hamlet's leash and harness from the guest room, then stuck her phone in her pocket. As soon as he spotted the harness, Hamlet uncurled himself from his spot beneath the coffee table and trotted out. Darla had his harness fastened and had just snapped on the leash when Nattie returned with the mailbox key.

"Here you go, *bambolina mia*," she said to Jake. Darla was amused to see that this key ring also sported a teeny version of the zebra-striped heart that hung from the woman's main set of keys. "I'll just lie down here on the couch for a little nap."

Leaving Nattie stretched out on the floral cushions, Darla headed out the door with Jake and Hamlet. It wasn't until they were in the elevator that she spoke.

"So you think something happened at the memorial

service that your mother isn't talking about? Maybe having to do with Alicia?"

"I'm not sure. I'm also not convinced it was Doris on that phone call a few minutes ago."

"Who would it be, then?"

"You heard that little 'hello' of hers," Jake reminded her with a shake of her head. "I'm thinking someone male, and someone she knows pretty well."

"You mean Billy?"

"Got it in one, kid. I'm going to see if I can't get hold of her phone when we get back so I can check her call log."

They cut across the lobby to the alcove that served as the mailroom, Hamlet leading the way. While Darla and Jake looked for Nattie's condo number, the cat sniffed at one particular box like a small dog in search of a buried bone.

"What are you doing?" Darla asked him with an indulgent smile. "Did someone get an order of pepperoni in the mail?"

Hamlet paused and shot her a very human look of disdain at the question, drawing a laugh from Jake.

"I think he understood you," she said as she found Nattie's mailbox and inserted the key. She opened the metal door, and then said, "Empty."

"Oh, my dear," a voice said behind them, "the mail doesn't come for another hour or so. Nattie should have told you that."

The speaker was a short, corpulent woman with hennaed hair lacquered to her scalp. Darla recognized her from the memorial service. *Nattie's friend, Mae.* The old woman gave them a friendly nod as she dropped off a letter in the outgoing box, and then caught sight of the cat at the end of the leash that Darla held.

"Why, this must be Hamlet," she said in an admiring tone, bending for a closer look. "My, he is a handsome fellow. Do you suppose he'll do a karate trick for me?"

"Oh, sorry, Mae, but Hamlet doesn't perform on command. He's a very independent cat."

The old woman made a disappointed face. "Well, maybe another time. See you girls later."

While that exchange had been going on, Jake had relocked the box again. "If I didn't know better, I'd say that Ma sent us down here on wild goose chase."

"I'm sure she just looked at the clock wrong," Darla reassured her as they left the alcove. "I'll go ahead and take Hamlet for his walk up front, like I planned. We'll see you back upstairs, unless you want to come along."

"No, I'll—"

She broke off as her cell phone rang. Looking at the display, she brightened a little. "It's Officer Johnston. Maybe he's got some news," Jake said as she pressed the talk button. "Martelli here."

The brief exchange that followed seemed a repeat of Nattie's phone call earlier and mostly consisted of "yes" and "uh-huh" on Jake's part. Darla listened impatiently to that portion of the conversation. As usual, Jake's expression gave nothing away, so she couldn't guess if it was good news or bad that Johnston was sharing. A few moments later, Jake hung up again and gave Darla a considering look.

"What?" she demanded.

Jake smiled a little. "It seems they've had a break in my case. Someone who was at the cat show finally checked out all the digital photos they took. They have a picture of someone hauling a cat in a carrier out of that door that led to behind the stage. It's date-stamped just about the time the attack went down. Johnston is going to send the photo to me in a minute so I can see if I recognize the person."

"That's fabulous news," Darla replied with a smile of her own. She glanced down at Hamlet and told him, "Don't worry, Hammy. We're close to figuring out who catnapped you."

Hamlet seemed less concerned about that, however, than by what was outside the lobby doors. He gave a tug on the leash in that direction, causing Darla to glance that way.

"What, did you spot a bird?" she asked him, only to give a little cry of surprise as she saw what had caught his attention. Despite the frosted palm-tree images on the glass, she could make out a car traveling along the half circle loop of the driveway.

A dark green Mini Cooper, convertible top down.

Darla's eyes widened. She couldn't see the driver, but she did glimpse a shock of bright hennaed hair bouncing like a cockatoo's crest over the steering wheel.

"Jake, quick—look! I swear I just saw your mother drive by," she said and pointed past the lobby door.

SEVENTEEN

THE PI'S GAZE FOLLOWED DARLA'S GESTURE, BUT BY THEN the little green convertible had already vanished. "Darla, are you sure? Why would Ma drive off like that?"

Darla shook her head. Then they exchanged knowing gazes as the identical thought occurred to them both simultaneously.

"The phone call!"

Jake shook her head. "I knew it! She sent us down here so she could sneak out to the parking garage without us knowing. If she wasn't my mother, I'd wring her neck for this little stunt."

Looking truly peeved, Jake hit a couple of buttons on her cell, putting it into speaker mode as it dialed. A moment later, Darla heard Nattie's voice, which sounded to her exaggeratedly carefree.

"Jacqueline, why are you calling? Is something wrong?"

"Yeah, Ma, something's wrong. Darla just saw you drive

off. Where in the heck are you headed, and why didn't you tell me, first?"

A nervous little laugh was the reply, and then Nattie said, "Why, I'm right upstairs. Darla must be mistaken."

Darla looked at Jake and gave her head a vigorous shake, mouthing the word "no." She'd not seen another green Mini in the parking garage the other night. It had to have been Nattie, she was certain.

And then the sound of a car horn and a muttered, "Eh, keep yer pants on," came through loud and clear on the speaker.

If looks could kill, Jake's cell phone would be six feet under, Darla thought. Even so, the PI's tone was surprisingly even as she shot back, "Good try, Ma, but we can hear the traffic. So, spill. Who called you, and where are you going?"

"Fine, I'll tell," the old woman huffed. "Billy needs my help. He wanted me to go to his place right away, so that's what I'm doing."

"Ma, if he needs help, he should call his attorney, not you," Jake clipped out. "So turn around and get back here."

"Jacqueline, I'm ashamed of you," the old woman cried, her voice loud enough to make Hamlet jump. "I taught you never to turn your back on your friends. Billy said I was the only one who could help him, and I wasn't supposed to tell anyone else. I shouldn't've said anything to you. Now, I'm hanging up."

"But, Ma, you can't—"

The phone went silent. Muttering a curse, Jake ended the call from her side.

Darla gave her a sympathetic look. "She's only going to Billy Pope's place. I'm sure she'll be back soon."

"Didn't you hear what she said?" Jake demanded, her expression one of true concern now. "She wasn't supposed to tell anyone where she was going. And that call we overheard—'yes, no, yes'? Someone was giving her instructions on what to do, and it might not even have been Billy. Something tells me she's about to walk into a boatload of trouble."

"Maybe Mildred knows what's going on," Darla hurried to suggest. "Your mother has been acting evasive ever since she got back from the memorial service. Mildred was with her all morning. We could go talk to her."

"Except that Mildred hasn't been on my most-trusted list since you saw her sneaking around with the cat. But you're right, kid; she might know something useful since she was with Ma at the memorial service. Any clue which condo is hers?"

"No, but I think she's on the second floor." Then, with a glance back at the mailroom alcove, she added, "Do you know her last name?"

"We can start with the first initial 'M' on the second floor.

Jake paused and then held up her phone. "Wait, I just got a text. It must be the photo from Johnston."

"You check that. Hamlet and I will look at the mailboxes."

Hamlet was ahead of her, however, rushing at a quick cat trot back into the alcove. Clinging to the leash, Darla hurried after him.

"All right, Hammy, help me look. First initial 'M,' and an address starting with a two," she said. But Hamlet was already pawing at the same mailbox that had interested him earlier. Darla bent to read the name.

M. Fischer, #2024.

It took her a moment to make the connection. "Jake, get in here! You have to see this."

"Yeah, well you have to see *this*," Jake countered as she walked in, phone clutched in her hand. "Johnston's photo came through nice and clear. Take a look and tell me who you see."

Heart beating faster, Darla squinted at the photo. A small figure with cat carrier in hand had been caught slipping past a knot of spectators whose attention was focused on the stage where Hamlet's video had been playing. The person's face was partially turned away, but the helmet of gray hair was clearly visible, as was her official purple FSA polo shirt. Darla zoomed in on the figure and saw a glint of silver that appeared to be eyeglasses.

She looked up at Jake and nodded. "Mildred." Then, pointing at the mailbox that had held Hamlet's attention, she clarified, "Mildred Fischer."

Jake, meanwhile, was still squinting at the photo. "This"—she waved the phone—"doesn't necessarily mean Mildred is our suspect. I seriously can't see her skulking around with a bottle ready to hit someone over the head. For all we know, she might have been helping out an exhibitor. And Sam would laugh herself to death if I called and told her to arrest that nice old lady because Hamlet was pointing a paw at her. Let's start by going to see if Mildred is home. Maybe she can shed some light on this."

But no one answered at number 2024.

"You don't suppose maybe Mildred's dead inside, do you?" Darla gingerly asked after they'd knocked and waited a good minute.

Jake pounded on the door one last time and then shook her head. "No, or else super sleuth here would be doing some kitty karate to bust open the door," she said with a gesture at Hamlet, who was sitting silently at Darla's feet. "My gut feeling is that if Ma is over at Billy's house, so is Mildred. We need to find a way to get over there now."

"I'll see if I can get hold of Tino," Darla promptly suggested, reaching for her phone.

For once, her timing was perfect.

"Hey, *chica*. What's shaking?" the young man exclaimed when Darla had identified herself. "You need a tour guide after all?"

"It's more important than that. I think Jake's mom is in

trouble—bad trouble—and we don't have any way to get to where she is. Can you drive over to Lauderdale Tropics condos right now and pick me and Jake up?"

"Sure, *chica*. I'll be right there."

"Thanks, Tino. We'll wait for you outside in the driveway. And hurry!"

Even before Darla had hung up, Jake was heading down the hall. "Go hold the elevator," she said as she unlocked the door to Nattie's condo. "I need to get something, and then I'll be right there."

She reappeared almost immediately carrying a large shopping bag with the Waterview Hotel's logo on it. "All right, let's get downstairs," Jake said as she rejoined Darla and Hamlet.

No more than five minutes had passed by Darla's watch when Tino came peeling into the drive. They didn't wait for him to climb out, but opened the doors themselves and hopped in.

"Hey, *chicas*. Looks like the whole gang is here," he said as he looked back at them. Then, glimpsing Jake's hard expression, he hurriedly corrected himself. "Sorry, I meant 'ma'ams.' Where are we going?"

"Take us back to Billy Pope's house, now," Jake told him before Darla could reply. Then, as he nodded and turned back around, she added, "And don't worry, '*chica*' will do."

Tino nodded and squealed out of the drive before Darla had finished belting herself in. Bracing herself with her feet against the front seat, she set Hamlet on her lap and wrapped her arms around him. The last thing they needed was to hit a speed bump and have the cat go flying.

"What's the trouble?" the cabbie said as they zipped down the residential street, retracing their route from the other day. "You want me to call my cousin, Ana? I got her on speed dial."

"Not just yet," Jake said. "But if things don't work out

well, we might need her and Johnston, and Detective Martinez, too."

They made the drive in what Darla figured had to be record time. Hamlet, his fur looking ruffled, hopped off her lap while she unbelted herself. Jake had already scrambled out and, shopping bag in hand, was standing in front of the metal intercom box, finger pressed to the call button.

"You want me to wait?" Tino asked as Darla climbed out.

She nodded. "I don't know what's going to happen here, so we might still need you. Plus, you're going to have to go back to the condo anyhow, since I kind of forgot my wallet."

"Hey, *chica*, I trust you. Say, what's your tall friend doing?"

Darla looked over to see Jake had left the intercom box and was examining the wooden gate. Darla and Hamlet joined her. "No one answering?"

"Not a peep. But look—there beside the garage. I think that's Ma's car."

Sure enough, what looked like the rear end of a small green vehicle was barely visible around the corner of the three-car garage. Darla nodded. "Cameras?"

"Almost certainly." Gesturing Darla to follow, Jake returned to the box and pressed the bell once again. Then, giving her head an exaggerated shake, she told Darla, "Let's go."

They went back to the cab, where Tino was waiting in the driver's seat, window down. "You said the other day that Billy Pope has a dock out back," Jake softly said. "Do you know if it's in clear view of the house?"

He nodded. "Yeah, he's right on the water. You can pretty well hop off your boat and walk right past the swimming pool over to the house."

"Sounds like our only choice. You think you can drive us back around to the launch to see if we can find someone who'll drop us off there?"

"Hey, *chica*, I can do you one better. My buddy Ricko

has a fishing boat he hires out. If he's there at the launch, he'll take you."

They piled back in the cab again, and Tino drove off. Jake, meanwhile, pulled out her phone again and dialed.

"I'm going to try calling Ma again and see if she can talk. I'm putting it on speaker so you can hear, but let me do all the talking. There's a good chance that if she does pick up, she'll have us on speaker, too, so whoever is there can listen in. And we don't want to tip our hand."

The phone rang twice, then Nattie's voice answered, "Hello?"

"Hey, Ma. It's me, Jake."

"Oh, hi, Jake. What do you want?"

Darla raised her eyebrows in alarm. She'd never heard Nattie use that nickname. Jake caught her glance and nodded. Obviously, her mother was raising a signal right off the bat.

"I just wanted to let you know that Darla and I decided not to wait for you to come back to go shopping. We called a cab, and we're going to head downtown and poke around in some of the shops. Is that okay?"

"Sure, sure," came Nattie's voice. "I should be back in time for you to take me to that fish place you talked about, and then we can watch another Gidget movie exactly like last night."

Exactly like last night. As in, with Mildred there? Darla thought.

"Sure, Ma, that sounds great," Jake said. "Anyhow, we're off to spend some money. I'm looking for a framed watercolor like the one we had in the guest room in the Thirty-Fourth Street house back when I was a kid. Remember how much I loved it?"

There was a small snort from the other end, and then Nattie answered, "Yeah, yeah, I remember. Your aunt Gianna painted it. She was talented, wasn't she? Well, I'd better go now. Love you."

"Love you, too, Ma."

Jake hung up and then put a hand to her forehead. "It's bad. She never calls me Jake, and she darn sure never says she loves me when she hangs up the phone. We've got to get into that house, and now."

"Don't worry, *chicas*, we're here," Tino called back to them.

He pulled into a damp, cobbled lot there on the waterfront. The parking area was squeezed between a high-end surf shop and a small shopping plaza complete with a real estate storefront, two seafood restaurants, and a souvenir stand. Ahead lay an open-air building and beyond that a series of finger piers—each with a dozen small boat docks branching off from a larger wooden wharf into the Intracoastal. Unlike the gleaming yachts and cigarette boats they'd seen the day before during the water-taxi tour, the vessels docked here were small fishing boats, along with a couple of personal watercrafts.

Tino parked in a spot near the open-air structure and hopped out. "Come on," he said as the two women and Hamlet climbed out of the back. "I see his boat, so he must be around here somewhere. Hey, Ricko!"

Ricko turned out to be a young Haitian man about Tino's age whose gleaming black skin contrasted with the yellow-orange hue of his bleached, shoulder-length dreadlocks. He wore cutoff blue jeans, a black bandana wrapped pirate-style over his dreads, and nothing else. He was sitting at a picnic bench next to the building sipping on an energy drink and munching chips.

"Hey, mon," he called back to Tino with a friendly wave, sending a shower of potato chip crumbs flying. "You bring me some clients?"

"Not exactly. These *chicas* need someone with a boat to drop them off at one of the houses a little ways up the water. Can you take them?"

Ricko rose from the bench and started toward them.

Standing, he towered over even Jake. "So, where you be wanting to go?"

Jake answered before Tino could. "Do you know Billy Pope's place? His is the yellow stucco home with white trim, with a matching detached garage, mother-in-law quarters, and a pool house."

He nodded, dreadlocks swaying. "Yeah, I know it. Why you need to be going there?"

"My mother is being held against her will there. We couldn't make it past the front gate, so getting in by water is our only choice. And I'm afraid we don't have much time."

"My rate, it be seventy-five dollars an hour, two hour minimum." Then, when Jake began to frantically dig in her pockets in hopes of finding some cash, the young man smiled and shrugged. "But for friends of Tino, I take you free."

"Thank you," Jake exclaimed. "Quick, we have to hurry."

"Okay, the boat be that way." He pointed to a cheerful white twenty-footer with blue stripes and a blue Bimini top, along which was mounted a row of fishing rods. Small, but probably pretty fast, Darla judged.

"Do you *chicas* need me to wait for you?" Tino wanted to know.

Jake looked at her watch and nodded. "Give us about forty-five minutes, and we'll either be back here, or be calling you to pick us up from Pope's place. If we haven't contacted you by then, call your cousin and tell her there's trouble."

"Got it. I'll wait right here," he said and pointed to the bench.

"Perfect. All right, Ricko, let's get out of here."

They hurried down to the dock, where the boat waited. Ricko climbed in first, and then helped Jake down the ladder. Even from the dock, Darla was aware of a faint but pungent and sweet scent drifting from the vessel. She shook her head, wondering if Jake could smell it, too. Apparently, Captain Ricko passed the time between clients by indulging in what, if he were living in California, would probably be euphemistically described as medicinal herbal therapy. She could only hope that he hadn't partaken in any so far today.

As Darla prepared to hand off Hamlet to Jake and climb in, however, Ricko stopped her.

"Wait, that black cat, is he coming on my boat, too?"

Darla nodded. "I know people think black cats are bad luck, but he—"

"No, no—the black cat, he be good luck on a boat," Ricko said with a smile. "But maybe you put this on him, just in case."

He reached into the boat's storage locker and pulled out a bright yellow mini life jacket. "My sister, she have one of those yappy dogs. I make him wear this on the boat."

Darla eyed the life jacket with no little alarm. Chances were Hamlet was not going to be as amenable as the yappy dog. Still, she nodded and then gave Hamlet to Jake before climbing in herself.

"You can sit right there," the captain said, pointing them to the bench in front of the console. Cranking the engine, he said, "Okay, now hang on to your kitty."

While he backed up the boat, Darla managed to fasten the life jacket on Hamlet. To her surprise, he seemed to accept it as another variation of his harness, for he squirmed only a little as she fastened the plastic squeeze clips that held the straps closed.

"Let's see what kind of a sailor you are," she told the cat as Ricko throttled the boat forward.

The first portion of their ride was in a no-wake zone, meaning that their progress up the Intracoastal to Pope's house was barely above an idle. Fortunately, Hamlet seemed to enjoy the water, sitting quietly between Darla and Jake as they motored along, whiskers flicking as he sniffed the fishy breeze.

"We could have swum it faster," Jake muttered, fingers beating out a nervous rhythm on her thighs.

"No worries," said Ricko, whose hearing was apparently as keen as Hamlet's. "Give it a minute, and then we can be moving into the main channel."

Jake nodded, but she didn't stop the tapping. To distract her friend a bit, Darla asked, "What was that you were telling your mother about wanting to buy a watercolor?"

"It was my way of trying to tell her we'd be coming by boat. When I was a kid, my Aunt Gianna took a watercolor class, and she decided to paint Ma a seascape as a surprise for her birthday." Jake managed a fleeting smile. "She brings it over, and Ma tears off the paper, and there's this painting of a big, out-of-proportion sailing ship that looked like it was about to crash into a lighthouse. I was ten years old, and even I knew it was ghastly. But because her sister made it, Ma insisted on displaying it. I'm hoping she took the boat hint."

Darla smiled a little. Then, pointing, she sobered, and said, "Look, there's Billy's place now."

Around the curve, she could see a glimpse of yellow stucco with a matching yellow pool house not far from the water's edge. Two craft were docked there: one, a fishing boat more than twice the size of Ricko's, and the other a small, sleek little motorboat with a wood veneer, the kind of boat that Darla had heard referred to as a runabout. Fortunately, the way the vessels were tied left a spot for Ricko to dock across the front of the pier.

"So how are we going to do this?" Darla asked as they drew closer. "Jump off the boat and storm the house?"

"That's all I've got," Jake said with a worried look. "Best case, Billy will call the cops on us for trespassing, and we'll be able to get Ma out of there. Worst case . . ."

"What's worst case?" Darla wanted to know, her grip on Hamlet tightening.

Jake shrugged and reached for the hotel shopping bag,

which Darla hadn't realized she'd brought aboard. "I don't know how bad it can get. Maybe it's nothing, but just in case, I brought along a little equalizer."

She reached into the sack, pulling out a familiar-looking glass scallop seashell sculpture. Darla stared at it, wide-eyed. "Where did you get that?"

"The Waterview Hotel gift shop," Jake said. "I bought it before we left the hotel, when I got that pillow for Ma."

Darla wasn't sure whether to be relieved or dismayed that Jake was armed with nothing more than a glass shell. Ricko dropped to an idle again and brought the boat toward the pier, then tossed a couple of fenders—the rubber bumpers that kept a boat's hull from smacking the dock—so that they hung over the side, and then maneuvered the boat across the front of the pier. Between the pool house and the height of the pier, which with a low tide required climbing up a few rungs to reach the dock, any view of the boat from the house was pretty well blocked. Unless someone was watching out the window and had seen their approach, chances were that no one inside knew they were there.

"I'm not going to tie off," Ricko said, simply wrapping a line around the ladder and tugging it to pull them closer. "As soon as you two ladies and the cat be on the dock, I'm taking off. But I'll stay nearby for a while, in case you need me. You can call me."

He told Jake his cell number, which she quickly programmed into her phone. Then, with a smile, he said, "I wish you good luck finding your mama."

Darla unfastened Hamlet's life vest. Maybe she shouldn't have brought him along; still, Hamlet had proved his mettle numerous times in the past. She handed the cat to Jake and clambered up. Jake in turn handed Darla the shopping bag, and then hefted Hamlet as high as she could. Lying on her stomach, Darla grabbed him and, fingers tightly intertwined in his harness, lifted him to the dock.

"Oof," she whispered to him as she sat up and settled him on his feet. "No more pepperoni snacks for you."

By now, Jake was safely atop the pier, too. Ricko gave them a thumbs-up and, releasing the line, quietly motored away from the dock.

"Now what?" Darla whispered.

Jake pulled out her phone and whispered back. "I'm going to call Ma, and let her know we're here. But first, let's get into the pool house so we're out of sight."

Keeping low, the two of them and Hamlet trotted up the dock and into what was the nicest pergola Darla had ever seen. Built of yellow stucco, it served as both an outdoor room in which to party and a means to shield the pool and its occupants from anyone cruising down the waterway. Though the pergola was open to the elements, a combination of white lattice panels and long white drapes gave an illusion of privacy. They could see the house from their vantage point, but with luck she and Jake would go unnoticed, at least for a while.

They crouched behind what looked like a kitchen island, complete with sink and cooktop, while Jake dialed Nattie's number. After what had to be several rings, Jake whispered, "No answer yet."

Then she shook her head and covered the phone's microphone with her hand, mouthing, *The line is open.*

Darla nodded. Maybe Nattie had managed to set her phone to vibrate and had answered it but been unable to speak. The question was, if Jake said anything, would someone other than Nattie hear it?

She could tell by Jake's uncertain expression that she was worried about the same thing. Finally, after a few seconds, she raised the phone to her ear again, and whispered, "Ma? Ma, can you hear me?"

"Of course, she can't hear you, Jake," a familiar voice said with a laugh. "You see, I have her phone."

Darla choked back a cry. The voice had come in stereo . . . from Jake's cell, and also from behind them. She exchanged looks with Jake, who shook her head in resignation and hung up the phone.

"All right, girls, I saw you duck behind that island," Mildred said from a few feet away. "There's no point in trying to pretend you're not there. So let's all go inside, where we can talk."

EIGHTEEN

"THE SHOES OF THE FISHERMAN," JAKE SOFTLY exclaimed. "Get it? Not Pope. Fischer!"

Darla nodded, for the same realization had just struck her. "Hamlet tried to tell us, but we picked up on the wrong person."

Jake, meanwhile, was reaching into the paper sack and pulling out the glass shell. "Okay, Mildred, we're coming out," she called to the old woman. To Darla, she hissed, "Quick, stick this in your waistband under your shirt, and then hold Hamlet in front of you."

Darla nodded and did as told. The glass was cool against her sunburn, but hardly comfortable. Whatever it was Jake planned to do with the sculpture, Darla figured she'd do her part to help should the need arise.

Jake waited until Darla gave her a thumbs-up, and then called out, "Say, Mildred, you don't have a gun or anything, do you? I'd kind of like to know before I stick my head up."

Mildred trilled another little laugh. "Actually, I do, but it's strictly for self-protection. I'm sure I won't need it today."

"Okay, just wanted to be sure."

Jake slowly straightened. Darla stood, too, making sure that the shell was securely in her waistband before picking up Hamlet and snuggling him up against her stomach. The cat loosed a small growl that Darla knew wasn't meant for her. She hoped for Mildred's sake that the woman wasn't foolish enough to try to take the feline a second time.

"Come on, come on," Mildred said, gesturing them forward. "You don't want to pass up a chance to see the inside of Billy's house. It's truly lovely."

Mildred was dressed in what Darla assumed had been her outfit from that morning: black slacks, white knit top, and a string of pearls. The only difference, presumably, was the small caliber automatic pistol she held at her side. She gave them a cheery smile, as if she were a hostess welcoming them to an afternoon soirée. As they drew closer, Darla saw that the usual speck of lipstick was missing from her front tooth.

Oddly, she found this little aberration more ominous than anything else that had yet happened.

"Oh, good, you brought Hamlet," Mildred exclaimed. "He is quite an exceptional cat. Now, go on in, but watch your step," she continued, pointing to the open French door. "You have to walk down a level once you're inside."

Another time, Darla would have been thrilled to tour her first ever mansion. Under the circumstances, however, all that registered was an expanse of white marble tile, beige walls and angled ceilings, and a scattering of modern art and furniture, accented with a few potted palm trees. But what really held her attention was a pair of burgundy leather love seats, which faced each other in front of a glass-tiled fireplace. On one love seat slumped Billy Pope and Alicia Timpson; on the other sprawled Nattie.

All were unconscious . . . or so Darla prayed. The alternative was something she didn't want to consider.

"Ma!" With that choked cry, Jake rushed toward the old woman. Gently, she shook her and tapped her cheek. To Darla's relief, Nattie briefly opened her eyes before her head lolled back and she nodded off again. Jake settled her more comfortably, then turned a deadly cold look in Mildred's direction.

"What have you done to her?"

"Oh, don't worry, I just slipped them all a few of my sleeping pills. I needed a little time to decide what to do, and it was too hard keeping an eye on that many people."

"Well, slight problem, Millie. You've got two more of us to deal with. That's five people you're going to have to bash over the head if you want to get rid of all the witnesses. Not to mention a guy with a boat and a guy with a cab both waiting to hear from us. If they don't get a call in"—Jake paused for a look at her watch—"five more minutes, they'll be phoning the cops to come out here. So why don't you do the right thing and let me bring in Detective Martinez to settle things once and for all?"

"I don't think so, Jake." Mildred gave her an equally cold look through her steel-rimmed glasses. "I might be old, but I'm not foolish, and I'm certainly not stupid. I don't want to go to jail for the rest of my life . . . which, given my genetic history, is liable to be another twenty years or so. I'm not sorry for doing something that needed to be done, even if a jury sees it differently. You don't understand. Ted Stein had to be removed, for everyone's sake. I'd kill him again if I had the chance."

While Darla shivered at Mildred's chilling words, Jake glanced at her watch again. "Four minutes, Millie."

"You're getting very annoying, Jake."

"Yeah, well, I tend to be that way with people who bash me over the head."

The old woman shot her a peeved look. "It wasn't me who hit you. That was Cindy, and it wasn't in the original plan," she said with a glance at the unconscious Alicia. "But, like they say, stuff happens. You and Hamlet were—what do they call it in the movies?—collateral damage."

"Three minutes, Millie," Jake coolly said, continuing the countdown. "Come on, you've seen it on television. The judge always goes a bit easier on you if you don't make a fuss over being arrested."

"You're bluffing. You don't have people waiting to call the police."

Barely had she spoken the words than Darla's cell phone abruptly rang a few notes of the old hit "Cat Scratch Fever." Juggling Hamlet so that she had a free hand, she pulled her phone from her pocket and glanced at the caller ID.

"It's Tino."

Jake shrugged. "Oops, a little early. Millie, what's your decision?"

By way of answer, Mildred raised the pistol. "Don't answer the phone, Darla, or I'm afraid I'll have to do something drastic."

Which meant it was their turn to call her bluff . . . except that Darla suspected from the expression of cool resolve in her eyes that the old woman meant what she said. Hamlet gave a soft *meow-rumph*, and Darla took a deep breath. Surely the cat-loving old woman wouldn't pull the trigger if there was a chance of hitting Hamlet. Still, Darla's fingers trembled as she hesitated over the phone's screen.

What to do? Answer, and have a couple of seconds to tell Tino they were in danger . . . and maybe get shot in the process? Don't answer, and pray Tino followed through with calling the police?

As she hesitated, the call went to voice mail.

Jake shook her head in mock dismay. "Guess you should have let her answer the phone, Millie. Not answering was the signal for our buddy Tino to give the police a call. You remember Officer Garcia from the cat show? Turns out she's his cousin, and he's got her on speed dial."

Mildred's expression went rigid.

"You girls have made things very difficult for me. Of course, most of the blame belongs to Nattie." She paused to give the unconscious old woman an angry look. "I could have taken care of Billy and Alicia and made it look like an accident. No one would have been the wiser, if she weren't such a silly old busybody."

"Busybody!"

Nattie's eyes popped open, and she sat up. "Busybody!" she yelped again. "Well at least I'm not a murderous old biddy who turns on her friends like a snake!"

Mildred's mouth dropped open. "You're awake! But—but the sleeping pills . . ."

Nattie snorted. "Like someone who used to be my friend once said, I might be old, but I'm not stupid. The minute I saw them two"—she jerked a thumb in Billy and Alicia's direction—"starting to nod off, I knew you'd try to slip me a Mickey, too, when you asked if I wanted some of yer coffee. I dumped it in one of those potted palms when you wasn't looking, and then I faked being asleep."

"Why, that is the sneakiest thing I've ever heard!" Mildred shrieked, the pistol now trembling in her hand. "All right—all of you, to the dock. We're going to take a boat ride. You girls"—she gestured the gun at Darla and Jake—"I want you to carry Billy and Alicia out there, too. You're young and strong. You can do it."

Jake nodded. "Sure, Mildred, we'll move them. Just keep calm. Ma, would you take Hamlet from Darla so she can help me?"

Keeping a peevish eye on her former friend, Nattie got up from the couch and went over to where Darla stood. Darla handed the cat over to her with a warning: "Keep his leash looped over your wrist the whole time."

Praying Hamlet would continue to behave, Darla joined

Jake at the other love seat, where Billy and Alicia still snoozed away, oblivious to all the drama. Neither was large, but unconscious they'd both be dead weight.

"We'll have to take them one at a time. Billy first," Jake told her, maneuvering so that they both had their backs to Mildred. "See if you can help me drag him up."

In an undertone, she added, "When I say when, be ready to hand me that seashell you're packing."

"Got it," Darla murmured back. More loudly, she said, "Maybe if you take one arm, and I take the other, we can pull him to his feet and prop him up between us."

"It's worth a shot," Jake agreed as they assumed position. "Ready on my count. One, two, three!"

By some miracle, they manage to drag Billy upright just long enough to each slip a shoulder under one of the man's arms. It was an awkward arrangement at best, given that Jake had to hunch over in order to stay even with Darla. Mildred, however, appeared pleased.

"Good work, girls. Now, out to the dock with him, and then you can move Alicia."

She picked her designer shoulder bag off the console table and slipped the strap over her head so that the purse hung securely across her chest. Then she gestured with her pistol. "Nattie, you and Hamlet lead the way."

The ungainly procession began moving in the direction of the French doors, which Mildred had earlier left open. The old woman glanced about her and smiled.

"What a nice day for Billy to take his daughter and friends on a little fishing trip," she remarked. "Too bad something will go wrong with the engine, and no one will be able to get to the life raft before the whole boat blows sky-high."

Darla stumbled and almost fell as she shot Mildred a horrified look. Was that how the old woman planned to eliminate any witnesses? Catching her look, Mildred smiled again and shrugged.

"It's amazing what one can find out on the Internet these days," she said, unknowingly echoing James.

Now, however, Darla could hear the faint sound of sirens drifting in on the light Intracoastal breeze. She doubted they signaled Officer Garcia's approach, since the cop would have nothing more to go on than Tino's suspicions that something was wrong at the Pope mansion. Still, the sirens served as a reminder that a call for help might have been made.

Mildred must have come to the same conclusion, for her smile promptly faded. She all but shouted, "Hurry, we don't have much time!"

By now, they'd made it past the threshold and were cutting across the lawn, bypassing the pool and pergola and heading straight for the dock. Out on the Intracoastal, Darla could see a familiar white-and-blue fishing boat idling a short distance upstream from them. Ricko was keeping an eye out, just as he'd promised. They had almost reached the pier when Jake stumbled . . . or pretended to.

"Hold up, Darla," she exclaimed. "I think I pulled something, trying to walk like this."

"Here, now—none of that," Mildred admonished in a frantic voice behind them. "We're almost there."

Jake looked over at Darla and nodded, and then mouthed the word, *Now.*

In a single swift move, Darla released Billy and reached beneath her shirt, pulling out the glass seashell sculpture. Jake let Billy go as well and snatched the sculpture from Darla's hands and swung about.

"Hey, Mildred—catch!" she shouted, and flung the glass shell at the old woman.

Mildred shrieked and reflexively dropped her pistol as she tried to avoid the incoming missile. To Darla's surprise, she almost did, suffering just a glancing blow off her shoulder.

An alternate for the 1960 U.S. women's gymnastics team, she recalled Nattie saying about the woman. Apparently,

Mildred had retained some of her youthful agility, since Jake's fastball pitch would have caught almost anyone else squarely in the gut. The shell, meanwhile, bounced a few times on the grass. Finally, it rolled to a stop next to Billy, its gleaming glass seemingly undamaged by such rough handling.

Not bothering anymore with trying to herd the hostages, Mildred reached down and snatched up the gun again. Shoving past Nattie, Mildred rushed for the dock and scrambled down the ladder. A moment later, an engine revved, and the small runabout went flying out into the channel, Mildred at the helm.

"Quick, we gotta stop her!" Nattie cried.

Jake was already ahead of her. Phone to her ear as she rushed down the pier, she was shouting, "Ricko, hurry! I need you to pick me up from the dock and follow the boat that just left here."

"Wait, what about me?" Darla demanded as she caught up with Jake at the ladder. "I'm going with you."

"Me, too," Nattie puffed once she reached the ladder, as well. "Me and Hamlet, we're gonna see this to the end."

"No, you're not," Jake countered as she started down toward the water. Looking back up at Darla, she clarified. "Neither of you are. Mildred's got a gun, and she's desperate. As soon as Garcia and the others show up, let them know what's going on. They should be able to send out a patrol to cut her off somewhere on the waterway."

Ricko, meanwhile, was pulling up to the dock.

"You must be the mama," he exclaimed with a smile, pointing to Nattie. "Don't be worrying. We take care of this."

Once the captain had wrapped the line around the ladder again to hold the boat steady, Jake hopped into it as lightly as Hamlet. "Let's get out of here."

The young man obliged, loosing the line and then pulling back the throttle so that the vessel nearly leaped from the water. Nattie and Darla stared after them in varying degrees of outrage.

"I can't believe my own daughter left me behind like that," Nattie cried as she set Hamlet down and handed Darla the leash. "Besides, I bet I know where old Millie is going."

"Where?"

Nattie gave a smug nod. "There's a private launch right before you turn up the New River. You can't find it unless you know where to look, because it's hidden by mangroves. When we worked on the water taxi, some of the kids would pull in there for a little recreation, if you know what I mean. I bet she'll jump out there and walk down to Las Olas to catch a cab."

"Well, then let's hop in the Mini Cooper and get there before she does," Darla urged her.

Nattie grimaced and shook her head. "We can't. That rotten old biddy stole my car keys from me. I think she's still got them in her pocket. We're stuck here."

"Maybe not," Darla exclaimed as she heard a sudden loud honking from the front gate. "Come on, I think plan B just pulled up!"

She hesitated, however, as she recalled Billy and Alicia. The former still lay upon the manicured lawn where she and Jake had dropped him, face peacefully pointed to the afternoon sun. While he didn't appear to be in any physical distress, he apparently wasn't going to be waking up anytime soon, either.

"Nattie, Alicia should be fine in the house, but we can't just leave Billy here."

"Eh, sure we can."

The old woman trotted over to the pergola and came back bearing one of those personal-sized beach umbrellas designed to clip onto the back of a chair. She popped it open and set it on the grass beside Billy, shading his face.

"There. Now he won't get sunburned. C'mon, Darla—let's go!"

With Hamlet galloping alongside her, Darla rushed around the side of the house past the garage and Nattie's hostage Mini. She could see a familiar cab sitting in front of the gate, horn still blaring.

"Tino!" Darla shouted, waving. "We're okay, but we need a ride!"

Letting up on the horn, the cabbie jumped out and rushed to the gate.

"Glad you're still alive," he called, clinging to the pickets like he was a prisoner. "When you didn't answer my phone call, I got worried and called Ana."

"Good," Darla panted out as she reached the gate. "Now you need to call her back and tell her Mildred Fischer admitted to killing Ted Stein, and that she's escaping on a boat down the Intracoastal. But first, we need you to drive us to where Nattie thinks Mildred is headed, just in case she outsmarts Jake and Ricko."

Nattie, meanwhile, had pressed the button to open the gate. Then, catching a glimpse of Tino, she frowned.

"That's the guy who yelled at me at the airport," she declared to Darla, bottom lip now sticking out at a mutinous angle. "I'm not getting into no cab with him."

"Hey, she was the one parking illegally," Tino protested in turn. "She deserved to be yelled at."

"Tino," Darla clipped out, "age trumps right in cases like this. Now apologize to Nattie so that we can get going."

She thought for a panicked moment that the cabbie was going to refuse, but then he gave a determined nod. "You're right. I should have been polite to an old lady. I'm sorry I yelled."

"Old lady," Nattie muttered, but to Darla's relief she gave a grudging nod of acceptance. "C'mon, let's get going."

Hamlet took the lead, leaping into the open cab door, followed by Darla and Nattie. Tino climbed back in, too, and slammed the cab door after him.

"All right, *chica*," he said as he pulled out onto the shaded street and handed Darla his cell. "You talk to *mi prima* and tell her what's going on. And, *Tia*—Auntie," he added to Nattie, who sat in the front seat with him, "you tell me where we're going."

Tino's phone was already dialing as Darla put it to her ear. A moment later, she heard what she presumed was Garcia's irritated voice on the other end.

"Darn it, Tino, I already told you I'd drive out there."

"Uh, Officer Garcia?"

"Who is this? Where's Tino?"

"Actually, this is Darla Pettistone . . . the lady with the black cat who went missing? Tino's driving, so he wanted me to explain what was going on."

"Hold it," Garcia cut her short. "I thought I was on my way to find you and your friends at Billy Pope's home, and now you're driving off somewhere?"

"Well, things got a little, uh, tense back at the house."

While Tino whipped down side streets and slid through yellow lights, Darla clung to the grab strap on the door and gave Garcia a rundown of everything that had happened after Officer Johnston texted the picture that had turned out to be of Mildred to Jake's phone.

Garcia listened in silence until Darla got to the part about a pistol-toting Mildred hopping into a boat and being chased by Jake and the Haitian captain. Then she said in a terse voice, "Hang on."

Darla assumed she put the phone down, for all she heard was a few moments of muffled radio communication before the officer finally came back on the line again.

"Okay, we've got paramedics heading out to Mr. Pope's place to check him and his daughter out, and I've got the sheriff's department sending out a boat to try to intercept the suspect, not that we have much of a description of the vessel to go on. You say Ms. Martelli has the suspect in sight?"

"She did, but that was fifteen, twenty minutes ago. I

haven't talked to her since." Darla paused and pulled out her own phone, pressing Jake's speed dial key. "Hang on, I'll try calling her."

But either Jake wasn't getting reception on the water, or else, more likely, she couldn't hear her phone ringing over the boat's engine, for the call went to voice mail.

"I can't get hold of her," Darla said. "But Nattie—Mrs. Martelli—is pretty sure Mrs. Fischer will be heading for a private launch she knows about. That's where Tino is taking us now."

She gave Garcia the cross-street information that Nattie had shared with Tino. The officer repeated the address, and then said, "I'm turning around and heading that way. You tell Tino he is not to approach an armed suspect. That goes for you two ladies, too. You stay out of sight and wait for the PD to get there. Understood?"

"Don't worry. All we're going to do is keep an eye on her until the police show up," Darla said, though she rather suspected that Nattie had visions of wrestling the gun from Mildred's hand and making a citizen's arrest. Her job would be to make certain Nattie made no such attempt.

Darla handed the phone back to Tino and gave Hamlet a nervous pat. He'd been remarkably calm through all of this, she realized. Was he confident that all would be well . . . or was he lulling them all into a false sense of security before he pounced? Tightening her grip on his lead—the cat had already seen his share of excitement over the past few days—she peered out the taxi window. From the change in skyline, it was apparent that they were nearing the Waterview Hotel, where everything had started.

"Stop—turn there!" Nattie shouted all at once, pointing at what looked like an alley.

Tino turned down what proved to be a narrow, sloping drive barely wide enough for two cars the size of his taxi to pass, and edged by almost impenetrable rows of tropical foliage. Through the windshield, Darla could glimpse a tangle of vines, coconut palms, mangrove trees, and lapping water. Near the launch site, the drive broadened into a roundabout where drivers pulling boat trailers could circle around and position themselves to back down the ramp. A couple of trucks with empty trailers hitched to them had already disgorged their vessels and were parked around at the far edges of the roundabout, half-hidden in the foliage.

Tino whipped the cab around and slid into an open spot behind one of the trailers.

"Good," Nattie said with an approving clap of her hands. "Mildred will have to tie off down there in the mangroves and walk back up the ramp. She'll probably go right past the cab and never even notice it. C'mon, let's go down to the water and see if we can see the runabout."

She hopped out before Darla could say anything. Tino grinned and glanced back her. "Guess we're getting out here."

Darla hesitated. On the one hand, if they all stayed huddled in the taxi and Mildred spotted them, they'd be trapped in the vehicle. On the other hand, skulking about the boat ramp could have its own set of dangers.

"Is it safe to be down there?" she asked Tino, suddenly more nervous about the local fauna than a retiree with a pistol. "Aren't there supposed to be alligators?"

"Don't worry. The water's too brackish here for them. But you might want to keep your eyes peeled for snakes."

Which was almost enough to keep Darla in the cab, trap or no trap. But gritting her teeth, she lifted Hamlet into her arms and slid out from the back of the taxi. She started down the ramp, glad she had on her walking shoes instead of sandals. The stone ramp was littered with pine needles and the occasional palm frond and even a couple of fallen coconuts. Nattie was ahead of her, already crouched behind a tangle of broad leaves. peering anxiously across the water.

For his part, Hamlet apparently was ready to hop into action, too, for he began to squirm in Darla's arms. "Fine," she muttered as she put him down. "You get swallowed whole by a python and see if I care."

"Psst!" Nattie called, and motioned her and Hamlet over. "I think I see the runabout headed this way. And look, she's slowing it down."

She looked in the direction Nattie pointed. Sure enough, there was the sleek craft with a silver-haired pilot at the wheel. Darla shook her head and gave Nattie an admiring look. It was obvious where Jake had inherited her knack for solving crimes. For all her endearing if annoying habits, the old woman was—what had Jake called Detective Martinez?—quite the smart cookie.

That, or she simply knew how to think like a criminal.

Tino was trotting down the ramp toward them, putting his phone back into one of his cargo shorts' oversized pockets.

"Hey, I just called Ana again," he told Darla as he crouched beside them. "She's still about five minutes away, but she's trying to get someone here now. What do you think we should do in the meantime—jump the old lady when she gets off the boat?"

Darla shook her head and pulled out her own phone.

"We can't risk it; she's got a gun. And you and I need to make sure Nattie doesn't do anything crazy, like try to confront her. I say we hide and wait for her to walk up the ramp. If we're lucky, the cops will get here before she reaches the street and stop her. But if not, we can hop back in the cab and follow her, and she'll never notice."

Swiftly, she dialed Jake again. This time, the PI answered, her voice barely audible.

"Where are you? Can you see Mildred's boat?" Darla asked without preamble.

"We're just passing that mansion with the red, white, and blue guest house . . . remember, the one we saw on the water taxi tour?" Jake said over the sound of Ricko's dual outboards and the splashing of water. "And I can still see Mildred's runabout, though she's a few minutes ahead of us."

Then, her tone growing suspicious, she added, "Why?"

"We want to make sure you don't lose Mildred when she tries to ditch the boat. She's headed toward a private launch ramp not far from where you can cut off the Intracoastal and head up the New River. The launch is behind a big clump of mangroves between two of the houses."

"And you know this because . . . ?"

"Because we're hiding behind that clump of mangroves, watching Mildred steer her boat in our direction."

She winced and held the phone away from her ear as Jake let loose with a few bad words that might have shocked even Ricko.

"What are you doing there?" the PI demanded when the first curse storm had passed. "You're supposed to be at Billy Pope's place!"

"Yes, but Nattie was sure she knew where Mildred was headed, so we had Tino drive us over here. We figured we could intercept her in case she got away from you. And don't worry, Officer Garcia and the other cops are on the way. We're just going to keep an eye on Mildred until they get here. Sorry—gotta go!"

Darla hung up before Jake could continue exercising her vocabulary and then turned her attention to the water. Even to her untrained eye it looked like Mildred was bringing in the small craft a little faster than was safe.

She said as much to Tino, who agreed.

"Unless she throttles it down, she's going to tear up that boat the minute she hits the ramp. If you don't want to be hit by flying shrapnel, we'd better ditch plan A and go take cover in the cab."

That was enough to convince Darla. Wrapping Hamlet's leash securely about her wrist, she grabbed Nattie's sleeve and tugged the protesting old woman back up the ramp.

"You can watch her crash from the taxi," Darla told her. "Now, come on. We need to get out of sight. You keep forgetting she's armed."

"Eh, she probably couldn't hit the broad side of a barn with that peashooter," Nattie said with a snort. Still, she climbed into the backseat of the cab alongside Darla and then joined her, kneeling onto the floor mats and carefully peering over the top edge of the door.

Unfortunately, their view of the launch was blocked by the wall of greenery, so that any witnessing of a crash would be limited to the audio. To that end, Tino turned the key and rolled down the taxi's windows partway. They heard the sound of the runabout's engine growing louder as Mildred drew nearer, and then a sudden silence as she cut the engine. Then came the sound of water lapping at the concrete launch as another boat's wake preceded hers.

All at once, Darla heard an alarming scrape and thud as the runabout hit the ramp and presumably skidded up onto the concrete.

"Now *that* is going to cost Mr. Pope some money," Tino observed in a low voice.

Darla shushed him and raised herself up a tiny bit more, hoping to get a better look at what was going on. She still couldn't see anything, but she heard the frantic rustle of branches. Mildred tying the boat off, she assumed.

"Here she comes," Nattie said with a sharp elbow to Darla's ribs.

Darla bit back a reflexive *oomph* and ducked a bit lower. Mildred couldn't have known that they'd guessed her destination, or that they were driving around in a cab. Even if the old woman spied their ride, surely she wouldn't think anything of it. That was, assuming she didn't glimpse a shock of hennaed hair bobbing in the window.

"Get down," Darla whispered and tugged Nattie out of the window just as Mildred came limping up the ramp.

Darla counted to twenty, waiting until she was sure the old woman had had enough time to pass them; then, gingerly, she rose up again and took a peek.

A furious Mildred stood outside of the taxi's window glaring back at her.

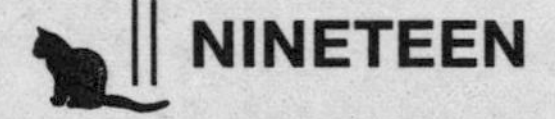

NINETEEN

AT THE UNEXPECTED SIGHT, DARLA GAVE A REFLEXIVE LITTLE cry. Nattie gave an answering scream of her own while even Tino, crouched on the front floorboard, uttered a startled yelp.

Mildred, meanwhile, grabbed the passenger-side handle and yanked the taxi's door open. "What are you doing here? Get out, all of you!" she shrieked, waving the pistol like she was directing a band.

She looked quite the worse for her boat ride. Her glasses were splattered with water spots and her helmet of gray hair was raked by the wind in all directions like Hamlet in midgrooming. Her pants were soaked to the knees from where she must have stood in the water tying off the runabout, while her once-white blouse boasted several streaks of dirt.

But the pistol still gleamed with businesslike authority, so the three of them hurried to comply with her demand. Fearful for Hamlet's safety, however, Darla left him on the floorboard of the cab. She gave him a whispered "Stay here, Hammy" before climbing out.

"I told you we should have jumped her when she got off the boat," Tino murmured in dismay as she lined up along with him and Nattie. "Bad move, hiding in the cab."

Nattie was the first to regain her composure.

"Guess you forgot I knew all about this launch, too," she said with a self-congratulatory air. "Now, why don't you give it up? The cops are on the way, and my Jacqueline and that good-lookin' Haitian fellow are gonna be here any minute, too."

"Don't be ridiculous." Mildred clutched her handbag to her chest, her grip on the pistol steady now. "I'm not going to wait here like some doddering old woman. I'm going to make a break for it, and you're coming with me as collateral."

Nattie crossed her arms over her narrow chest and gave her friend a look of challenge. "No, I ain't."

Mildred's eyes began to water behind the steel-rimmed glasses, while her expression grew more frustrated. "I'll shoot you, then, and I'll take Darla with me, instead."

"Eh, why don't you take Tino? He's got a taxi, so he can drive you right outta here."

"Hey, bad idea," the young man protested before Mildred could reply. "I get real nervous driving if someone's pointing a gun at me. Oh, and the boss is gonna get really ticked at me if I get stiffed on this fare."

"No, no. That's a very good idea," Mildred said with a thoughtful nod. Then the sound of a fast-approaching siren set her off again. "You, cabbie, get inside," she exclaimed, waving the pistol again.

With a look of resignation, Tino started around to the driver's side.

"Now, you two girls stay here," Mildred demanded as she reached for the passenger door. "And, Nattie, don't you even think about trying to follow me again."

"Okay, but can I at least have my car keys?" the old woman shot back. "I'm gonna need them when I go get my Mini from Billy's place."

Mildred gave her an annoyed look but with her free hand reached into her shoulder bag and dug around. She made a little sound of distaste as she pulled out the keychain with its dangling zebra-striped heart.

"Here you go," she said, and tossed it toward Nattie. Pulling open the passenger door, she added, "And if I see you or Darla trying to follow me this time, I'll—*eeeek!*"

It happened almost simultaneously. Mildred opened the taxi door, and Hamlet launched himself from inside it like—as Darla later described it to James and Robert—an Olympic gymnast executing the perfect vault. He stuck the landing literally, front paws wrapped around Mildred's neck and rear claws digging into her chest.

"Eeek!" she shrieked again, though this time her scream was muffled by Hamlet's furry head against her mouth. The pistol fell with a clatter onto the stone drive, and Nattie swooped down to pick it up.

"I told ya, Millie, give it up," she said with a cackle, training the weapon on her former friend. "I got yer gun, so don't you try running off."

Glasses askew and looking like she had a fur stole draped about her, Mildred nodded gingerly and raised her hands. Hamlet, apparently satisfied that the humans could take it from there, released his grip on Mildred and dropped lightly to the ground again. Leash trailing behind him, he strolled over to where Darla stood and looked up at her with his patented *I'm a good kitty* expression.

Yes, you definitely are, Darla silently told him as she reached down to catch hold of his leash.

Not that the feline would have heard the words even if she'd said them aloud, for sirens blared now at the top of the ramp. She could see blue lights flashing through the surrounding foliage as well, while the sound of numerous car doors opening and slamming again filled the air. Apparently, the cavalry—meaning Garcia and company—had finally arrived. Even better, Darla could hear the sound of Ricko's boat approaching the launch.

But her relief was short-lived when, as soon as the sirens cut off, a man's voice barked through a bullhorn, "Police! Drop your weapon now! Drop it!"

Five uniformed officers, guns drawn, were slowly marching down the boat ramp toward them. The one with the bullhorn turned out to be Officer Johnston, while Officer Garcia led the other four. All of them had their weapons trained on Nattie, who was still enjoying her moment in the sun playing Annie Oakley.

"Nattie, they mean you! Put the gun down and get away from it!" Darla shrieked in sudden panic, visions of the old woman falling in a hail of gunfire rushing through her mind. She'd read about innocent bystanders being shot down by mistake while the police were sorting good guys from bad. And the fact that Nattie happened to be wielding a weapon at the moment tended to put her into the latter category.

"Officer Garcia, please don't shoot!" Darla shouted when the old woman remained unmoving. "That's Jake Martelli's mother. She disarmed your suspect just as you and the other officers arrived."

"Hey, Ana!" Tino shouted. "She's right—don't shoot! It's this *loca* old lady in the glasses you want!"

"Eh, keep yer pants on," Nattie called as, seeming to snap from her momentary paralysis, she bent and set the gun on the ground. Then, arms raised high, she took a few steps back, and said, "Look, no gun."

Garcia edged forward, her own pistol still at the ready. Motioning one of the other officers to retrieve Mildred's weapon, she waited until it was safely out of the way before moving in closer. Her gaze swept Darla, Nattie, and Tino, the latter of whom gave her a big grin and thumbs-up.

"Hey, *prima*, glad you got here. This *loca* lady"—he pointed at Mildred—"she tried to kidnap me!"

Garcia shot her cousin an annoyed look. "Don't worry, Tino. She would have gotten sick of you and tossed you out after a couple of blocks." Then, turning her attention to Darla, she said, "Nice to see you again, Ms. Pettistone. I assume that's the famous lost cat, Hamlet?"

She nodded, remembering that the cop had yet to see the famous Karate Kitty in person.

"Officer Garcia," another, familiar voice called from the direction of the launch. "It's Jake Martelli. I was in pursuit of Mrs. Fischer by boat and followed her here. May I approach?"

"The more the merrier, Ms. Martelli," Garcia replied, though her displeased tone belied her welcoming words. "Come up where we can see you, and make it fast, if you don't mind."

Jake, soaked to the knees just as Mildred was, came sloshing up the ramp. Garcia looked at her. "Were you in that boat alone?"

"No. I convinced a local fishing guide to play taxi for me," Jake said. "He had customers waiting, so he dropped me here at the launch and took off again."

Darla suppressed a knowing smile at that. She figured that the prospect of losing paying customers wasn't Ricko's reason for bailing. More likely it was his reluctance to get near the local constabulary.

Garcia motioned Jake to join the rest of them. The PI gave Darla a look that said, *We'll talk about this later*, and then stood beside Nattie. Though she put a protective arm around her mother's shoulder, Darla suspected that Jake was more in the mood to wring Nattie's neck.

Officer Garcia, meanwhile, holstered her gun. And while Johnston and the other officers still remained on alert, they also put their weapons away, much to Darla's relief. The last thing they needed was for everyone to go O.K. Corral there.

"Mrs. Fischer," the cop said to Mildred, who had been huddled near the taxi clutching her purse, "you're under arrest for the murder of Ted Stein, as well as for numerous counts of kidnapping and attempted kidnapping. Now, I'm going to handcuff you and search you, and then I'm going to read you your rights. You'll cooperate with me, right?"

"Yes, yes," Mildred replied in a small voice, body hunched and looking suddenly a good decade older than her true age. "Maybe Billy will help me pay for a lawyer," she added, the comment drawing a disgusted snort from Nattie.

Mildred straightened and obligingly moved away from the taxi as Garcia approached. Then, before any of them realized what was happening, Mildred took a few running steps toward the vehicle and dove for its hood, doing a handspring that sent her up and over the cab and landing on the ramp beyond it. From there, she took off at a run toward the water, presumably intending to take off in the runabout again.

Darla stared after the old woman, aware that her mouth was hanging open. *Did I just see what I think I saw?* Mildred may have once been a high-level gymnast, but she was over seventy now. Still, the undeniable proof that her abilities were largely undiminished lay in the set of small handprints that marred the dusty hood of Tino's taxi.

Darla wasn't the only one to question what she'd just witnessed. The sight of a septuagenarian performing such a stunt held the cops in stunned silence for a few crucial moments while the old woman put distance between her and them.

Only Nattie shook her head in resigned satisfaction. "I told you she was a gymnast," she reminded Darla.

Then Garcia gave her head a hard shake and broke into a run.

"Stop!" she shouted after Mildred, rushing that same way. The other cops leaped to attention as well, joining Garcia in the foot race.

But Mildred's string of luck abruptly changed from good to bad. Before she could get more than halfway down the ramp, something plummeted from the palm trees above the old woman. A heartbeat later, Mildred lay prone on the ground, as if felled by an unseen fist.

Garcia reached the spot where the old woman sprawled and bent over her for a quick look. A moment later, she straightened.

"Quick, call the paramedics," she shouted to Johnston.

Nattie, meanwhile, was staring in satisfaction at her unmoving friend. To no one in particular, she remarked, "I told you ya gotta watch out for those falling coconuts. One hits you on the head, and it's lights out, permanent-like."

"IT BASICALLY BOILED DOWN TO THE MONEY," JAKE EXPLAINED THE NEXT morning as she, Nattie, and Darla ate a late breakfast on the deck of Porto del Sol diner. Hamlet curled comfortably under the table, waiting for an errant bit of egg or ham to fall his way. So far, he'd been disappointed.

Taking another bite of what was listed in the menu as the Hot, Hot, Hot Omelet (made with three different kinds of peppers), the PI went on, "Sam wasn't willing to tell me much more, but I got some of it from Garcia. Plus I paid a little unofficial visit to Alicia and Cindy last night, as well. Apparently, Mildred was gunning for both Ted Stein and Billy Pope, and Alicia didn't realize it until too late."

"So Billy Pope was involved in the lien situation after all?" Darla asked. "But, I thought he was a multimillionaire."

She glanced again at the front page of the morning paper that she'd brought along to breakfast. Next to an account of a national political scandal was the headline *Former Olympic Hopeful Arrested in Murder.* But that was already yesterday's news. That morning, one of the headlines on Darla's favorite news sites now proclaimed, *College Prostitution Scandal Broadens*. A subheading suggested this was a *Possible Tie to Cat-Show Murder*.

"'Was' is the key word," Jake replied to her question. "When the real estate boom went bust, so did Billy. He managed to keep up appearances for a long while, but things were getting tight. Ted was just a greedy opportunist who saw a chance to make some easy money. You saw the copy of that letter that went out from the condo board. Mildred missed a payment on her association dues, and Billy and Ted were threatening to foreclose and sell the place right out from under her."

"But could they do that for just a few hundred dollars in debt?" Darla asked between fruity bites of her Cuban-style French toast.

Jake shrugged. "A lot depends on how the association agreement is worded but, yes, there have been cases of people actually losing their homes over missed fees. And since Ma's friend Billy was a former real estate mogul, he knew all the ins and outs."

"He's not my friend anymore," Nattie muttered, poking at a barely touched plate of biscuits and gravy. "We might as well hold a memorial service by the pool for him, because he's dead to me."

She punctuated that last with the universal finger across the throat gesture.

Jake gave her mother a sympathetic look. "Anyhow, Billy and Ted blackmailed Mildred into helping them skim some of the association money in return for not foreclosing on her. They ran it through her bank account, so by the time it got to them, it was all clean and fresh."

"But how was Alicia involved?" Darla wanted to know. "She was there at the mansion, drugged up on the couch with Billy, and the way Mildred talked, she had to have known something."

"Believe it or not, Alicia was the heroine in all this. She and Ted had been an item for a long while, until she found out about his illegal activities. And she pretty well blamed him for involving her father in the plot."

Jake paused for another bite of omelet, and then went on, "Alicia couldn't blow the whistle on their little scheme without bringing down the authorities on both of them, so she figured she'd try her own style of blackmail to get them to stop. What better way to make a cat-show judge and a cat breeder look bad than to have them accused of holding another cat for ransom? Unfortunately, she wasn't as good at blackmail as her father and her boyfriend. It all blew up in her face."

Darla dropped her fork onto her plate and shot her friend a startled look. "Wait! Are you saying that Alicia was responsible for Hamlet's catnapping?"

"She orchestrated it, yes. Mildred and Cindy did the actual grunt work for her. Cindy snatched Hamlet and handed him off to Mildred, who stashed the carrier under a table next to a couple of other cats until she could sneak Hamlet out of the exhibition hall. Then she handed him off to Cindy again. Cindy's job was to bring Hamlet to Billy's suite, where she'd already arranged to meet Ted. That part went off without a hitch."

"That's why Mildred volunteered to help me find Hamlet!" Darla realized. "She must have hidden him in the section of the hall that she claimed she searched. But how did she get him outside later, when the show volunteers were searching all the carriers?"

"It seems she quote-unquote *borrowed* the show paperwork for another black household cat and walked out with Hamlet, bold as brass. And since she is well known as a volunteer on the cat-show circuit, it never occurred to anyone to question her."

Darla picked up her dropped fork and took another considering bite. "Don't tell me—the whole wingtip photo thing was part of the blackmail? Take a fake selfie of Billy and Hamlet, then threaten to publish it if Billy didn't stop his evil ways, so to speak."

Jake nodded. "Ted was all in on that, because he was worried Billy was starting to have second thoughts about the foreclosure and money-laundering scheme, anyway. Alicia didn't let on that she knew he was a partner in Billy's racket. And he also didn't know that Alicia had learned about the Minx Connection from Cindy."

Darla gasped. "Surely Cindy wasn't—"

Jake shook her head. "Not her, but a couple of her friends had hooked up with Ted and couldn't get out of the situation. Between that and the whole kitten-breeding thing, Cindy was on the warpath against our buddy Mr. Stein already. So even though she and her mom were pretty much at odds all the time, it didn't take much persuading by Alicia to get her daughter to help out."

"'The enemy of my enemy is my friend,'" Darla quoted. Then she shook her head. "It sounds like Alicia could have shut both of those guys down with her little plan. So why did Mildred up the ante and murder Ted?"

"I got that," Nattie broke in, tone still sour. "Some people just need killing. Not that I'm giving her a pass," she added when Darla and Jake stared at her, "but I kind of see her point. Besides, I don't think it was the foreclosure thing that got to her. It was the whole kitten-breeding scheme that made the old biddy crazy. You know how them cat people are about unethical breeders."

"So much for a relaxing vacation," Darla muttered. Then, with a look at Hamlet, she added, "And someone is slacking off on the job. Remember that first book Hamlet snagged when he was settling into his personal bookstore there at the show? *How the Grinch Stole Christmas* sure didn't have anything to do with what happened."

"Actually, it kind of did," Jake said, coming to the cat's defense. "You know that veterinarian who was first responder when I got smacked? You told me his name is Dr. Navidad, right? As in, *Feliz Navidad*."

"Christmas," Darla agreed. "All right, but who was the Grinch and what did he steal?"

"Cindy confessed to me that the main reason she set up the Cozy Kitty faux massacre was to cause a commotion while she stole some sort of animal sedatives out of Dr. Navidad's bag while everyone was distracted. She'd been around the rescue folks long enough to know what she was looking for. But it didn't occur to her that the good vet would be the first one on the scene when the cat's owner raised the hue and cry."

"I guess that makes sense," Darla said with a shudder, not wanting to think what might have happened had Cindy actually stolen the drugs and used them on Hamlet, or even Jake.

"Anyhow," the PI finished, "the cops are still sorting out a whole laundry list of charges. I don't know who's going to get slapped with what, but between Billy and Alicia and Cindy and Mildred, I imagine Fort Lauderdale's legal community is going to be busy for a while."

Hoping that the laundry list didn't include her and Jake having to make another trip to Florida as witnesses, Darla said, "We've got a few days left here in Fort Lauderdale before we have to fly back. What's the plan now?"

Jake grinned back at her. "Plans? We don't need no stinking plans. We're supposed to be on vacation, remember? You want me anytime before our flight takes off, you'll find me on the beach."

TWENTY

"YES, JAMES, THERE'S A LOT MORE TO THE STORY THAN what you read online, but it's just too much to go into on the phone," Darla said, feet up on the railing of Nattie's balcony as she spoke into her cell. "We'll be home tomorrow afternoon, so I'll give you the full scoop then."

James sighed, but all he said was, "Very well, but be assured I will expect a detailed account of all that transpired. Now, if you would care to hold the line, Robert wishes to speak to you for a moment."

"Hey, Ms. P.," came Robert's youthful tones a moment later. "I can't believe that Hamlet, you know, solved another murder."

"Yeah, I thought being in Florida was going to be a vacation, not another chance for him to prove he's smarter than us helpless humans," she agreed with a rueful look at the feline in question, stretched out on the chair beside her. Changing the subject, she asked, "So, tell me, since you're our official barista, what do *you* think of the new coffee bar?"

"It's, like, really sick! I tried out all the machines and stuff, and it all works great. We'll be ready to start brewing coffee as soon as you and Ms. Jake get back."

"I can't wait to see it," Darla said before having Robert put James back on the line to talk shop for a few minutes.

By the time she had hung up and come in from the balcony, the two Martelli women were bickering over the best way to store condiments.

"Whadda you say, Darla?" Nattie asked as Darla joined them. "Do you keep your ketchup in the refrigerator, like regular people, or in the pantry, like my know-it-all daughter?"

"Sorry, Nattie, but I'm with Jake on that one. There's nothing worse than cold ketchup."

"Ha! Nothing worse except maybe food poisoning," the old woman darkly muttered.

Jake grinned. "Ma, I've been doing this for more than thirty years, and I haven't ended up in the ER yet."

"Well, there's always a first time," she declared, standing on tiptoe to reach into the cabinet for the bottle Jake had put there and then transferring it into her refrigerator.

Darla and Jake exchanged amused glances, and then the latter glanced at her watch. "Time to pick up the newest member of the family. Ma, can I have the keys to the Mini?"

Nattie immediately forgot their squabble. "Sure, *bambolina mia*," she said, trotting over to the counter, where she'd left the zebra-heart keychain. Handing it off to Jake, she said, "You girls go on, and I'll clear a little spot for the kitty in the bedroom while you're gone."

"Thanks, Ma," Jake replied, giving her mother a fond kiss atop her hennaed head. "We'll be back soon."

Half an hour later, she, Darla, and Hamlet pulled into the parking lot of Tropical Adoptables' headquarters located in the industrial part of town. The building—a tiny converted home painted purple and yellow with silhouettes of dogs and cats stenciled across the front—was situated between an auto repair place and a fencing company. A clever bit of trompe l'oeil added to the front door made the entry look like an open doghouse, complete with a grinning pooch peeking out at them.

Marie, the animal-rescue worker whom Darla and Jake had met at the cat show, rose from a little brick patio area, where she'd been repairing a broken planter box. She brushed the dirt from her bright pink Tropical Adoptables T-shirt and gave them a big smile.

"Hello again, ladies . . . and Hamlet. We've been waiting for you." Turning to Jake, she went on, "Ms. Martelli, I have your paperwork inside. You've been officially approved to adopt one of our precious fur babies. Are you all ready to pick up Trixie and take her home with you?"

"All set," Jake agreed, beaming as she shoved her mirrored sunglasses back onto the top of her head and waved a plastic bag from the local pet superstore. "I double-checked this morning to make sure the airline could allow her on our flight tomorrow. They said yes, so all I have to do is call back and confirm."

"Wonderful. Come on inside." Marie ushered them into what had once been a parlor, and which now served as an office and waiting area, complete with a small selection of pet supplies for sale. Another volunteer in a Tropical Adoptables tee—this one a bald, middle-aged man—sat behind the desk with a phone scrunched between shoulder and ear as he typed on a computer keyboard. He gave them a friendly smile before returning to his task.

"We've had a busy week. The cat show gave us a little boost of publicity, and we've adopted out double our usual number of cats and dogs since the weekend." With a nod to Darla and Hamlet, she added, "Oh, and Ms. Pettistone, I saw Hamlet's recommendation for our rescue group on your store's website. We certainly appreciate the plug."

"You're very welcome. All of us at Pettistone's Fine Books are firm believers in rescue." Then, as the sounds of eager barking and meowing drifted to them, she added, "Sounds like you've got a whole herd in here. How many dogs and cats do you keep at a time?"

Marie sighed. "We can only handle maybe a dozen dogs, and that's if they're mostly puppies or small breeds, along with fifteen or so cats and kittens. But we have quite a few more in foster homes. Now, let's go see Trixie."

Marie slid open the door to a room marked, appropriately, "Cats." A knee-high gate lay across the doorway while a taller, circular net pen took up most of the room. Inside the pen were a couple of cat towers, three kitty hammocks, and a dozen rubber balls and catnip mice, along with litter boxes, food, and water. In the midst of this, four adult cats and nine kittens—Darla managed to count them all—were holding what looked like a feline circus. And three-legged Trixie was in the center ring, flopped on her back and spinning like a top as she battled one of the catnip toys.

"I'd forgotten how cute she is," Darla exclaimed while Jake knelt down by the mesh and began tapping her fingers on it to attract the kitten's attention. "Hamlet, don't you agree?"

Hamlet surveyed the feline collection with a cool green gaze. The adult cats—two orange tabbies, a calico, and an odd-eyed white—glanced up at him but prudently did not engage. To Hamlet's credit, he did not hiss or otherwise indicate disapproval, though the slight twitch to his tail told Darla he'd rather be elsewhere.

Trixie, meanwhile, had realized she had visitors. Dropping the stuffed mouse, she leaped to her three feet and crouched, ready for action. She spied Jake and promptly bounded in her direction, followed by a posse of three other kittens.

Jake laughed. "I guess we know who is cat boss around here. Hamlet, I think Trixie is going to give you a run for your money."

"She's a pistol, all right," Marie agreed. "I'm sure the two of them will get along great."

Darla rolled her eyes at this, not quite as confident as Marie on this matter. Hamlet, meanwhile, gave a small *meow-rumph* that she translated from catspeak to mean, *In your dreams, volunteer lady.*

Unaware that she'd just been dissed by a cat, Marie leaned over the mesh to give Trixie a quick scratch behind the ears before straightening again. "Good. Let's get the adoption fee paid, and then we'll send you ladies on your way."

"Mommy, look!" a small voice called from the doorway. "There she is, the kitty from the cat show!"

Darla turned to see a round-faced girl with blond pigtails standing with an equally blond and even plumper woman whom Darla presumed was her mother. The child was perhaps nine or ten years old, wearing a pink plaid jumper over a white T-shirt. As her mother hefted her over the gate, Darla saw in surprise that one of child's legs had been amputated above the knee. In place of the missing limb, she wore a metal prosthesis, which ended in a molded foot. Upon that tiny plastic extremity was tied a pink ballet slipper to match the one that the child wore on her other, flesh-and-blood foot.

The little girl was already headed toward the cat pen, her gait steady if slightly rolling. She caught sight of Marie and gave her a big smile.

"I saw you at the cat show. I've come to get my kitty now."

"That's great," Marie said with a cheery smile, gesturing the girl's mother to join them. "I'm finishing up with these ladies right now, but you look at the kitties all you want. And when I come back, you can sit down inside the pen and play with them to help you decide."

"I don't need to look," she said with a little girl's lofty

air. "I already picked out my kitty. I want that one," she said, and pointed at Trixie.

Marie raised her brows in dismay. "Oh, honey, do you mean the little Siamese girl?"

"Yep," the girl said with a firm nod. "She's just like me, so we can be bestest friends forever. Right, Mommy?" she asked, turning to her mother.

The woman smiled and shook her head. "Chelsea hasn't stopped talking about this cat since we went to the show," she told the volunteer. "Her father finally agreed she could adopt her, so here we are. I was really worried that the poor little thing might not still be here."

"Of course she would be here, Mommy," Chelsea corrected her. "Nobody wants a kitty that's missing a leg. No one 'cept me. Can we take her home now, Mommy? Can we?"

"Oh, honey," Marie softly repeated, her face flushed now with agitation, "I don't know how to tell you this, but little Trixie already has been adopted."

"No, she hasn't. She's right there," Chelsea said with impeccable logic.

Darla shot a look at Jake, who was staring down at Trixie as Marie shook her head and glanced helplessly over at the girl's mother for support. Chelsea's mom rushed over. "Now, Chelse, it's not the end of the world," she said, catching the girl by the shoulders and giving her an encouraging hug. "Look at all the other kittens there in the pen. They all need homes, too."

"But I want Trixie," the girl whispered, a large tear rolling down her cheek as she stared miserably at the ground.

"Uh, Marie," Jake spoke up, "small problem here. I finally got a callback from my landlady. She said she won't waive the no-pets rule for me, even if I give her a deposit. So I hate to say this, but I can't adopt Trixie after all."

"Jake, are you sure?" Darla exclaimed. "I know how much you wanted her."

"Yeah, she's a great little cat, but rules are rules." Then, with a look at Chelsea, the PI added, "But luckily for Trixie, it looks like there's someone else who can take her home."

Chelsea slowly raised her head, her lips still quivering. "You really can't adopt her?" she whispered.

Jake shook her head. "No, I can't. It stinks, but that's the way it is. But if you haven't decided you'd rather look at the other kittens, then maybe you can adopt her, instead."

Chelsea's face broke into a wide grin. "Mommy, Mommy, the lady says I can have Trixie after all!" she cried and turned to grip her mother in a big hug.

"Why, that's just wonderful," the woman said, pulling the girl to her. Over the top of the child's blond head, she mouthed the words *Thank you* to Jake.

Jake shrugged and pulled her sunglasses back down. "Guess there's no reason to hang around any longer. Thanks, Marie, and good luck with your rescue work."

"No, thank *you*," Marie replied, sniffling just a little. "And Darla, it was great meeting you and Hamlet. I'll be sure to bookmark your website."

Darla nodded. "Hamlet will be glad to help if you ever need his assistance plugging another event. Just send us an email."

They had reached the doorway when Jake abruptly halted.

"I almost forgot, I bought this for Trixie," she said, reaching into the plastic bag and holding up a pink collar liberally studded with rhinestones. "Chelsea," she called, "how do you think this would look on your new kitty?"

Chelsea looked up from the kitten she was snuggling to her chest, and exclaimed, "It's beautiful, like diamonds. And pink is my favorite color."

"Well, it's probably Trixie's favorite color, too. So why don't I give it and all these other kitty things to you to give to her as a happy adoption present?"

"Mommy, can I?"

Her mother raised a hand in protest. "Oh no, we couldn't."

"Really, you'd be doing me a favor," Jake countered, handing the bag off to Marie. "We're leaving tomorrow, and I wouldn't have time to take them back."

"All right, then. Chelsea, tell the nice lady thank you."

"Thank you," the girl obediently echoed, waving one of Trixie's paws at her. "Trixie says thanks, too."

Jake gave a curt nod and glanced at Darla. "C'mon, kid," she muttered. "Let's get out of here before I start bawling like a baby."

Darla didn't need any further encouragement, for she was already wiping away a few tears of her own.

They hurried back to the Mini Cooper, Hamlet trotting alongside them. At the driver's door, however, Jake paused and then tossed the zebra-striped keychain over the top of the car to Darla. "You mind driving us back?"

"Not at all," she said, and quickly swapped places. Once they were settled inside, Hamlet crouched between them on the center console and, once his leash was securely fastened to the driver's seat headrest, Darla turned to her friend.

"You know, everyone thinks you're so badass, but you're just a marshmallow inside," she exclaimed. "That was such a noble thing to do."

"Yeah, yeah, whatever," Jake said with a wave of her hand. "You can mail me my good conduct medal. Anyhow, I'm sure Hamlet's pretty pleased that he'll still be the lord of the manor back home."

"I'm not so sure. I think he rather liked Trixie."

"Well, either way, it wasn't meant to be. So let's stop yapping about it and head back to the condo."

Darla nodded and cranked the engine, and then glanced at her watch. "It's almost lunchtime," she said as she pulled out of the lot. "How about we call Nattie and see if she wants to go to that Cuban restaurant again?"

"Here's a better idea. How about we hit one of those surf

bars we saw on the water-taxi tour? They all have outdoor seating, so Hamlet should be allowed in."

Darla considered that a moment and then shook her head. "It's the weekend. Too many people, and the music will be too loud. Hamlet would be miserable."

"I suppose we don't have to take him with—*ouch!*"

Darla looked past Hamlet to see Jake rubbing the side of her head. "What happened?"

"I think Hamlet just slapped me," she said in disbelief.

Darla had paused at a stop sign, so she had time to shoot a stern glance at the feline. He sat crouched with his paws tucked innocently against his chest, his attention seemingly on the road ahead, but as if feeling Darla's gaze on him, he turned his head and gave her a slow blink.

Darla stifled a snicker and returned her attention to the road. "Hamlet says he didn't do it," she told her friend. "You must have gotten your hair caught in the seatbelt or something."

"Yeah, it was 'or something,' all right," Jake muttered, but she was smiling as she said it.

Darla thought for a moment, and then said, "I've got an idea. How about we give Tino a call? He can haul all four of us around town in his taxi for a couple of hours. Of course, the first stop has to be at his sister's bakery."

"Good idea, we'll need a couple of bags of Cuban pastries for sustenance," Jake agreed. "And we can always stop somewhere for Cuban coffee, too."

"How about we take Nattie to the surf shop and see about signing her up for a lesson?" Darla suggested, getting into the spirit of things. "And after that, we can have Tino take us to one of those bars, and Hamlet can snooze in the taxi while we have piña coladas or something. What do you think?"

"Sounds like fun," Jake said as she turned to the cat. "Hamlet, are you in?"

Hamlet roused himself to a seated position again, balancing like a pro on the console. And then he raised one paw. Darla and Jake exchanged glances before bursting out laughing.

"Fist bump!" they chorused, touching knuckles over Hamlet's head before each lightly brushing the cat's paw.

"Looks like we're all bros now," Darla exclaimed in triumph, putting her hands back on the wheel. "I can't wait to tell Robert. What do you say, Hammy?"

Hamlet merely blinked again, and then purred.

"[An] unusual and appealing series."
—Richmond Times-Dispatch

FROM *NEW YORK TIMES*
BESTSELLING AUTHOR

ELLERY ADAMS

BOOKS BY THE BAY
MYSTERIES

A Killer Plot

A Deadly Cliché

The Last Word

Written in Stone

Poisoned Prose

Lethal Letters

PRAISE FOR THE BOOKS BY
THE BAY MYSTERIES

"[A] great read."
—Lorna Barrett, *New York Times* bestselling author

"[A] terrific mystery."
—*Fresh Fiction*